The clear air began to fill with choking white billows of gun smoke. "Attack! Charge!" Ben yelled. Crouching, he began methodically firing in the direction of the darting figures in the night.

"Charge!" he repeated, this time leading the attack. A dozen soldiers joined him. Ben reached the top of the hill and looked down on a small knot of Comanche milling about in confusion.

Ben started firing as he walked downhill, ignoring the surge of battle around him until a warrior yanked out a knife and slashed at him. Throwing up his gun arm blocked the thrust that would have ended his life.

He winced as blood flowed along his forearm, then ignored the pain and began fighting back, his life in the balance. Reaching out, Ben grabbed a sinewy throat with his left hand and squeezed. The Comanche twisted and thrashed about, then used his knee against Ben's belly to force himself back. As the Indian stumbled away, Ben lifted his pistol and fired.

This time he knew his target was dead.

"He's gettin' 'way!" shouted a soldier. "Thass him! Black Horse!"

Ben lifted his pistol and fired until the hammer fell with a dull metallic click on a spent chamber. Ben silently cursed his bad luck, although the weapon didn't have the range needed to bring down the escaping Comanche chief. But the rifles of his soldiers did. Ben wasn't sure which of the four privates who opened fire on Black Horse shot the chief from horseback, but one did.

Black Horse lay sprawled on the ground, dead. Ben was experienced enough to know Comanche raiding in West Texas wouldn't stop because of one chief's death, but it would slow.

And it did.

BOOK YOUR PLACE ON OUR WEBSITE AND MAKE THE READING CONNECTION!

We've created a customized website just for our very special readers, where you can get the inside scoop on everything that's going on with Zebra, Pinnacle and Kensington books.

When you come online, you'll have the exciting opportunity to:

- View covers of upcoming books
- Read sample chapters
- Learn about our future publishing schedule (listed by publication month *and author*)
- Find out when your favorite authors will be visiting a city near you
- Search for and order backlist books from our online catalog
- Check out author bios and background information
- Send e-mail to your favorite authors
- Meet the Kensington staff online
- Join us in weekly chats with authors, readers and other guests
- Get writing guidelines
- AND MUCH MORE!

**Visit our website at
http://www.kensingtonbooks.com**

SWORD AND DRUM

Karl Lassiter

PINNACLE BOOKS
Kensington Publishing Corp.
http://www.kensingtonbooks.com

For Margaret Vardeman. Words will never be enough to thank you for being such a great mother and grandmother.

Satanta, in the presence of Satank, Eagle Heart, Big Tree, and Woman's Heart, in a defiant manner, has informed me that he led a party of about 100 Indians into Texas, and killed 7 men and captured a train of mules. He further states that Chiefs Satank, Eagle Heart, Big Tree and Big Bow were associated with him in the raid. Please arrest all of them.

/s/ Lawrie Tatum, Indian Agent
letter to Colonel Benjamin Grierson,
commander Tenth Cavalry, Fort Sill
27 May 1871

Failure

May 1, 1861
Jacksonville, Illinois

"You can borrow more money," Alice Grierson said. She sat with her hands folded in her lap, a book of poetry on the small maple table beside her. The confidence she had shown earlier in her husband had begun to fade. She touched her severe bun of dark brown hair, patted it firmly into place and then stared unwaveringly at Ben, her deep brown eyes not blinking.

"From whom? The banks have cut off all credit. My brothers are in dire straits, also. I would never think of asking my sister Mary for money, even if she had it to lend. You know she's not quite right in the head. Your parents are kind enough to let us stay here without paying room or board, but they have no money to spare. Who's left?"

Benjamin Grierson studied his wife and saw that she was sorely vexed. Her jaw was set and her eyes never wavered, as if they were spears impaling him where he stood. He hated feeling as if he were a schoolboy who had done something wrong.

"Your father," Alice said. "He might—"

"My father didn't want me to go into the dry-goods business in the first place," Ben said. "I wish I had remained a music teacher, but we both know there's no money in that." Ben went a little dreamy thinking of the earlier years when he had been a bandleader and had given lessons in both piano and clarinet. None of his students had been particularly good, nor had they paid promptly or fully, but he had enjoyed the challenge and the music.

"He won't give you the money because you didn't petition the governor strenuously enough to get that postmaster's position for your brother." Alice sat a little straighter in the chair and then made shooing motions to chase off their young son, Charlie, eavesdropping from the hall. "Go look after your brother," she told the boy. "He needs his diaper changed after his nap."

"Mama, that's all he does," Charlie said, lisping slightly. "Do I have to?"

"Go on," Ben said gently. "Do as your mother says. We need to talk." He waited for Charlie to go.

"Since my father didn't want me to go into dry goods, it wouldn't behoove me to ask anything of him," Ben said, knowing logic would only make Alice angrier. "I don't like the turn of our fortune any more than you do."

"You spent far too much time campaigning for Mr. Lincoln," she said, as if this trumped all his logic.

"He won Illinois handily. I'm pleased I had some little part in that." Of all the men who had ever run for the presidency, Abraham Lincoln was, in Ben's opinion, the finest. But the elder Grierson was a dyed-in-the-wool Democrat and this had further widened the rift between father and son.

"If Mr. Lincoln's so beholden to you, why don't you ask him for a job?"

Ben Grierson licked his lips, then launched into relating the broad aspects of the letter he had received from Governor Yates. Ben had campaigned equally as hard for his friend

Richard Yates as he had for Lincoln, but political activities had come at the expense of his business, as much as he hated to admit that Alice was right. If he hadn't left the day-to-day running of the business to his brother John, they might still be raking in the profits. John was not much of a businessman or, as far as Ben could tell, much of anything else.

"I received a letter from the governor," he began, skirting the issue until he found an indirect way to present the details.

"This doesn't have anything to do with all those awful books you've been reading, has it?" Alice looked accusingly at him, then across the small sitting room to the desk where Ben had spread out a fan of textbooks on strategy and tactics so he could skip from one book to another quickly. "When you were in the militia you were a trumpeter, not a soldier. Not a real soldier at all. Don't go putting on airs."

"I know I wasn't much of a cavalry soldier," he said. Ben closed his eyes for a moment and rubbed the side of his head. How he hated horses! When he was eight years old, he was kicked in the head by a horse and had lain unconcious for two weeks, his despairing mother hovering by him the whole while. When he finally regained consciousness, he was partially blind for another two months. His mother kept him in a dark room until vision finally returned in his left eye. Perhaps it had been an act of God that restored his vision, as his Episcopalian parents had thought. Ben thought his brother John was closer to the truth, saying he was too stubborn to remain in bed for too long. The only evidence of his mishap now was a huge scar on his cheek hidden by his thick, bushy black beard.

"No, you're not much of a soldier. What does Governor Yates want of you? A position in the government? Clerking jobs don't pay well, but anything is better than having you around all day poring over those useless books and not earning a red cent."

His wife's condemnation stung, but there was a kernel of truth hidden in what she said. Alice never minced words.

"Richard wants me to deliver messages."

"A courier? That's all? It cannot pay too well."

"Nothing at all, actually, but I can be of service," Ben said. "And I'll receive provisions and a place to sleep. That will relieve a little of the burden on your parents."

"Well, yes," Alice said. Then she eyed him critically. "You're not going to do something foolish like enlist in the Army, are you?"

"Dear, I have no intention of sneaking off to smoke and carouse. You know me better than that."

"You smoked before we were married," she said, glaring at him as if he still enjoyed this vice. "And you talk of going to the theater often."

"I enjoy the music. You do, too."

"Not in such depraved surroundings." Alice sniffed and looked at the open book of poetry beside her, then began reading without another word. It was so hard being the moral compass with such depravity all about. Ben heaved a deep sigh, went to her, and kissed her chastely on the cheek. His wife mumbled some vague farewell, and he set off to carry documents for the governor, feeling a trifle sinful about the chore because Alice, with her lightning-quick mind, had once again seen through to the real nature of the chore.

Ben picked up the dispatch bag from the governor destined for Colonel Prentiss, the commander of the Illinois Volunteers. He saw no reason to burden his wife with the added detail that Prentiss, with whom he had campaigned vigorously to get Lincoln elected, had offered him the position of lieutenant and aide-de-camp.

It was similarly an unpaid position, but with circumstances throughout the country moving in such a perilous direction, Ben felt more useful in the Army than simply idling about his in-laws' house when he wasn't searching futilely for a new job.

He went outside and hesitated on the top step of the porch. His new position offered a better opportunity to provide for his wife and young sons, but it required him to ride this accursed horse. He went down the four whitewashed steps, one by one in measured cadence to a silent drum tattoo, feeling as if he were mounting thirteen steps to a gallows instead. Ben did his best to gentle the frisky beast, then hastily mounted and turned the horse's head in the direction of Springfield and Colonel Prentiss's bivouac.

It might not be so bad working as an aide-de-camp if the job didn't require him to do much riding. After all, the Illinois Volunteers were infantry soldiers, not cavalry.

Benjamin Grierson gave the horse its head and struggled to hang on as it galloped away.

Secesh

"General Harney is not in command," Captain Lyon said harshly. He glared at Ben Grierson, daring the lieutenant to contradict him. Not sure of protocol, Ben did not come to attention but simply stood, his tall, wiry frame signaling just a hint of readiness to bolt.

Ben looked around, as if he could find some hole to dive into until this blew over. He saw nothing to relieve his worry that Nathaniel Lyon was getting ready to set a match to a keg of powder that might blow all of Missouri into the secessionists' hands. Colonel Prentiss was back in Cairo, trying to whip the remainder of his eight ragtag regiments into a semblance of order. Ben had thought this brief courier's mission would be a relief from the discipline of Prentiss's encampment and the sorry state of his recruits. The leather pouch with the readiness reports from Prentiss to Harney weighed a ton now that Ben had blundered into this dangerous situation steered by an officer obviously bent on proving himself in battle.

"I am sure that the general would not approve of a move against rebels in St. Louis without proper support and diligent planning," Ben said, picking his words carefully.

"Your problem is that you avoid conflict, Lieutenant," Captain Lyon said. His barrel chest rose and threatened to split the blue woolen uniform apart. Lyon growled like a bear and then rested his hand on the hilt of his saber. "I am short of staff since the general took most of the regimental officers with him on his inspection tour. You will ride with my command and you will fight as if you mean it, because your very life will be on the line when we engage the secesh."

"There're secessionists scattered throughout the city," Ben said. "General Harney knows that military action against them, in force, will tilt the rest of the city's population to the rebel cause. We need to maintain control and keep the state free. Let the local police deal with the rebels."

"The state of Missouri will remain free because men of honor are willing to fight and die for that noble cause," Lyon declared. His chest expanded to the point where the brass buttons on his uniform were about to pop. He held out his right hand so the bright morning sunlight caught the gold ring he wore. "Do you see this, Lieutenant?"

"A ring," Ben said, confused by the abrupt change in the captain's thoughts.

"Not just 'a ring' but a West Point ring. I am a regular Army officer, not a political appointee. I spent four years studying the art of war and will not stand by idly while the secesh thumb their noses at me and my country! You are out of line suggesting that I misunderstand the general's position."

"Respectfully, sir," Ben began, but the stocky, powerful captain roared like a wounded lion. Ben fell silent, staring at the raging officer and realizing how much Lyon imitated his namesake.

"We attack! Muster the men, Lieutenant. Get them mounted for the attack. We will flush the secesh from Camp Jackson on the outskirts of town. We will ride victorious this day or know the reason!"

"You're running quite a desperate risk, Captain," Ben said.

"The only risk is giving the secesh time enough to flee, to shrink back into the population where we will never find them until they strike at us from the shadows! If we cut out the vile cancer that they are now, the rest of St. Louis might survive. Do your duty, Lieutenant, or I swear I will see you court-martialed!"

"Yes, sir," Ben said, coming to attention and saluting smartly. He considered what he ought to do. Although Captain Lyon outranked him, he was technically serving Colonel Prentiss and was not in the officer's command. After all, he had only brought a packet of papers for General Harney. The dilemma caused Ben to waver. Harney was on an inspection tour, Prentiss was miles off in Cairo, and from the way Lyon turned florid as he called to his sergeants to assemble the troopers into platoons in preparation for battle, Ben feared he himself might end up as the recipient of a summary execution.

He had written Alice telling her of the sorry state of the Union soldiers and how he wished he could do more, but her answer had been curt. She had yet to forgive him for accepting the aide-de-camp position with his friend, although he had used his most skillful arguments to show her the inevitability of war. If the shooting began in earnest, he wanted to be in the forefront, where he could fight for Illinois and the Union and protect his family. But Captain Lyon was wrong in his attack, no matter how many secesh lurked at Camp Jackson on the outskirts of St. Louis. Fighting rebels was one thing, but holding the United States together as General Harney—and Abraham Lincoln—wanted was a horse of a different color.

Ben rubbed his hindquarters, painfully reminded of the long hours he was spending astride the miserable sway-backed animals Colonel Prentiss requisitioned. The saddle was more wood than leather, pinching him in embarrassing locations.

He'd get the knack of riding for long days soon. Soon. But not yet. He had only been Colonel Prentiss's aide-de-camp for nine days.

That was too soon to die.

Ben considered returning to Cairo to tell Prentiss what was happening, but he held back. That smacked of desertion. He was no coward, but Lyon would report it that way. Desertion under fire was punishable by hanging. The vision of Alice stoically watching as the executioner placed a knotted hangman's rope around his neck prior to opening the trapdoor on the gallows haunted Ben. The disgrace would be too much for a proud woman like Alice.

What would his two boys think of him?

Ben swung into the saddle and rode to the front of the infantry column, already marching from camp in the direction of the rebel nest. Feeling awkward, he rode as best he could to overtake Captain Lyon. The mounted man berated a sergeant walking at quick time.

"Faster, we must go faster. We cannot give the rebels a chance to escape us!"

"Sir, we're doin' our dangedest. If 'n we keep at this pace, we'll be too tarred out to fight."

"You will fight like the fine soldiers I know you to be!"

"Sir, the sergeant has a point," Ben said. "Wouldn't it be better to send a scout ahead to be certain the, uh, secesh, are still in their camp? If they've retreated, we'll need the men to be rested enough to pursue."

"Finally, Lieutenant, a good point. Ride on ahead. Report back."

"Sir? I meant for someone else, someone who can—"

"A half hour, Lieutenant Grierson," Lyon said forcefully. "That's all the time you'll have to get the lay of their camp, tally the opposition we'll face, and then report back to me."

"Yes, sir," Ben said, realizing how wrong he had been to bring up this point, since it required him to ride faster and farther than anticipated. Fighting didn't bother him, but the riding did. He pulled down his cap to shade his eyes, leaned forward, and put his spurs to the horse's flanks.

The roan shot off like a Fourth of July rocket, forcing Ben to hang on for dear life. He knew better than to gallop the horse too far, but he wanted to get out of sight of the captain and his relentless determination to stir up trouble. The secessionists were everywhere, making General Harney's job all the more difficult. After Lyon's attack, public opinion might sway toward the Federals, but Ben had a gut feeling that this would only split the St. Louis populace even more. Missouri had to remain loyal to the United States or the entire West would be cut off.

Ben drew rein as he came to the top of a ridge and wiped sweat from his forehead. The day was warm, but his condition came more from exertion than outright fear. Spread throughout the hollow at his feet were dozens of tents pitched with rifles stacked in neat military pyramids in front of them. Not even Colonel Prentiss's headquarters company showed such military discipline—and these were supposed to be riffraff gathering into a mob. For a brief instant, Ben wondered if Captain Lyon might not be right and the general wrong. They should snuff out such dedicated rebellion now rather than letting these men—soldiers without uniforms—spread their poison throughout Missouri.

Taking a quick head count, Ben wheeled about and trotted away. All the books he had read about tactics rushed back now, details swirling like leaves caught in a millrace. Before he reached the Federal column he had mentally edited his report and had a detailed recommendation worked out for the attack.

"Sir!" Ben called, throwing Captain Lyon a quick salute. "Forty secesh are camped a mile down the road. All are well-armed, but we can take them because they camped too close to the river. If we force them back, they have to retreat across a tributary to the Mississippi—and it's a broad one."

"Didn't see any ducks among them, then?" asked Lyon, a gleam in his eye. The smile on his lips showed no humor.

"If they try swimming, they'll have to abandon those Brown Bess rifles they're sporting," Ben said. He recognized the arms as having been around for many years. The secession-ists also had a few Kentucky muskets. In some ways, they were better armed than Lyon's infantry. Surprise and mili-tary discipline would have to carry the battle against supe-rior firepower.

"What do you recommend, Lieutenant?"

"If a squad fires on them from the left flank, they'll turn in that direction thinking that it is the major threat," Ben said. "Then we attack with our main force against the side of their line."

"We hit them hard and drive them into the river," Lyon said, rubbing his hands in anticipation.

"That'll work, Captain," Ben said. He pictured the fight in his head. The pre-emptory attack would bring the secesh out to form a line to face their attackers. Then the soldiers would strike with their main force, robbing the rebels of position and forcing them to shoot through their own ranks or break and run. If they ran, they would be cut down in retreat. Otherwise, the Federals would let the secesh escape across the tributary and mop up the remainder on dry land.

Ben Grierson liked the plan and said so.

"I'm glad you approve," Captain Lyon said sarcastically. "Give the orders, sir!"

Ben was taken aback by the officer's attitude but obeyed. He spent a few minutes directing the sergeants so they would get their troops into position for the battle without blunder-ing into their own ranks. Ben had read much about the casualties caused by frightened men who did not understand the battle plan, having been told only to fight. More often than not, they fired on their comrades.

"You're taking too long, Lieutenant," called Lyon. "Get them moving!"

Ben hastily gave the final orders and saw that Lyon already had a platoon moving into position. Heaving a deep sigh, Ben found himself curiously calm, considering this was his first real battle.

Ragged gunfire told him that Captain Lyon's men had opened fire on the secessionist camp too early, allowing the rebels to swing out in a vee formation, defending their own backs while firing directly into the attacking Federal troops.

Benjamin hesitated, took in the scene of confusion, and saw his left flank beginning to sag before being driven back. Without consciously realizing it, he rode forward, yelling and waving his pistol about like a madman. The blue-coated troopers saw this, rallied, and rejoined the attack, forcing the secesh back.

Amid the caustic gunsmoke and choking smell of freshly spilled blood, Ben Grierson led the attack. By the time he reached the edge of the secesh camp, the fight was over. Camp Jackson had fallen.

"Well done, men," Captain Lyon congratulated his troops when they assembled after the skirmish. His men let out a loud cheer. "Now let's move these rebels into town where we can put them where they belong. In jail!"

Another cheer went up. Ben felt less sanguine about this move on the captain's part. The guerrilla force they had captured, some forty men, were better kept away from a city where their friends might rally to their rescue. But Lyon turned a deaf ear to this warning as he force-marched his prisoners on the road straight into St. Louis.

"Captain, send a courier ahead to bring out a larger force to guard the prisoners," Ben urged. "Or wait until the general returns. We can keep the prisoners away from town until then."

"I am capable of getting these secesh to a prison without appealing to civil authorities."

"Don't try to hog the glory," Ben warned.

"You are out of line, sir!" raged Captain Lyon.

"I couldn't care less if you win a medal for this day's fight, but I beg you, don't dangle these prisoners in front of their friends in St. Louis. You'll be throwing raw meat to a hungry wolf. Rebel sympathizers will have to rescue their friends."

"Let them try and be damned," said Lyon.

Before Ben could argue the point further, he heard a sergeant giving the command for his troopers to prepare to fire. As he had feared, a crowd grew around their column as they marched into the city, and the identity of the prisoners became common knowledge in minutes.

"Free them, you butcher!" shouted a man in the mushrooming crowd. He reared back and let fly with a stone, forcing Lyon to duck.

Ben tried to countermand the captain's order and failed, his command drowned out by the report of a dozen muskets discharging and the shrieks of anger and pain from the crowd. The conflict quickly turned into a massacre with Captain Lyon in the vanguard, his sword slashing and turning bloody with civilian blood.

Promotion and Secession

May 15, 1861
Cairo, Illinois

"It's good to see you again, Benjamin." John Charles Frémont thrust out his hand for a firm shake. Frémont was almost as tall as Ben but far more handsome, his olive complexion, light blue eyes, and curly hair more befitting a dandy than The Pathfinder.

"It's been a while, General," Ben Grierson said, eyeing his friend's epaulets. "Your promotion was well deserved." He knew even Frémont's new rank would not afford him easy entry into the Grierson home; Alice looked askance at the man because of his background. To Ben it hardly mattered that John Charles's parents had not been married. The man had proven himself a brave explorer and the finest proponent of Manifest Destiny in the country.

"I wish it had come under different circumstances," Frémont said.

"You look tired, General."

Frémont glanced around. Colonel Prentiss bustled about across the command headquarters, trying not to seem too curious about the new general in charge of the Western Army talking privately with his aide-de-camp. But Ben had already reported fully to Prentiss, who had sent the story up the chain of command of what Nathaniel Lyon had done in St. Louis.

After the report, events had moved swiftly, bringing Ben back to the Illinois Volunteers, and Frémont to Cairo.

"It was a long ride, Ben. I couldn't believe it when the President chose me for command, especially under such trying circumstances."

"Lyon should have been relieved of his command! I hope you'll see fit to punish him for what he did!" Ben flared. He sucked in a deep breath and tried to calm himself. Usually, he didn't fly off the handle like this, but Lyon had done everything wrong and now the Union was going to pay the price.

"Calm down and tell me what you think. I read your report. It was quite temperate, considering the twenty-eight deaths among the civilians. I know how you feel about such useless violence, but I need to know your impressions if I am to ably command several hundred thousand men."

Ben's eyes widened. He knew the Union had a considerable force in the West but had not realized his friend would command so many. His admiration for Frémont grew by leaps and bounds. They had met during the 1860 campaign for president. Frémont had been the first Republican candidate in 1856 and, as such, Ben had fully supported him in his futile bid for the post. John Charles had been disappointed when the party chose Lincoln over him for the next election, but his party loyalty had never wavered as he and his wife, Jessie, campaigned in both Missouri and Illinois for Lincoln. Now it had paid off with a command vitally important to the United States.

"Lyon should never have gone after the secesh, as he called them. When he did capture them, he foolishly herded them into St. Louis where their allies could cause trouble.

I'm not saying Lyon wasn't defending himself and his men by firing into the crowd, but he should have avoided the entire sordid situation."

"Calm logic is not part of Major Lyon's makeup."

Ben stiffened. He knew the Army had had two choices. General Harney could either have court-martialed his errant captain or promoted him.

"Did he get a medal, too?" Ben asked acidly.

"No, but the promotion came quickly." Frémont sagged a little from fatigue. "Almost as quickly as Missouri's vote to secede. Governor Jackson is already enlisting state militia for service with the Confederacy."

"No!"

"My father-in-law heard immediately and made certain I got Jessie away from St. Louis. There are distinct advantages to having Thomas Hart Benton as a father-in-law."

"The most powerful man in the Senate," murmured Ben.

"Not quite powerful enough, it seems. Even his eloquent rhetoric couldn't sway Claiborne Jackson. The legislature's decision hasn't been made public yet, but will soon." Frémont laughed without humor. "There's hardly anyone on either side of the question who doesn't know the result."

"Lyon precipitated the secession of an entire state? This was what the general feared. And Lyon was promoted!"

"I read between the lines of your report and the one filed by Lyon. You acquitted yourself well, old friend."

"The captain—the major—did not follow the best line of attack at Camp Jackson. If it hadn't been for the guerrillas' inexperience in battle, Lyon would have suffered defeat at the camp. Considering all that happened later, that might have been for the best."

"I agree. Tell me everything about the battle. I need to learn what I can of rebel tactics since it appears that I will be going up against a Mexican War veteran. Governor Jackson has enlisted Sterling Price to be the head of his militia, and I know little of his preferences."

"Were the secesh in Camp Jackson under Price's orders?" asked Colonel Prentiss, coming up from where he had been straining to eavesdrop. His curiosity had finally gotten the better of him, but Frémont did not seem to mind the intrusion.

"I have reason to believe they were—that is, Senator Benton does, based on everything he has seen and heard."

Frémont went to a map spread on a large table and motioned that Ben should trace out the progress of Lyon's attack on the rebel camp. Ben saw red Xs already marked across it and wondered if these were military targets, enemy positions, or something more. He quickly outlined how the attack should have proceeded. Both Frémont and Prentiss listened silently as he explained his strategy.

"You have the making of a fine officer, Ben," Frémont said. "I'd find a spot for you on my staff but you'd be wasted in an office. With such instinctive command of tactics, I'm sure Colonel Prentiss can better use you in the field. We will need all the level-headed officers we can find if we are to win this fight."

Ben started to protest. There was no position he would rather have than to be on the Western Commander's staff. He might even become a fully paid officer, able to send home money to Alice and the boys. But he saw that Frémont already prepared to leave without making the offer.

"Thank you for letting him stay in the Illinois command, sir," Prentiss said as he saluted Frémont.

"You'd better be sharp, Colonel. Benjamin Grierson will have your position some day."

"I'm not angling for that, sir," Ben quickly said. "Unless the colonel receives a deserved promotion to general, that is."

"A soldier and a diplomat. You'll go far, Ben, yes, you will." General Frémont stepped back, waited for Ben and Prentiss, returned their salutes, and then left. As he went through the camp, he picked up a phalanx of staff until it looked as if flies were buzzing around a tasty morsel wearing gold braid.

"He's right, Ben. I *can* use a man with your ability," Colonel Prentiss said. "Let me outline what I have in mind."

Ben Grierson's head still spun from so much praise from such a high-ranking officer. John Charles was his friend, yes, but he had been speaking as a general. He barely listened as Prentiss detailed his first assignment.

First Command

June 2, 1861
Elliot's Mill, Kentucky

Benjamin Grierson rubbed his hands on his pants legs, then looked around to see if any of his men noticed his nervousness. As much as he appreciated Colonel Prentiss's faith in him, he realized how little he really knew of military command, of life and bloodshed in battle. The small skirmish at Camp Jackson had been a revelation to him, and he had acted instinctively to take command when the troops flagged. But Nathaniel Lyon had been the officer in charge. If the fight had become protracted, his experience would have saved his soldiers. Ben hated to admit it, but his foolish charge without knowing what he was doing might have lost the battle—and lives. He had been lucky and nothing more at Camp Jackson.

"No, no, that's wrong. Lyon was a bullheaded fool wanting glory. Nothing more," Ben said to himself as he looked out over the prow of the steamship bearing him and his two companies of infantry up the Ohio to Kentucky.

"How's that, sir?" asked his sergeant, a boy hardly eighteen and still one of the oldest soldiers in the volunteer company. Sergeant Willie Carruthers had already seen more combat than Ben, in spite of being so much younger. For a frantic moment, Ben wanted to turn command over to Carruthers. Then he came to his senses. Any show of weakness or indecision on his part would race through the soldiers like some debilitating plague. That would kill more than any error he might make in the heat of battle.

"I'm not used to riding on a boat. The motion is making me a little uneasy," Ben lied, hoping this would cover the real cause of his nerves.

"You reckon we'll see much action?" Sergeant Carruthers asked.

"I don't know, but I doubt it," he answered. "Kentucky is neutral."

"Then why're we goin' to Elliot's Mill? We weren't told nuthin' back in camp."

Since General Frémont had taken over the headquarters of the Illinois Volunteers for his own command post, the flow of information had almost stopped. What little Ben learned was more grapevine rumor than actual fact. Colonel Prentiss spent more time with Frémont and less with his troops, putting a burden on his untrained officers to discipline and drill green recruits to prepare them for combat. Ben had worked hard with his men, following what precepts he could from his books, and had been chosen for this mission.

"The secessionists are kicking up a bit of a fuss," Ben told his sergeant. "It's our job to stop them and make certain Kentucky remains neutral."

"Be good if they saw the light and threw in with us," Carruthers said. Ben swallowed hard. How young the sergeant looked!

"That's why I want my orders followed instantly and completely. We will not have a repeat of the slaughter in St. Louis."

"That Major Lyon is somethin' of a hero among the men,

sir," the boy told him hesitantly. "Truth to tell, I admire the way he went and got them secesh. But you were there. You know what happened."

The steamboat whistle blared as the boat slithered over a sandbar, forcing Ben to grab a stanchion to keep from falling overboard. The pilot expertly maneuvered the paddle wheeler closer to a dock.

"Prepare the men to disembark. Make certain they don't leave any equipment behind. We might find ourselves needing it all."

"Yes, sir," Sergeant Carruthers said, starting away. The boy stopped, then, flustered, turned and saluted. "Sorry, sir. I ain't used to this salutin'. Not yet."

"Dismissed," Ben said, wanting to agree. He had written Alice telling her of his discomfiture at being saluted all over the camp and having to remember to salute his superior officers first, but she had not yet had time to respond. For a moment, a smile crept across Ben's lips. His young boys were good but a bit more discipline would suit them even better. Should he have them salute him? When he was in uniform?

"All ready to march, sir," came the sergeant's shrill voice.

The steamboat banged hard into the dock and four men hastily fastened the heavy hawsers to posts to keep the boat secure against the strong river current.

Ben walked down the gangplank and found his orderly waiting with his mount. The best part of the river trip from Cairo had been not riding a horse. He got into the saddle and started his own quick scouting mission while his soldiers disembarked. The few roustabouts greeted him cheerily, and he saw no trace of the insurrection against the Union that had so worried Colonel Prentiss.

"Sergeant, get the men moving down yonder road," Ben said, seeing a signpost indicating the way to Elliot's Mill. He had spent hours on the trip memorizing maps of the terrain and had found them sketchy at best. Having the road so well marked aided his quick advance.

An hour later, Ben halted his two companies of men and surveyed the mill noisily grinding away. A few workers moved sacks of cornmeal onto a wagon, but nowhere did he see an encampment matching that of Camp Jackson. Knowing his experience was limited, Ben preferred to err on the side of caution.

"Sergeant, send out four parties to scout the mill. I want a report in ten minutes, so choose your quickest runners."

"Yes, sir." Carruthers chose the men at random, or so it seemed to Ben, but the soldiers dashed off to obey, leaving him to study the terrain and compare it with his map. The map might have been of Detroit for all the resemblance it bore to Elliot's Mill. Ben quickly decided on the best way to array his men so they could deliver devastating fire without exposing themselves to return fire.

"They're back, sir," Carruthers said. Four red-faced, panting men hurried through their reports.

Ben listened in silence and tried to keep from smiling. He was a soldier now and should fight the enemy. But he was more than a little relieved when all four of the soldiers reported that the secessionists had turned tail and run before the Union force.

Ben ordered his men to camp at the mill that night and formed them into choral groups to sing some gospel and even a few bawdier tunes to bolster their spirits. He only wished they had brought along some instruments. They could have had a victory concert.

Later, after the sentries were posted and the main body of his troop had bedded down for the night, he wrote Alice of his first command and how anticlimactic it had been. He concluded the letter with a heartfelt belief that the war would soon be over and that the secessionists lacked any real military muscle or will to fight.

Cat's-paw

"Good to see you back, Lieutenant," greeted the sergeant who had served him so ably two months earlier. Sergeant Carruthers had remained in Cairo when Colonel Prentiss and Ben Grierson had been reassigned to a command in southern Missouri. Colonel Prentiss had brought Ben back to the center of Frémont's power.

"Glad to be back, even if it is for a short time. Are they treating you well?"

"Couldn't be better. Me and the boys, we had braggin' rights when we got back from Elliot's Mill. None of the rest have so much as seen a secesh." Carruthers grinned broadly, tobacco-stained teeth apparent. The young sergeant had taken up a noxious habit. Ben considered mentioning it, then decided not to. Let the boy have his vice.

Ben started to point out that they hadn't either encountered any enemy, not at Elliot's Mill. But he held his tongue. Boys like this would see battle soon enough. He had been seriously wrong when he wrote his wife that the war would be over quickly.

The Confederates' decisive victory two weeks earlier at Bull Run had shown that this would not be a short conflict. Ben tried to find some solace in his error by telling himself how little he knew of military matters or political ones. Illinois politics were certainly not those of the rest of the nation, where every state had its own goals and ways of living.

"If you're lookin' for the general, he's over in the command HQ." Carruthers pointed using his middle finger. He saw Ben staring at him and smiled sheepishly. "Shot my trigger finger off right after we got back from the mill. Danged fool thing to do, but I was cleanin' my musket, not payin' a whole lot of attention and—"

"There's no need to explain. I'm sure you will deliver worse injury to the enemy," Ben said uneasily. Over and over he saw evidence of how poorly trained these soldiers were and how badly they needed someone to take firm control of their instruction. He had been lucky that the secessionists had fled if his top sergeant knew so little about firearms.

"Thanks, sir. If you need an aide, keep me in mind, will you, sir?"

Ben nodded, returned the boy's salute and walked slowly toward the HQ building. Frémont had renovated it but not the soldiers in his command. That boded ill for the Union should they face a determined enemy, as McDowell had at Chinn Ridge. Ben had gone over the snippets of information about Bull Run and had decided McDowell had done well, but green troops had been his downfall.

He paused on the steps of Frémont's command post and looked around. All he saw were green troops.

"Benjamin!" came the cheery greeting from inside. "What are you doing here? Doesn't Prentiss have enough to keep you busy?"

"General Frémont, good to see you again, sir." Ben remembered to salute his friend and worked to get all his thoughts in order. His mind had drifted to the problems of training, but now he had to present his colonel's case quickly. He had been around enough command centers to know that Frémont might not have more than a minute or two, even for an old friend.

"Come in. I have to meet with my staff in a few minutes, but tell me why you're back in Cairo. It's so good to see you!"

"Sir," Ben said, finally getting his wits about him. "Colonel Prentiss is unhappy with being sent to southern Missouri. He feels the command position is beneath his—"

"Benjamin, please," Frémont said, looking harried. He had dark circles under his pale blue eyes and his usually ebullient nature had faded like dyed cloth left in the bright sunlight. "Lay it out for me without all the fine words. Prentiss is upset that I put Grant into command over him, isn't that it?"

"I know nothing about Colonel Grant, sir, but you cut right to the heart of the matter. Colonel Prentiss felt he deserved promotion and that being stationed in southern Missouri was a slight."

"Grant's a good soldier, solid and daring when he has to be. I see great things ahead for him."

"The colonel feels shut out of decision making, sir," Ben said, still hunting for the argument that would get his commander back into the mainstream. "There's scant rebel activity and with Grant in overall command, there's no chance to perform greater service to the Union."

Frémont looked distracted. Ben saw a major beckoning to the general.

"I've got to start the staff meeting. Look, Ben, would Prentiss be more favorably inclined with a command in Kentucky? You know the area. He sent you there on the Elliot's Mill raid. Could his expertise help there?"

"Do you mean would he be happier in Kentucky than in southern Missouri?" Ben thought a moment and then nodded. Kentucky was still neutral and was closer to Prentiss's Illinois home. He thought homesickness was as much of the colonel's problem as being skipped over for command the way he had. Ben wondered at Frémont's decision to place Grant in charge of so many soldiers after hearing Prentiss's ranting, raving appraisal of the man and his sorry character.

"Good. I'll issue the order transferring Colonel Prentiss to Kentucky. Give my regards to Alice when you write her," Frémont said, shaking Ben's hand and then hurrying off without waiting for a proper salute.

Ben stood for a moment, watching his friend retreat into the closed meeting with his top officers. He had done as Colonel Prentiss asked and had gotten him a transfer from a dead-end command, but he didn't feel right about it. Even worse, he couldn't figure out what had gone wrong.

Collision of Wills

August 10, 1861
Cairo, Illinois

Ben Grierson stood behind his colonel. To say he was ill at ease was an understatement. He would rather have faced the Confederate General Jeff Thompson down in Missouri, with all his guerrillas and irregulars flocking about the small regular army unit the rebel commanded, than to be here now.

"You don't understand, Colonel," Ulysses Grant said, his voice slurred slightly by alcohol. "You're not in command. I am. I outrank you!"

"General Frémont put me in charge." Prentiss thrust out his jaw and bumped up against Grant, daring him to make a scene. They looked like two schoolboys about to have a playground scuffle. Ben saw his friend's miscalculation but couldn't warn him quickly enough.

Grant, disheveled and looking as if he had already fought a long war, shoved the colonel back a step. Not content, he followed aggressively and shoved him again, harder. Prentiss was so startled that he made a misstep and fell onto his behind. Looking up at the dark-bearded, looming Grant made him furious.

Prentiss leaped to his feet and swung. His fist lightly grazed Grant's cheek.

"That's the way it's going to be, eh?" growled Grant. "Let's settle this once and for all." He stripped off his shabby uniform coat and tossed it onto the floor. In shirtsleeves, he squared off for a bout of fisticuffs.

"Colonel, please," begged Ben. Prentiss shrugged him off.

"He insulted me. I was put in command of those troops, and he ordered them back to southeastern Missouri."

"Where they could find a decent fight. You were running off with them to Kentucky. There's no fighting there. I'm up to my ears in guerrillas in Missouri!" Grant stepped forward and punched, his fist hitting Prentiss in the chest.

Before a real donnybrook could start, Ben stepped between the men and held up his hands.

"Please, gentlemen. You're officers. Don't behave like barroom brawlers."

"That's what he is," cried Prentiss. "Look at him! Smell the liquor on him!"

"If I wanted more to drink, I'd run off to Kentucky where they make good whiskey," Grant said.

In spite of himself, Ben had to smile. Ulysses Grant showed pluck and wasn't going to back down, no matter what. Ben saw the traits that Frémont valued in the man, but this was not the time, place, or method of settling such a dispute.

"Can we save the fighting for the rebels?" Ben asked. He thrust out his elbow to keep Prentiss from rounding him for another jab at Grant. Ben faced the truculent Ulysses Grant unflinchingly. This stopped the officer's attack for a moment, but he kept his fists raised as he took Ben's measure.

"You're mighty bold for a lieutenant," Grant said.

"You're mighty foolish for a colonel," Ben shot back.

This brought a more than a smile to Grant's lips. He laughed outright. Then he brushed crumbs from his thick beard and looked a bit more thoughtful but didn't retreat a step.

"Might be we can settle this matter if we can find Frémont," Grant said. "He's the one who gave me overall command."

"Not of my troops!"

"Yes, of yours!" shouted Grant, ready to fight again.

"Please, if you will promise not to maul one another, I'll find General Frémont," Ben said, keeping between the battling officers.

"You've got a brave aide-de-camp there," Grant said to Prentiss, shouting over Ben's shoulder. "You don't deserve him."

"He's my friend. It's you—"

"Gentlemen," Ben said sternly, as if he were disciplining his two small boys. But he was on unknown ground. Neither Robert nor Charlie had ever acted this poorly. He waved frantically when he saw Frémont and his entourage hurrying across the parade ground. Frémont hesitated, considered the situation, then came over.

"What's going on?" John Frémont glared at the tableau. "I've got a war to plan—"

Under his breath so only Ben overheard, Grant said, "Planning's all you ever do."

"General, there is some confusion as to the role of the colonels," Benjamin said, heading off a flurry of angry words from both Prentiss and Grant. He wanted to maintain as much calm reason as he could between the hotheaded officers.

"What happened?" Frémont asked, frowning. "Out with it. You first," he said, pointing to Prentiss.

For ten minutes, with only occasional outbursts from Ulysses Grant, Colonel Prentiss explained his position.

Finally, Frémont cut him off. "I'm sorry for this confusion, Colonel, but Grant's right. He does have overall command."

"We're both colonels!" blurted out Prentiss.

"Well, technically, that is true, but he has time in rank over you." Frémont looked as if he had eaten something that disagreed with him.

"You can't—" began Prentiss.

"I'm actually glad you are both here," Frémont said. "This might clear up the confusion of command. It's my honor and privilege to announce your promotion to brigadier general."

For a moment, Ben wasn't sure whom Frémont addressed. Then it became clear. Brigadier General Grant glared at his rival.

"You can't do this! I'll take the matter up with Governor Yates!" cried Prentiss.

"You didn't let me finish, General Prentiss."

"What's that?"

"You have also been granted a promotion."

"Then I can get my men back!"

"I . . ." Frémont faltered, and Ben understood the reason. If Grant had seniority as a colonel over Prentiss, he maintained that seniority as brigadier general.

"Sir, perhaps a larger command will be forthcoming. The Illinois Volunteers is hardly a large enough detachment for a general," Ben said.

Frémont looked at him with gratitude.

"He is so right, General Prentiss. While General Grant maintains command in the field, you are hereby ordered to Chillicothe where you will be responsible for training all Illinois troops."

Prentiss puffed up at this, but Ben went cold inside. He had given Frémont the idea of giving Prentiss a promotion, but Frémont had effectively stripped him of real command by assigning him a staff position behind the lines. General

Grant's prestige and power soared, while Prentiss's was maintained only by sleight of hand.

Even worse, Ben remained Prentiss' aide-de-camp without pay. He saw no future for a lieutenant on the staff in Chillicothe. None at all.

Promotion

The ride from Cairo had been taxing for him, but Benjamin Grierson tried to look relaxed. He had no idea why Governor Yates had ordered him to the capital in this fashion. It was unusual for the governor to issue such a summons, but even General Prentiss had not argued when Ben showed him the letter he had received.

"Lieutenant Grierson to see the governor," he said to the secretary guarding the governor's office. Ben stood at attention, eyes ahead, although the man staring at him was a civilian and not due this sort of respect. Still, he felt he had gained the upper hand by the way the secretary shot to his feet and hurried to the door. The man gave a quick knock and stuck his head inside.

Ben couldn't hear what the governor said, but the secretary popped out and held the door for him.

"Governor Yates will see you right away, sir."

"Thank you," Ben said, more curious than ever why he was summarily called to the capital.

Richard Yates pushed aside a stack of papers and came around the desk, hand outstretched.

"Ben, so good to see you. Come in, please, sit down."

"It's good to see you, too, Governor," Ben said carefully. Before he had accepted the post as Prentiss's aide-de-camp he had felt comfortable calling the governor by his first name, but somehow the uniform separated them and made this meeting more formal than it would have been under less trying circumstances.

"A cigar, Ben?" Yates opened a box and held it out.

Ben hesitated. He knew what Alice thought of such vices, but the subtle tobacco odor rose to tantalize him. It had been months and months since he had indulged in a cigar. He took one, inhaled deeply, and cut the tip off. The governor waited patiently to light it for him.

He puffed briefly, reveling in the sensuous feel of the smoke passing across his lips.

"Thank you, sir."

"There's no need for such formality, Ben. Not in the office."

"Thank you, Richard. I appreciate such courtesy."

"You always were a stickler for protocol."

"Alice encourages it," Ben said.

"Do you write her regularly?" Yates asked unexpectedly. "You said you would when you accepted your current position."

"Why, yes, I did—and I do. At least once a week and sometimes more often. The past few weeks have been rather dull, and I have written her almost every day." Ben puffed a few more times on the cigar. Perhaps Alice was right. Anything this luxurious must be sinful.

"I have followed your career closely, you know."

"No, Richard, I hadn't known."

"I have, and I must say I have been delighted at your progress."

Ben sniffed in disdain at such fulsome praise. He had

been assigned garrison duty after the single foray to Elliot's Mill. The war seemed to be passing him by as General Grant chased down Sterling Price's forces throughout Missouri. General Prentiss rummaged about Kentucky, futilely chasing secessionists, and John Frémont planned his fantastical, complex campaigns that would bring the South to its knees. Even Nathaniel Lyon continued to range across the country-side chasing down his secesh foes.

Ben Grierson had been a garrison soldier and nothing more.

"You are a modest man. You don't realize how well you have trained the men in your regiment."

"It's hardly my regiment, Richard. They are quickly sent to join Grant's forces. I hardly have time to learn their names."

"General Grant thinks highly of you, Ben."

This took him by surprise. After he had broken up the fistfight between Grant and Prentiss, he had thought his career was over. It had certainly careened into a cul-de-sac when General Prentiss had been transferred to Chillicothe. He had not even followed his mentor, but had been stranded in Cairo as a training officer.

"I didn't realize that," Ben said honestly.

"It gives me great pleasure to give you these," Richard Yates said, reaching to a small box on his desk. He flipped it open. Inside gleamed major's pips. "Your sacrifice and devotion to duty is being rewarded, Major Grierson."

Mixed emotions flowed through him.

"This is a great honor, sir. Richard. It is especially so for a training officer."

"I've spoken with Prentiss and Grant on this matter and both agree your talents are wasted in garrison duty. If you will accept, command of the Sixth Illinois Cavalry is yours."

"I don't know what to say, Richard," he mumbled. Ben found the conflicting emotions to be almost overpowering. Promotion meant he would have a major's pay to send back to Alice to help support her and the boys, but he had been given command of a cavalry regiment. That meant more time in the saddle than he preferred.

"I accept, sir," Ben heard himself say.

"Excellent. Illinois and the Union could use a thousand more men of your ability and patriotism." Richard Yates pumped his hand and then turned more somber. "There is one other item I find it my duty to pass along."

Ben sat a little straighter, the cigar burning unnoticed between his fingers. He knew the preamble to cheerless news when he heard it.

"It's John Frémont," the governor said. "No, not that," Yates hurriedly said when he saw the shock on Ben's face. "He's not injured. I know the two of you are friends, and I certainly know him socially. That's why I wanted to be the one to tell you, as a mutual friend. He's been removed from command due to his lack of success against the rebels."

"He's a good man," Ben said, a little relieved that Frémont was all right. Another part of Ben felt great relief. Frémont planned endlessly but never quite delivered the victories in the field. A more action-oriented commander would be good for the Union. "John Charles will find a new post and serve ably."

"I'm sure he will," Yates said, the smile returning, "but his star is setting and yours is rising, Ben."

Ben opened the box and looked at the major's insignia. For a brief instant his eyes betrayed him and he saw general's stars. Then he closed the box. Being a major, even of cavalry, was honor enough.

Rout

November 2, 1861
Jefferson City, Missouri

Ben Grierson hunkered down by the banked campfire and scratched in the dirt with a twig, rubbed out the wiggly lines, and started over for the sixth time. He looked up when Sergeant Carruthers sauntered up and looked over Ben's attempt to make a map.

"You still plottin' 'nd plannin', Major?" the young sergeant asked. He scratched himself, his missing finger obvious. He shoved his injured hand under his wool uniform to keep it warm as new arctic-cold wind whipped down from the north. "You better not think too much or you'll end up like General Frémont."

"His fault is being too much of a visionary," Ben said. Frémont's problem had been more political than military, it turned out. Ben had learned that his former mentor had issued an emancipation proclamation, which had horrified Lincoln. The president feared such a decree, freeing slaves in Missouri, would push non-secessionist slaveholders into Confederate hands. And it had. By the time Lincoln had rescinded the order and replaced Frémont, Missouri had seceded and once-neutral Kentucky had become a fierce battleground.

That expanding conflict had seen the demise of his other mentor, too. Ulysses Grant had quickly replaced Prentiss when it became obvious Prentiss was not aggressive enough pursuing rebel guerrillas.

"Grant wants action, not thinkin'," Carruthers declared, as if this settled all war matters. "Will we see action soon, Major?"

"Sterling Price is moving a lot of men and matériel through here, going east toward the Mississippi for some sort of campaign. We have to be cautious in how we proceed."

"The men trust you, sir," Carruthers said.

"All sixteen of them?" laughed Ben. "I'm flattered. We'll see how they regard me after we mix it up with the rebels."

Ben scuffed out his last map. His scout had returned with sketchy information about a small band of guerrillas outside Jefferson City. Not sure what the rebels were up to, Ben vowed to find out. All the way through Missouri he had skirmished with rebel forces but had never fully engaged. He heaved a deep sigh. Being in a cavalry unit had one benefit. If he couldn't outfight the enemy, he could outrun them.

"Orders, sir?"

"Get the men mounted, Sergeant. We're going to find out what Price is doing." Ben's horse stood saddled and waiting for him. He took a few seconds to fish out a lump of sugar for the animal, patted it, and then climbed into the saddle. Other cavalry officers assured him he would get used to being astride a horse for hours on end. He wondered when this might occur.

He wheeled his horse about and went to the head of the small column. Having sixteen men allowed him to move fast, but he couldn't stand and fight any significant force. Right now, Grant wanted intelligence returned to his Cairo headquarters about Sterling Price and the size of his army.

Too many rumors clouded the issue, and Grant was not a man to wait patiently. The way Ben read the general, he was everything John Frémont was not.

They rode silently through the dawn until they came to a side road skirting Jefferson City. Ben signalled Carruthers to take this rutted road. As they made their way along it, he saw evidence of the recent passage of horses.

A lot of horses.

"Sir?" Sergeant Carruthers rode alongside. "You seein' what I do?"

Ben looked up from the hoofprints. He felt a surge of anticipation when he saw four thin gray spirals of smoke from campfires rising above the stand of sweet-gum trees a hundred yards ahead.

"Reckon there must be a bigger force than the scout reported," the sergeant said.

"Might be they joined up with another batch of guerrillas," Ben said, more to himself than to his sergeant.

"What do we do, sir?"

"Take eight men, and go around to the far side of the camp."

"Sir, there's got to be a hunnerd rebels!"

"About the right number for a fair fight," Ben said, his mind working like a machine. He estimated their chances and saw they were good, in spite of being sorely outnumbered. "Don't let the men stop firing. I want a lot of lead flying until I give the order to stop. Do you understand, Sergeant?"

"I hear you, Major. General Grant wanted some spirited fights. This is gonna be one of the most spirited. I jist hope it's not us what end up bein' spirits."

"Courage, Sergeant," Ben said. His heart raced but outwardly he was calm. He felt much as he had during the assault at Camp Jackson. This time was different in one respect, however. He was in charge. If anything went wrong, he, Major Benjamin Grierson, would be court-martialed.

Ben drew his pistol, cocked it, then reached back into his

saddlebags and pulled out a second pistol. He thrust this one into his belt and waited patiently as Carruthers took his squad to the far side of the rebel camp. When he figured the sergeant was in position, Ben launched the attack with a loud cry, "For Illinois, for the Union, for victory!"

Hooves clattering, guns blazing, he led the charge through the center of the rebel camp. The startled guerrillas were still half-asleep. A few poked about making breakfast. What sentries had been placed around the camp failed to note the Union cavalry advance until it was too late. Ben personally shot one guard, then switched pistols because the cylinder of the first came up empty.

Shouting at the top of his lungs, he led his eight men to the middle of the rebel bivouac and joined with his sergeant's force coming from the opposite direction. Ben signaled that they should retreat at right angles to their entry, cutting the camp into quarters with the attack.

What return fire he received was minor and disorganized. In less than an hour, Major Grierson and his sixteen men marched out eighty captured rebels. He had scored an impressive victory without a single loss.

Rebellion in the Ranks

December 10, 1861
Camp Yates, Illinois

"I tell you, Major, the men're gettin' mighty uneasy. They can't take no more neglect." Sergeant Carruthers shifted nervously from foot to foot as he stood in front of his company commander. He looked more like a schoolboy waiting for punishment than a veteran soldier missing a trigger finger and more than one tooth.

"Have you taken this concern elsewhere?" Ben Grierson asked. He and the sergeant had an understanding that worked well, up to a point. Ben was not a man to force into decision over political matters, although his entire life had somehow devolved into such pursuits. He had been reassigned to the Camp Yates training brigade, in spite of his successes for Grant in southeastern Missouri.

"The men, well, they sorta picked me to speak up for them. We been together fer a spell and they think I got special influence with you."

"You came to me rather than to Colonel Cavanaugh. That's

not the proper chain of command. He's regimental commander and can address their concerns."

"We ain't got concerns, Major. We got problems. Like as
not, we don't have enough food. Blankets? What the boys don't
get from home they don't get. Some of 'em are freezin' and
we ain't even fightin'."

"General Grant needs recruits who know which direction
to fire."

"They ain't learnin' sich things here, not from the colonel."

"Don't be disrespectful," Ben snapped, although he
agreed. It was bad for morale if he allowed a noncom to
speak ill of his commander.

"He don't deserve respect. Where is he now, Major? You
tell me."

Ben leaned back in his creaking chair and studied the
sergeant. They had been through several battles and he had
requested Carruthers when he discovered he had again
been assigned to train raw recruits. He couldn't tell if this
pleased Carruthers. Probably not. They endured the same
savage conditions that troops in the field did, only without
being shot at. Since Colonel Cavanaugh had assumed
command, desertions had more than tripled. Ben hardly
knew which faces would be familiar every morning at assembly.

"The colonel has been called to Springfield for, uh, important business."

"We know why he's there. He's throwin' fancy-ass parties
and dinin' on cavvy-are and thick steaks while we're starvin'
in the cold. Sir."

"You tread perilously close to insubordination," Ben
warned. What rankled the most was Cavanaugh's inability to
keep his partying from the troops. By a wild stretch of the
imagination, what he did might be considered useful. The
politicians and their wives whom he wined and dined were
the ones the Illinois infantry and cavalry depended on for

supplies and replacement troopers. Should the politicians falter, the entire state might be in peril.

Major General David Hunter had been given Frémont's command and had retaken St. Louis, only to be replaced by Henry "Old Brains" Halleck, who was too engrossed in fighting to the south ever to care what Cavanaugh did in Illinois. Ben had lost all his contacts save Ulysses Grant, with whom he exchanged letters sporadically.

In spite of the general's carousing, Ben found himself liking Grant more and more and the officers over him less and less. Halleck was a decent enough garrison commander but lacked Grant's aggressive military style, just as Colonel Cavanaugh lacked any interest in his men if his own career could be advanced.

"Sir, all I'm sayin' is that the men don't like sittin' 'round the post starvin' and freezin'."

"The weather is too inclement for drill and target practice," Ben agreed. He knew marksmanship was out of the question since they hadn't received either powder or bullets in two weeks. But dry-firing gave the men some idea of what they had to do when they received ammunition and decent muskets.

"They want you to—" began Carruthers. Ben cut him off.

"They need a morale builder. That shipment headed west. The one with the broken-down wagon."

"What of it?" asked Carruthers. "There weren't no food or rifles."

"Only musical instruments," Ben said with gusto. "Just the thing to keep the men occupied. Find out how many play an instrument and give them ones from the cargo. If any others know how to read music or sing, assemble them into a choir."

"Sir, I—"

"That was an order, Sergeant," Ben said sternly. He rubbed his cold hands together in anticipation of some decent music again. How he missed Sundays with Alice and the boys, playing the piano and singing.

"What are you, Major? A music teacher?"

"I have done that, Sergeant. It is a noble profession."

"Didn't mean to say it wasn't." Carruthers started to speak again, then saluted and left in a hurry. Ben rummaged through his desk and found a packet of music that could be adapted to trumpet, fife, and drum. He had neglected to inventory the instruments in the abandoned wagon, but knew he could make do.

He fussed about for fifteen minutes to give Sergeant Carruthers time to dispense the instruments, then went out into the blustery winter afternoon. Ben had to smile when he saw the ranks of men holding their instruments and looking bewildered.

"Gentlemen, welcome to the Sixth Illinois Cavalry band practice. You hold your instruments because Sergeant Carruthers believes you can play them. Let's see."

For an hour he listened to horrible squawks and screeches that slowly turned into a semblance of music. When this happened, he began the men marching as they played. It pleased him that their close-order drill was greatly improved with the music allowing them to keep in step.

Ben halted the ragged band and congratulated them on their expertise.

"We will assemble tomorrow and practice a few of the songs I have discovered in my sheet music."

"Major," called a private toward the middle of the rank. "We don't want to be here."

"Nonsense. You have the makings of a good band. Practice will take off the rough edges. Soon enough you'll be playing concerts for the entire post."

"It's the damned colonel," the man protested. "We don't like the way he flits off and leaves us on our own. We signed up to fight, not to stand around."

"You have not been standing around, Private," Ben said coldly. He felt the mood of the men and did not like it. "You have practiced drilling today, receiving and obeying orders."

"Hell, Rafe got confused a couple times and hit them sour notes."

"Everyone knew it—and so did Rafe," Ben said, not knowing who had spoken or who out of the fifty men Rafe might be. "So you will learn other things you will need to know to fight the secessionists."

"We don't want Cavanaugh leadin' us. We want you, Major!"

This was greeted by a rousing cheer. Ben was disappointed to see that Sergeant Carruthers joined the men. He had feared this was the message the sergeant had tried to bring him earlier and the one he had tried to deflect.

"A-ten-shun!" Ben bellowed. Seeing the men come to a semblance of attention, he stepped onto the boardwalk in front of his office and faced them. "You are soldiers and will obey lawful orders. You do not choose your officers."

"The Johnny Rebs do," muttered a man to Ben's left. Ben started to berate him, then realized he had to ignore this small insurrection if he wanted to put down the larger one brewing that might destroy the entire regiment.

"You are under my orders and I am under Colonel Cavanaugh's. General Grant wants it that way, Major General Halleck wants it that way, and President Lincoln expects our complete obedience. There are fine officers in this grand and glorious army defending the republic. There are other officers who are not so fine," Ben said, sensing he had the men's attention. To deny men like Cavanaugh existed would be to lose the recruits' loyalty with a blatant lie. "Good or bad, brilliant or foolish, however, they are officers and *you will obey them all*. By God, if you do not, I shall see you courtmartialed! If you disobey orders, I will see you shot! Do I make myself clear?"

Carruthers muttered, "Yes, sir."

"Sergeant, these men shall assemble tomorrow morning after mess to play *decent* music. Now, have them police the parade grounds and then dismiss them so they can clean their musical instruments."

Ben spun in a smart about-face and went inside, not wanting to hear the muttered comments on his little speech. He shared their feelings about how inept Colonel Cavanaugh was as commander, but Cavanaugh was the commanding officer of Camp Yates and would be obeyed, if not respected.

Or Benjamin Grierson would know the reason.

Replaced

April 9, 1862
Camp Yates, Illinois

"Another batch of 'em sent on their way," Sergeant Carruthers said, rubbing his nose with the hand missing the trigger finger. He sneezed like a cannon discharging. The spring brought with it diseases Ben Grierson could not identify, but it seemed as if his trainees, and the few permanent staff under his command, contracted every one.

"I know," Ben said, watching as the soldiers marched out smartly, cadence perfect and maintained by the tune they played as they left. Every regiment he had dispatched into the field kept a small band for morale. He wished enough musicians had remained behind to bolster his spirits.

"You're lookin' mighty down in the mouth, if you don't mind my sayin' so, Major," Carruthers said. "The missus not writin' back?"

"Oh, Mrs. Grierson is keeping up a steady stream of letters." He smiled, remembering the Christmas visit she, Charlie, and Robert had paid the camp. It was hardly a fitting reunion, but he was so glad to see them. In the flesh was far better than a thousand letters, and it had been troublesome when Alice left. Watching her ride off had set into motion all his doubts.

Ben felt the war was passing him by. Shiloh, Pea Ridge, the fall of New Orleans, the defeat of the Confederate fleet at Memphis—all had happened while he sat safe and sound in the dusty, drafty building at Camp Yates. The men he trained fought in those battles, and he remained behind, twiddling his thumbs and trying to think up new and better songs for them to play as they trained.

His early victories had deluded him into thinking there was a career for him in the Army, even if it was astride a horse in some cavalry unit.

"Not many officers in these here parts for you to carouse with, sir," the sergeant pointed out, "especially with the colonel gone all the time." He swallowed hard when he saw Ben's expression. "Maybe carouse wasn't the right word."

"Socialize," Ben supplied.

"Yeah, that's what I meant, Major," the sergeant hastily said.

Ben shrugged. Camp Yates was hardly the crossroads of the war. General Grant had moved south. Rumor had him attacking Vicksburg as soon as he put down that devil Nathan Bedford Forrest. The Confederate general had fewer than a thousand horse soldiers but made life impossible for Grant. There wasn't a secure supply line running from Illinois into Missouri that the wily guerrilla general had not attacked. As Union forces pushed farther south, winning their costly Pyrrhic victories at places like Prairie Grove, Nathan Bedford Forrest began raiding on home ground with the full support of the civilian population.

Still, Ben couldn't complain too much. He had made friends with another general who came to inspect the troops. The fiery, red-haired William T. Sherman had returned several times as much to socialize, as he had pointed out to Sergeant Carruthers, as he had to supervise the training offered by Ben and to accept the recruits into his division.

Ben mopped his forehead and stuffed his handkerchief, embroidered by Alice for him as a present, back into the front of his wool jacket.

"We'll be getting more recruits soon, Sergeant," he said.

"Recruitment's down, Major. That's what I hear."

Ben squinted. The sentry in a wood tower at the corner of the camp signaled that a considerable number of men was approaching. For a fleeting moment, he wished it might be a sneak attack by Forrest. He had studied the reports and felt he knew how the man's mind worked, how he formed his guerrilla attacks, and the secrets to his success. Then he knew this could never be. Even if Nathan Bedford Forrest struck this far north, Camp Yates was not much of a target. With the last regiment already on the road, marching south to join Grant's army outside Vicksburg, all the Confederate general would find here was a handful of men and no supplies at all.

As usual, Colonel Cavanaugh was away from the post furthering his own career and trying to get a transfer back East where the real fighting was. But unless Ben guessed wrong, Cavanaugh sought a staff position in Washington, D.C., rather than a combat command.

"Fancy that," the sergeant said. "Looks like you'll get a chance to do some socializin' after all, Major."

"Have the cook prepare a special meal in the officers' mess," Ben ordered. "Entertaining the governor will be a true honor."

He smoothed his uniform as he marched out onto the parade grounds to wait for Governor Yates to step down from his carriage and see the training camp named after him.

"Ben!" called the governor hurrying forward, hand outstretched.

"Good to see you again, sir," Ben said. He saluted, although he didn't have to, since Yates was a civilian, and then shook hands. "I ordered the cook to whip up something special."

"I didn't mean to put you out," the governor said.

"If you'd come this morning, we'd've had a brass band to greet you."

"I've heard of your training techniques. The field commanders think highly of the men you send them."

"The recruits are devoted and patriotic," Ben said. "All I hope is that they have learned enough to keep themselves alive and win the war for our great state."

"Illinois is proud of them—and you, Ben." Yates put his arm around the officer's shoulders and steered him away from the carriage where they could talk in private. "I am on my way to Cairo to meet with General Sherman. When I mentioned I was stopping here to see you, he entrusted me with a special mission."

"Special mission, sir?" asked Ben. "What might that be?"

Richard Yates grinned ear to ear.

"I'm not the only one pleased with your performance. The general has authorized me to tell of your promotion to colonel."

"Colonel, sir?"

Yates cleared his throat. "The reason I wanted to speak in private rather than announcing it before the entire post is that Colonel Cavanaugh has been relieved of command."

"I see, sir," Ben said. He had known it would be a matter of time before Cavanaugh either found his way higher up the chain of command or slipped to the bottom. From what Yates said, he wasn't sure which it was, though he hoped Cavanaugh would never command a fighting force.

"General Sherman wants you to accept command of the Sixth Illinois Cavalry."

"Command, sir?"

"Although he didn't tell me—perhaps he will when we meet—I suspect he and General Grant have great plans. Plans you will play a great part in."

"Colonel Grierson," Ben said softly. Alice would be so pleased. And he might finally receive an assignment that utilized his full talents, even if it was as commander of a cavalry unit.

"Yes, Ben. Colonel Benjamin Grierson. Congratulations." Yates beamed and again shook Ben's hand like it was a pump handle.

Nighttime Requisition

April 30, 1862
Cairo, Illinois

"Mighty fine-looking men, sir," said Lieutenant Sam Woodward.

"You've done wonders with them," Ben Grierson told his new adjutant.

"Me, sir? Hardly. You had them ready for honing. Even then, I can't take much credit. That sergeant of yours— Carruthers—is a wonder."

"We make a fine team, Sam. All of us." Ben grinned as the band struck up a tune. The somewhat ragged marching turned into precision that would have been the envy of any West Point company of cadets. "But we're going to have a time of it, if General Sherman really does order us into battle. What are we to do? Throw rocks?"

"Didn't the general give any hint about that, sir?" asked Woodward. "He can't expect us to fight without muskets."

"The general's a man after my own heart. A teetotaler, also, but I can't make him understand our position here. After Shiloh he's been given whatever he wants. Supplies, reinforcements, anything." Ben sighed deeply. His own promotion had been a wonder, especially when he found out that Cavanaugh had been forced to resign after Governor Yates had been presented with a petition signed by all thirty-seven other officers in the regiment. Only Ben had not signed—they had not burdened him with their action after he had pointedly told the recruits he would not mutiny against "Old Cav" last year.

Today Ben almost wished Cavanaugh was still in charge of the Sixth Illinois Cavalry. The paperwork had doubled for him, even with Sam's help, and the training had been unrelenting. Coupled with Sherman's promise of action soon, Ben lay awake nights worrying about arms for his troops.

"He has his own ways, sir," Woodward said. "I found a supply order that might interest you." The adjutant reached into his uniform and pulled out a rumpled, sweat-stained paper.

Ben scanned it quickly. His eyebrows rose.

"Sharps carbines with ammunition?"

"One hundred fifty of them, sir. That'd go a ways toward arming a cavalry unit."

"Like the Sixth Illinois Cavalry," Ben said, mind racing. "Who is to receive these fine rifles?"

"Why, sir, we are, if we move fast enough." Woodward grinned wolfishly.

"It's your duty to cut through paperwork for the unit, Sam," Benjamin said, "but if I take your meaning, you want to steal these rifles."

"Requisition while the paperwork is being processed, sir. It's not apparent to me which unit was supposed to receive the Sharps rifles. That means it's as likely to be us as one of Sherman's which'll get the arms."

"The armorer isn't likely to release the rifles. He might even intend to sell them on the black market. In fact, he probably is, since he worked so closely with Cavanaugh."

"Steal what is going to be stolen? That's not the way I'd

put it, sir," said Woodward. "We intend to use them, soon if General Sherman is to be believed."

"I cannot condone theft from a Federal armory, Lieutenant," Benjamin said sternly. "However, I see nothing wrong with you, Sergeant Carruthers, and me driving a wagon for pleasure this evening."

"Who knows what valuable items we might find, sir? I like the way you think!"

"How can I ever tell my wife I've become a thief?"

"In a good cause, sir." Sam pointed to the soldiers drilling with wood stakes instead of rifles. "When we ride into battle, it's better if they are holding proper weapons."

Late that night the Sixth Illinois Cavalry received fifteen crates of new Sharps carbines.

That Bushwhacking, Jayhawking Traitor

June 18, 1862
Memphis, Tennessee

"Good to see you back, sir," greeted Lieutenant Woodward.

Ben Grierson returned his adjutant's salute as he slipped from horseback to the solid ground. He refrained from rubbing his hindquarters in front of his fellow officer, although he suspected Samuel Woodward knew his distaste for horses and how his anatomy never quite adapted to the regulation wooden saddle.

"How'd the meeting go, Colonel?"

Ben saw how anxious Woodward was to learn of the orders given him by General Lew Wallace. Wallace had occupied Memphis after several fierce skirmishes, but had his hands full trying to maintain city functions while holding down the secessionists. From what Ben had seen of the general, the man was a capable administrator but had little stomach for combat. The entire meeting had been over in a few minutes, as far as Ben was concerned, since he cared little about Wallace's political ambitions or literary endeavors.

"There's a Confederate detachment raiding an area not far from the city," Ben said. "General Wallace has ordered the Sixth Illinois Cavalry into the field to prevent any significant force from attacking and reoccupying Memphis."

"Excellent, sir," Woodward said. "Actual orders."

Ben smiled crookedly. They had been dispatched from Camp Yates on little more than hearsay of General Grant's wishes, but Wallace had greeted them warmly and had never asked for written orders or how they had commandeered the steamer *Crescent City* to reach Memphis.

"Those Sharps rifles ought to come in handy. You've had the men clean them again?"

"Yes, sir. And Sergeant Carruthers rustled up more mounts."

"I trust your use of the word 'rustled' is vernacular rather than legal." Ben saw how Woodward hesitated answering. "Never mind. We are a cavalry unit. Without horses we would be . . ."

"Infantry," Lieutenant Woodward finished, grinning. The only way to requisition for the Sixth seemed to be on the sly. "Orders, sir?"

"Mount the troops. We'll patrol south of the city where the rebels were seen yesterday morning."

Ben helped himself to a dipper of water, wished he had time to soak his rear end in hot salt water, then mounted again. He patted his horse on the neck, urging it to the head of the column. Along with his companies from the Sixth, he had accumulated four more companies from the Eleventh Illinois. Three hundred troopers, all ready for battle with him at the lead. Ben shivered a little in anticipation, then gave the order to move out.

They rode slowly, his scouts ranging ahead. By evening, the scouts brought back the news he had anticipated.

"A goodly force, Colonel," reported Sergeant Carruthers. "Looks to be Jeff Thompson."

Ben stiffened hearing this. Jeff Thompson had made a career out of annoying Ulysses Grant. If not for the Confederate general, Grant would have swept through Missouri and recaptured it quickly.

"Where's his camp?" Ben asked.

"Not 'round here, Colonel. Might have hightailed it over to Hernando."

Ben spread out his map of the region and saw that Hernando was a Mississippi town twenty-five miles south. Pursuit of a force led by a Confederate general into more firmly held Southern country would be risky.

"He's expecting supplies or reinforcements on the Mississippi and Tennessee Railroad," Ben speculated, after thinking about Thompson's motives. "He's not retreating; he's waiting to launch an attack. Thompson is planning to retake Memphis."

"Should we report back to General Wallace to warn him, sir?" asked Woodward.

"What would you do, Sam?" Benjamin asked. He had taken a shine to his adjutant, but still had to figure out what the officer might do if the going got tough.

"Our orders are to interdict Confederate troops, sir. We go after Thompson. Offense is better than defense."

"It could prove quite a fight," Ben pointed out. "Sergeant Carruthers, how many men does Thompson have in his command?"

"Can't tell, sir."

"Then we should find out firsthand," Ben said. "If we ride all night, we can reach Hernando by daybreak."

In spite of disliking the constant rocking motion of the horse beneath him, Ben led the Sixth Illinois Cavalry and the rest of his command the twenty-five miles to Hernando, Mississippi, and arrived an hour before dawn in time to hear a distant train whistle.

"Full gallop!" ordered Ben, his arm sweeping down in the

direction of the railroad tracks. Although his troopers' horses were tired, they responded well. They crossed the tracks and found a deserted Confederate camp.

"Sir," panted out Woodward, "looks like they're not far ahead. Some of the fires are still burning."

Ben nodded and grimly set about the pursuit. General Jeff Thompson's capture would be quite a feather in his cap. As he rode, Ben saw a decrepit sign saying that he was nearing Coldwater Station. If Thompson waited anywhere, it would be at a railroad depot, while he waited for supplies and reinforcements.

With his troopers somewhat scattered by the helter-skelter advance, Ben had to trust his soldiers not to panic when they saw what he did. A Confederate force of at least one hundred guerrillas swung about, ready to fight. They had been warned of pursuit and had left their camp to come here to meet the train. Any chance of taking them by surprise had long passed.

"Fire, fire, fire!" shouted Ben, pulling out his pistol. He found himself in the thick of battle, shooting into the butternut-clad irregulars and even wheeling about to let his horse rear and kick out at the Confederate soldiers. The snap of Sharps carbines told him his "appropriation" of the rifles had not been in vain. White smoke from the carbines rose and mingled with the musket smoke from the rebels.

Ben's pistol came up empty, forcing him to rely on his cavalry saber. The heavy sword proved awkward, but he scattered more than one knot of the enemy as he charged forward, swinging fiercely. Before he knew it, the firing had died to a deathly quiet.

"What's wrong?" he demanded. "Lieutenant Woodward, what's wrong? Why aren't they firing?"

"Sir, the enemy's in full retreat. We won."

"Where's Thompson? I want Thompson!"

"Sir, that way," cried a bloodied cavalry trooper. "I seen him ridin' off. A great big gray horse."

Ben grabbed a carbine from one of his soldiers who'd had his horse shot from under him. Without a word, he charged in the direction taken by the fleeing enemy general. He heard Woodward issuing orders for a full company to follow.

Ben wanted Jeff Thompson so bad he could taste it. Without his expert leadership, the Union's advance throughout the South would be far easier. Grant would have a free hand in laying siege to Vicksburg, and Missouri would again come under Union control. All Ben had to do was capture or kill one man.

"There, ahead! I see him!" cried Ben. "You bushwhacking, jayhawking traitor! I've got you now!" He lifted the carbine to his shoulder and fired at the fleeing Confederate officer. The recoil almost unseated Ben, forcing him to flail about wildly and drop the carbine. By the time he recovered his seat, the soldiers around him had opened fire. He wasn't sure whose bullet was responsible, but a Union slug took the big gray out from under the rebel general.

Ben saw Jeff Thompson hit the ground hard, roll, and come to his feet clutching a pistol. Two of the Sixth Illinois Cavalry rode down on the general, but he fired on both men, halting their advance. By the time Ben had reformed his troopers and ordered a new attack, General Thompson had faded into the woods. An hour's search failed to flush the wily rebel from wherever he had gone to earth.

Ben felt a curious mixture of elation and despair. His men had killed three, wounded seven, and taken another nine rebels as prisoners, even if he hadn't captured Thompson.

"Sir," said Lieutenant Woodward, "the men found a big supply dump behind the Coldwater Station depot. They're destroying danged near fifteen thousand pounds of bacon and a passel of other supplies, things we can't take back with us. You'll get a medal for this, Colonel. Mark my words."

"A medal for destroying supplies but letting a general escape? I don't think so, Lieutenant." But Ben still felt pride in the performance of his soldiers.

Even better, both Lew Wallace and Ulysses Grant applauded his raid and rewarded him with more challenging missions.

Recognition

July 4, 1862
Memphis, Tennessee

"Well done, Colonel," said General Sherman. "You've run that rascal ragged. I couldn't have done better myself."

"I failed to capture General Thompson, sir," Ben said, trying to keep the bitterness from his voice. He saw right away that Sherman noticed it. The redheaded general smiled broadly.

"That's the attitude I like to hear, Colonel. You've run him off, but you didn't drive a stake through his foul heart! You'll get the chance to remedy this failure. I assure you of that."

"He's a traitor, sir," Ben said hotly. "He was commander of the Missouri militia and he organized guerrillas after the state seceded rather than remaining with the United States." His words took on a curious ring as they rattled around Sherman's office, now empty after long hours of planning with his staff.

"He's not the only one," Sherman said. "Loyalty to one's state has put many a decent man on the wrong side in this war." Sherman snorted in disgust. "Too bad some of the ones who stayed on the right side didn't up and quit."

Ben knew Sherman had a dislike of Lew Wallace that went deeper than Wallace's failure to reinforce the general's position during the battle of Shiloh. Their personalities clashed. When both were in the same room with him, Ben always felt as if he were caught between opposing armies. Strangely, though, Sherman and Grant did not arch their backs and start spitting like fighting cats in spite of their huge differences.

Grant was a known tippler and carouser. Sherman was his opposite, both pious and a teetotaler whom Alice would gladly welcome into their home. Grant was dark-haired and somber, whereas Sherman was fiery-haired and effervescent, always bubbling over with enthusiasm. In Ben's eyes, though, both shared the same trait: brilliance as military commanders. Counting each as his friend mattered greatly to him.

"Let's have dinner. I've had my orderly find the best victuals in all of Memphis for you." Sherman ushered Ben through a door at the side of the office into the general's personal quarters. After living in cold camps and riding long, wearying hours every day, the room looked like a mansion to him. But Ben knew these were austere compared to many commanders. He couldn't help remembering how posh Colonel Cavanaugh's quarters had been at Camp Yates, and he hadn't been half the officer that William Sherman was.

"That's very kind of you, sir. I can certainly appreciate something more than salt pork and hard bread with maggots poking their snouts out before I bite."

"Think nothing of it, Colonel. I want to keep you sharp, especially after the good work you did at Germantown."

"General Grant decided not to use it as a headquarters, sir," he pointed out. Ben had been lucky to convince many of the Southern planters to support the Union by driving off rebel troops intent on burning those planters' cotton fields.

"During war, headquarters are apt to change without notice. I'm lucky to be here in Memphis long enough to kick off my boots and enjoy a good meal. As you know, there's been considerable turmoil in the ranks, Colonel," said Sherman, signaling for his orderly to begin dinner service.

"How do you feel about McClellan being replaced by Halleck as commander of the Army of the Potomac, sir?"

"McClellan was too tentative. I'm not sure 'Old Brains' is any better, but his promotion certainly has kept us moving about here in the West. General Grant took Halleck's HQ at Corinth and assigned me here."

"And you've called me back from patrol, sir," Ben pointed out. He sampled the turtle soup and almost fainted. It was superb. He tried to remember when he had eaten such fine food and couldn't. He had to write Alice right away to let her know of this tête-à-tête with General Grant's right-hand commander, but he wrestled with whether to mention the quality of the food since he wasn't certain, even after sending most of his colonel's pay, she and the boys were thriving. The war interrupted vital supplies, especially among the civilian population.

"Let your men enjoy a short furlough. They're camped at the racetrack, aren't they?"

"Yes, sir. Keeping them from betting on the outcome of races has been difficult."

"Not from the sounds coming this way. How did you find such good musicians? I have half a mind to steal them from you so I can put on a decent concert."

"There are plenty of music halls in Memphis, sir," Ben said longingly.

"Indeed there are. When we finish the meal, let's take in a show. There's one playing called *Daughter of the Regiment* that I hear is quite fine."

"In a saloon, sir?"

"Music hall. There's no need to drink if you are intent on listening to the fine vocal performances and watching the sprightly dance."

Ben let General Sherman convince him to attend, although he knew Alice would never approve. She would think he was slipping into the dark pits of sin, but he resisted the temptation to smoke a cigar, although it was offered him. And the performance was every bit as good as the general had intimated.

Later, in his quarters, Ben wrote his wife of the dinner and Sherman's generosity without quite mentioning the musical. He yawned and started to fold the letter, then decided to complete it so it could be on its way early in the morning.

Of the fights and the men he wrote in detail, of Sherman and the dinner he told what he thought she ought to know, and then finished: "The only adverse factor in returning to Memphis is the multitudinous Negroes. They are a restless, shifty, indolent lot. Though I will do my sworn duty as a Union officer and fight to the death to obtain their freedom, as no man should be held as chattel, such sacrifice is wasted on them."

He finished the letter with a flourish, then signed and sealed it so he could put it in the mail pouch for morning post. Ben stretched again and lay on his hard bed, thinking of Sherman's words of praise, the fine meal, and the show that had been his reward for chasing Jeff Thompson deeper south.

What would Sherman and Grant think if he captured the elusive Southern general? Ben's dreams were pleasant although they involved endless riding.

Ambuscade

September 7, 1862
Olive Branch, Mississippi

"The men deserve the rest, Colonel," Samuel Woodward said. "If you keep pushing them too hard, the horses that aren't broken down now will be. And the men'll be less able to fight."

"Cavalry shouldn't be left afoot," Ben Grierson said to his adjutant. "But we are deep in enemy territory."

"Not that deep anymore, sir, thanks to you. Hernando's only a few hours' ride away, and you helped wrest it from the Confederates."

Ben had to disagree. Two days earlier they had mixed it up with a band of secessionists in that town and captured twelve rebels. Because that dozen had been subdued did not place Hernando safely in Union control. If anything, the secesh were even more active. Ben wasn't one to let his imagination race away with him, but he felt eyes on him constantly. But when he would turn, there was nothing but forest—ominously silent forest protesting the intrusion of so many Union bluecoats.

"What does the scouting report say about Olive Branch?" Ben asked.

Woodward shrugged and shook his head, showing that nothing untoward had been reported.

Ben worried even more.

"Walk with me, Lieutenant," he said as he started a slow circuit of the camp. As he and his adjutant passed the troopers, he saw smiles and even affection for him in spite of the ungodly pace they had endured the past month. They had made a hundred-mile sweep through enemy-held territory, raiding and destroying supplies—doing to the Confederates what Jeff Thompson and Nathan Bedford Forrest did to the Union. In three skirmishes, the Sixth Illinois Cavalry had killed two men and taken twenty others as prisoners. Nothing but praise radiated from General Sherman's pen in reply to his every report, but Ben still felt uneasy.

Sam Woodward was right. The men ought to get a chance to rest for a day or two in Olive Branch. The area had never reported rebel activity, not like that in Hernando, and it provided a decent base to make a new sweep down through Mississippi searching out more supplies to capture and patrols to ambush.

It was so peaceful here.

"How far is it to the edge of the woods?" Ben asked.

"Looks to be twenty yards, give or take, sir," Woodward said.

"A cavalry assault would have the rebels on us in seconds. How are the sentries posted?"

"I left that to the company sergeants, as usual, sir. What's wrong, Ben?" Woodward asked in a low voice. "It's not like you to get so jittery."

"It's nothing but fatigue. But humor me. Be certain the sentries are kept alert. Double up, have them patrol in crisscross patterns so they have to acknowledge one another occasionally."

"They might shoot their partner, sir."

"Risk it. Tell them to be alert to anything moving in the woods. And I want Old Barber saddled and ready at all times."

"That's not good for your horse, sir. Better to give him a rest, too."

"Perhaps you're right." Ben shucked off his white duster and gave it a snap, sending clouds of brown grime into the air. "I could use a bath, but that's out of the question." He pulled the dirty linen duster back on and paced slowly through the camp, speaking to the men and listening to whatever they might have to say.

He had hardly spread out his pallet in preparation for a quick nap when his ears pricked up. Reacting out of pure instinct rather than his more usual coolly collected information, Ben Grierson shouted, "To arms! We're under attack!"

His words mingled with the first volley fired from the forest. Then came a rebel yell that ripped at his ears and tore at his nerves. Benjamin shouted for his orderly, but the man was nowhere to be seen. Grunting, he heaved his light saddle onto Old Barber. The horse had seen his share of combat, but still flinched at the nearness of the rifle fire.

Swinging into the saddle, still wearing his white duster, Ben trotted into the center of his encampment for a better look. Bullets whizzed past his head, but he never flinched. He saw that the stretch of forest that had spooked him earlier was the center of the Confederate attack.

He sucked in his breath when he saw wave after wave of rebel soldiers pouring out. He winced as a bullet ripped through his pants leg but left his flesh untouched.

"Sergeant Carruthers, form a line to the right flank. Fire at will. Lieutenant Woodward, take command of the center." Ben guided Old Barber to the left flank, where total confusion reigned. It took a few minutes before he restored military order and formed a double line to return fire. But he saw this wasn't good enough.

His small command faced better than four hundred men.

"Advance on my command, now!" he cried. Ben twisted

as a hot bullet tore at his duster, trying to blast it off his body. "Advance, fire and advance!" He was at the forefront of the attack, forcing the rebels to retreat into the woods.

Ben knew better than to press the assault without issuing orders to his other officers. His small segment of soldiers would be cut off from support unless Woodward or another of his lieutenants had the balls to attack, also.

"Dig in, men. Pile up limbs, get behind mounds of earth. Don't give up one inch! Fire at any good target, make every shot count."

Seeing the men were settled into a stiff defensive position, Ben rode through the lines to where Samuel Woodward struggled to keep his men from retreating. The center had sustained the worst of the attack.

"There are hundreds of them, sir," Woodward gasped out. "You saved our bacon with your attack. I'm sorry but I couldn't support you."

"I see your problem." Ben twisted around as another bullet cut through his duster.

"Sir, you make a mighty fine target on your horse and wearing that white duster."

"Let them fire all they want. Our men need to see that I am in command and not afraid. Ouch!" Ben jerked his hand around as another slug tore across his knuckles. Sluggish blood oozed from the wound.

"Please, Colonel," begged Woodward.

"Here they come again. Don't let them break your line, Lieutenant!"

Ben galloped behind the lines to be certain officer and noncom alike understood that they fought a defensive battle. It looked like four hundred rebels were attacking, and that many more might be lying in ambush, waiting to pare up his command should one flank or the other overextend itself.

For an eternity, blue and gray fought ferociously, exchanging volleys, until Ben saw his opportunity. The rebel commander had fallen into a pattern, believing Ben would never counterattack. His rush forward, quick fusillade, and retreat proved uneven, with a clump of men lingering toward the center, exposing a portion of his command to assault.

"Forward, attack! Charge!" cried Ben, sending Old Barber leaping over the line on the left flank. Some of his troopers got onto their horses and joined him. Others remained on the ground, but they attacked on his order, too.

The startled Confederate commander tried to reform his ranks, but his men were out of position and lacked the battlements, crude as they were, that had enabled the Sixth Illinois Cavalry to survive a two-hour siege.

Ben felt Old Barber falter for a moment and then plunge ahead. Bending low to avoid the tree limbs, Ben fired left and right. He heard one rebel gasp as a bullet struck him, but Ben was riding too fast to know if he had killed the man.

When he had penetrated fifty yards into the forest, he swung around, grouped his men, and attacked again, this time sweeping at right angles to their original advance. This drove his men into the center of the Confederate ranks, splitting them as easily as a wedge splits a wood rail.

"They're runnin'," came the cry. "Them Johnny Rebs're runnin' like the cowards they are!"

A cheer went up. Ben wiped sweat and blood from his face, startled to see that the sweat was his but the blood was not.

"Regroup," he ordered. "Back to our encampment. Fall back and regroup!"

The soldiers had tasted victory and wanted to pursue the fleeing enemy, but Ben knew better than that. Their ammunition supplies were running low and pursuit into the twilight, on enemy ground, where no foe had been reported, was suicidal.

"Are you all right, sir?" Lieutenant Woodward rode up, looking worried.

"Report, Lieutenant. What's our status?"

"Twenty casualties, sir. But it looks like we've killed

forty of them bastards and another thirty have surrendered." Woodward frowned and added, "Old Barber's taken a couple bullets, sir."

Ben examined his horse and found the shallow crease wounds to be insignificant. His horse had come through the fight virtually unscathed, as he had.

Ben Grierson pressed his handkerchief against one of Old Barber's wounds to stanch the blood, knowing he would have to explain to Alice how he had come to ruin her fine embroidered gift. But this battle felt different. His men had proven their courage and skill in the face of overwhelming odds. He felt only elation at this victory.

Recognition

September 17, 1862
Memphis, Tennessee

"What have you done, Benjamin?" asked Alice Grierson. "This is most unusual, isn't it?" The woman frowned, then reached out to corral Charlie and Robert to keep them from running loose in General Sherman's headquarters.

"I haven't done anything, dear," Ben said. "If I had done anything wrong, the general would never have suggested I send for you and the boys while I'm recuperating."

Alice sniffed. "Skinned knuckles is hardly a wound requiring much doctoring, though you did get your handkerchief mighty bloody."

"The heat of battle," he said vaguely, never having told her he had used the cloth to bind his horse's wounds. "I'm sure the general called the Sixth back for rest and recuperation. We'd been fighting for some time, cutting quite a swath through the enemy."

"I heard about that, Benjamin," Alice said in a softer voice. "You are so foolish." She smiled almost shyly. "So brave, too."

"There you are!" came Sherman's booming voice. "This must be the lovely Mrs. Grierson. So pleased to meet you, ma'am. The colonel is a lucky man. And these two? You're Charles," Sherman said, singling out one boy accurately. "That means you're Robert."

"Yes, sir," piped up Robert. "You a real general?"

"I am," Sherman said, beaming.

"I want to be a general, too."

"I'll see that your application for West Point is given the highest priority, then," Sherman said. He saw Alice's reaction to this. "We need the finest among our men to fight this battle, ma'am. Your son is certainly one. But then he has a father who is also in that exalted rank."

"Sir?" Ben wasn't sure why his commander had invited them all here.

"Come along. The officers are waiting."

Ben and Alice exchanged glances. He shrugged, not knowing what Sherman meant. The Grierson family trailed the fiery general out into the humid afternoon. The instant they appeared, the Sixth Illinois Cavalry band struck up a lively tune.

"This way," Sherman said, escorting Alice and letting Ben follow on his own as they mounted the assembly platform where the general could address the assembled troops.

Benjamin stared out over almost a thousand soldiers, many of them in his unit but even more from other regiments. Sherman pointed to chairs for Alice and the children, but let Ben remain standing beside him.

When the band's last note died, General Sherman stepped forward.

"This is a brutal war," he said in a loud, echoing voice that reached even the last soldier in the last rank clearly. "Brother fights brother. Families are torn apart. It is not a war we were prepared to fight, but a select few have risen to the challenge."

Sherman signaled his aide-de-camp, who hurried over carrying a long polished case.

"An example of Colonel Grierson's fine work has just entertained us. His regimental band might not be the best, but it is certainly the loudest." He waited for the ripple of laughter to die. "We are all better served that Colonel Grierson did not remain a music teacher but became a blue-ribbon, first-water cavalry commander. Because of him, General Grant has prosecuted the war along the Mississippi River with fewer casualties than expected."

Ben squirmed a little at this. He knew his shortcomings. Jeff Thompson still raided with his guerrilla force, and Nathan Bedford Forrest had become Grant's major adversary. Trying to stop Forrest and his cavalry was harder than nailing a gob of jam to the wall. Whatever small victories he had achieved meant nothing, since he had not captured or killed the South's two most able generals.

"Colonel Grierson's spirited fight at Olive Branch proved again his bravery and skill." Sherman nodded to his aide-de-camp to open the case. Grierson flinched as the afternoon sunlight reflected off the long silver tube inside, blinding him momentarily.

"Colonel Grierson, it is my pleasure to present you with a small token of esteem for your military acumen." General Sherman took a silver-plated carbine from the case. "For your gallantry in combat, sir. I thank you, and your country thanks you."

A spontaneous cheer went up, starting with the Sixth Illinois Cavalry and spreading quickly. Ben tried to keep from smiling as he took the carbine but couldn't. He looked back and saw Alice beaming in pleasure at him and his boys almost too excited to sit in their chairs.

It was his finest day in the Army.

Timidity Punished

December 28, 1862
Holly Springs, Mississippi

"Van Dorn is moving along this road, Colonel," Ben Grierson told his commander. Colonel John Minzer scowled, ran his fingers along the edges of the tattered map spread on the icy ground between them, and finally shook his head.

"We can't know that. If we commit a detachment, they might be ambushed."

"General Grant's supply lines are being cut every day by Van Dorn. We've been ordered to stop him. He's the most able general the South has operating in the region."

"That's why I am cautioning you, Ben, against precipitous action. We must keep our force intact."

"For what purpose? To parade about smartly?" Ben tried to hold his anger in check and failed. He had not liked being assigned a secondary position to Minzer, but Grant had to follow protocol. John Minzer had seniority on him by several months.

"I don't like your attitude, Colonel," Minzer said sharply.

"And I don't like sitting here, letting Van Dorn range

freely to destroy Grant's supplies and keep a decent campaign against Vicksburg from happening."

"I can relieve you of your command, sir," Minzer said, his lower lip quivering. "Will you obey my orders?"

"Will you let me stop Van Dorn? He's on this road. I can catch him and make certain he pays dearly if he remains in Mississippi."

"You might be General Sherman's fair-haired boy, but to me you are nothing but a failed businessman from Illinois. You know nothing about warfare, in spite of a few accidental victories. The meanest private in your company knows how to follow orders better."

Ben seethed. He knew better than to continue this argument, but the opportunity to drive Van Dorn's force ahead of him like a herd of cattle was slipping away with every instant.

"I know how to follow orders, Colonel Minzer," Ben said fiercely. "You do not. General Grant ordered us to end Van Dorn's raiding."

"I am doing so, but not in a fashion you approve of," Minzer said smugly.

"How're you going to stop that devil?" came a deep voice.

Ben blinked. He thought he and Minzer were arguing in private. Minzer was so caught up in himself that he didn't notice a third man had joined their circle to stand behind him.

"Caution, sir. We advance to be certain Van Dorn doesn't lay any traps for us."

"Like he did at Pea Ridge?"

"I don't know about that, Colonel. All I know is—" It finally hit Minzer that Ben was standing across from him at attention, his lips pulled into a thin, tight line. Grierson had not spoken.

"Earl Van Dorn is a capable general. I figured you had the balls to slow him or maybe even stop him. I see I was wrong. Grierson, what would you do?"

"Pursue immediately, General," Ben said, his eyes locked on Ulysses Grant's.

"My men are starving and are reduced to throwing insults at the rebs because they're short on ammunition. That's Van Dorn's dirty work. You want to sit on your fat behind, Colonel Minzer, while my troops get shot up?"

"Sir, I didn't know you were in camp." Minzer spun about to face Grant.

"You don't know anything, Colonel. Nothing!" Grant roared before Minzer could argue. "I'm massing 80,000 troops for a siege. If Vicksburg is to fall, my men have to be better supplied than the rebels behind those walls. You are more of an impediment to my assault than Van Dorn and Forrest together, Colonel!"

"I must protest, sir," Minzer said, regaining some of his composure. "You don't know all the facts."

"Grierson, what did you want to do?"

"Pursue, sir. We might not capture General Van Dorn, but the Sixth Illinois Cavalry can keep him on the run and unable to cut your supply lines."

"I disagree. I don't think the Sixth can do it." Grant glared at Grierson, then turned to a smirking Minzer. "I think an entire brigade can do it with the right commander. Minzer, you are relieved of command. Grierson, use the entire brigade in any fashion you choose, but by damn, I'll replace you, too, if you don't stop their flow of supplies and keep them from destroying mine!"

Ben grinned, then saluted smartly. "Your orders are understood fully, sir. I'll make life hell for the Confederates."

A brigade. He had command of an entire brigade!

Brigadier

January 23, 1863
Somewhere in Mississippi

"My musket ball's frozen, Colonel," complained a private crouched a few yards from him. "If it don't warm up soon, the rest of me'll get all froze up."

"Quiet," Ben Grierson said. "They'll be along soon. Your voice carries for miles in this cold air."

"Glad somethin's able to move," the soldier grumbled, then fell silent when Ben glared at him.

Sam Woodward moved quietly and crouched beside his commander, where they could both keep a good view of the half-ice, half-mud road.

"Scouts tell me the supply train's on its way. It'll be here in another few minutes."

"Any idea what the rebs are carrying?" Ben asked. "I could do with some fresh meat." He laughed, sending a plume of silvery breath into the frigid air. "I could do with *any* meat. I swear, the cold is so bad nothing will poke a nose from its burrow until spring."

"Wish we could do the same," Ben's adjutant said.

Ben drew his pistol and nodded to Woodward, who quietly left and took his position down the road. They had worked ambushes like this a dozen times before to good effect. Grant had given him a mission, and Ben had taken it to heart. If his cavalry couldn't run down the enemy supply trains, then he went to ground and waited for them to slip into a crossfire.

He had lost count how many rebels he had killed and captured and how many tons of supplies he had denied the Confederacy. His only regret over the past few weeks was his inability to lock horns with either Earl Van Dorn or Nathan Bedford Forrest. Those two generals continued to hamper Grant's effort to mount a significant siege on Vicksburg.

"There," someone whispered. The single word carried like a bullet through the still, cold morning air.

Ben gripped his pistol and half-stood, peering around the tree trunk hiding him from sight. He caught his breath. This was a decent target. He counted four heavily laden wagons, with the promise of several more around the bend in the road.

His men had been properly trained and knew better than to fire too soon. Ben waited until the first wagon came even with him before stepping out, pointing the cocked pistol straight at the driver and calling, "Halt! Halt or die!"

The startled driver's hands went up as if they had been fired from a cannon. He dropped the reins, but the mules weren't convinced anything was wrong and kept pulling. Ben took two quick steps, jumped into the driver's box, and snared one of the reins. He tugged back and yelled, "Whoa!"

One mule in the front team obeyed, the other didn't. This caused the wagon to pull sideways along the road, blocking the way for the others. If Ben had planned it this way, he couldn't have done better.

"You are my prisoner, sir," Ben announced. "Who's in command of this detachment?"

"Dee-tachment?" The driver lowered his hand and scratched his head. "I'm a teamster, not a soldier. I get paid in kind."

"Smart man," Ben said. "Confederate scrip is nigh on worthless."

"Surely is," the driver said, nodding. "The only good use for it is to put a bale or two on the campfire. I kin git my hands warm that way."

As he exchanged pleasantries with the driver, Ben watched Woodward and the rest of his men seize the remainder of the supply train. It was another successful raid, with more supplies seized, and not a casualty on either side.

"Sam!" he called, standing suddenly. "Horses!" He looked at the driver, who shook his head and looked a tad frightened. He wasn't expecting a cavalry detachment to defend him.

"We got a company mounted and ready, Colonel," Woodward shouted back.

To his surprise, the lone rider galloping along the road wore a Union jacket. In this fierce weather, that said nothing about his loyalties. A jacket taken in battle kept a man warm, no matter which side of the war he fought on.

"Colonel Grierson!" called the man. "Message from the general."

Ben motioned for the man to ride up. He was almost eye to eye with the courier as he stood in the driver's box.

"Here you are, sir."

"Which general sent it?"

The courier blinked, wiped off ice turning to water from his face and finally said, "Not real sure, Colonel. Think it's both."

"Both?"

"General Grant and General Sherman."

Ben took the packet and studied the wax seal on the envelope.

General Grant had sealed it. He tucked his pistol under his arm, then broke the seal and hastily read the contents.

"What're our new orders, Colonel?" asked Sam Woodward.

"You've got that wrong, Lieutenant," Ben said, folding the letter.

"We're being recalled, sir?"

"Both Grant and Sherman have nominated me for promotion." Ben waited for the import to sink in. His adjutant let out a loud cry and threw his hat high into the air.

"Hip hip hurray! General Grierson!"

Even the rebel driver joined the cheers.

At the Beginning

April 17, 1863
La Grange, Tennessee

"How was the visit with Alice and the boys?"

Ben Grierson had come by steamboat from St. Louis to Memphis and had ridden hard once he had received his orders, taking him away in the middle of a well-deserved leave to see his family. But his return to the Sixth Illinois Cavalry had just taken a pleasant turn.

"John!" he cried, embracing his brother. "Your appointment came through! They never told me."

"I'm your quartermaster, like it or not," John Grierson said. He peered at his brother's shoulders but said nothing.

"I think the promotion has been blocked," Ben said. "Grant and Sherman put me in for a star, but Hamilton has to agree, also, and we have not been on good terms."

"Then you will receive your promotion soon," John said. "Hamilton has been replaced by General Hurlbut. You know him, don't you?"

"I consider him a friend," Ben said cautiously. He didn't want to count on his star before it became official, but if his brother was right, he would start a constellation on his shoulders sooner rather than later. Hurlbut was a good officer. "But what difference does a promotion make when we are in the middle of a grand new campaign?"

Lieutenant Woodward stood quietly until Ben motioned him over.

"Good to see you back, sir. I'm sorry your leave was cut short."

"It's for a good cause. Brief me, Sam. Is this finally the start of Grant's assault on Vicksburg?"

"Yes, sir. He's marching 40,000 men through a swamp to attack from the left flank. On the river, Admiral Porter has a ship with guns aplenty to provide cover for supply barges coming from New Orleans."

"And our part?"

"No supplies are to get through to any Confederate command, sir," Woodward said. "We are to cut communications, destroy railroads and supply dumps, and take as many prisoners as quickly as we can."

Ben laughed. "General Grant wants me to become Nathan Bedford Forrest!"

"We might encounter him, sir," said Woodward.

"We'll show him the temper of fine Union steel. Prepare the brigade. We ride immediately."

"The men are well provisioned, Ben," said John. "Each has a Sharps carbine, a hundred rounds of ammunition, a revolver, and a saber, and you even have artillerists with six two-pound guns."

"Food?"

"Hardtack, salt, coffee, sugar, and bacon for every man."

"Then there's nothing to slow us down." Ben rubbed his hindquarters. After the battles he had found over the last eight months, the idea of being astride Old Barber for long hours no longer seemed as daunting. But would the aching ever go away?

He mounted and led his thirteen hundred men south toward the Tallahatchie River, engaging the Confederate forces three times in as many hours before crossing the river and camping in a driving rain. But Ben felt good about the quick travel. His men had shown again their ability to ride and fight to victory, no matter how tired.

Butternut Guerrillas

April 20, 1863
Louisville, Mississippi

"I don't know, Colonel," said Sam Woodward, chewing on his lower lip. "Looks to be mighty dangerous if any of the boys get caught. Bad enough to be taken prisoner when you're in uniform. If they get caught wearing Confederate uniforms, they'd be shot as spies on the spot."

"Then again, might be the civilians wouldn't pay them a second glance. Where we're riding, we're surrounded by enemy. Blending in will be safer than being sighted." Ben Grierson sat on the small camp stool in his tent, a map stretched out on the cot he used more as a desk than for sleeping.

"Forrest is around, sir," Woodward said.

"This ploy will make it easier to track that devil down," Ben said. "I won't order any man to wear the Confederate butternut, but a scout would have a real advantage."

"Understood, sir. That's why I asked. We got nigh on a hundred wanting to scout. I chose twenty."

Ben laughed in delight.

"I knew I could count on them—on you, too, Sam." He folded his map until a large section of Mississippi was exposed. "Here's where we'll be going. Fast, hard, deadly. Let's start at Louisville, south of Starkville. The rebs think that's theirs since it's in the middle of the state. Let's shake them up and prove how vulnerable they can be."

"Fast, hard, deadly, Colonel," Woodward said. He made his way out of the tent and began barking orders.

Ben folded his map and packed the items he would need. No supply train now. That was in his brother John's hands back in Memphis. His cavalry regiment would live off the land. If they couldn't carry it, they'd steal it. And if they didn't carry or steal it, they didn't need it. He made certain he had two spare loaded pistols tucked into his saddlebags, then hefted them and went to find Old Barber already saddled.

"Let's give 'em hell, sir," his orderly said.

"Watch your language, Private," Ben said automatically. His mind rode down the pike and into enemy-held Louisville. It was going to be a good day. He felt it in his bones.

He mounted and rode the length of his column, talking to the men, taking their measure, and seeing that they were as eager as he was for the coming jaunt. Ben stopped in front of the twenty Confederate-uniform-clad soldiers.

"You lads won't forget which side you're on, now, will you?" he joked.

"Colonel, the Sixth Illinois Cavalry's got the best danged band on either side of the Mississippi. No way am I gonna give up my trumpet."

"Might be reason for the rest of us to go to the other side," quipped another, "since Davis's playin' is so pitiful."

"Scout ahead," Ben said, "and report any significant enemy troops. If you don't find any, keep riding, and we'll catch up with you."

"To Louisville!" cried the sergeant leading the butternut guerrillas.

Ben let his newly outfitted scouts get a start before moving his column out. He rode with more confidence, and the expectation built when he neared the outskirts of Louisville without being warned by his butternut guerrillas.

"Pistols only," he ordered. "We don't stop as we go through occupied territory unless we can destroy supplies."

"Ready, sir. What about the scouts?" asked Woodward.

"Speak of the devil," he said. "Here they come." Ben took their report, pleased at how openly they rode through enemy territory to find the supply dumps and to estimate armed resistance. When the sergeant in charge had finished his report, Ben said, "Shuck off those uniform jackets but don't get rid of them. They'll come in handy later."

"Sir," said the good Illinois native sergeant in a fake Southern drawl, "if I find myself a Confederate officer's jacket, kin I wear that? Always wanted to see what it's like to be an officer, even if it's for the wrong side."

"This is war," Ben said. "Lead us to the warehouses."

With a whoop, the sergeant wheeled about. At a dead gallop, Ben's regiment rode through Louisville streets and went directly to the stored goods, meeting only token resistance.

"Here it is! Torch it, men!" he ordered when they reached the warehouses piled high with the Confederate supplies.

A bullet tore past him, causing Old Barber to rear. As the horse came to his back legs, Ben saw the lone Confederate soldier and fired three times. One of the rounds caught the young man in the head, straightened him up, and then dropped him to the ground. Ben felt a momentary pang of regret, then found himself dodging more bullets.

He made certain his soldiers set fire to the supplies before ordering a retreat down Louisville's main street. As they tore through the town, they shot at anyone shooting at them. Before he reached the far side, Ben had found two more, smaller supply depots and torched them, too.

When his column exploded out of the town and into the

countryside, he took a quick head count. Not a single casualty. In the distance, flames leaped skyward as Louisville began to burn.

"Well done, men," he shouted so the entire column could hear his praise. "Now let's *really* show the rebels war!"

Railroad Tracks

April 25, 1863
Newton, Mississippi

Ben Grierson sat astride Old Barber, waiting impatiently. They had fought their way south from Decatur and outraced all Confederate pursuit. Ben had almost hoped that Nathan Bedford Forrest would get wind of their furious raid through the middle of Mississippi and come after them. He itched to take on the slippery Confederate general, but Ben's scouts had found no trace of him or Jeff Thompson. Even Earl Van Dorn was nowhere to be seen. This let the Sixth Illinois Cavalry have its way, save for isolated pockets of rebel guerrillas who put up only a small fight. For the sake of his men, that was good.

It was bad for Ben's sense of accomplishment. He had to remove Forrest from the field if he wanted to truly aid Grant and Sherman. With the overall command of the Union Army in constant flux, it was more important than ever that those two shine in the eyes of Washington, and not only because they were friends. Ben had every confidence in President

Lincoln, but he was a thousand miles away—and everyone knew bad news traveled twice as fast as good.

"Well?" Ben called. Sergeant Carruthers looked up from where he had put his ear against the sun-heated railroad track. He pointed, using the hand with the trigger finger shot off. Then he held up his little finger to signal the train was only a minute away.

Ben passed along the word to the rest of the cavalry troopers waiting impatiently on either side of the Southern Mississippi Railroad. He had worried that he might fall into a trap, with Confederate soldiers loaded onto the freight train, so he had sent units from his regiment on diversionary raids. Captain Forbes had taken Company B to attack the Mobile Railroad at Macon, and Major Graham had already performed his mission of burning a tannery supplying bridles and saddles, and had rejoined the column.

With the lesser raids, Ben sought to fool the Confederates into thinking this principal stretch of track, running all the way across the South, was safe from him.

He heard the distant clatter of a heavy steam engine straining along the tracks. Carruthers had felt the vibrations a minute earlier and had not been wrong as to their cause. Ben drew his pistol and laid it across the saddle in front of him. Old Barber pawed the ground, ready for the fight. Ben shared the anticipation. Every supply dump he burned, every saddlery or ammunition factory destroyed, every rebel taken prisoner weakened the South and their ability to fight just that much more.

"Here she comes!" someone shouted.

Ben glanced up the track. Two men put their backs into chopping away at trees so they would fall across the rails. He began to worry that they would be too late after he spotted the tall white plume of steam coming from the engine's smokestack turn to black as the engineer saw the danger and had the stoker working double time so they could run the blockade.

The trees fell with stately precision to land hard on the tracks, blocking the engine. The woodsmen kept chopping until two more thick-boled trees crossed the tracks. By now the engineer saw the futility of bulling his way through and applied the brakes. Sparks the size of copperheads leaped from the wheels gripping the steel rains, and a screech so loud it momentarily deafened Ben cut through the swampy air.

"Twenty-five cars," shouted Woodward, doing the preliminary count. "Might be a passel of soldiers guarding the train!"

Ben had already lifted his pistol and fired several times when he saw a rebel poke his head up past the engineer and try to swing a rifle about. Ben's bullets ricocheted off steel and sang away into the swamp, their tiny melody blending with the shriek of tortured metal as the heavy train skidded past him and into the first of the trees.

"Drop it!" Ben shouted at the guard in the engineer's compartment. He had winged the man and forced him to try to fire his musket one-handed. Ben saw the man's eyes go wide as he peered into the leveled pistol and then came to a conclusion.

A fatal one. He tried to wrestle his rifle about to discharge it. Ben cut him down. The guard sagged, sat down, and then tumbled from the engine as the huge locomotive finally ground to a halt. The stench of burned metal hung in the air, mixing with the rotting vegetation and other swampy odors. But Ben was relieved to hear the buzzing of the voracious insects again. The wrenching noise of steel on steel as the engine braked had not permanently deafened him.

"Get down," Ben ordered the engineer. "Spill the head of steam and get down here."

A long, loud whistle sounded as the stoker vainly tried to signal someone—anyone—of their plight. Ben cut short the stoker's attempt to warn any nearby militia with an accurate shot to his shoulder. The stoker jerked about, howling in pain.

"Both of you, get down. Now!"

From farther down the line came the sound of a spirited gunfight. Old Barber crow hopped, anxious to get into the middle of the battle.

"You two, put these prisoners to work," Ben called when the men who had been chopping down the trees came back at a run. "Get all the dried limbs you can and stack it along the tracks."

"No, Colonel, don't," pleaded the engineer. "It'll take a month to fix. Longer. I got a family to feed."

Ben hesitated, but only for an instant. The man's plea fell flat. Ben had been hardened by too much spilled blood. Would Nathan Bedford Forrest or Jeff Thompson worry about a Union engineer's family? He doubted it.

Seeing the engineer and stoker safely under the watchful eyes of the advance guard, he put his heels to his horse's flanks and trotted along the train. He spotted the danger right away. Sam Woodward had been right in his count of the freight cars laden with supplies, but he had forgotten to mention the next three, crowded with soldiers set to defend this booty.

A dozen rebel bodies lay draped over the windowsills of a passenger car. Not a pane of glass remained intact, though most looked to have been broken out some time earlier. His men had formed a line near the edge of the wooded area and delivered a potent fire into the car. Splinters flew with every new fusillade until there were more holes than solid wood left in the parlor car.

"Give up. Surrender and your lives'll be spared!" Ben called.

A couple bullets whined past him, but he ignored them.

"How do we know this ain't a trick?" came a deep Southern drawl.

"On my honor as an officer," Ben said. "For you that means little, but to me it is everything. I am an honorable man."

"Stop them boys of yers from shootin'," came the request.

Ben passed the order along to remain watchful but not to shoot. A solitary figure rose within the car, holding a handkerchief that had been white once. Now it was mostly stained with blood.

The man hobbled to the end of the car and came onto the passenger platform. Ben caught sight of the captain's bars on the man's shoulder, the one that wasn't completely soaked in blood.

"I got a carload of boys who deserve better than to be cut down," the Confederate captain said.

"Give me your parole and I promise fair treatment for them."

"If 'n we surrender, we don't do nuthin' agin' the Confederacy," the captain said.

"Agreed."

"Come on out, men. This here colonel's given his word. You give your parole and do as you're told. You promise not to fight ag'in the Yankees and they'll let you go on home."

Ben swung about in the saddle to be certain none of his men were getting itchy trigger fingers. He saw that their rapid sweep into the midsection of Mississippi had given them confidence in their abilities. They didn't need to kill the enemy, not if a Confederate soldier was surrendering. If anything, it enhanced their reputation with every Johnny Reb that gave his parole and was no longer a threat.

And this day they got seventy-five rebels to throw down their arms and swear not to fight against the Union again.

"Watch over them," he ordered his adjutant. "Sergeant Carruthers! How's the supply situation?"

"Colonel, we took a bit of what's in there but mostly we're gonna have to burn it. Too much flour. A lot of other worthless stuff, more suited for city folks."

Ben nodded. This was a supply train on its way to Vicksburg. If it had gotten through Grant's feeble blockade, the city could have held out for an added month.

"Any ammunition?"

"Nuthin' we kin use."

"Cut open the bags of flour," he ordered. "Put a keg of gunpowder in the same car and leave a fuse out."

"Whatever you say, Colonel," Carruthers said, not understanding the orders but willing to follow them.

"What of the track?"

"Got eight rails pulled up and piled on the firewood."

"Set fire to them. Melt those rails. And toss the cross-ties onto the fire to keep it good and hot."

"They're painted with creosote, Colonel," said Carruthers. "That's gonna make one big stink."

"After we blow up the supplies, that will be a minor problem, Sergeant. Get to it!"

Ben gave orders to Woodward to move out with their prisoners. Although they had pledged their parole not to fight against the Union again, Ben had to get them to safety through the swampy terrain along the railroad.

Soon, only a handful of men remained.

"Mount up and get out of here," Ben ordered. "No matter how far you ride, it's not going to be far enough."

Sergeant Carruthers scratched his head and looked at the thread of gunpowder he had laid running to the cars carrying the bags of flour. After a few minutes of savage ripping with his bayonet, flour hung in the air like some strange white fog. The sergeant reached into his pocket and pulled out a tin of lucifers and went to stroke one.

"No, don't!" shouted Ben, but it was too late.

Sergeant Carruthers dragged the match along the sandpapered side of the tin. The spark caught the floating particles of flour and set off an explosion so violent that it blew Ben off his horse. He landed hard, unable to do anything but stare up at the sky for several minutes. His senses returned slowly, and he painfully sat up.

The rebel supply train burned from one end to the other due to the ignition of the flour. When the fire reached the gunpowder, a secondary blast rocked the marshy ground.

Ben sucked in a painful breath and fought to get to his feet. He had tried to stop Carruthers from making the deadly mistake and had failed. Ben had seen one too many granary explosions not to be wary—and to think it smart to use the flour as part of the explosive. He had almost outsmarted himself, and the sergeant was blown to kingdom come because he had failed to properly warn the man.

"Colonel!" cried Woodward, galloping up. His face was a mask of dirt and worry. "Ben, are you all right?"

Ben Grierson dusted himself off. "I'm still in one piece, but Sergeant Carruthers is dead."

"I'll get a burial party for him."

"That won't be necessary," Ben said. The heat from the burning train drove him back as he turned to face it. The supplies in those cars would burn for hours. By the time the ruined train and tracks cooled off enough to permit retrieval of what remained of Carruthers's body, every militiaman in the area would be on their necks. "We'll be a dozen miles south by the time it would take to bury him. The sergeant would prefer us to destroy another train."

"In his memory," Woodward said.

"In his memory," Ben confirmed. He swung into the saddle. Old Barber wobbled a little under him but both recovered quickly, then set off on another forced ride deeper into the heart of the Confederacy in their hunt for supply lines to disrupt.

Attack, Always Attack

April 28, 1863
Brookhaven, Mississippi

"Pemberton is panicking," Ben told his assembled officers. "He's sending out troops on both rail and along the roads to find and stop us. We've cut too big a swath through Mississippi to ignore, and if we keep destroying Confederate supplies, General Grant will crush Vicksburg."

"Wouldn't Pemberton want to keep his troops closer to Vicksburg to fend off Grant?" asked Colonel Loomis of the Sixth Illinois Cavalry.

Ben smiled. "We're too big a thorn in his side. Over the past three days we've destroyed more supplies than any other Union command during the war."

"And prisoners, sir. Don't forget the prisoners," said Lieutenant Woodward. He beamed at their success.

Ben had to laugh aloud at his adjutant. "The lieutenant is writing paroles as fast as he can and is still falling behind. That's why Pemberton wants to stop us. Supplies, troops—we are driving a knife into the gut of the Confederacy."

He settled a little and looked at the map spread in front of him. His finger traced the hundreds of miles his regiment had already come. Captain Henry Forbes had been unable to entice rebels to chase him and had gotten stuck on one bank of a river, unable to cross. Ben had considered sending Forbes reinforcements, but the pressure of cavalry troops on his back trail forced him to keep on the move. It might prove advantageous having Forbes separated from the main body, if the captain had his wits about him and found small targets to attack. From what he had seen of his junior officer, Ben wasn't sure Forbes was up to the task.

"We can take Brookhaven," Ben said. "We'll ride directly, but Colonel Loomis, I need you to decoy the cavalry coming behind us so hard."

"Adams, sir," said Woodward. "Colonel Wirt Adams is the rebel commander."

"Anyone know him, other than by name?" He looked around the circle of gaunt, tired faces. Ben pushed his officers hard, and they pushed their soldiers even harder. So far, their lightning strike through Mississippi had been successful, taking the pressure off Grant for a spell. But they moved so fast they encountered enemy officers no one knew. Many of the officers with Ben had gone to West Point with their Confederate counterparts, but as the war dragged on and both sides relied more and more on native talent, it became harder to second-guess the opposition.

That worked against Ben. It also worked for him. He was a musician and businessman, not a soldier. All he knew came from books he had read, common sense, and an innate ability to get the most out of his soldiers. The West Point graduates might have the experience, especially those who had served during the Mexican War, but he wasn't bound by tradition or some general's outdated methods.

"He's probably in General Bowen's command, directly under Pemberton."

"Good. That means we're forcing Pemberton to commit troops to find us that could be better used elsewhere." Ben's finger stabbed down on the map. "We could engage Adams. However, I have a yen to ride directly for Brookhaven and victory, gentlemen!"

In an hour the regiment was in the saddle, and in two they swept through the sleepy Southern town.

Brookhaven wasn't as quiet as Ben had expected. Too many men came out, looked around with a keen eye, and vanished.

"Sir," called a scout. "There's a supply dump at the edge of town. Rifles. Lots of rifles!"

Ben knew then that he had ridden into a Confederate stronghold. He quickly dispatched his soldiers to round up anyone who might be a rebel guerrilla. It took only a few minutes to flush considerable resistance. The sporadic crack of rifles grew until it became a constant barrage.

"There," Ben shouted, getting his men spread out in a skirmish line. "A reb cavalry unit!" He mounted a charge directly through the heart of town, veered down a side street, and raced to the corrals where the enemy struggled to get their horses saddled.

As they fought, Ben emptying first one pistol and then the other, he saw a two-story building nearby flying a Confederate flag. This was either a regional HQ or served some other significant function. The firefight ended as quickly as it had begun, the rebels surrendering hastily.

Ben saw the rebels were ill-equipped, which didn't make sense since his scouts had reported a cache of rifles at the other end of town. Then he saw women wearing white caps peering from the second story of the building.

"Hospital!" Ben called. Everything came into focus for him now. These soldiers were responsible for moving wounded and dying to the hospital and had not expected to be caught up in a prolonged fight themselves.

"Checking it, sir," reported a captain, who led a squad

into the front door. A few minutes later, the officer returned. "I spoke with the doctor in charge. Doctor Maury was quick to surrender."

"See that they are treated well, Captain," ordered Ben. "How many are there?"

"Almost two hundred, sir."

"Two hundred prisoners," he said laughing. They had hardly fought before the reb soldiers gave up. "Lieutenant Woodward will be busy for quite a while taking their paroles."

"Yes, sir," the captain said. "One orderly asked if we were going to burn the trestles and bridges outside town. The railroad runs nearby."

"Thank him for the information. Captain, you're in charge here." Ben assembled what he could of his regiment and rode from town, finding the railroad tracks angling away from Brookhaven. He led his men along the roadbed, pointing out places for his troopers to pull up loose track and destroy the rails on hot fires built from railroad ties. Eventually Ben reached a trestle spanning a sluggishly flowing bayou.

"Burn it. Make sure both the trestle and that bridge yonder are destroyed," Ben ordered. His men fell into their economical, well-practiced routine of pulling up tracks and moving railroad ties to the trestle to burn it into the creek. He took a company, backtracked along the railroad into Brookhaven, and found the depot.

"Deserted, sir," came the report. "There was a rebel training camp. It's all abandoned, too."

"Burn it all," he ordered. Ben waited for his men to begin the arson, then rode to the town's main street. The citizens were now in the street. Some glared at his soldiers, but most were chatting friendly enough, showing that they saw nothing wrong with the way he treated them.

"How's Lieutenant Woodward doing?" he asked the command company sergeant who had replaced Carruthers. Sergeant Zeiss saluted, then gave a succinct report.

"Needs more ink. Too many parole forms to fill out 'fore we leave."

"He knows what to do. Able-bodied soldiers first, then the wounded and others." Ben swung around in the saddle when a cry went up among the townspeople. Flames from the burning railroad depot leaped far into the sky, sending fiery sparks to buildings dozens of yards away. Brookhaven was in danger of being burned completely to the ground.

"Fire brigade!" Ben shouted. "Sergeant Zeiss, organize the men. Don't let the fire spread to the rest of town."

Ben personally kept the citizens back as his men began the backbreaking work of putting out the fire they had started, working first on adjoining buildings and then, after almost an hour of moving water from the railroad water tank and the bayou, putting out the last of the fire in the depot. Only charred timbers remained, small gray tendrils of smoke rising lazily in the still afternoon air.

"Who's mayor?" Ben shouted. A man shuffled forward, with his hat in his hands though he tried to look fierce. "Sir, my apologies for jeopardizing your town in this fashion. The depot and armory were our targets, not structures belonging to civilians."

"You put out the fire," the mayor said, stunned at what was happening. "You could have let Brookhaven burn."

"Sir, we are all Americans. The resolution of this war will show that. Again, please accept my apologies." Ben looked up and saw two of his butternut guerrillas galloping hard down the street. To his amazement, they drew angry shouts from the town's residents.

"Sir, Adams's cavalry is on the way. Do we engage?" The scout, Sergeant Surby, threw Ben a sloppy salute.

Ben judged his men to be too exhausted for real combat. Putting out the fire had taken its toll, as had the rest of the raid.

"Have you seen any other units, besides Adams's?" he asked, considering the chance for a fight.

"Might be Colonel Richards comin', too," Sergeant Surby reported. "Same fella who gave us such hell a week back in Tennessee. I got into a little discussion with a gent out on the road, and he thought that was who's on our tail."

"Bugler," Ben called. "Blow assembly. We're moving out *now*." As much as he wanted to tangle with Adams, he wasn't going to be slowed down by a small cavalry unit until Colonel Richards's men arrived. He had sent Forbes out to feint toward Fayette, but none of the Confederates had taken the bait and had stayed after his main force.

The regiment quickly mounted and moved out in a ragged line. As they left, Ben rode to the mayor and said, "Again, my apologies for inconveniencing you, sir."

"It's war," the politician said stoically. Then he thrust out his hand and reached up to shake Benjamin's hand. "Thank you, Colonel. Thank you for not destroying Brookhaven."

Ben shook and hoped that the mayor's own side wouldn't do any more damage. Adams and Richards might take it into their heads that the mayor had aided and abetted their enemy.

He got his regiment moving to the railroad and then back east at a brisk pace for almost eight miles. It was sundown now and travel, even along the level railroad tracks, was chancy in such marshlands. Moreover, the Sixth Illinois Cavalry had earned a rest.

They had fought well, destroyed enemy matériel, and had done a bit, just a little, toward winning the war through their decent treatment of Brookhaven's populace. It was a good day.

Forty Barrels of Rum

April 30, 1863
Bogue Chitto, Mississippi

"Burn it. Burn it to the ground," Ben Grierson ordered his men. Four soldiers slid from their horses and hurried to be the first to set fire to the railroad depot.

As they toiled to start the fires, Ben looked along his brigade's back trail. Fourteen days they had raced through Mississippi, chased by half the Confederate Army, or so it seemed at times. The past three days had been the worst for him, never resting, always on the move, because of Wirt Adams and Colonel Richards so tenaciously closing in. Lieutenant General Pemberton had sent such sizable cavalry units to stop the raiding that Ben had come to the conclusion that the rebel troops were either inept or unlucky. After hearing tales of Adams's reputation as a cavalry commander, Ben honed the question down even finer. Either the CSA had been unlucky or the Sixth Illinois Cavalry had been very, very lucky. Adams had shown himself to be a clever, competent officer. Ben felt boxed in by his adversary's tactics and knew this mission had to end soon, one way or another.

He wanted to sit around and brag about this daring raid rather than rotting away the rest of the war in some Confederate prison—or worse. Although he did not dwell on it, Ben knew he could die as easily as any of the others in his command.

One other item rankled greatly. He still hadn't engaged in a face-to-face fight with Nathan Bedford Forrest. The one cavalry commander whom he grudgingly admired had remained in Tennessee to raid and harass the Union forces. At least, he had not made it to the Mississippi River to give General Grant more trouble in his anticipated attack on Vicksburg. When that port and its garrison fell, the entire river would be securely under Union control.

"All done, Colonel," called one of the soldiers. The blaze caused Old Barber to shy away. Ben didn't blame his horse one bit. Even a single extra degree of heat on such a sultry day made his sweat turn toxic.

"Down the railroad tracks, toward Summit," he decided. "Lieutenant Woodward!" he called. "Any word from Surby?"

"The butternut guerrillas are already scouting ahead for us, sir," came his adjutant's report. "I expect them back within a few hours."

"Move out," Ben decided. He could stand by and watch the Bogue Chitto depot burn or his troops heat the tracks over intense fires to melt them into useless steel pretzels, but Ben felt the pressure of the chase. Until he had better intelligence about the size and composition of the units he faced, he was better served keeping the Sixth on the move. That tactic worked for Forrest; it would work well for Ben Grierson.

The column trotted out. Ben didn't have to tell his men what to do as they followed the tracks; they pried loose rails and dragged them away to throw into swamps, or just knocked out rivets to leave dangerous tracks that might derail a careless engineer's train.

Ben reached for his pistol, then relaxed when he identified the man wearing the Confederate uniform riding pell-mell toward them and waving like a maniac. Sergeant Surby skidded to a halt and approached his commander at a more sedate pace, but his face was dotted with perspiration and his horse was flecked with lather. His Confederate uniform was plastered to his body, showing how hard he had ridden in the heat of the day.

"Colonel, there's another town ahead. Just skirted it since I wanted to check on troops to the west."

"Summit?" asked Ben. "That is supposed to be the next town along the railroad."

"That's the name," confirmed Surby. All too often, the maps were incomplete or even outright wrong. "But there's a big force in Osyka. Not sure we want to engage. They got soldiers, and they got civilian support. We'd have to grow eyes in the backs of our heads to win a fight there."

"Who's in command?"

"Don't rightly know. I kin ride that way and find a picket wantin' to swap a few lies."

Ben realized their raid had been spectacularly successful so far. It was time to head for safety. If he began angling to the southwest, he could avoid Osyka and the enemy directly in front and behind him. An all-out ride would allow his troopers to reach Baton Rouge, which was securely in Union hands.

"Shuck off that uniform jacket, Sergeant," Ben said, coming to a decision. "Ride with us as a bluecoat, for a change."

"My privilege, sir!"

As they entered Summit, Ben noticed something strange and inspiring. The Southern civilians weren't hostile. In fact, they welcomed his soldiers. It made him believe the war might be over soon, Shiloh notwithstanding.

"No looting, and no gunplay unless you're fired on first," he ordered. "Find supplies we can use but don't take them. Ask for them."

"What about military supplies, Colonel?" asked one of his lieutenants.

"Destroy them, of course. But be certain they *are* military. The entire town looks clear of Confederate forces."

Ben dismounted and greeted the mayor warmly and spoke with him for some time until he heard three soldiers whooping in glee.

"Please, Colonel, don't—" began the mayor. Ben ignored him and went to see what the troopers had unearthed under the boardwalk.

"Forty barrels, Colonel," crowed a private. "We got ourselves forty barrels of rum!"

"Let's celebrate, Colonel. We kin—" began another.

"Destroy them. Break the barrels open and pour the rum into the street!"

"But, Colonel. We deserve a little nip. There's 'nuff here for all of us to have some."

"Do it, Private," Ben said coldly. "No soldier in my command will fall victim to such vile stuff!"

Amid great grumbling, the soldiers set about their sorry duty of getting the barrels from their hiding place and rolled into the street. Ben thought he saw tears in one soldier's eyes as he used an axe to cave in the end, sending a river of fragrant rum gushing into the dirt street.

As he watched, a woman came up to him, looking prim and proper.

"You are the commander of these men, sir?" she asked.

"Ma'am, I am." Ben touched the brim of his hat.

"Sir, if the North wins this war and you should ever run for President, I will *order* my husband to vote for you!"

"Thank you, ma'am," Ben said, fighting to keep from grinning ear to ear. When he saw the last of the barrels drained, he stepped out and bellowed, "Troop, mount! We're moving out right away!" He turned back to the woman, saluted, then climbed into the saddle and led his disgruntled soldiers out of Summit and away from the heady aroma of the spilled rum.

The grumbling stopped as they rode along the railroad. Ben ordered his men to remain in the saddle rather than constantly dropping down to destroy more tracks. They sensed his need for haste to leave Summit behind and to reach . . . where?

"Sir, we got company," reported Surby. "It might be Captain Forbes coming in from Fayette."

"Might it be R.V. Richardson?" Ben worried that the approaching troopers could be the Confederate cavalry unit dogging his trail.

"Might be, but I doubt it, Colonel. You're gettin' a bit spooked, ain't you?" Sergeant Surby studied his superior. "We been puttin' a lot of land behind us for the past two weeks."

"I am not losing my nerve, Sergeant," Ben said coldly. "Richardson or my captain?"

"Don't rightly know if you kin call Henry Forbes yers," Surby said in his fake Southern drawl, catching the signal from another of the butternut guerrillas ahead along the tracks, "but that's him. He's joinin' up after moseyin' all around the countryside."

Ben rode ahead and saw that his scouts were, as usual, right. A battered-looking Captain Forbes reported of his feint toward Fayette and then his blundering about in a swamp for two days.

"We're riding directly for Baton Rouge, Captain," Ben told him. "You can rest your troops there."

"We're not riding straight out, Colonel?"

Ben looked at the captain for a moment, then asked, "What have you heard?"

"We spied on more than one enemy picket. Grant's attacked Vicksburg. I wondered if we were being ordered back north to join him."

Ben let out a loud cheer that echoed through the piney woods. He settled down, grinning ear to ear.

"We've done our job, Captain. If General Grant needs us for more, the Sixth Illinois Cavalry will carry out his orders to the letter."

After a difficult crossing of the Comite River, Ben Grierson rode into Baton Rouge amid great acclaim. Over two weeks, he and his men had marched six hundred miles through the heart of Mississippi, killed or wounded more than a hundred Confederate soldiers, had Adjutant Woodward parole five hundred, and seized a thousand head of horses. But his real triumph came through CSA Lieutenant General Pemberton sending more than 38,000 troops to stop him, troops that could have been used to defend Vicksburg.

Those were the numbers, but the ones that pleased Ben even more concerned his own casualties. Three of his men had been killed, seven wounded, and nine were counted as missing.

The Sixth Illinois Cavalry had struck a devastating blow to the Confederacy.

Fame and Humility

May 27, 1863
Port Hudson, Louisiana

Ben Grierson felt the pressure of commanding so many troopers. After the normally hard-bitten General Sherman had praised him to the skies for the two-week-long raid driving a cavalry saber through the belly of Mississippi, he had not only become a national figure but had also received command of the First Cavalry Brigade, Fourth Division, Department of the Gulf. Trying to maneuver not only his own Sixth Illinois Cavalry but the Seventh, along with the Second Massachusetts, First Louisiana, and Fourth Wisconsin Mounted Infantry, required abilities he had not exercised before.

"We can do it, sir," Samuel Woodward told his superior with some confidence. "If we can make life hell for Pemberton at Vicksburg, we can take Port Hudson."

"I'd feel better if we were back in those miserable swamps destroying railroad tracks," Ben said. "I'd feel even better without those reporters breathing down my neck."

"I can get rid of them, sir," Woodward said. "They'd prefer a tour of the New Orleans whorehouses to being in the field."

"No!" The very idea offended Ben. "They can stay, but this campaign is going to be a protracted one."

"Why, sir? General Banks has more than enough men to take Port Hudson, with our cavalry support."

Ben snorted in contempt. He had nothing against the commander of the Department of the Gulf, but the man had black troops. How Banks could ever think he could depend on such slackers in the heat of battle was a mystery and put even more of a burden on Ben's shoulders. Tearing up the railroad tracks between Port Hudson and Clinton and cutting off supplies going to Vicksburg would do more to help Ulysses Grant's assault. That was the fight where Ben wanted to commit his gallant soldiers, not fighting twice the battle, his own and that of the Negro soldiers.

"Pass along the orders to assemble. General Banks wants to begin the assault soon."

"Yes, sir," Woodward said, looking strangely at his superior.

Ben sat and stared at the campaign plans drawn on his map. A sharp, determined cavalry attack might be Banks's only chance to capture Port Hudson without having to lay siege to the town, tying up troops for long weeks until the Confederates inside starved.

He folded his map, tucked it into the front of his uniform, and left his tent. The sun poked above the banyan trees in the swamp to the east. His troops would swing south and then ride directly west in attack on Port Hudson. He had spent the prior day with officers from General Banks's staff determining the most vulnerable routes to the front door of the Mississippi port city. Ben mounted and rode slowly to the head of his column, studying his men without seeming to do so. They were nervous enough without thinking he was judging them and finding fault. His job as commander was to praise; let the sergeants chew out the men and keep them in line.

They had learned to fight a guerrilla war, but this was a more standard cavalry assault. He had to rely more heavily on the new units under his command. But Ben knew they would not fail.

They couldn't. Not with so many reporters watching his every move. The fame that had come his way after the Mississippi raid was now more of a burden than the Confederate guns he faced.

The tiny knot of reporters was kept in safety by Sergeant Surby and others whose scouting talents weren't needed today. Ben returned the scout's sloppy salute and rode on.

The brigade moved out, getting into position as Banks's bugler sounded charge. Ben passed the order down to his own bugler, then led the attack on the southeastern corner of the fortress protecting Port Hudson. Before he had ridden for two minutes, cannon began thundering and hunks of the landscape began exploding into the air. He continued until he had drawn enough fire to allow elements of Banks's infantry to advance, then fell back, still drawing fire.

"Casualties?" he barked. Reports came back. Minor. He launched a second attack and a third until he was deafened from the cannonade and disoriented by the smoke and dirt hanging in the air.

"Pull back," Ben ordered. "Regroup."

"Sir, we're starting to lose mounts. Forty so far," Captain Forbes reported. "We're still just beyond the range of those guns, but those poor black devils are taking heavy fire."

Ben saw that Banks's black infantry units marched repeatedly into the teeth of cannon and rifle fire from Port Hudson's ramparts. He watched attack after attack fail, but the troopers did not break and maintained their order even when it became apparent they were trapped and unable to retreat to regroup.

"We can't let them fight that well and die for it," Ben said. He had never expected Negro soldiers to show such courage under fire. And he was not about to let any Union battalion suffer the casualties they were taking without trying to aid them.

Ben launched a widespread assault that was turned back, but the Negro soldiers succeeded in escaping the withering fire from the fortress.

At the end of the day the Confederates still held Port Hudson, but Ben wrote Alice that he had seen the bravery of the Negro regiments and had settled the matter of their good fighting abilities in his mind for all time.

Back in the Field

June 6, 1863
Clinton, Mississippi

"No more tracks runnin' south, Colonel," reported Sergeant Surby. "We done ruined 'bout all the rail lines in these parts."

Ben hardly heard the report as he dismissed the scout, all decked out in his butternut guerrilla uniform again. After being repulsed repeatedly at Port Hudson, General Banks had finally resigned himself to a protracted siege, freeing Ben's brigade to range again throughout Mississippi. Ben had wasted no time heading north toward Clinton, hoping to be part of General Grant's campaign against Vicksburg.

There was hardly a mile of track that had once run from Port Hudson to Clinton that his brigade hadn't destroyed. Sending the butternut guerrillas out to flank his progress northward allowed them freedom to cut telegraph wires and to engage in small skirmishes to keep the Confederates off balance. Ben felt he had done more good back in the field than his entire unit had by charging futilely against Port Hudson's battlements, in spite of being routed after a four-hour fight when his brigade ran low on ammunition outside Clinton three days earlier.

"What are you thinking, sir?" asked Captain Forbes. "I've seen that look before."

"Clinton is still in rebel hands," Ben said. "We've cut off all supply routes. What's to keep us from capturing the town?"

"We ran out of ammo before, sir," said Woodward, "and Clinton has been supplying Port Hudson. That means they have a powerful lot of supplies piled up that they can use for their own defense. Fact is, they even have an ammunition factory in the town."

"We're better armed now," Ben said. "The troopers have plenty of ammo from the supply wagons that reached us this morning." His brother John had come through with the supplies in the nick of time. Without the supplies, Ben would have been forced to break off his expedition.

"That'd be a bold move, sir," Forbes said. "What does Banks think of it?"

"Why, if he knew, he would approve," Ben said, coming to a decision. Deep in his gut, though, doubt gnawed. Was he launching this attack because he had been driven off and that had hurt his pride, or could he really break the back of an important Confederate supply depot? Maybe he could borrow some of those black soldiers fighting so well for General Banks. Or maybe he could argue himself out of the fight if he sat around thinking long enough.

"Prepare the men for battle. We're riding into Clinton. Let's take us a city!"

The fight before had been protracted and brutal, Ben unable to make any headway after his brigade ran short of ammunition. But resupplied, he was certain they could drive through the center of the town. When Clinton fell, Port Hudson would go quickly, and possibly, even Vicksburg.

They rode slowly to a point on a low hill looking down

into Clinton. Every detail of the town's defense had been etched into Ben's memory from the earlier fight. Nothing had changed. A hundred muskets poked out over earthen ramparts, guarding entry.

"Captain Forbes, go to the left flank and wait for my attack. Have the Seventh and the Massachusetts wait in reserve. After we've drawn a few volleys, attack. We will fall back. The rebels will think they've run us off and that you're too late to the attack. The remainder of the brigade will strike decisively when their attention is drawn to you, Captain."

"A dangerous plan, sir," Lieutenant Woodward said. "We have to believe they'll concentrate fire on Forbes and not counterattack on your position when you withdraw."

"Let's see if it works." Ben hesitated. "Are all those reporters safely out of the way?"

"Most of them are back in camp, sir," said Woodward. "They weren't told of any action today."

"Good. They make me nervous poking about, asking foolish questions." Ben fished about in his saddlebags and got out his spare pistol. "Victory, gentlemen, let's ride to victory!"

As Ben led the charge directly into Clinton's defenders, he felt a bullet warm his arm. Another creased his leg. But he kept riding and shooting until both pistols were empty. Less than fifty yards from the town's defenders, he read the determination in their eyes. That made him even more resolute.

"Back, retreat!" he shouted. From the corner of his eye, Ben saw Forbes's two companies swinging to attack from the flank, apparently too late. As he retreated halfway back the distance he had come, all fire died. The Confederates concentrated on Forbes and his troopers, thinking they had easy targets now.

Ben lifted his arm and gave the signal. Two regiments, fresh and unbloodied, swept past to smash into the Confederate ranks. He took time to reload, and saw that the men from the Sixth Illinois Cavalry accompanying him had similarly reloaded. He wheeled them about and rejoined the battle in support of the two regiments battling furiously against the stubborn Confederates.

His head jerked to one side as a bullet drilled a hole in the brim of his hat. But Ben saw a small gap in the defenders' rank and made for it. His men streamed after him, whooping, hollering, and firing their carbines the best they could at a dead gallop. Old Barber strained, jumped, and cleared the dirt battlement, and Ben found himself surrounded by gray-clad men on all sides.

He fired until his pistols were emptied, then drew his saber and slashed as wide a path through the defenders as he could. In the heat of battle, he never saw the resistance slowly fading away. Finally, he was left alone, sword weighing heavily in his hand.

"Where'd they go?" he asked, still caught up in the rush of battle.

"Retreated, sir, or just plain routed," called a lieutenant whose face was so covered with blood and grime Ben couldn't identify him.

Ben calmed down, mopped sweat from his face, and came away with a dirty hand. But no blood. He patted his jacket and found bullet holes. Only vague recollections of the rounds remained. Ben reached up to check the hole put into his hat brim by another slug, but couldn't find it. His memories of what had happened didn't jibe with the evidence—except that the Confederates had broken and run.

Clinton was open to him. At last.

"Report. What casualties did we take?" Ben felt a curious disconnection from the reports trickling in now that the immediate danger had passed. He knew his officers were reassembling their men and trying to regain order. Attacks always spread the brigade over the battlefield, making it hard to press an assault past a few simple commands.

"Eight dead, sir, and twenty-eight or thereabouts wounded too badly to ride. Another fifteen missing."

Ben didn't even know who had reported the casualties to him. He turned and motioned for the heart of Clinton.

It wasn't until the sun sank behind a line of trees that Ben regained his senses. By then, the railroad depot had been burned to the ground and a steam locomotive destroyed. Huge mounds of ammo were destroyed, along with the factory manufacturing them. Even a woolens factory was destroyed. No new uniforms for the rebels. Clinton had been taken out of the war, virtually ensuring the fall of Port Hudson.

And Vicksburg.

Ben Grierson felt no triumph at this victory. Before, there had been a thrill of fear and anticipation in every engagement, but this time there was only a fugue state he could not explain.

He wondered if he was losing his edge—or his mind.

Siege and Star

June 14, 1863
Port Hudson, Louisiana

"This is a terrible place to die," complained Ben Grierson. He looked around. A fetid wind blew sluggishly against a sheet dangling from a tree limb. This formed the better part of his tent. For furniture he used empty ammunition cases and slept on a cot propped up with rocks on one end and his saddle at the other. The ground was marshy, and if the insects ever stopped buzzing and biting, Ben wasn't sure when that was. Morning, night, and twilight, the hungry bugs never stopped swarming around his face. He swatted at a particularly hungry mosquito and smashed it into a bloody spot on the back of his left hand.

"The price of success, sir," Lieutenant Woodward said. "If you hadn't taken Clinton away from the Confederates, there'd still be need for us in the field. As it is, the siege of Port Hudson is the only real assignment we could have drawn."

"Grant's bogged down at Vicksburg," Ben grumbled. "Pemberton might have retreated before Grant and Sooy Smith's troops, but they never beat him decisively. Now that Pemberton's retreated behind Vicksburg's walls, it might take the rest of the summer to force a surrender."

"General Banks isn't doing any better here, sir," Woodward pointed out. "Even with our entire command at his disposal, he can't convince the rebels to surrender."

"I wonder who's starving whom," Ben said. He rubbed his belly. Even the officers were on short rations. For all Banks's abilities as an officer, supply was not one he held in high esteem. He had never been convinced that an army traveled on its stomach. And Ben had to admit it might not be true. All the growling bellies in his brigade might deafen the Port Hudson defenders and force them into surrender.

He laughed at this small joke but didn't share it with his friend.

"So, Sam, how are the men faring? For them this is almost rest and recuperation."

"Not many cotton much to garrison duty. Other than patrolling the lines to be certain General Gardner doesn't try to send out couriers with communications intended for other Confederate commanders, they have nothing to do but get into trouble."

Ben heaved a deep, heartfelt sigh of resignation. "The composition of Banks's infantry is all wrong," he said. "They're Easterners and fight differently. He ought to have Westerners fighting. That would end the siege quick as a rabbit." He leaned back, hiking his feet on an empty crate. "He ought to have more Negro troops. They fight well in this wretched heat and don't seem to mind the insects."

"It's not likely for General Banks to get any reinforcements, sir," Woodward said. "He can't even fill out a proper requisition for supplies. I've done what I can, but I'm doing the paperwork for the entire Department of the Gulf."

"Put in a requisition for our brigade, then," Ben said. "And for five hundred fly whisks." He whacked at another hungry mosquito intent on drilling into his flesh and drinking his blood.

Ben looked up as a messenger hurried over. The private looked no older than fifteen or sixteen and frightened at reporting to a brigade commander.

"Yes, son?"

"I, uh, you Colonel Grierson?"

"I am." Ben wondered if he had ever been in such awe of an officer. He couldn't remember ever feeling that way about any of the men he knew. He hobnobbed with generals—Grant and Sherman he counted as close personal friends—and he knew governors and the President. For him, such power seemed normal.

"Got this for you. Lookit the seal on it, sir. I mean, I couldn't help seeing it."

Sam Woodward took the letter from the boy's shaking hand. His own eyebrows arched as he passed the envelope along to Ben.

"Now what can President Lincoln possibly be sending me? It's been a spell since we sat down for a good talk," Ben said in as level a voice as he could. In spite of hobnobbing with presidents, he felt a growing excitement. He broke the wax seal on the envelope and then quickly scanned the letter inside. A smile brightened his face. "I certainly have something to write Alice about now."

He handed the letter to Woodward, who read it before looking up.

"This is certainly long overdue, sir. Congratulations—Brigadier General Grierson!" his adjutant cried.

Fortune, Misfortune

July 18, 1863
Vicksburg, Mississippi

Ben Grierson leaned against the rail of the paddle wheeler, his view from the Texas deck inspiring as the renamed *Imperial* steamed up to the dock in Union-held Vicksburg. Pemberton had surrendered on July 4 to Grant. Hearing of this, Gardner had relinquished command at Port Hudson four days later, his only term of surrender being to speak with Ben Grierson. They had reminisced, as much as generals on opposing sides could, of the fight and how Gardner "had ambushed you where you did not go and waited for you till morning while you passed in the night."

"That's a mighty pleasing sight," Ben said with satisfaction. Huge chunks of fortification had been blown away by Admiral Porter's barrage from the river, and much of the city still smoldered after the intense fighting, no matter that the persistent fires had been fought for two solid weeks.

"Yes, sir," said Sam Woodward. "Do you reckon General Grant will be waiting for you at dockside?"

"He said he'd have a brass band playing every song I'd ever heard and some I hadn't," Ben said, laughing. "I'd settle for the band being in tune rather than trying too hard to impress me."

"You deserve any accolade you get, sir," Woodward said. "I think it's a tribute to you that both Grant and Sherman fought to get you assigned to their command and away from General Banks's."

"My luck's finally changing. I wish Alice and the boys could meet Simpson," Ben said, referring to Grant. "I'm not sure Alice would like him, not the way she does Sherman, but he's an honest, forthright man. That's a commodity sorely lacking in many officers."

"Especially the West Point graduates," Woodward said with just a trace of bitterness.

"Don't be too harsh in your judgment, Sam," Ben said. "We've seen some good officers and some, well, let's say they were overly timid. But they're not here. We are."

"*You* are, sir. Look! There's the general!" Woodward pointed to a tight knot of blue-clad officers, their braid glittering in the afternoon sunlight. "That's got to be Grant. Who else would sport that much gold braid?"

"Perhaps it's not General Grant," said Ben. "He dislikes standing on formality as much as I do. It could be Sooy Smith. I've heard he delights in his rows of medals so much that he stands in front of a mirror every morning and counts them, just to be sure he hasn't gotten a new one overnight."

"Has he earned them?" asked Woodward.

Ben ignored his adjutant's question. He had no reason to deal with Sooy Smith and every right to be in Grant's command. The fall of Vicksburg sealed the Confederacy's fate in the West. All that remained were a few battles to be fought back East. If he understood the way Grant thought, he would be assigned the mission of sweeping through Tennessee and cleaning up the last pockets of resistance while the main army swept eastward to catch Lee between the Army of the Potomac and Grant's full force, now released from the siege of Vicksburg.

"Come along, Sam. This is a fine day, a lucky day for me."

"Careful, sir, getting to the gangway. Those bales of supplies are like a forest."

Ben heard the horses at the prow protesting the loud steam whistles and the change in tempo of the side wheels. He weaved his way through the bales and came out on the starboard side, waiting for Grant and the brass band to greet him.

"Lead your horse," urged one of the ever-present reporters. "That'll make for a good story."

"Sorry," Ben said as he turned to the reporter who had dogged his steps since Clinton fell. "I'll let my orderly deal with the horses."

He lurched as the steamer banged into the docks. A frightened horse reared and began pawing the air. Ben jumped up and caught the horse's bridle, trying to control it. The whites of the horse's eyes showed in fear as it continued to fight. A hoof lashed out and caught him in the leg, sending him reeling. He grabbed a railing an instant before he would have tumbled overboard into the turbulent Mississippi River.

"That would have made a fine scene," he said as Woodward helped him stand. "Imagine a general taking a tumble into the river with a brass band watching?" Ben laughed and took a step. His leg buckled under him and his face blanched as pain washed over him like a choppy wave from that muddy river.

"General, are you all right?" asked Woodward, concerned.

"Can't seem to stand. Support me, just a little, Sam."

Woodward tried not to be obvious about the way he buttressed Ben, but Grant noticed immediately as they hobbled off the boat.

"That was a nasty kick the horse delivered you," Grant said. "Are you all right, General Grierson?"

"I . . . yes, sir." Ben put his weight on his good leg and saluted. "Thank you for inviting me to Vicksburg. It's an honor to be in the city you conquered."

The brass band struck up "Battle Hymn of the Republic" and drowned out Grant's words. He shrugged and let the band finish their somewhat grating rendition.

"From what I've heard of your brigade's band, they are much better."

"Your men are fighters, sir," Ben said. Then he smiled in spite of the pain. "So are the soldiers of my Sixth Illinois Cavalry."

"Let me give you a tour of this fair city's fortifications, General," said Grant, "and we can discuss your future. I don't want it to be a secret that I can use a man of your fighting ability, but Will Sherman wants you in his command so you can cut the heart out of resistance in Mississippi."

Ben settled himself in the carriage next to Grant, stretching his leg out stiffly. It throbbed only a mite now, not enough to bother him as he considered his future. He saw he had to choose carefully, since it was obvious Grant was offering him any position he desired.

As Ulysses Grant pointed out the Vicksburg salients, they spoke of where the war stood and where Grant wished it to go.

After an hour, Ben had come to his decision.

"Sir, it would be a grand opportunity serving with either you or General Sherman."

"I hear the 'but' in your voice. You're a national hero, Ben, after your raiding through Mississippi. I don't know how widely reported Gardner's comments were after he surrendered at Port Hudson, but Pemberton almost accused you of singlehandedly causing the fall of Vicksburg. He seems to want to ignore my part." Grant laughed, his gravelly tone turning a tad frivolous. "You can have any command you want—except mine!"

"General, never that. My ambitions are more limited. I'd like to be assigned to Tennessee."

"You still have a hankering to tangle with Nathan Bedford Forrest?" Grant saw the answer on Ben's face and laughed. "You say your ambitions are limited? It'll be easier defeating Lee, Jackson, *and* Longstreet than bringing that guerrilla bastard to bay."

"That's part of it, sir. I want to be closer to my family also."

"I'll have orders cut directing you to serve in Hurlbut's command. If there's a cavalry commander in the Union Army that can stop Forrest, you're the one!"

"Thank you, sir."

"The *Imperial* is heading on upriver to Memphis with twenty-eight Confederate officers destined for prison in Detroit—none of them were willing to give their paroles. Report to Stephen Hurlbut, and I'll expect to hear word of Forrest's capture within the month!"

"Sir," Ben said, grinning, "that's not ambitious, that's *impossible*."

"Impossible for a brigade commander. That's why I'm requesting that Hurlbut make you cavalry chief for the Sixteenth Army Corps. If you can't run down Forrest with three brigades and eighty-six hundred men, I don't know who can."

Ulysses Grant let Ben out dockside. As the general drove off in the carriage, Ben started back up the gangway, only to have his leg give way under him. Waves of pain threatened to close in around him until Sam Woodward hurried to help him.

Even appointment as commander of so many men—and being closer to his family—did nothing to assuage the pain as the riverboat made its way to Memphis.

Injured

January 6, 1864
Memphis, Tennessee

Ben Grierson tried to walk, leaning heavily on his cane. Even with this support, his leg buckled under him and sent him reeling into his desk. The crash caused Samuel Woodward to come running.

"General, are you all right?"

"You worry too much, Sam," he said, flopping heavily into his chair.

"You're white as a ghost. Your leg's not getting any better."

"It's no worse," Ben said, trying to put his injury into better light. "Some day soon I ought to be able to ride again."

"You can't even travel in a carriage."

Ben closed his eyes and tried to regain control of his rampaging emotions. His anger knew no bounds, and it was anger at himself more than anyone else.

"If it hadn't been for my cavalry boots, it would have been worse." Ben couldn't help reflecting on how he had been kicked in the head when he was eight years old. Not walking was better than being in a coma or being blind in one eye.

As that thought crossed his mind, he wondered if being blind wasn't better. He had been unable to ride and take the field against Nathan Bedford Forrest. As a result of his injury, Ben had been forced to send orders into the field from his desk in Memphis. Worse, Grant's chief of cavalry, William Sooy Smith, with five regiments, had been placed in temporary command of operations. Never had a greater mistake been made in war. To catch a badger like Forrest required an officer with daring. Sooy Smith had been nothing but timid. Forrest had raided with impunity and had penetrated within fifty miles from Memphis, intending to establish his headquarters in Jackson.

Sherman had fought Braxton Bragg at Chattanooga and had finally defeated him, opening the route to Atlanta. But Ben felt useless because of the way Forrest cut railroad lines and interrupted Union supply lines vital to Sherman's efforts. Of all the Confederate commanders, Ben wanted to face Forrest most to test his mettle. And he sat behind a desk while Sooy Smith pussyfooted about.

Timid. That word burned in Ben's brain. Sherman had thought Sooy Smith was "timid" at Shiloh, and Ben had disregarded his impetuous friend's characterization until he had witnessed it firsthand. After months of chasing after Forrest, Sooy Smith had failed repeatedly.

"Sam, I want you to take command in the field. Ignore Sooy Smith's orders. It's the only way we are going to box in Forrest."

"Sir, I'm only a lieutenant."

"It won't matter," Ben insisted. "A friend of mine will be transferring in soon."

"Colonel Hatch?"

"Edward is a good man, a fine cavalry officer, and we share a great deal when it comes to ideas for command."

"I'll keep the brigade fighting until Colonel Hatch assumes command." Woodward hesitated, knowing this was only part of what ate at his commander. "Sir, any word from your wife?"

"Alice is still back in Chicago. I'm afraid my sister Susan is not doing well." During the autumn Susan's two sons had contracted dysentery and required protracted attention before they died. Since then, Susan's mental condition had become increasingly precarious. He worried because of the strong trait of insanity that wound through his family tree that had left too many Griersons in asylums.

"Your sons are well, though," Woodward said. Sam knew how Ben worried about Charlie and especially Robert, growing up without their father's presence.

"They are. I wish my family could spend more time here in Memphis, as they did around Christmas."

"Everything will work out, sir," Woodward said with more confidence than he felt.

"Yes, of course it will. The war goes well for the Union," Ben said, but again sadness descended on him. He felt useless sitting at his desk, hurting from a pointless injury, longing for his family, knowing Nathan Bedford Forrest ranged at will throughout Tennessee. Soon, Ed Hatch would be in command and would be more than a match for Forrest.

Ben closed his eyes and tried to imagine the leg pain away.

He failed.

Disaster

February 26, 1864
Memphis, Tennessee

Ben Grierson looked up for the papers stacked all over his desk. He shifted uncomfortably to place his leg back on a pillow propped on a low stool beside his chair before turning his full attention to his visitor. From the look on General Sooy Smith's face, Ben knew what the man had come to report.

"General," greeted Sooy Smith. The small, weaselly looking man's pale eyes darted about as if he sought refuge. Ben already worked to keep his anger in check.

"How bad was it?" he asked, knowing what Sooy Smith was going to say from the expression on the man's face.

"Forrest whupped us good, Ben," Sooy Smith said. Ben bristled at being called by his given name. He and Sooy Smith were equal in rank, but there any equality ended.

"If I remember the orders General Sherman issued, he warned that Forrest was likely to attack with 'vehemence.'"

"That's certainly true," Sooy Smith said. "I went to Meridian to flush that devil out, but discovered he was at Collierville."

"That explains why Sherman marched into Meridian with twenty thousand troops and had to spend five days destroying the cantonment," Ben said acidly. "He expected you, but when you never showed up, he returned to Vicksburg."

"I engaged Forrest near Oklona," Sooy Smith said, growing angry.

"I know. My Second Brigade led the retreat, having been assigned rear guard duty."

"Hatch was unable to command, and I didn't trust Lieutenant Colonel Hepburn to field his force adequately."

"My force," Ben said angrily. He stood, his leg throbbing but better now that fury gave him added strength. "My forces led your retreat. How dare you put them in that position?"

"I lost over three hundred soldiers," Sooy Smith said, his lips thinning to a hard, tight line. A muscle in his jaw began to jerk and quiver. "And two thousand horses. I lost men and horses and supplies. We fought him. We fought hard, and not everything was a complete disaster. Rumor has it that Forrest's brother was killed during my campaign."

"If you'd stood and fought at any point, you would have defeated Forrest himself," Ben said. He fought to contain the fury raging inside him, fueled by the throbbing in his leg and the way nothing had gone right. "I've seen Sherman's reports, I've seen those from my adjutant, I've seen those from other officers. You failed, General, because you would not engage."

"He—"

"You've reduced my force to nothing but green recruits. Two thousand men who had no idea of combat were placed in jeopardy because of you. And the sorry thing is, *they would have won* if you had engaged Forrest!"

"You are wrong, General."

"I'm not wrong that Forrest's guerrillas are raiding within a few miles of this very headquarters. You failed to contain and destroy him, and he's expanding his influence throughout Tennessee."

Sooy Smith sputtered, stamped his foot, then spun and left without another word. Ben watched him go. He took a few seconds to calm down, then shouted for his orderly.

"I'm taking back command of my brigade," Ben said. "Pass the word to the officers. I want my regiment drilled, trained, and ready for the field. Let it be known that Nathan Bedford Forrest will fall!"

His orderly swallowed hard, nodded, then did a quick about-face and left.

Ben tested his leg and found it adequate to the task of pacing. This had not been a good day. He had expected the report from Sooy Smith, already having the details from other sources, but hearing it directly still angered him. He hobbled to his desk and looked at the latest letter from Alice.

She and the boys were visiting Alice's parents, taking a break from nursing his sister. He wanted to hear about Susan, about the boys, about their day-to-day life. All Alice could write about was her fear that he was smoking, cursing, and carousing with his fellow officers. Ben crumpled the letter and hurled it across the room. Nothing was going right today.

But it would. Stopping Nathan Bedford Forrest would be the start.

That Devil Forrest

June 10, 1864
Brice's Crossing, Tennessee

"Sir, the men are about ready to fall from their saddles," Sam Woodward reported. "We need to take a day or two for rest."

"No," Ben Grierson said adamantly. "Forrest cannot be allowed to slip through my hands, not now, not when he is so close. If Sooy Smith hadn't botched his entire campaign, this one wouldn't be necessary." Ben swallowed rising bile and added, "Fort Pillow might not have fallen, either."

Nathan Bedford Forrest had attacked Fort Pillow almost a month earlier and had slaughtered the hapless defenders. Ben had been in the field then, getting his injured leg used to the rigors of all-day riding, but had not heard of the fort's attack until too late to lend support. Once he had arrived, he had spent part of the day helping count bodies. There had been more black defenders than white—226 black and only 168 white. He had seen no evidence that any man in that command had faltered for a moment, not until death took him.

That determination, especially on the part of the Negroes, had fueled Forrest's savage slaughter.

Subsequent engagements with Forrest had proven elusive. The man always zigged whenever Ben zagged until Ben began to wonder if Forrest had spies on his staff. Such spies had hardly been needed when Sooy Smith was hunting for Forrest, but Ben sent out his butternut guerrillas and had dozens of other scouting parties constantly alert for the enemy's movements. Repeatedly, he had come up with a handful of smoke and nothing more.

"We can take the time, sir," Woodward insisted. "General Sturgis is reinforcing us. We don't need to bear the brunt of this hunt. He's in command, after all."

Ben winced as if his adjutant poured salt into the wound. Sturgis had been placed in overall command because of Sherman's failing confidence in Ben.

"That's the point, Sam. He's reinforcing us. He's not serving in our stead." Ben studied the map and wondered where Forrest hid. The man knew every nook and cranny of the state better than any cavalry officer on either side of the war.

"Our recruits still haven't been well enough trained. Sooy Smith left us in dire condition. I'm sorry, sir, but there was nothing I could do about that. And Colonel Hatch—"

"Never mind, Lieutenant," Ben said briskly. "Rehashing our past does nothing to assure our future—or send Forrest to perdition."

"Sir, we *have* to deal with it. We have fewer than two thousand men and only about three hundred horses that aren't broken down. You know what General Sherman said."

"I know, Sam, I know. He was less than charitable, thinking Hurlbut and I were malingering."

"He replaced Hurlbut, sir." Woodward gently reminded Ben that he had suffered a similar fate by having Samuel Sturgis placed in overall command. The volatile Sherman did not tolerate failure lightly, and failing to bring Forrest to bay presented a major impediment to further Union activity.

The Confederate guerrilla's small units nipped and bit at even large elements of the Union Army.

"Sturgis might be here to replace me," Ben allowed, "but he's already found that Hurlbut was doing the best he could after Grant siphoned off most of the cavalry for his own use."

"And you, sir. In spite of your injury, you've done the best you could."

Ben idly rubbed his leg. For once it actually felt better in the afternoon than it did in the morning. The pain was almost gone, and he had resisted the surgeon's advice of taking a little nip of whiskey to deaden the pain. If Alice had caught wind of even a suggestion of this medicinal application of alcohol, she would have been inconsolable. He had blamed his leg injury long enough. It was time to ride as he had done before when he had raced through the heart of Mississippi, taken prisoners, and destroyed Confederate supplies.

"There," Ben said finally. "We can lay a trap for him at Brice's Crossing."

"Why there, sir?" Woodward frowned as he studied the map. It was the same one Ben used, but he saw no way his commander could be so certain from the scant details marked on it.

"We think alike, Forrest and I. Only I am not prone to wanton slaughter. If he offers his surrender, I will accept it, and rest assured I will not have the others in his detachment executed, either."

"Aren't you jumping ahead of yourself?" asked Woodward.

"We'll have him, Sam. Forrest will ride headlong into our ambush. Sturgis can back us up should pursuit be necessary. If our troopers lack horses, then we become infantry. I don't care if Sturgis claims the credit for his artillery, for his infantry, or even for his cavalry. As long as Forrest is defeated, I will be content." He turned the map around and began outlining his plan for trapping Forrest.

After the briefing, Lieutenant Woodward hurried off to pass along the orders. Ben stared at the map for a few more minutes, turning over in his mind everything that might go wrong. When he realized that just about everything might, he gave up. The time for timidity was past, and had been gone since General Sooy Smith was relieved of his command. No matter how reckless this plan, it would please William T. Sherman.

It would also please Ben Grierson because he would capture Forrest. Ben hurried to mount his horse and prepare for the fight. It was going to be a desperate one but one which his soldiers could win.

"Sure 'nuff," whispered one trooper to another near Ben's position in the woods. "There's a whole bunch of them gray bastards movin' up."

Ben held his breath as four Confederates rode to the ford on the far side of the river, alertly hunting for any sign of their enemy. They had to be Forrest's advance scouts. The men spread out and studied the banks of Brice's Crossing for any trace of hoofprints that might warn of a trap. Ben had been adamant that his men remain on this side. Let Forrest cross the river, then attack. That forced the crafty cavalry commander to retreat back across the river where his men would be slowed and vulnerable, even to inexpert fire from Ben's recruits.

The four scouts retreated into the woods on the far side, only to return with the leading elements of a larger cavalry detachment. Ben caught his breath when he saw the bearded man riding to one side.

Forrest!

He prayed that none of his soldiers got buck fever and fired too soon. He knew his officers had impressed on every man the importance of waiting for the command, but nerves could get the better of any of them and ruin the ambush. If

Forrest did not cross the river before the shooting started, he needed to only fade away into the forest to escape again. That left Ben and his brigade to cross the river in pursuit and possibly find themselves in the same trap they now laid for the Confederates.

Ben played through songs in his head to divert himself and to keep from crying out the order prematurely. He was an anxious as any of the rawest recruits cowering in the shrubs, waiting for the enemy to ford the river.

A company came across and then another, with Forrest riding beside the unit's captain. joined them. Although most of the force waited to cross the ford, Ben knew better than to bide his time. Capture Forrest, and the battle would be a victory.

"Fire!" he shouted. "All fire!"

A ragged volley rang out. For a moment it hardly appeared that any Union bullet struck a Confederate target. Then the enemy's horses began to shy and dance about as more hot lead seared past. What Ben's men lacked in marksmanship they made up for in determination. Ben didn't see any man flagging.

Until Forrest snapped out a command.

Ben had expected the Confederate general to attempt an escape back across the river. He did the opposite. He charged.

Forrest only had a pair of companies with him, but they were veterans and used to combat. The same couldn't be said for Ben's men. Many turned and broke ranks when confronted by the guerrilla general's bold attack.

"Charge!" Ben mounted and led a counterattack straight for Forrest, but was driven back by withering fire. To Ben's dismay, Forrest made no effort to retreat. Rather, he urged the remainder of his men to cross the river to this side to reinforce his position.

"Keep firing!" Ben shouted as he was forced to withdraw. He signaled to bring up General Sturgis's men. A successful sortie was the only way to keep his own men from being pushed back and giving position to Forrest.

General Sturgis's men came charging through the gaps left in Ben's ranks, but they were soundly repulsed by Forrest's cavalry.

"Sir, we're running short of ammunition," came the dismaying report.

Ben swallowed hard. He had Forrest pinned between the river and the front of his gun sight. Letting him go now was outrageous!

"Charge!" Ben ordered again. Fewer than a hundred men responded, mostly veterans he recognized from earlier campaigns. But they were pushed back, too, when they ran out of ammunition and had to seek sanctuary among the ranks of Sturgis's infantry. The artillerists had not had sufficient time to establish their positions, and the cannons were useless against Forrest.

"He's got all his men on this side now," Woodward reported. "More are joining him. He started with a thousand but he's rumored to have five times that."

"He sent out smaller units to harass us. Now they're all coming back together here," Ben said. His heart sank as he stared at utter defeat.

"What do we do, General?" asked his adjutant.

"Fall back and resupply," Ben ordered. "We can't give way now. We have to stop him once and for all."

The order passed quickly down the line, but Ben's worst fear was realized. Forrest was not content to sit out a lull in the fighting and let Ben get more ammunition from supply wagons behind the line. He launched an all-out assault that threw every one of his men against the weakest part of the Union line. Sturgis's men folded like a bad poker hand, and Forrest expertly routed what remained of Ben's cavalry. The Union soldiers on foot had no chance to fight, were out of ammunition, and were peering down the barrels of Confederate carbines.

"Fix bayonets! Charge!" ordered Ben. Only a handful of men obeyed. That handful died in a bloody fusillade.

Ben was forced to retreat and let Forrest, with his entire troop, race through the middle of his line to vanish in the woods, beyond any possible capture.

"How many mounted troopers can we muster?" Ben asked, still thinking of pursuit. He did a quick count himself and his heart fell. He had started with three hundred horses that couldn't have traveled three days before keeling over. He had half that now. Worse were the casualties among his men.

"Here he comes again!" went up the warning cry.

Forrest's repeated attacks sent the Union Army running down the road toward Ripley, throwing away their packs and rifles in their panic. To Ben's dismay, Forrest did not withdraw even then. He pressed his advantage with a renewed attack.

"Retreat," Ben said tiredly, knowing they had no choice. Sturgis was losing artillery to the Confederates and was unable to do anything about the losses.

For the rest of the afternoon, Ben retreated, trying to keep the relentless Forrest from turning the rout into a complete debacle.

Although Forrest stopped his attack north of Ripley, the Union retreat continued, leaving behind 2300 casualties with the loss of 14 artillery pieces, 250 supply wagons and 1600 soldiers taken prisoner.

It had taken the Union forces ten days to reach Brice's Crossing from Memphis. To Ben's eternal shame, it took only three days to retreat to the safety of that city.

Recruits

December 21, 1864
Ripley, Mississippi

"They don't appreciate what I can do," grumbled Ben Grierson. He looked up, startled, when he realized Sam Woodward had entered the tent without him noticing. The patter of freezing rain against the canvas tent had masked his adjutant's entrance, and nothing stopped the cold wind from sneaking under the tent walls to chew at his leg. He rubbed it and wished it didn't turn so stiff in cold weather, then realized he was lucky to even have it. A week earlier the entire division had been so bogged down that he worried they would freeze to death.

"No, sir, I don't believe they do."

"Always the comfort, Sam. Thank you," Ben said, shivering a little. He pulled a blanket up around his shoulders. "Ever since they transferred Hatch and that division to Rome, I've been struggling to find something worth my while."

"You foraged up two thousand horses while you were

visiting your family, sir," Woodward said. "That gives Colonel Winslow enough mounts for a real fight."

"A good man, Winslow," Ben said, but he really wished he had his full corps in the field, rather than allowing Sherman to take the better part of his command. The march into Georgia was important, but the fight in Mississippi was not over. Even transferring his command to Nashville had not put him any closer to the real enemy.

Forrest.

The name sneaked into his dreams, taunting him. Let others talk of how adroit Stonewall Jackson was as a cavalry commander. He didn't hold a candle to Nathan Bedford Forrest—and their one meeting had been disastrous for Ben and his command. Somehow, General Sturgis had kept his command and Ben had not been disciplined for the staggering loss when they had expected swift victory. Forrest was both lucky and clever, but he could be defeated.

Sherman found his match in Joe Johnston, but Ben wanted to tangle with Forrest again. With fresh mounts, a month of resupply, and only the weather as an enemy, he had rebuilt his command slowly and almost painfully. His letter to Sherman complaining of both Sooy Smith and Sturgis had been well-enough received, but the crying need for reinforcements in Tennessee and Missouri had shut off any possible flow of new soldiers to his command.

Worse news came when General Howard robbed him of many men to go after Sterling Price. Ben had fewer than two thousand men now, but segments of the war around him went well. Thomas had been victorious against Hood at Nashville, forcing the Confederates to retreat. Their only supply line was the tempting Mobile and Ohio Railroad.

"Three brigades, that's all I have for this campaign," he complained to Woodward, "but it will be enough. Colonel Winslow has fresh mounts, and Karge and Osband are willing fighters."

Ben did not add "unlike Sooy Smith" since his adjutant understood. But Ben wished he still had Edward Hatch in his command. They could cut the South into pieces in nothing flat.

"What of your Pioneer Corps, sir? I'm not sure they would be understood farther up the chain of command."

"Is there a single one among the fifty I recruited not willing to work?"

"Sir, uh, they are civilians. To use them as engineers to build our roads and to repair telegraph wires is, uh, unheard of."

Ben's lips thinned to a line. "Your real complaint is that they are Negroes."

"Sir, I'm only pointing out problems that might arise should any of them be captured by Forrest."

"I remember the massacre at Fort Pillow all too vividly," Ben said. "If anything, that memory serves the Pioneer Corps well, giving them added reason to work doubly hard. I have spoken with them. They know the punishment they are likely to receive if they are captured. They're not deterred because many of them were slaves."

"Escaped slaves are always harshly treated," Woodward said.

"These blacks cannot fight for the freedom of their brothers using force of arms, but they are willing workers. We need roads and telegraph lines as we move through the South."

"It seems strange, sir," said Woodward. "We burn bridges and blow up railroad depots and they come along behind to rebuild."

"To rebuild for freedom, Lieutenant." Ben shivered a little, then stared at the map in front of him. His finger traced out a half-dozen lines on the map, all lightly penciled in. Every path he took led to a single town.

"We'll find him there, Sam. Verona."

"Who, sir? Oh," his adjutant said, realizing the enemy who was never far from Ben's thoughts.

"Let's march for Verona. I want him captured by Christmas." He took a deep breath of the bitingly cold air and said, "That would be a fine present, indeed. Nathan Bedford Forrest all trussed up in ribbons and chains."

Cold Revenge

December 25, 1864
Verona, Mississippi

The cold rain wormed its way under his slicker and soaked his blue woolen uniform, but Ben Grierson hardly noticed. His keen eyes peered through the sheets of rain blowing southward. His brigade had ridden in worse weather from Tupelo, but he felt exhilarated at being so close to Forrest. He felt more than the cold and wet in his bones—he felt the Confederate cavalry commander's nearness. He had carefully studied how Forrest had split his men into small squads, some as small as five or ten guerrillas, then sent them ranging far and wide, to mask the rebel's base.

Tracing the patterns showed how Forrest would gather the smaller units together here at Verona. From raising hell all over Mississippi and Tennessee, Forrest could again make a significant attack northward.

Nashville? Possibly he intended to retake the city. Memphis? That would be a blow to the Union, having a city considered secure attacked and "liberated" for the South. Frankfort or even some other city in Kentucky might be Forrest's new target. Anything that robbed Sherman of troops in Georgia was good.

Anything that supported Hood as he licked his wounds after losing the Battle of Nashville was even better from the Confederate viewpoint.

"I've got him," Ben said.

His brigade commanders were already splitting off from the main body, moving to either side of the rebel camp at Verona. Ben knew that patience could win a battle, but against Forrest, speed and viciousness of the initial attack mattered more. He hummed "John Brown's Body" to himself several times as he tried to pass the time, letting Karge and Oband get into position. When he couldn't stand the anticipation anymore, Ben gave the signal.

His unit let out a whoop and splashed through knee-deep mud in the direction of Nathan Bedford Forrest's camp.

Ben's attack flashed past sentries too miserable and cold to respond quickly. Their minds were on home and hearth, family, and Christmas. Ben concentrated only on getting as many of his men into the middle of Forrest's camp as he could, all with carbines blazing.

Ben had seen units withdraw from the field. He had seen others disintegrate. Forrest's startled soldiers simply evaporated. One minute, they were struggling to find their muskets; the next, there was only mud and rain left.

"Where's Forrest?" Ben called. He had ordered all his scouts to find the Confederate commander. Impatiently riding around the vast camp assured him he had not mistakenly raided some other gray-clad cavalry officer's camp. He saw the long lines of supply wagons—more than two hundred— Forrest had taken from General Sturgis. Railroad cars brimming with supplies Hood needed desperately sat on a siding. And a bit of searching through warehouses on the outskirts of Verona gave up eight thousand British rifles.

"Where's Forrest?" Ben repeated until every soldier in his command had heard his request.

"Sir," reported Woodward, "we've looked and he wasn't in town. We're questioning some of the captured soldiers, but we're not getting anything from them. It's possible they don't know."

"Damnation," Ben said, then bit his lower lip. Alice wouldn't appreciate him using such language.

"The raid was successful, General," Woodward said earnestly. "Look at how much we've recaptured, how much we're denying Hood. Without these supplies, he won't be able to fight effectively until spring."

"The war will be over by then," Ben said, wiping sleet from his face. He smiled and said, heart lighter now, "You're right, Sam. I may not have caught Forrest, but we've single-handedly ended the war up and down the Mississippi. There's no way the Confederates can mount a real attack without these supplies."

Ben looked around, his eyes falling on a warehouse brimming with artillery shells and other ammunition.

"Set fire to that," he said, pointing. "This is Christmas Day, and I think we'd all appreciate some decent fireworks."

"Yes, *sir*!"

The explosions continued well into the evening as Ben continued his expedition through the South again, destroying 100 miles of railroad track, bridges, 95 railroad cars, and warehouses filled with arms and eventually captured more than 600 prisoners with a loss of only 27 killed and 93 wounded. John B. Hood's fighting capability was at an end because of Ben Grierson's 16-day, 450-mile raid.

But Forrest was nowhere to be seen.

Grant, Lincoln, and Two Stars

February 8, 1865
Washington, D.C.

Ben Grierson dropped his salute and thrust out his hand, shaking warmly. "General Grant, so good to see you again," he said.

"And you, Benjamin, and you. Glad you could make it from Louisville so quick."

"I'm always at your command, sir," Ben said, looking around the train depot and into the city beyond. The bustle of the nation's capital was even greater than he remembered from earlier visits. He only wished his wife and boys could be here, also, but he had left them in Frankfort, much to Alice's chagrin. With Ulysses Grant's invitation—order— Ben could forget about Alice's growing distaste for military life and being apart so much. At least, he could forget her concerns for a few minutes as he reveled in the attention given him by the general commanding all the Union's military forces.

"I wish that were true. I could use a cavalry officer like

you to chase down those damned rebs," Grant said. "Since Lee lost Jackson, his cavalry has been piss-poor."

"You're doing a good job of keeping them dancing about, General," Ben said.

"You've done your part, General," Grant said. "Hood has been replaced by Joe Johnston. That doesn't make our friend Sherman any happier, but Johnston's lack of supplies surely does. Thanks to your raids in Mississippi."

"I never stopped Nathan Bedford Forrest," Ben said.

"Benjamin, my good friend, only the end of the war will stop that one. I appreciate your service." Ulysses Grant reached into a side pocket and pulled out a small wooden box. He hesitated, then handed it to Ben. "You'll want these before we meet the President."

Ben opened the box. His eyes went a little wider.

"Thank you, sir. I didn't realize I was up for promotion."

"Sherman and I have pressed constantly," Grant said. Ben heard a little more in what the officer said. He had to inquire.

"Who's been opposing my promotion?"

"There are only so many posts available for a major general," Grant said. He spat, reached into his other pocket, and took out a small silver flask. He knew better than to offer Ben a swing from it. After he rinsed his mouth with the whiskey, he said, "Tread carefully around Sheridan. I've locked horns with him more than once, and he has a brigade of men who think he walks on water."

"General Custer?" Ben asked.

"Pin those stars on your shoulders, Ben. Here, let me do it. Your hands're shaking something fierce." Grant stepped closer, took the new stars, and expertly attached them to Ben's shoulder epaulets. "Don't do this often enough to men who deserve it." Grant stepped back, saluted Ben and said, "Major General Grierson, the President awaits."

They rode in Grant's carriage through the muddy streets until they reached the White House. Ben's sharp eyes picked out the sentries walking their rounds and the reinforcements out of sight unless someone looked for them.

"Is this usual?" Ben asked.

"There have been rumors," Grant said. "If the South can't win on the battlefield, they may try other routes." Grant spat out the carriage window. "We'll bring them down soon enough."

"Am I returning to chase Forrest?" Ben asked.

"Probably not. Your new post is commander of cavalry, Military Division of West Mississippi. General Canby had asked for Avrell to command his cavalry, but I convinced him you were the better man. He found it mighty hard to argue after a few minutes of persuading."

Ben tensed. Grant had an abrasive way about him.

"Don't worry. Canby's a good officer. I've told him to take Mobile, then drive through Alabama. You'll have twelve thousand cavalry to whip into shape for that little jaunt."

The carriage clattered to a halt at a side door of the White House.

"Go on, Benjamin. President Lincoln wants to talk to you. Me, he wants to get off my behind and stop Lee."

Ben jumped down from the carriage, anticipation mounting. It had been years since he had spoken with Abraham Lincoln back in Illinois.

"Congratulations, Benjamin," Grant said.

Ben saluted, and Grant grunted and snapped an order to his driver. The carriage rattled off. Taking a deep breath, Ben went to the side door, entered, and waited for a servant to take him to the President.

After more than an hour's audience with President Lincoln, Ben went on to meet Secretary of War Stanton and several of his top advisors. All in all, Ben had a splendid time and spent the remainder of the day writing Alice describing it and the future he saw for them after the war.

Nothing

May 26, 1865
New Orleans, Louisiana

"Are you going to bring your family down, sir?" asked Samuel Woodward. "Since there's no real fighting any longer, it would be safe for them to travel, even for a pregnant woman."

Ben nodded distantly, lost in thought, but it wasn't about his family or his wife's condition. Alice wouldn't give birth for another three months, but travel was out of the question, even on a riverboat. Better that she stay where her family could help her and the boys. Ben wished he could see Charlie, though. Nine years old was a good age, but then Robert was four, and that wasn't a bad age, either.

Only his age was bad. He was too old to start a new career and not likely to go any farther in the military. If anything, he was likely to be mustered out now that the war was winding down. General Canby hadn't needed any cavalry in his assault on Mobile. That city had surrendered quickly once it was obvious more than fifty thousand men were going to be hammering at its gates. The days of Grant's long, tedious siege of Vicksburg were long past.

New and less savory days were upon them all, now that Lincoln was felled by a coward's bullet.

"Sir?"

"Oh, sorry, Sam. I was thinking of other things. Alice, you say? No, she'll stay in Illinois until the birth. I'll try for a command in Kentucky or Tennessee, if the one Grant mentioned in Texas is not forthcoming. It would be too much to ask for one in Illinois."

"You're sure to get a command soon, sir. What other cavalry officer has your impressive record?"

"Ah, I know now why I've kept you around for so many years, Sam. You're good for my spirit, not to mention being the finest adjutant any commander could want." Ben chewed on his lip, then stroked his long, full black beard as he thought. "If I don't get a new command, I want you to consider transferring to some other unit. The Army needs men like you, and I would be a millstone around your neck."

"Sir, men like you *are* the Army!"

"General Grant has recommended me for command in Texas. The fighting is almost done there, so it would be garrison duty. Still, there is something to be said for such duty. I can finally assemble a decent regimental band!"

"Not likely, sir, not with the Comanche and other Indians kicking up a fuss the way they are. No settler is safe in Texas."

"Quell the rebels, fight the redskins," Ben said. "That would be a challenge, one bigger than trying to track and engage Nathan Bedford Forrest. He was only a rebel. The Comanche and other wild tribes are born in the saddle. I've heard them described as being the closest creatures to centaurs we are likely to see on this planet."

"You're the man to outride and outfight them, General,"

said Woodward. "With the war over, the push westward is going to begin again. Anyone homesteading on the other side of the Mississippi River's not going to take kindly to Indian raids."

"The ultimate cavalry unit, but will they let a volunteer officer serve?" Ben asked, more to himself. It sounded good, and Grant had said he would do what he could. The loss of Lincoln had unsettled the government, but the military chain of command remained much as it was at Appomattox. How Ben wished he could have been there six weeks earlier to witness Lee's surrender and the death of formal Southern rebellion. Pockets of resistance spurred by Lincoln's murder remained throughout the South and would for months to come, but eventually even the most recalcitrant rebel would see the futility of continuing the fight.

A knock on the door of his office made Ben look up. He brightened.

"This might be the courier I've been expecting."

Lieutenant Woodward let the private in and took the sealed envelope from him and passed it over to Ben. For a moment Ben stared at it as if it might develop fangs and bite him. Then he ran his fingers around the edge and let out a hiss like a steam locomotive.

"It's from Sherry-dan," he said contemptuously. "I was afraid of this. After all he said, Grant was forced to let Sheridan choose." He used a letter opener to slit the sides of the envelope and withdrew the orders inside. He looked up at his friend forlornly.

"He gave the Texas command to Custer," Woodward guessed.

"His good friend George Armstrong Custer," Ben confirmed. "Damn him! Damn them both!"

Ben sat back, shocked at his own outburst, but he had no reason to hold in his anger.

"Where are you assigned, General?" asked Woodward.

"Either Kentucky or Tennessee would put you closer to your family."

"Nowhere," Ben said bitterly. He threw the orders on the desk and then drove his letter opener into the sheet. "I have no orders. Sherry-dan has consigned me to limbo."

Birth of Another Grierson

August 27, 1865
Jacksonville, Illinois

Ben Grierson jumped at every creak of the house and every rattle of chains and squeak of leather outside.

"Boys, be quiet," he said to the boisterous Charlie and Robert. "You'll have a new sibling soon, but your mother needs quiet now."

"Are we gonna have another brother?" asked Charlie. "We never knew Kirkie."

"No, you never did," Ben said, trying to force the memories of John Kirk Grierson from his mind. The baby boy's death had been a shock and one he and Alice seldom mentioned. Both of them preferred to look ahead rather than back at the sadness of their firstborn's unfortunate death, virtually at birth.

"How long you gonna be around, Pa?" asked Robert, looking up at him. "And when are you gonna put on some weight? You're skinny as a rail!"

Ben had to laugh at this. His boys lacked any of the skills of a diplomat. He was down to 145 pounds but felt fit enough. Being home and away from the political intrigues rampaging throughout the South because of Andrew Johnson's vacillation and refusal to confront the Republicans' punitive Reconstruction policies was enough, but being away from Phillip Sheridan's orders counted for more. Sheridan had assigned him to Major General Woods's command in the Department of Alabama at some unspecified post. Ben could only assume it was as a minor functionary and that he would soon lose his stars. With luck and help from his friends, he might get a regular Army commission, but that required considerable political string-pulling.

He intended to see Sherman at his St. Louis headquarters on his way to his post in Alabama after all was settled with Alice and his new child.

"I'll stay as long as I can," he told Robert. "My orders aren't specific when I'm to report. General Canby told me to come ahead and not to worry."

"You liked him, didn't you?" asked Charlie. "I can tell. But you don't like General Sherry-dan." His son did a passable imitation of him vilifying Sheridan.

"General Canby is a fine officer. So are Grant and Sherman," he said, ignoring Sheridan—or wishing he could. Ben turned at a new sound from the direction of the bedroom. He caught his breath.

"Is it?" he called, seeing the midwife coming out, wiping her hands. She was smiling.

"General, you have a fine-looking daughter."

"A daughter," he said in wonder. In their usual fashion, they had discussed the matter of a name. "Alice and I decided to call her Edith Clare—Edie."

After three boys, he and Alice finally had a healthy nine-pound daughter.

No Prospects

January 15, 1866
Jacksonville, Illinois

"This is nothing to be despondent over, Ben," Alice Grierson said as she looked over the letter. She held Edie in her other arm. "You've served your country well. It's now time to move on to other things. You do have a growing family." The way she said that made Ben look up, alert to her tone. There was a hint of desperation in it—or was it bitterness?

"I haven't many prospects, dear," he told her. He sat in his favorite chair but it felt different now. His frame had changed, perhaps. He was certainly many pounds lighter than when he had used this chair every night before the war. "John and I were going to raise cotton with Sam, perhaps in Mississippi or Alabama, but Sam has chosen to remain in the Army. It's easier for a lieutenant than a major general to find a post."

"What do you know of growing cotton, anyway?" scoffed Alice. She began nursing Edie, modestly placing a small linen nursing cloth over the baby's head.

"What do I know of running a store or anything else? I

cannot believe it, but I was well-suited to be a cavalry officer."

"You still don't like horses," she said.

"No, can't say that I do, but I understand them. And I understand the men who fought from horseback." He settled down a bit more in his chair, aware of the lumps and spots that poked into his gaunt frame. If only he had met Nathan Bedford Forrest a second time, without General Sturgis being in command. Ben was sure he would have run the Southern guerrilla leader into the swamps and perdition. As it was, Forrest had surrendered to Canby without a decisive cavalry battle.

"You must be persistent and not mope about the house, Benjamin," Alice said sternly. "You have a wife and three children to support." She hesitated, then said firmly, "I will *not* move back in with my family or any of yours."

"I understand, dear," he said, but what eluded him was what he might do to earn a decent living. All that he had tried, other than soldiering, had ended in disastrous bankruptcy.

Ben went to his writing desk and began scribbling out a letter, putting all his heart and hopes into it. He felt as if this was his last, best chance.

Testimony

March 2, 1866
Washington, D.C.

Ben Grierson sat behind the wide oak table, staring across it at the senators and congressmen of the Joint Committee on Reconstruction. His old friend, Richard Yates, now an Illinois senator, sat on one end of the panel. He winked at Ben, then motioned for him to go ahead with his testimony, although the chairman still spoke with two aides and had not paid Ben any attention.

Clearing his throat got their attention.

"Gentlemen, your summons to testify comes on the heels of five years in the service of the U.S. Army and after numerous letters being exchanged with my brother and sister."

"Your brother John's a captain in the quartermaster corps, is he not?" asked one of the panel.

"That's correct, sir, in Memphis."

"What is his appraisal of the progress of Reconstruction?"

"I share his opinions on this, sir. The Southern slave owners do not show any remorse for their actions. Indeed, they demonstrate nothing but contempt for Northern ideals and governance. Should any of them be allowed to gain power, I fear a second war will be the result."

"Harsh words, General Grierson," said another on the panel.

"They put on airs and long for the days when their plantations were populated with slaves," Ben went on. "My brother calls them secesh—secessionists. They have not learned any lesson from the war, nor have they changed their philosophy."

"What of the freemen?"

"Sir, at one time I thought blacks to be shiftless and unworthy of Union blood spilt in their behalf. After seeing units fighting, after seeing how nobly they fought at Fort Pillow, I have changed my opinion of their military abilities."

"You used some Negroes as part of your division, didn't you?"

"Not as combatants but as sappers. The Pioneer Corps, as I called them, rebuilt roads and bridges, strung telegraph wire, and put back together the railroads I was entrusted to destroy. The fifty men working for me never flagged in their duties and showed great bravery during combat. There is not a one of those men I would not trust with any chore, no matter how difficult."

"What of other freemen in the South? Have you seen them after they were emancipated?"

"Sir, I have seen their cheerfulness as they work. My sister Louisa has nothing but praise for their determination to make do with very little. Most have made the transition from slave to freeman wonderfully, but again I repeat, they must be protected from their former owners if they are to succeed in their ventures. None of the leaders of the Confederacy should be allowed any position of power until they have proven themselves worthy of trust. Give them back power too quickly and they will work strenuously to reintroduce slavery to the South. Their only regret is that they did not have the military and political power to carry out their designs."

"This is at odds with the leniency President Johnson advocates," said another of the panel.

"I do not formulate policy, Senator. You asked for my observations. Where power has returned to those who ruled the South with an iron hand before the war, society is tending toward slavery again. The freedmen are chary about moving far from the only homes they have known. This will work against them should Southern power be regained by Southern hands, especially those who served in the Confederate Army."

"So how can Negroes prove themselves?"

"That is not for me to say, sir. Reconstruction rests in your capable hands. I have come to believe the black man is capable of any chore or position of authority and is equal in all ways to a white."

"Would you serve in the Army with a Negro?" asked another.

"Yes, sir, I would," Ben said without hesitation.

The testimony went on for some hours until Ben was excused. As he left the chamber, he saw his old friend, William Sherman. The fiery red-haired general greeted him with a slap on the back.

"I heartily approve of what you had to say, Benjamin," Sherman said.

"It's good to see you again, General." Ben smiled almost shyly. "Since I've been mustered out, I suppose you're no longer my superior and I can call you William."

"Would you remain in the Army, given the chance?" asked Sherman, his eyes fixed intently on Ben to judge his sincerity.

"I've spoken of this with Alice. We both agree that a career in the military is closer to my heart than any other profession."

"Simpson and I have worked with the congressional delegation from Illinois," Sherman said. "Your Senator Yates is quite the politician."

"A good friend, too, though he seems to have taken to imbibing a bit more since he left Springfield and came to Washington."

"A bit?" Sherman laughed without humor. "The man and the bottle are constant companions, but he is a true friend. He shepherded a petition through Congress and got President Johnson to sign it. Should you accept, you will be made brevet major general of volunteers—and colonel in the regular army. This means you'll be eligible for $1500 back pay as a general before beginning your regular pay as colonel."

Ben caught his breath. A regular salary would go a long way toward paying off debts from his ill-fated business venture before the war. Sam Woodward had mustered out finally and had gone into the cattle business in Mississippi, but Ben had been cool toward a partnership with his old adjutant. Nothing in the civilian world held the attraction of the cavalry. Moreover, he could build Alice the home she yearned for so. She deserved it after almost five years of separation.

"That would be good, General," Ben said. "I feel there is a secret organization in the South that must be stopped before a second rebellion springs up. The Freedman's Bureau should be defended fully by the army until this threat is eliminated."

Sherman grumbled a bit under his breath and stared straight at Ben.

"You see clearer than most of the men in that room. Your old foe Forrest is behind a great deal of the mischief."

"I can stop him, given the chance."

"No, Benjamin, this time he won't ride at the front of an army column. He will sneak about in the dark like some vile roach. But that doesn't mean your talents won't be needed elsewhere."

"What do you have in mind, sir?"

Ben Grierson listened to all that William Sherman had to say and liked it very much. It was good being back in the army, albeit reduced in rank to colonel.

The Tenth Cavalry

November 16, 1866
Fort Leavenworth, Kansas

Ben Grierson looked across the parade ground to the flagpole with Old Glory flapping fitfully in the chilly autumn wind. Winter wasn't far off, and there had been snow flurries most of the day. He wished the carriage bringing his family would arrive soon. He had been on the post for almost three months, after General Grant had given him command of the Tenth Cavalry, and missed them greatly.

The sound of a sergeant barking out commands as he drilled his squad echoed across the grounds. Ben turned to watch as the sergeant called an abrupt halt because a mounted officer purposefully rode in front of the squad, then stopped. Such irritation had been a constant way of life because the Tenth was composed of black soldiers with white officers. This officer was assigned to Major General Hoffman's staff. The post commander had shown nothing but disdain and even utter contempt for the black soldiers.

Ben walked to where his sergeant put the men through close-order drill. They looked sloppy, but not a one had been on the post before the beginning of the week. Recruitment was slow for an all-black unit, and the officers responsible for getting men signed up often fell down on the job. Ben had berated Captain Davis in Memphis repeatedly but the man still sent recruits ill-suited for military life. Ben envisioned the Tenth Cavalry as being an elite unit, with only the finest men serving in it. If a man had been a slave and could not read, he would be taught. But Ben wanted only the most dedicated freedmen.

"Captain," Ben called to the mounted white officer. "Have you seen my adjutant?"

"Woodward?" The captain sneered. No one in the Tenth was well liked, making Ben feel a tad guilty for enticing Sam Woodward back into the Army. Sam's brother had died of cholera, leaving him with eight hundred acres of cotton to harvest. Weevils had taken much of the crop. While Ben hoped his own inducements had lured Sam into the Tenth, he knew the personal loss and outright failure of the farming venture had much to do with his return.

"That's Lieutenant Woodward," Ben said coldly. He had tried to gently nudge the captain into moving so the sergeant could continue his marching drills. Seeing that was not going to work, he became more direct. "Move so that my sergeant can continue his training."

"Training? That what you call it? We call 'em Grierson's brunettes, you know. You can't train monkeys to be soldiers."

"You are proof of that, sir," Ben said, his anger hardly in check.

"You calling me a nigger?" The captain rode over, hand resting on his saber.

"I am calling you a small-minded, bigoted fool."

"I'll see that General Hoffman hears of this!"

"Be sure to use small words so he can understand you, Captain," Ben said. He jumped out of the way as the captain cruelly put his spurs to his horse, causing the animal to bolt. If he hadn't moved, Ben would have been trampled.

"Sir, you surely are treadin' on dangerous ground with that one," the sergeant said. "Quicksan', that's where you're walkin', Colonel."

Ben spun and shoved his face within inches of the sergeant's.

"These men are woefully trained. You will march them to and fro until they are in step, can perform any close-order drill sequence required of them, and are proficient with a carbine. Do I make myself understood, Sergeant?"

"Yes, suh."

Ben waited for the sergeant to whirl around and get the men double-timing across the grounds before he let out the air he had been holding in his lungs. He was still stinging from the recruit that had deserted within days of arriving at Fort Leavenworth. If that hadn't been bad enough, another from the Tenth had been arrested in Leavenworth City by the civil authorities and jailed. Sam had spent the better part of an hour arguing with the marshal before freeing the private from the town hoosegow.

The Tenth's soldiers were served inferior food and had inferior quarters, and Ben knew his sergeant would never get this squad onto the firing range for practice because they didn't have ammunition to spare. How he was supposed to field an army under such conditions was a constant challenge. He almost wished—just for an instant—that Sheridan had not wrangled command of the Seventh for his fair-haired boy general, George Custer, and that Sherman had prevailed in putting Ben in charge. But the politics was obvious. Grant and Sherman against Sheridan, against Sherry-dan the vindictive.

His mentors were not politicians, cozying up to the men in Congress. Both Sherman and Grierson were blunt military men, more likely to speak their mind than to use honeyed words.

"Colonel Grierson!" came the loud cry. He glanced over his shoulder to see General Hoffman striding out from his office. If the man's attitude could affect the weather, there would be a snowstorm at any instant. Ben had never seen the post commander look colder or less cordial.

"Grierson, you will not insult my staff behind my back."

"Then I'll do it in front of your face, General," Ben said. "What happened to my requisition for decent rations for my men?"

"Your men? Your *men*? You call that sorry bunch of darkies men?"

Ben stepped forward until his face was inches away from the general's. Hoffman had pushed him too far this time.

"They are soldiers in the Army of the United States of America and will be spoken of with the same respect as any other soldier. Sir."

"You do not order me! I'm bringing you up on charges, Colonel. I'll see you busted down to the ranks. You'll be bedding down with those animals as a private by the time I finish! Such insubordination! I—"

"I trust General Sherman will be on the court-martial board. And General Grant. And General Canby. My good friend Senator Yates will want a full report for his committee, also. How many reporters ought to be present? The ones from the *St. Louis Globe*?"

Hoffman turned red in the face and he began sputtering. He knew how well liked Ben had been by the reporters. They had made him into a national figure after his bold, successful raids through the heart of Dixie at a time the Union sorely needed heroes.

"Representatives of the Bureau of Refugees, Freedmen and Abandoned Lands might find such a trial enlightening, also."

"What's the Freedmen's Bureau got to do with this?" General Hoffman was sweating now. His face was turning redder by the instant. Ben hoped a blood vessel would pop and relieve Fort Leavenworth of such a bigoted commander.

"They maintain a Complaint Register. Many of my soldiers are freed slaves and anyone denying them their freedoms is entered into that Register."

"You will address me as sir or General Hoffman."

"Yes, sir." Ben was willing to give in to this extent, but refused to allow the man to bad-mouth soldiers just because they were black. Hoffman hadn't seen the evidence at Fort Pillow where so many had died fighting.

"We need not pursue this matter, unless you continue to be insolent, Colonel."

"No, sir, we don't need to continue this discussion." He looked past the general and saw the carriage pulling through the gates. "What we need to discuss are quarters for my family."

"There are none available," Hoffman said.

"Then I must exercise my right to move the family of an officer junior to me so my wife and three children can be adequately quartered. Should I chose which officer to evict, sir?"

"I . . . do as you please, Colonel." General Hoffman stormed off, cursing under his breath.

Ben felt no satisfaction in the exchange, but he did in greeting Alice, his two boys, and young daughter. With them on the post, he felt less alone.

In Concert

January 30, 1867
Fort Leavenworth, Kansas

"Colonel, it doesn't look good. We can't recruit enough men, and as to officers . . ." Sam Woodward's voice trailed off.

"Eighty men," Ben Grierson mused. "I had hoped for five times that many by now. And only seven officers. I understand why it is hard to find career officers. This is certainly looked upon as a dead-end assignment."

"General Hoffman and the other officers don't help. There's not a man in the Tenth on speaking terms with anyone else on this post. Any of our officers that go into the officers' mess are isolated. I've seen—experienced personally—Hoffman's staff getting up and moving away when any of us sit down to eat."

"I want you to make the rounds, Sam. Go recruit personally. Light the fire under our recruiting officers in Memphis and St. Louis. This isn't a good time to travel, I know, but the Tenth Cavalry will be disbanded unless we get more men."

"Sir, I've heard Colonel Hatch would be willing to sign on."

Ben shook his head. His old friend was up for a promotion, if it could be called that.

"I got a letter from him a few days ago. Edward's going to be given command of the Ninth Cavalry. He and I will be equally looked upon as pariahs." Ben laughed without humor. "The only bright spot is that Alice is satisfied with our quarters, which are quite sizable." He didn't elaborate. Woodward knew they were quartered away from the rest of the officers, as if the color of Ben's command might rub off on the other families.

"I'll see what I can do, sir. But you need to address morale among the men."

"I've been thinking about that," Ben said. "I passed out musical instruments a few days ago. I'm off to see if I can't squeeze a tune or two out of the men."

"When do you want me to leave, Colonel?" asked Woodward.

This time Ben's laugh was genuine.

"Oh, can't wait to get away from all the sour notes they're likely to play? Go right away, Sam. Take a few days' vacation in St. Louis before you get down to serious recruitment. You deserve the leave."

"Yes, sir. And good luck." This time Woodward was the one smiling ear to ear. "You'll need it. I've heard the men playing their harmonicas and trying to sing."

Ben gathered a pile of sheet music from his desk. He doubted any of the men in the Tenth could read, much less read music, but he wanted to find a simple tune for them to practice. He leafed through the stacks as he wandered outside. He had ordered his company sergeant to assemble the men, but was distracted by the sounds of music drifting on the cold winter air.

He walked around the building to the rear of his office

and saw close to the full detachment working to play a tune. And it wasn't too bad, considering he had thought them all to be ignorant of horns, drums, and other implements of musical torture.

"Very good," he said, clapping in appreciation. "I didn't know I had a company of musicians."

"Yer jist sayin' that, suh," said the sergeant.

"Try this little ditty," Ben said, humming "Lorena" and keeping time with his hand so all could see.

"We know that 'n," the sergeant said.

And they did. They were a little ragged and the sour notes grated, but Ben ignored that and actually began to enjoy the concert. From the corner of his eye, he saw other troopers gathering, white soldiers come to listen. The musical repertoire was limited, but no one seemed to notice or care, any more than they did that the men playing with such gusto were black.

Transfer

July 30, 1867
Fort Riley, Kansas

"Well?" asked Alice Grierson. "Have you heard from Lieutenant Woodward yet?" She paced back and forth in front of Ben's desk. "Anything?"

"Not yet, dear," Ben said. "I'm sure Sam will let us know soon."

"I can't believe it. Such a handsome man staying unmarried for so long. I'm going to move Lieutenant Carmichael from his house to give to Sam and his wife," she said, going over all the machinations in her mind. Alice had become adroit at dealing with the junior officers since arriving at Fort Riley.

For his part, Ben was willing to leave such chores to her, in spite of her being pregnant with their fifth child. He had organized five companies of soldiers over the summer, mostly thanks to Woodward's good work in St. Louis. The quality of recruit had gone up and retention was higher than among units composed of only white soldiers. Even better, Ben noted less drunkenness among his troopers. The only complaint he had was the up-and-down quality of the Tenth's band. As he sent companies out on patrol, he had to break apart trained men to go along with recruits. That sapped his musicians, but this was minor. Finally, his men were safe-guarding Indian Territory and sporadically skirmishing with the Kiowa, Comanche and, increasingly, the Cheyenne.

But he was as anxious as Alice to see the woman Sam was marrying. He wanted some good news after hurrying back to Jacksonville to be at his father's bedside when he died in May.

"Sir, got a dispatch for you," the regimental orderly said, sticking his head into the office. He waved the sheet about.

"From Lieutenant Woodward?" asked Alice, hurrying to take it from the private.

"Can't say, ma'am," the private said, although Ben knew he not only could read but probably had already spread the news throughout the regiment.

"No, how dare he!" Alice stamped her foot, then let the letter flutter to Ben's desk. He quickly scanned it.

"Me and mine will consist of myself and trunk and noth-ing more," Woodward had written.

Ben looked up and shrugged. "Sam and marriage don't look to be good partners."

"Men," Alice said, as if the broken engagement was Ben's fault. She stormed from his office, letting Ben return to train-ing reports from Captain Alvord, newly in command of Company M. He needed another company in the field imme-diately to protect the Kansas-Pacific Railroad from hostile Indians since he had already dispatched three others to Fort Gibson. It would be good having Woodward back, married or single.

First Death

"The railroad's in that direction," Sergeant Christy said, pointing. His dark face shone with sweat from the hard ride and hot Kansas sun. "Don't see any Cheyenne but that don't mean they's not lurkin' about, suh."

Captain George Ames mopped at his own face, then tucked the dirty rag away in the front of his soaking uniform.

"Don't much care about the railroad, Sergeant," he said. "Where's the river?"

"Saline River's over yonder," the sergeant said. "We goin' to take a break, suh?"

Captain Ames saw that Company F was dragging in the sultry heat, its horses nigh on broken down and the soldiers in little better condition from exertion.

"I'd go, but the colonel's a stickler for staying on patrol." Captain Ames looked up to see a tiny puff of dust coming in their direction. Fort Riley was better than twenty miles off, but Colonel Grierson showed up unexpectedly to be certain none of his officers slacked off.

Ames had served under worse commanders and wasn't up to open rebellion like Nordstrom and Vande Wiele, but then they clashed more with Grierson over their treatment of their soldiers than anything else.

"Sir," Ames called, saluting as the colonel rode up. "What brings you out here?"

"I decided to get away from the fort for a spell," Ben Grierson said. The politics of being in charge of so much intrigue and backbiting got to him, and he missed the dust of the trail and the chance to look out at the untrammeled prairie. His sister Louisa had romantic visions of what the frontier was like, and nothing he wrote of the hardships did anything to dispel those notions.

But this was where he belonged, not back in the fort behind a desk listening to interminable disputes between his officers over petty matters.

"Long way to get out of the fort, Colonel," Ames said.

"What sign have you found of the Cheyenne?" Ben asked. "Ever since the Medicine Lodge Council back in July, it's been peaceable enough, but I feel the tension."

"Suh, it's 'bout like a pot gettin' ready to boil," Sergeant Christy said. "Ever' single Indian we find's sweeter 'n sugar, but I always ride off thinkin' I'm gonna get an arrow in the back."

Ben nodded. He trusted his noncoms more than the officers when it came to reporting the mood of the Cheyenne. He had been to numerous meetings with their chiefs and knew how polite they could be. After enough pipe smoking, they would agree to anything—if he supplied the tobacco.

He had to smile a little. Alice realized what it meant to an Indian if he refused to smoke a pipe. That was tantamount to a declaration of eternal enmity and would set the entire prairie ablaze in war. But she still complained about the stench clinging to his uniform from the tobacco and did what she could to air out his jacket after every meeting.

Then Ben sobered. The Medicine Lodge back in July had

been amicable and the Cheyenne had sworn peace forever and ever. But from the reports the train crews telegraphed back—when the telegraph lines had not been cut—he knew the Cheyenne itched for a fight.

"All clear along the tracks?" Ben asked.

"Yes, sir," said Captain Ames. "I recommend we ride to the river to water the mounts and cool off. Nothing's stirring at this time of day. Too hot."

Ben swatted at a horsefly.

"Almost nothing's stirring," he corrected. He caught another and held it in his closed fist, then let it go. Buzzing crazily, the fly vanished into the bright sunlight. "Lead the way, Sergeant."

Company F rode slowly in the hottest part of the day, but Ben felt something more than heat prickling up and down his back. He couldn't get Sergeant Christy's words out of his mind—every time Christy turned his back to a Cheyenne, he wondered if he would catch an arrow.

"Suh, we got comp'ny," Christy reported, riding back toward them. "Couple dozen Cheyenne. They's all decked out in war paint. That's no huntin' party."

The words were hardly out of his mouth when loud whoops sounded and a dozen Cheyenne appeared over a low hill on their left flank. Arrows whizzed through the air, followed by a dozen rifle shots.

Captain Ames shouted orders, swung half his troop about, and returned fire. The carbines barked over and over, filling the hot, still air with dense smoke until vision was almost impossible. Ben drew his pistol but held off firing to see what effect Ames's counterattack had.

Shrieking, the Cheyenne retreated over the hill and vanished from sight.

"Company F, after them!" Captain Ames led the way, Ben hanging back to one side of the double column. He felt uneasy chasing the handful of braves without a better knowledge of what lay on the other side of the hill.

Barely had Ames and the squad with him crested the low hill than it sounded as if they had returned to the battle of Vicksburg. Ben was deafened by the hundreds of rifle reports; he shouted to Ames to retreat, but the captain tumbled from horseback, clutching his hip.

Ben never hesitated. He galloped forward and reached the point where he looked down into a hollow. His heart caught in his throat when he saw half a hundred braves. The Cheyenne had lured Ames into following, foolishly thinking he would get a quick, easy victory. He had fallen into their simple trap like a raw recruit.

"Sergeant, never pursue an Indian until you know where he's going and what's waiting for you," he called to William Christy.

"Unnerstand, suh," Christy said, hardly pausing as he positioned his men along the top of the ridge in a double line so the front could fire while the rear reloaded. They could switch off, letting the front reload, giving steady fire into the Cheyenne.

Ben fired rapidly, taking one brave from horseback. The Cheyenne crashed into the ground and dropped the feathered stick he carried. Ben swallowed hard. This was definitely a war party. The brave had intended to count coup, showing his courage against an enemy.

"We're being ringed in, Sergeant," Ben said. "Deploy a squad to cover our rear."

"We got 'nuff ammo fo' a while, suh," Christy reported, "but if they keep up this heah attack . . ."

"They're falling back," Ben said. He waited to see if the Cheyenne were leaving or if they had merely regrouped. The answer came like lightning. It took the better part of twenty minutes to fight off the Indians' renewed attack.

"Suh, they don't give up, do they?" Sergeant Christy bled from two scalp wounds, one threatening to blind him in the left eye.

"Neither do the soldiers of the Tenth Cavalry," Ben declared. "The Cheyenne will *not* prevail!"

"Heah they come 'gain," Christy said. The sergeant fired his carbine until it went empty, then reached to pick up another that had been dropped by the private next to him. That soldier sat on the ground, clutching his belly where an arrow had pierced his gut.

"Sergeant!" shouted Ben, but his warning came too late. Or maybe no warning would have been adequate. The Cheyenne charged straight up the hill as if they had singled out William Christy.

The black sergeant swung the rifle around but it misfired. Dirt in the action forced him to struggle to clear it. Then he died under swarming Cheyenne and flashing, slashing knives.

Ben ordered a retreat, as much as they could, forming a tighter circle atop the hill. Again they drove back the Cheyenne. For six hours Company F fought, until after sundown. Only then did the Cheyenne warriors break off their attack and slip silently into the night.

Captain Ames thrashed about on the ground, feverish from his wound. Ben ordered a travois made to take the officer back to Fort Riley, but Sergeant Christy he slung over his own horse to return to the fort for a proper burial.

The Tenth Cavalry had sustained its first combat death. Ben Grierson knew it would not be the last.

Court-martial

"It's a waste of time," Ben Grierson grumbled to his friend, Edward Hatch. "The Cheyenne have violated every part of the Medicine Lodge Council and are scalping any settler they find. Why should I be here?"

Colonel Hatch stared across the parade grounds at the officers' mess where the court-martial was to be convened. He saw the interest that had been taken made it impossible to lightly dismiss the matter. Reporters from half the country had swooped down like vultures to cover the trial of such a notable military figure.

"You're right, as usual, Ben," Hatch said, "but I suspect something else is eating at you. How is Alice?"

"She'll deliver our child any day now," Ben said. He smiled ruefully. "Am I so transparent that you see my real thoughts? Perhaps that's why the Cheyenne run me ragged. I need new tactics. They know what I'm going to do before I do it."

"Our hands are tied by Sheridan," Hatch said with some heat. "He gives the orders. We have to follow them."

"I wish Sherman was in charge of the Indian problem," Ben said. "He never worried about what people thought as much as he did about getting the job done. And he has some affection for the redskins."

"Affection or admiration? The general's a clever man and appreciates that in others."

Ben nodded in agreement, finding it hard to keep up his side of the conversation. His mind buzzed with too many other things, important things.

"There's Sherry-dan now," Hatch said, giving the name the same mocking inflection Ben used. "Looks fit to be tied."

"Why not? His boy general is on trial and *I* must sit in judgment."

"Desertion is serious enough that even Sheridan can't ignore it."

"Desertion is only part of it," Ben said tiredly. The ride from Fort Riley had worn him down, although it hadn't been that far. Every mile he rode toward this court-martial was a mile away from Alice and his command. The Tenth Cavalry had become a force to be reckoned with on the prairie while Custer's Seventh was, at best, lackluster.

Ben hoped that it was true that a leader's character reflected all the way down to the lowest ranks. That meant removing Custer and replacing him with a less flamboyant, not-so-impulsive commander would improve their field record.

"An open mind," Ben said to himself, but Hatch heard.

"That'll be hard to do, after all I've heard. But if anyone can give him a fair hearing, it'll be you, Ben. Too bad I'm not on the court, too. Custer's given me my share of woe."

"Trust me, Edward, you wouldn't like it any more than I do." Ben shook hands with his friend, then marched across the parade ground to the small cluster of officers sitting in judgment. As a group, they entered the officers' mess to begin the proceedings.

The court-martial found George Armstrong Custer guilty on all counts of absence from his command without leave and conduct prejudicial to discipline and good order. Punishment included suspension from command and rank for a year and forfeiture of pay.

But Ben cared little about Sheridan's protégé. By the time the court-martial was over, he was the father of a new son, Benjamin Junior.

New Territory

May 5, 1868
Fort Gibson, Indian Territory

"Alice and the family will like it here," Ben Grierson told his adjutant. He sat on a ridge looking across the grassy valley to the distant Fort Gibson. The post spread out over acres and acres, with only a small part marked with a palisade.

"Those are the officers' quarters, sir," Woodward said, pointing to the structures some distance from the palisaded fort. "Next to them is the bakery. A hospital is down the road a pace."

"I thought Kansas was lovely, but this land is a place where I might stay." Ben took a deep breath. "It only looks peaceful, I know," he said. "Sherman didn't order us to Indian Territory for no reason, not with the Cheyenne and Arapaho attacking any wagon train or settler they find."

"The Five Civilized Tribes are peaceable enough now," Woodward said.

"The Cherokee, some of them at least, fought against us in the war. I've heard tell that Stand Watie was the last Confederate general to surrender."

"He's given up his Southern ways, along with his slaves," Woodward said, "but he and John Ross are locked in a fight for control of the tribe. It's no secret that Sherman favors the Ross faction. So does Grant."

"We're here to protect them all," Ben said, marveling at how times changed. The Osage, along with the Comanche and even the Apache, were intruding in the western part of Indian Territory and destroying peaceable villages.

"We're a buffer between the Indians in Texas and those to the north and west."

"Caught between a rock and a hard place," Ben said, laughing. "That's our duty." He let out a gusty sigh as he surveyed the land again. It was so beautiful, so peaceful. It was hard to believe this had been the site of intense fighting during the war—and after.

"Your orders, sir?" asked Woodward.

"Assemble the Tenth Cavalry right away. We'll begin patrols at dawn tomorrow. There won't be any more trouble in Indian Territory, or I'll know the reason!"

Reservation and Starvation

July 10, 1868
Indian Territory

"There's no reason for you to come along, Colonel," Lieutenant Colonel Davidson said, his jaw set and his eyes straight ahead. "I am capable of leading my company without your supervision."

Ben Grierson held his anger in check. He and Davidson had argued endlessly over the last few months because of the man's continued mistreatment of his recruits and the sub-rosa machinations trying to keep Ben on detached duty at Fort Leavenworth so Davidson could command the Tenth Cavalry. Both men had been brevet major generals during the war, but Davidson's promotion predated Ben's, making him Ben's superior—if their brevet ranks had stood.

As colonel in the regular army, Ben outranked Davidson, and this rankled.

"Consider me an observer. General Sherman wants to be sure the terms of the treaty are observed."

"They should never have signed a treaty with those savages," Davidson said angrily. "Who can believe a word they say? So what if they put their marks on a treaty? They'll have new chiefs next week who won't honor the treaty."

"Are you questioning what Congress has authorized?" Ben asked in a soft voice. He tried to plumb the depths of Davidson's disloyalty. He knew the man looked upon his soldiers as being less than any white. One recruit had arrived covered in ulcers. Not only had Davidson ordered him to immediate duty, he had singled him out for punishment. The man had lacked any skill, being illiterate and physically debilitated. Ben had seen that the recruit was nursed back to health and had watched his training closely. This had not sat well with Davidson, who rightly took it as a personal affront, especially when the recruit turned out to be the best horn player in the division.

For two cents, Ben would have transferred Davidson out of the Tenth Cavalry, but Sheridan perversely blocked any such move, assuming that if Ben wanted the man sent elsewhere then he was in precisely the spot to give Ben the most trouble. So Lieutenant Colonel Davidson remained in the Tenth.

Ben saw the scout galloping up before Davidson noticed, and this irritated the brigade commander even more.

"Suh, we got a whole bunch of them Injuns," the scout said. "'Bout a dozen of 'em, all camped over yonder." The scout pointed in the direction of a mist-cloaked valley where a stream meandered down the floor and provided both water and decent hunting.

"War paint, Corporal?" asked Davidson.

"Suh?"

"Was this a war party?" Davidson asked sarcastically. "You can tell, can't you?"

Ben held his tongue.

"Suh, they ain't no warriors. Look to be starvin' half to death. But they got rifles."

"They might not have ammunition for them if they are

skin and bones," Ben suggested. "Corporal, can you show me where they're camped?"

"Suh, I don't rightly know if that's sich a good idea."

"Don't worry, Corporal," Ben said. "I'll have you with me."

The corporal grinned, then quickly hid the smile when he saw how Davidson glared.

"Continue your patrol along this path, Colonel," Ben said. "We'll catch up later."

"As you wish, sir," Davidson said with ill grace.

As the larger force rode off behind Davidson, the corporal asked, "Why you always baitin' that po' man, Colonel?"

"He does it to himself, Corporal. And you will not pass judgment on your officers. Lead on."

"Yes, suh."

Ben kept his eyes peeled for any trouble, but saw nothing but the gently rolling green hills of Indian Territory—this was all Creek land. But the dozen men huddled at the creek, tearing away the flesh of a single small rabbit, were Cheyenne.

Ben rode within twenty yards, then halted, signaling the corporal not to advance until the men in the camp allowed them. It took the better part of ten minutes, but Ben was in no hurry. The corporal got a bit antsy, but there was no danger that Ben could see. The Cheyenne were hunters and from their haggard appearance, not very good ones.

Finally, one brave strutted out as bold as brass.

"What do you want?" he demanded rudely.

Ben looked at him for a moment, to enforce the notion of who was in charge, then said, "Why aren't you on the reservation? Your chiefs have agreed that your people not stray."

"No food," the brave said. "We starve."

"Suh, he might be talkin' straight," the corporal said. "I know them folks ain't gettin' the shipments they was promised."

"Buffalo soldier speak truth," the warrior said.

Ben looked over at the corporal. He had heard the Indians use this term for the black soldiers before, always as a compliment. He wasn't sure if it had to do with their hair or the way they fought to the last. It may have been for both reasons, but having the corporal with him added to his credibility.

"Leaving the reservation creates great trouble," Ben said. "I must escort your warriors back, but I promise to do what I can to get the food and clothing guaranteed by the treaty."

The brave said nothing. He glowered at Ben, taking the officer's measure.

"Will you honor the treaty, honor your chief's promise, if you have enough food for your family?" Ben asked. He waited for the response. He could almost hear the Indian's belly grumbling from lack of food. It took a while, but the Cheyenne brave nodded once.

"We will ride with you. Corporal, do you have any trail rations? Here. Add yours to mine. These men need the strength to return to their homes."

Ben tossed what food he had to the brave, who also accepted the corporal's meager victuals. From the way his eyes widened, this might be more food than any of the braves had seen in quite a while.

"Ammunition? You give us ammo?"

"We'll escort you to your reservation," Ben said. "No ammunition."

This caused a stir among the other braves who had edged closer when they saw their leader had been given food. They argued among themselves for a moment, then the brave who acted as spokesman said, "We go."

Ben saw the conditions on the Cheyenne reservation and wrote a long report to General Sherman telling of the misfeasance in delivering food and clothing. He doubted even Sherman could do anything about the Department of War's supply chain, but unless the United States lived up to the treaty, he saw nothing but endless fighting ahead.

A New Post

January 6, 1869
Medicine Bluff, Indian Territory

"I keep being amazed by the beauty of the land," Ben Grierson said. Sam Woodward sat astride his horse beside him, looking down across the river and up to the buttes nearby. "I thought Fort Gibson was pretty, but this post will be like paradise." He had found a pleasant valley at the edge of the Wichita Mountains that looked perfect for a new post. Both Cache River and Medicine Bluff Creek supplied pure water that was far more palatable than that at Fort Gibson. Game abounded, and Mount Scott would be a perfect spot for a sentry point to look out over dozens of square miles, should anyone try to creep up on a fort.

Not far off on the plains roamed a herd of buffalo Ben estimated at more than ten thousand.

"Alice wants to move on, sir?" Woodward asked.

Ben had to laugh.

"Not really. She finally got our quarters squared away so Edie won't get into too much trouble as she explores. And the boys like Fort Gibson. But what they want—what I want—isn't important."

"Orders, sir?"

"The Arapaho and Cheyenne are pretty well content on their reservations. The Bent brothers from their trading post along the Arkansas River engage in constant trade with them and provide good service not only for themselves and the Indians but everyone else on the Santa Fe Trail. But the others . . ." Ben's mind wandered as he thought of the Kiowa and Comanche rising up against two of the Five Civilized Tribes. Both the Choctaws and Chickasaws complained bitterly that they were losing cattle, horses, and even women to the raiders. General Sheridan worried more about them now than he did the Indians further north. For once, Ben agreed with the newly appointed commanding general of the Department of the Missouri. Fort Gibson was too far east to be of aid.

"Camp Wichita is a good name for the place," Ben said.

"Sir," Woodward interrupted. He pointed to a pair of scouts from Captain Alvord's Company M riding hell-bent for leather. Three other companies of the Tenth Cavalry were scattered throughout the valley, exploring to see if they should locate the post elsewhere.

"What've you found?" Ben asked as the two scouts came up.

"Suh, we got a whole bunch of them Comanche down in the hollow. Looks like they got themselves prisoners, too."

"How many prisoners?" asked Woodward.

"Six, suh. And there's 'bout ten of them Comanche."

"Report to Captain Alvord immediately," Ben ordered. "Tell him to come up slowly with a full show of arms. Don't shoot unless fired upon." He took a deep breath. "Don't fire unless he sees trouble."

"Whass that mean, suh?" asked the other scout, his dark eyes fixed on Ben. "You thinkin' on goin' ahead of us?"

"I've never parlayed with Comanche before," Ben said. "Reckon it's about time to see what we're up against."

"Wait for Company M, sir," Woodward urged.

"Summon the other companies, too," Ben told the scouts. "Same orders."

The two scouts hesitated, then rode off, leaving Ben and Sam Woodward behind.

"If they have prisoners, they're a war party, sir," Woodward warned.

"Let's find out. It would be wrong to assume they're criminals, although they might well be," said Ben. He rode off, letting his adjutant catch up.

They rode steadily toward the Cache River. Ben was aware that the Comanche immediately saw them and wondered if the Indians had also spotted the scouts. As much as he counted on the frontier skills of his scouts, he knew the Comanche were probably better.

"A dozen, sir? There's a hundred!"

"Stay calm, Lieutenant," Ben warned. "It's too late for us to go in shooting, so we will talk."

They stopped a respectable distance from the Comanche camp and waited until an older brave walked out, slightly dragging his left leg. From the way he moved, Ben thought this was an old injury. The man had to be a chief of some regard from the way the other braves deferred to him.

"You are far from your lands in Texas," Ben said, looking around.

"We have no land," the chief said. "We have none, we have all."

"You're on Choctaw land," Ben said. He made no move for his pistol when the warriors flanking the chief hefted their rifles. He shook his head slightly to keep Woodward from making an untoward move.

"Our land."

"Choctaw land," Ben insisted. "We must talk."

"You big chief?"

"I am a big chief," Ben said. He heard Woodward hiss a warning, but Ben thought the Comanche could read insignia. "I will only speak to another big chief. You are a big chief." Ben said it flatly, as if he recognized the Comanche. He saw the way the Indian puffed with pride at being so identified.

Ben and Woodward dismounted and went into the Comanche camp, surrounded by dozens of the armed warriors. As they went to a campfire to sit and pass a pipe around, Ben saw the prisoners his scouts had mentioned. All six were Choctaw.

The Comanche chief puffed at a pipe, then passed it to Ben.

"No."

The Comanche stiffened. His eyes turned to stone.

"You refuse?"

"You have not fed your visitors. You keep them tied like animals. Release them, give them food, and send them on their way. Then I will smoke with the big Comanche chief."

"They are slaves taken in battle," the Comanche chief said harshly.

"You are mistaken. They are travellers, visitors, guests of the mighty Comanche."

"Sir," warned Woodward. "The others are getting ready to lift our scalps."

"I am a heap big chief," Ben said forcefully, not backing down. "Release the Choctaw."

Throughout the camp came a stir, like a soft breeze building into a tornado. The Comanche warriors hurried to their horses and grabbed their rifles, and bows and arrows.

"Alvord's company?" wondered Woodward.

"Companies D, E, and L, also, unless I miss my guess," Ben said quietly. Along the far side of the Cache River he spotted Company L deploying, with Captain Gray waving his arms about like a windmill. In a few minutes, three hundred soldiers would surround the Comanche camp.

The Comanche chief spoke rapidly with several of his lieutenants. Argument raged back and forth until the chief turned back to Ben.

"Our . . . guests go." He held out the pipe.

Ben saw the rawhide bonds of the six Choctaw severed by flashing knives. More than one Comanche warrior fought to keep from driving his knife into the belly of the prisoner he had just freed, but all resisted the urge. Seeing they were free, the prisoners wasted no time hightailing it to the safety afforded by the Tenth Cavalry. Only when they were out of the Comanche camp did Ben take the pipe and puff on it, taking part in the ritual.

It was the first time he had met the Comanche. It wouldn't be the last.

Raiders and Bootleggers

August 20, 1869
South of Fort Sill, Indian Territory

"No way I can sweeten it, Colonel. We lost them," reported Captain Alvord. "I'm not sure where they went after they burned that settler's house and stole his horses. They were like smoke. They just upped and disappeared."

Ben Grierson closed his eyes and tried to ignore all the aches and pains rampaging through his body. He had been in the saddle too long chasing the Kiowa and Comanche raiders. For over a week, Company M had been after the Indians, and they still didn't know which tribe the raiders belonged to, much less the identity of their war chief.

"Are you recommending that we return to the fort, Captain?"

"I'm saying we haven't got much chance of finding the Indians responsible for the raids, sir."

So much had happened in the past few months. Camp Wichita had been established at Medicine Bluff and then renamed after General Joshua Sill, a West Point classmate of Phillip Sheridan killed during the war. The name rankled

Ben because Sheridan had chosen it, but also because he had wanted the camp named for a friend of his who had died during the Battle of the Washita, Joel Elliot. The tussle over the naming had not lasted long. Sheridan was in command.

In the midst of the squabbling, Alice discovered she was again pregnant. Fort Sill was a work in progress, but Captain Alvord's wife had done as much as she could to make life easier—about the only other officer's wife to even speak civilly to Alice. Living in a tent was not proper for an expectant woman, but no other quarters were available. Their sixth child. It hardly seemed possible, and Alice was not taking it well.

Putting aside his marital tribulations, Ben thought on how the Indians had been raiding and where they were most likely to run now that an entire company of the Tenth Cavalry was after them.

"They're going home," he said finally. "They have nothing to gain and everything to lose by staying north of the Red River. They want to find their tribes on the Texas plains and brag about their victories."

"The scouts haven't spotted them moving in that direction, Colonel," Alvord said. "If we commit troops there, it might come back to bite us if they attack elsewhere."

"We go straight south. As hard and fast as we can ride, then we look again. They might be moving slower to avoid drawing attention. Whether they are Kiowa or Comanche, they'd be noticed by Choctaw or white settlers."

"You can see a mighty long way in that land, sir," Alvord pointed out. "We need more than a company of men to spread out, if you mean to cover that much territory."

It looked like a fool's errand to Ben, too, but returning to Fort Sill was hardly any more appealing to him at the moment. His oldest son, Charlie, would be at the fort soon after a semester of schooling in Chicago. He was fourteen and could be a great help to his mother.

"More than I can right now," Ben said.

"Sir?"

"Sorry, Captain, I was thinking aloud. Order the troopers south. Fast."

They rode hard until just before sundown, when a scout spotted a lone wagon crossing the prairie, a back wheel wobbling precariously.

"Who'd press on like that and not stop to fix the wheel, sir?" Alvord wondered.

"We won't find the Indians," Ben said, resigned to this small failure. "We've covered more than forty miles today and there hasn't been so much as an eagle feather found showing they've been through this part of the territory." He felt a bit of regret. Stopping a raiding party didn't mean much, but letting one escape back into Texas only fueled future raids. The braves would brag about easy theft and counting coup, then show off their stolen horses. That would pull other Comanche and Kiowa like iron to a magnet.

"Should we offer our help, Colonel?" asked Alvord.

"Deploy your men ahead and to the flanks, Captain. If there is gunplay, they are to attack."

"Gunplay, sir?"

"I can't tell until we search that wagon but something is being smuggled under our noses."

"Guns, sir?"

"Let's find out," Ben said, leading a squad forward while Captain Alvord sent out elements of his company to circle the wagon. Ben had ordered the soldiers into position more to give them practice than because he expected a fight. The man driving the wagon couldn't run—there was nowhere to go on this tabletop-flat prairie. His decrepit wagon was being pulled by a team of mules. Even with the exhausted horses ridden by Company M, the greenest soldier could run down a man trying to escape on a mule.

If he had suspected the man of something illegal before, Ben knew he had struck a nerve when he rode up. In the twilight, the man didn't notice them until Ben's squad was almost on top of the driver.

The man let out a yelp, threw down the reins, jumped from the driver's box, and tried to run away. Ben signaled and four soldiers rounded up the fleeing miscreant before he had sprinted a dozen yards.

"Why did you run?" Ben asked. The man was short and powerful, and refused to look him in the eye. He was more like a caged wild animal than a human being, but the four troopers recognized this and kept close to prevent a new escape attempt.

"Thought you was Injuns. Or thieves. Lots of road agents out here."

"I haven't heard about highwaymen. This is a desolate location for a thief. A road agent might sit by the road for days waiting for someone to drive by with a load like yours. What are you freighting?"

"Nuthin'. Ain't got nuthin' in there."

Ben motioned for Captain Alvord to peel back the dusty canvas.

"Mighty strange looking 'nothing' you are carrying," Ben observed. "Are those barrels filled with illegal intoxicants?"

"Hell, no, Colonel," the man protested. "I got ten barrels of rum!"

"You need not examine the cargo to be sure it's rum rather than some other whiskey," Ben said sharply to his captain. "Tip over the barrels and pour out the contents."

"Yes, sir," Alvord said. He issued the orders. Ben thought the captain looked a bit wistful as the gallons of rum sank into the thirsty ground alongside the road.

He might not have stopped the Comanche raiders, but he had interdicted a bootlegger. A small victory. Enough small victories lead to larger triumphs.

Portents

"There's no reason to stay here, Colonel. We been burned out twice in the past three months. Them redskins come swoopin' down, set fire to the barn and the house, and then stole the livestock. I lost eight horses and damned near twenty head of cattle." The settler took a deep breath, as if he were reloading for another verbal barrage, but Ben Grierson cut him off.

"Mr. Jonas, I understand how dangerous it has been living out here. That's why the Tenth Cavalry is patrolling constantly now. I have six companies who think Fort Sill is only a myth—and that's their headquarters."

"Don't care if them black soldiers of yers *live* on the prairie, Colonel. They're not doin' nuthin' to stop the Comanche or Kiowa. Don't know which is worse. Think it might be the Kiowa."

"Indian Territory is vast and there are only so many of us," Ben pointed out patiently. "Have you seen any Indian raiders in the last few days?"

Jonas turned and pointed to his half-rebuilt house. The sun shone off the bald spot on the top of his head, shiny with sweat in spite of the chilly morning air.

"See that, Colonel? It's gettin' around to bein' put up again. If them heathens were anywhere near, they'd be here quicker 'n lightning and burn me out again. I sent the wife and kids over to her sister's place, down the road ten miles. Not any safer there, mind you, but there's more of them. The brother-in-law's laid up with a busted leg, but can still poke a rifle out a window if the need arises."

"Has your brother-in-law been raided?"

"Only once, last spring," Jonas said. "That was damned near enough for him, but he ain't got much in the way of a backbone. My wife's sister is the one what wears the pants in that family, if you ask me."

"Thanks. I'll be sure to have a patrol come by as often as possible to look in on you, Mr. Jonas."

"Prefer it if you'd leave a few of them. I kin use some help getting the roof done again."

Ben smiled sympathetically, then mounted and rode briskly from the settler's yard. His expression turned sour fast as he rejoined the main body of the Tenth Cavalry with him.

"You hear his story more 'n once, suh?" asked a corporal, grinning broadly. "Ever' last time I come by, I have to hear Mistuh Jonas's swallered-by-whale stories."

Ben had to laugh. "I hope he gives you a dipper of water to ease the agony."

"Yes, suh, that he do. His missus is even kinder. Sometimes I get a piece of pie from her. Surely do wish I could hep out more."

"Don't we all, Corporal, don't we all," Ben said. The scout trotted off when Ben dismissed him. Ben rode around the resting troopers, studying them and liking what he saw. Men like General Hoffman might denigrate Negro soldiers, but no unit at Fort Leavenworth could hold a candle to the men of the Tenth Cavalry.

He had been in the field with them for almost two weeks, riding hard, dashing from hither to yon and back, vainly hunting for Kiowa raiders. From everything Ben had learned, the Comanche had pulled back and weren't likely to be raiding northward from Texas into Indian Territory until the spring. But the Kiowa were as active now as they had been in April, when they had come north to hunt buffalo and raid any settlement along their path.

"Where now, sir?" asked Captain Alvord. "We usually ride east to Jonas's in-laws."

"South, Captain," Ben decided. "The Kiowa are still here. They might not have raided in a week or two, but they're around. I feel it."

"By now, they've headed back into Texas, along with the Comanche. They're getting ready for winter. For someone living in a tepee, winters are mighty fierce."

"The Kansas winters were bad enough at Fort Leavenworth," Ben said. "I've heard the weather is milder to the south."

"Way south, sir. Down around the Gulf of Mexico it doesn't hardly snow. But in the Panhandle, well, sir, I've heard the Staked Plains are prone to as fierce a winter as anywhere you'll ever see."

"Why are the Kiowa still here?" Ben wondered aloud. To the captain, he said, "South, entire company, as fast as we can ride."

"It'll be good training, sir, but we won't find any Indians."

By midafternoon, Alvord ate his words. Company M overtook a band of a dozen Kiowa raiders. After a brief, fierce skirmish, the Indians hightailed it.

"What do we do, sir? You want us to pursue?" asked Alvord.

Ben considered for a moment, then pulled out a map of

the territory and pressed it flat as he studied the locations where Kiowa had been spotted.

"That way," Ben said, pointing east. "This might have been a small party."

"A dozen warriors, sir? I doubt that. Most of the raiders don't travel in packs larger than this."

"That way, Captain. Be sure the men have their weapons ready for a protracted fight."

"There won't be anything there, Colonel," Alvord said.

And he was wrong again.

This time Company M found more than fifty Kiowa in a hollow. Word of the cavalry patrol had reached the Indians already, possibly from the dozen warriors Ben had run off earlier, and they were prepared for a fight. They got it.

Ben let Alvord deploy his men in a skirmish line and advance slowly in the face of the concentrated fire. Alvord ordered his men to withdraw, reload, and then engage the Kiowa again. As the soldiers fought, Ben watched the Kiowa, studying their tactics and knowing the fight was going to be over quickly. Before Alvord realized it, his men were firing into an empty camp. The Kiowa chief had retreated, leaving a few braves to fire as fast as they could to give the illusion of more in the camp.

"We've run them off, sir," Alvord reported a half hour later. "Four wounded, one a sergeant. No deaths, not on our part."

"How did the Kiowa fare, Captain?" Ben asked. He suspected he already knew the answer.

"If we hit any of them, they got the bodies out. No proof we even winged one of the red devils."

Ben walked through the abandoned camp, feeling a hollowness in his gut at what this meant. The Kiowa were staying late in Indian Territory for a reason. He wished he knew more of what transpired down in Texas. Were the Comanche forcing the Kiowa to hunt for new land, or were the Kiowa chiefs simply planning something far more deadly for the settlers?

Ben knew he had until spring to resupply, recruit, and train. Captain Alvord was right about the Kiowa wanting to ride out the winter in their traditional land.

Kicking Bird

January 11, 1870
Indian Territory

"What!" Ben Grierson jumped to his feet. "You can't be serious. The Indians never attack in winter." He looked past Lieutenant Woodward to the gentle arching snow drifting up against the flagpole in the middle of the parade ground. Sam hadn't bothered closing the door behind him because he was in such a rush to bring the bad news.

"Sir, it's true. It's a big raid, too."

"Kiowa?"

"We think so, sir. From the reports, it might be Chief Satanta."

Ben fumed. He hadn't worried enough about the possibility of a Kiowa war chief leading a raid in the dead of winter. Alvord had doubted the Kiowa would attack—and Ben had agreed.

If it had to be a Kiowa violating years of behavior, why was it the worst of the lot? Satanta had done nothing but create woe around Fort Richardson, causing the Texas commander to complain that Ben wasn't patrolling heavily enough.

Ben's response had been accurate, truthful, and not appreciated in the least. Colonel James Oakes of the Sixth had filed
a formal complaint against Ben in an attempt to get more of
the Tenth Cavalry to patrol the north boundary of the Red
River. As delighted as Sheridan must have been receiving a
complaint about Grierson, he had supported him, knowing
the vast area the Tenth had to cover and how futile it was trying to interdict Kiowa raiders along the Red River.

If Oakes had every man in the Sixth on patrol, as he
claimed, and had not stopped the Kiowa warriors from ranging north at will, a thousand times as many soldiers would
not stop them.

"What happened?"

"A Texas drover was attacked. He lost forty head of cattle,
and the Indians stole all the belongings of the cowboys."
Woodward couldn't keep from smiling. "They even stole
their shirts and pants and left them in their union suits."

"That ought to make any Texan madder than a wet hen,"
Ben said. "What response has there been from Camp Supply?"

"Major Kidd has taken all four companies into the field to
chase down Satanta, sir."

Ben rocked back in his chair, thinking hard. Kidd had no
chance to run Satanta to the ground. The companies in
Kidd's command were poorly trained and had never done
well on the firing range. As hard as Ben worked, stressing
discipline and expertise in soldiering, some recruits never
came up to snuff. Unfortunately, many of them were at the
supply dump for Fort Sill.

"How many men can be ready for the trail in thirty minutes?" Ben asked.

"You can't go after Satanta yourself, sir. He's too far away
now to catch him. If Major Kidd can't run him down, there's
no way you can, even with better-trained soldiers."

"Was Satanta desperate to stage a midwinter raid, or have
the Kiowa changed their tactics? It's hard enough keeping
them penned up during the spring and summer. At least we

can follow the buffalo herds and stand a decent chance of finding them and running them back to Texas, but if they venture out in the dead of winter, there's no way we can bottle them up. They might be anywhere."

"Do you intend to follow him all the way back into Texas?" Woodward stared at Ben with eyes wide in amazement.

"No, I'm not going after Satanta. Let Kidd do what he can. I fear all he'll get from the Kiowa is laughter at his feeble efforts to stop them. I'm going directly to Kicking Bird's camp. I know where it is and that he's likely to be there."

"I'm not sure the old chief controls the young bucks any longer, sir," said Woodward. "Satanta's raid shows that."

"I need to know if Kicking Bird will try to stop the younger warriors or if he is egging them on. Get the troopers assembled, Sam. I need to tell Alice I'm going."

"She's not going to like it, sir. Not with little George feeling so poorly."

Ben knew that his wife had had nothing but trouble with Theodore McGregor "George" Grierson. He had been a robust ten pounds at birth last August, but had remained puny from some infection in the autumn and still had not recovered. At least his family had a decent house now, and Alice and the children were no longer quartered in a tent. But Ben did not seek reasons for leaving the fort; they found him.

"If Kicking Bird is amenable to a truce, it means a lot of settlers and drovers will keep their belongings—and their scalps." Ben sighed, then pulled on his heavy woolen coat and went to talk to Alice. She was a good Army wife. She would understand.

The cold wind slashed at his face like an unhoned razor. Ben wiped his dripping nose and wondered if he had brought along his son George's latest bout of chilblains. Not only did his nose drip, but his hands and feet swelled, making riding more difficult for him than at any time since he had been kicked on the riverboat. He blinked hard and cleared his eyes enough to see the thin wisps of rising smoke down in the valley.

Kicking Bird camped a mile across the Red River in Texas. It had been a hard ride, but Ben was glad he had made it, over Alice's objections. There were more than two hundred Kiowa in this camp. Using a rule of thumb, Ben figured Kicking Bird had more than eighty warriors with him.

Was Satanta among them?

Ben led the patrol down the hill to find out. Woodward had mustered only forty troopers on such short notice. That worried Ben, not only because he rode with fewer than he intended, but also because it meant supply and readiness were lacking at Fort Sill. The Tenth Cavalry needed a summer of full supply and hard training to make it the best unit west of the Mississippi.

With the Kiowa raiding through the winter, Ben knew training was going to be difficult for his men. It would be in the field, in the saddle, under fire.

The soldiers riding into the camp caused quite a stir. Ben saw the braves reaching for their rifles. He wondered if gunrunners were supplying them. Some of the weapons were newer and better than those his men carried. Comancheros were responsible for much of the illicit weapons and whiskey trade, but they were harder to catch than the Indians since they also traded with white settlers for items unobtainable otherwise. The very people at risk from the Indians refused to turn in the illegal traders because of the goods they got from them.

Ben looked neither right nor left as he rode proudly into the Indian camp. Children rushed out, hesitated, then darted up to touch his leg or boot with the handle of their knives. They were practicing counting coup. He ignored them and they dropped back when a middle-aged man came from a tall tepee and stood, blanket pulled around his broad shoulders.

Kicking Bird had a large scar on the side of his face, one that twisted his eye into a perpetual cheerful wink. But there was no friendliness in the man's stance.

"Why do you come?" Kicking Bird asked.

"Why do you send Satanta to steal cattle?" Ben shot back, equally as rude.

"I do not send him," Kicking Bird said, his tone softening. "Why do you think this?" The chief knew Ben could bring down five hundred men on his camp, should he order it. It was time for Ben to soften his own stance.

"You are Kicking Bird, the greatest chief of the Kiowa." The chief nodded immodestly as Ben spoke. "Who would dare go against the great chief's word if Kicking Bird ordered him to remain peacefully in camp for the winter?"

"Come, we will talk," Kicking Bird said more formally. Ben dismounted and handed the reins of his horse to his orderly. The young soldier looked pale at the sight of so many armed Kiowa around him.

Ben hoped none of the men in his detachment did anything foolish. For the most part, the Kiowa respected the buffalo soldiers as much as the Sioux and Cheyenne did. All his men had to do was stand by and not look too frightened.

The tepee was filled with smoke, little of it curling to the tall top and escaping the smoke hole. Kicking Bird seemed not to notice the stifling air. He shucked off his blanket and sat by the fire. Ben saw the chief was older than he had first thought from the way his body soaked up the heat.

He sank to a spot opposite Kicking Bird and waited for the formalities. An hour after passing the pipe and talking of small matters, Kicking Bird got to the meat of Ben's visit.

"Why do you seek Satanta?"

Ben explained the raid and how forty head of cattle had been stolen.

"It is wrong taking a man's clothing. Satanta should have killed them first."

Ben almost choked when he heard that, but Kicking Bird did not sound vindictive. He had simply stated a truth.

"The belongings taken from these men will be returned."

"The cattle will also be returned," Ben insisted. He saw this was not likely to happen. Satanta had driven off the cattle and many were probably slaughtered, and the meat dispensed throughout the tribe, within a few hours.

"You must speak with Satanta about this," Kicking Bird said. "He is a chief, too. I can only parley."

"If I find him, I will arrest him. If you see him before I do, perhaps you can rein him in. Keep him south of the Red River and there will be no reason for me to imprison him."

Kicking Bird nodded sagely. He understood the deal Ben was making. In return of guaranteeing no more raids by Satanta, Ben promised not to relentlessly pursue Satanta until he caught him.

Ben worried that Kicking Bird would realize how difficult such a capture might be in the middle of winter.

They sparred verbally a while longer, then smoked another pipe. Ben left the Kiowa camp feeling that Kicking Bird would do all he could to restrain the hotheaded braves in his tribe. For the moment. But come spring, the cork would blow out of the bottle.

Ben had to be content with gaining a couple months' respite. And the return of the drovers' clothing.

White Thieves

Ben Grierson put his hands on the high stacks of paper to hold them down as a fitful wind blew through his open office door. As the wind died and the sultry heat descended once more, Ben leaned back. He almost wished he had let the breeze carry away the reports detailing repeated attacks by the Kiowa chiefs, Satanta and Satank. Ben had tried to determine which was the more vicious of the pair and found that they were each engaged in a contest to top the other.

After Satanta stole a dozen horses, Satank stole fifteen and scalped a settler. When Satanta scalped two settlers, Satank robbed a train and set fire to the passenger cars.

The heavy spring rains had brought the waist-high grass springing up to furnish sweet fodder for Indian ponies starved all during the winter. Strong horses meant the Kiowa could range farther and cause even more devilment.

"What is it?" Ben almost snapped off Woodward's head when his adjutant came into the office. From his expression, the lieutenant was bringing even more bad news.

"Sorry to bother you, sir, but there's been a report of a new raid. Not ten miles off."

"They're getting bolder. Who was it? Satank? He has the most to prove since his band is smaller."

"Neither of the Kiowa, sir," Woodward said. "White thieves. Horses stolen from a corral."

"Not Rafe Harding again?" Ben closed his eyes and moaned. Harding was a loudmouth, but he had plenty to complain about. The Indian raids had cost him livestock almost every week. The settler had reached the point of demanding a vigilance committee be formed to stop the thefts. Having a wild-eyed pack of fear-crazed, trigger-happy settlers galloping around the countryside was the last thing Ben wanted.

"I'll take a company," he said, coming to a decision. "I might have to smooth his ruffled feathers. It'll sound better coming from the post commander than it would from a subordinate."

"I can do it, sir," Woodward volunteered.

"You've got plenty of paperwork to catch up on. Sherrydan's sending us all the supplies we can use and plenty we can't. Don't let up on keeping a decent inventory. He's sure to ask for a complete accounting." Ben had heard of other commanders being inundated with worthless equipment and supplies. They had let it rust or simply dumped it, then been called on the carpet when the inspector general could not find the supplies accounted for. These were the kinds of political shenanigans Ben hated most, but they were the ones he expected from Sheridan. Relations with him had been even more strained after Ben had sat on the court-martial board that had found Custer guilty.

"I'm going crazy from garrison duty, sir."

Ben grinned. "I outrank you and I'm going crazy, too."

Ben considered stopping by the nice palisade house that had been built some distance away from the parade grounds and telling Alice that he was going out on a patrol, then decided against it. The children were playing outside, and she was inside taking a short nap. Ever since George was born and Alice had nursed him through the difficult winter, her health had been more fragile. Almost as fragile as their relationship.

Ben assembled his troopers and led them out of Fort Sill, heading for Rafe Harding's land grant. The sun was hot for this early in the year, but once he was away from the fort, the wind picked up and provided some cooling. He kept his braided hat pulled down to shade his eyes as he rode.

Everywhere were signs of life popping up from the prairie, turning a desolate brown plain into lush green ocean. The gorgeous land was ripe for Kiowa raids and thundering herds of buffalo—and rustlers. With the settlers had come cattle and horse thieves and bootleggers. Ben appreciated the Indian raids. That had been their way of life for centuries. The only new element was who had their horses stolen.

The white horse thieves were stealing from their own kind, as well as from the Five Civilized Tribes. They were a parasite sucking the blood from those who contributed their lives to make this primitive land into civilized territory.

As he rode, he got madder by the mile at the bootleggers and white horse thieves making Indian Territory their exclusive domain.

"Wait here," Ben ordered when he neared the Harding spread. Unlike many of the settlers, Rafe Harding had never been burned out, possibly because of his proximity to Fort Sill. The smoke would have alerted the soldiers and brought out a patrol quickly. Sneak thieves stealing horses in the middle of the night had hours to get away and weren't as likely to rouse the ire of the Tenth Cavalry.

Until now. Ben vowed to put an end to such depredation, especially within a day's travel of the fort.

"What do you want?" Harding demanded. He was a florid

man missing two teeth in front. He clutched a shotgun as if
he had his fingers around some rustler's neck and was throt-
tling him to death.

"I need any information you can provide about the horse
thieves. Were the horses taken from that corral?" Ben pointed,
hoping that Harding would look in that direction.

"They damn well were." The settler's piglike eyes never
left Ben. "You can't come take any of them for your soldiers." His tone indicated he was less than impressed with
having black soldiers come to his aid.

"After they drove the horses from your corral, which direction did they go?"

"North. I followed the tracks for about a mile before I lost
them."

"Thank you. I don't promise we'll get your horses back,
Mr. Harding, but we'll try."

"Get off my land," Harding said, waving his shotgun
around wildly now. "Go on, git!"

"Makes it hard to do right," the lieutenant in charge of
this company said when Ben rejoined the column.

"No, it doesn't," Ben said sharply. "We have our duty, no
matter what he says or thinks about us." He snapped the
reins and got his horse trotting northward. The tracks were
already disappearing as the grass sprung back and the dry
earth beneath shifted with the restless wind.

For twenty minutes they rode before Ben lost the hoofprints, but his best trackers went to the ground and started
their bloodhound-like work. The spot where Harding and
Ben had been confused proved to be a quick turn to the west.
The horses had been taken to a shallow stream a few miles
away for watering.

"We got 'em, suh," a scout said, grinning ear to ear. "They
thought they was safe, so they stopped ridin' hard. Bet they
ain't a mile off." The scout turned and pointed up the stream.
"That way. Not more 'n a mile."

"Two," said his partner.

"A silver dollar sez you ain't right," said the first.

"Gentleman!" Ben spoke sharply. "There will be no wagering. That is against regulations." He saw that neither was the least chagrined at his rebuff. They whispered for a few seconds, probably finalizing the bet. The first scout acted as spokesman.

"We come to think they is one and one half miles from here, suh."

"Very well. Thank you for your excellent work." Ben summoned the lieutenant over and laid out the attack. He doubted they faced more than a handful of men, and Ben had a full fifty men for the attack. It would provide decent training and give the newer soldiers experience in the field.

Splitting his force against horse thieves was one thing, but Ben would never launch such an attack on the Indians without more information against Satank or Satanta. The Kiowa fought as if they had ten times their strength, rode faster and harder than any but the best in the Tenth Cavalry, and were knowledgeable when it came to the tactics used by the cavalry.

Twenty minutes later, his company divided into four squads and in position, Ben rode up the stream toward the horse thieves' camp. The thieves had been napping in the hot afternoon sun, under their supply wagons and in the shade of a stand of salt cedars.

One horse thief came awake, rubbed his eyes, and then let out a yelp of warning as he went for his rifle. Ben lifted his pistol and squeezed off a shot. The bullet tore through the thief's arm. He grabbed for the wound to stanch the flow of blood, yelping even louder than before.

"Surrender!" Ben shouted. "You are all under arrest! Resist and we'll cut you down!"

A dozen soldiers fired their carbines, all without orders. But they were such poor shots, they didn't hit anyone they aimed at. The volley brought the rest of the horse thieves awake and convinced them to surrender.

"Hold your fire!" Ben bellowed. He heard the lieutenant repeating the order. "They've given up!"

He counted eight horse thieves and more than forty horses penned in a crude rope corral. Harding's Circle H brand shone on the rumps of five of the horses. Ben did not recognize the brands on the others.

"What's in the wagon, Lieutenant?" Ben asked.

"Got ourselves some bootleggers, Colonel," came the answer. "The barrels are marked as being whiskey."

"We will need it as evidence. But not all of it. Destroy all but one barrel of that vile liquid," he ordered. Even returning to the fort with one barrel would offend Alice, but he needed it to cinch the conviction against these men. The horse thieves realized how lucky they were to be captured by the cavalry and not a band of vigilantes who would have strung them up on the spot.

But they weren't happy at all when Ben saw to it they were each sentenced to five years in a federal prison for bootlegging and horse stealing.

The Long Chase

June 12, 1870
Fort Sill, Indian Territory

"Sir?" Captain Alvord peered into Ben Grierson's office. "Have you got a minute to spare?"

"Come in," Ben said, glad for the break in the endless torrent of paperwork that flowed across his desk. Sam Woodward took care of much of it, but still a veritable mountain of paper required the post commander's signature. Requisitions, transfers, promotions—so many trivial items took Ben away from the important functions of the fort. Relying on his officers' reports about training and preparedness only added to his paper.

"I've found something curious, sir. At least I think it might be."

Henry Alvord was not a man who showed much inquisitiveness about the world around him. Ben could hardly wait to hear what had finally perked up his curiosity.

"Sit down, but don't block the breeze coming through the door, Captain," Ben warned. It was hot enough that he had shed his heavy wool jacket, but still his shirt clung to his body from the gallons he sweat in the tiny office.

"Have you authorized dispatch of the mules, sir? The ones we had in the corral to the east of the fort?"

"What do you mean?" Ben perked up. He had expected something trivial.

"I needed a team to pull a wagon going out to Camp Supply. The two privates came back and reported that the corral was empty. There weren't any mules to be seen."

"I haven't ordered anything done with the mules. We need them for our supply wagons."

"That's what I thought, sir, so you can imagine how I felt when I personally checked. The privates were right. The mules are gone."

"Did someone leave the gate open?" Ben asked.

"The gate was secured, sir. That's why I thought you might have sold the mules or sent them somewhere else."

"Assemble your company, Captain. Someone's stolen seventy-three mules belonging to the U.S. Army!" Ben grabbed his uniform coat and slid into it. Then he fastened his gun belt around his middle, making certain the pistol was fully loaded. He did all this on his way out of the office. By the time he reached the corral, his orderly had his horse saddled and ready for him.

"Tell my wife I've gone on patrol," Ben ordered. "I don't know how long I'll be away."

"Put a week's rations in yer saddlebags, suh," the orderly said. "You want more, we got to get them wagons rollin'."

"This will do. I'll either recover the mules or be back inside a week." He trotted to the center of the yard, waited for Alvord to assemble Company M, and then led the way out of the post at a brisk canter.

He reached the empty corral only a little before the rest of the company, but it was long enough for him to see what Alvord and the two soldiers had not. Stuck in the closed gate was a single feather with three notches precisely cut into one side.

"White Horse," he said under his breath. "I'll catch you and string you up, you mule-stealing devil!"

"Sir?" asked Alvord. "Are you sure the mules were stolen?"

"Kiowa war party," Ben said tersely. "I recognize that feather as the calling card of a young chief named White Horse."

"I've heard of him, sir. A nasty fellow, by all reckoning."

"Get the scouts on his trail. How hard can it be to track down a Kiowa raiding party herding seventy-three of our broken-down, balky mules?"

Ben found out how difficult that task could be. White Horse had a few hours' start on him, but they were adequate for the artful thief to mask his trail using a half-dozen different techniques. Ben persisted and doggedly chased White Horse fully a hundred miles southward over the next three days to the Red River before losing him. Even then, Ben kept his scouts hunting for any clue, no matter how tiny, as to the direction taken by the Kiowa chief, for more than three hours before ordering a halt.

Company M returned to Fort Sill in silence, no one daring to speak for fear of igniting their colonel's wrath. Ben Grierson simmered the entire way, for the four days it took to return, as angry at having the mules stolen from under his nose as he was in not capturing White Horse. Such a failure on the part of the Tenth Cavalry now meant the Kiowa would become bolder in their future raids.

Ransom

Ben Grierson tried not to grind his teeth as he waited for the Kiowa chiefs to arrive. They had been given safe access to the fort by the new Indian agent, Lawrie Tatum. After the past two months of raids and killing, Ben wanted the chiefs strung up rather than allowed into his post under a white flag.

Chief Big Tree had scalped a woodcutter near the fort six weeks earlier, then shot and killed a Mexican herder. If that hadn't been bad enough, white horse thieves had shot up Ben's house. Luckily Alice and the children had not been inside at the time. He thanked his lucky stars for insisting the Tenth Cavalry have a decent band. Otherwise, Alice would have begged off attending the concert that had been in progress when the horse thieves had opened fire. Still, their bullets had broken a mirror and several knickknacks about the house.

Chasing them down had been difficult, but all the men in

his command realized the importance of deterring such violence in the future.

In spite of such an outrage, the Kiowa had been his primary concern for most of the summer, with their endless forays across the Red River and into Indian Territory. Ben began tapping his foot impatiently when he touched his pocket where a letter from Colonel Mackenzie, the new commander of Fort Richardson, accused him of selling rifles to the Indians. The only rationale for such a wild claim that Ben could determine was to find a scapegoat for Mackenzie's inability to stop the Indian raids.

Such a charge was groundless and would be dismissed, but Ben knew the protest would be filed in General Sheridan's office and would be pulled out some day when he least expected it.

"When are they getting here?" Ben asked impatiently.

The Indian agent shrugged. "You know the Indians. They operate on their own time."

"I don't like having these particular chiefs in my fort—other than residing in my stockade."

"Please, Colonel, it took quite a bit of negotiation to get them to agree to this meeting." Tatum took off his glasses and cleaned them for the hundredth time with his handkerchief. The man was short, slender, and had the perpetually harassed look of a bureaucrat about him. Other than this obvious case of nerves, Tatum had been efficient enough, but not to Ben's liking.

Ben thought that Tatum gave away too much to make his mark as the new agent. There wasn't any way this side of perdition that the Kiowa chiefs would agree to stop raiding, but they would lie and promise Tatum anything he wanted to hear in exchange for presents. They would accept the government's largesse, then go about their business of turning the prairie into a bloody grassland from the Red River north to the Dakotas.

"There they are. Is the officers' mess cleared out?"

"As you requested, Mr. Tatum." Ben touched the letter from Colonel Mackenzie in his jacket pocket, then let his hand drift down to rest on the hilt of his saber. He watched the three arrogant Kiowa chiefs ride in. One he recognized immediately from the feather tucked into his braided hair. Three notches had been cut along one side—this was White Horse, the raider who had stolen the mules from under his nose.

The other two he guessed at. Lone Wolf was the oldest of the trio and Satanta was the haughtiest, looking down his Roman nose at the soldiers and their barracks. Ben could almost hear the chief's thoughts on how easy it would be to attack this fort, kill all the soldiers, and steal the horses.

"Welcome, great chiefs," Tatum greeted.

The three dismounted and stood in a line, arms crossed on their broad chests, their dark eyes cold and foreboding. They said nothing, forcing Tatum to ramble on nervously, trying to elicit some response.

"This way," Ben said, taking command. He spun and walked toward the mess hall. If the three remained, they would look foolish. By turning his back on them, he showed his disdain for them. Ben fought to keep the small smile of triumph from his lips when he heard the Kiowa hurrying after him. He lengthened his stride just enough so they couldn't close the distance without running. That would be unseemly and make them appear to be nothing more than his servants trailing behind.

Ben walked through the door into the cooler mess hall where the largest table had been set with cups filled with water. He went directly to the head of the table, not caring where Tatum positioned himself among the Kiowa. He turned, pointed imperiously to the long benches, then sat before they could scramble to sit ahead of him. Again he made it appear he was giving orders to them and that they were obeying.

The chiefs were fuming now but held their anger in check. Tatum looked perplexed at their attitude and at Ben's, not understanding the silent power play going on.

"We have business to conduct. Mr. Tatum will explain. Be so good as to tell our esteemed visitors what you require of them, sir."

Ben forced the pace of the meeting and kept the Kiowa off balance just enough to be uncomfortable. He saw how they exchanged looks, as if trying to decide whether they ought to walk out or continue the meeting. When they didn't budge from their benches, Ben knew they wanted something that Tatum was willing to yield.

He half listened to Tatum droning on about the responsibility of an Indian agent and how much it meant to him to be of service to all Indians. Ben was more interested in Satanta. Of the three, he was the most composed—and undoubtedly the most dangerous. The chief kept his emotions in check while both White Horse and Lone Wolf gestured grandly and tried to cow Tatum with their belligerence.

"We are all agreed, then, gentlemen," Ben interrupted, not sure if anyone agreed to anything in this room other than wanting to put an end to his enemy with knife or pistol.

"Colonel, please. I haven't made my proposal yet," Tatum said.

"That was next on the agenda," Ben said, hoping the agent would finally get around to the purpose for the meeting.

"We are willing to offer ransom for the six prisoners, as you requested."

"What!" Ben was outraged at such a proposal. Pay ransom once, and a precedent was established. The Indians would know they could get what they wanted at any time by taking more hostages.

"Colonel," warned Tatum. "This has been approved at higher levels."

Ben calmed down, but saw that he had lost his control over the meeting. Satanta knew that whatever Ben said now would be ignored by the agent—and that their superiors agreed.

"The six captives will be released in exchange for six wagons of trade goods."

"Want rifles," White Horse said.

"No!" barked Ben.

"He's right," Tatum said quickly. "We will give only blankets, food, and cooking utensils."

The dickering went on for more than an hour, during which Ben said nothing. He studied Satanta closely, taking the man's measure the best he could. The Kiowa war chief was a cool customer and Ben knew this wouldn't be the last time they met. If he didn't find Satanta, the Kiowa chief would definitely seek him out.

The trio of Kiowa chiefs finally departed, a signed pardon for their kidnapping in their possession and a time and place set for the exchange of prisoners for supplies.

"It had to be done, Colonel. Mackenzie hunted for Satanta's camp where the six are being held and couldn't find it. Even with every man in the Tenth Cavalry searching, there was no hope to find the captives. We're getting back two women and four children. We're saving them from a terrible life of slavery. Please understand, sir."

"I understand, but I don't have to like it," Ben said. He stared at the empty spot on the bench where Satanta had sat. He made a silent vow to return Satanta to Fort Sill—in chains.

Benzine-board

September 26, 1870
Fort Sill, Indian Territory

"He's abusing his position again," Ben said grimly. "The man gambles every minute of the day. If he pursued Lone Wolf or Satanta as diligently, we wouldn't have any Kiowa north of the Red River to worry about. What other choice do I have but to court-martial Major Kidd?"

"Sir, that's a big mistake," Sam Woodward said. The adjutant chewed his lower lip as he thought. "Kidd's popular among the other officers. Even Alvord likes him."

Ben had to consider this matter carefully. Alice tried to get along with the officers' wives, but they were icily polite and nothing more to her, never including her in their activities and showing up at get-togethers she held strictly because she was the commander's wife. Only Alvord's wife could be considered a friend of the family, and if Ben took action against a friend of her husband's, that might reflect adversely on his own family.

Ben did not want to see Alice and his children become social pariahs. Life on the frontier was difficult enough.

"He's not a good officer. His record is poor," Ben went on. "He parleys with the Kiowa, then believes anything they tell him. Kicking Bird has lied repeatedly to him and Kidd even believes Satanta's tall tales."

"That might be true, Colonel, but Kidd isn't as bad as the others you are recommending for court-marital." Woodward held up the list Ben had prepared and read it slowly, double-checking the reasons for the court.

"If Cox and Armes vanished from the face of the earth this very minute, no one would notice. But Sheridan wants Graham court-martialed. He is a wild one but always accomplishes his mission."

"So this is from Sheridan's headquarters?" Samuel looked even more uncomfortable at the notion of Ben adding to a list sent by Sheridan.

"Only Graham. I thought it was worthwhile to add the others. Kill all the birds with one stone, as it were."

"Including Kidd. Sir, I have to counsel against it."

"You think my morals are getting in the way of maintaining control over my cavalry?"

"How you came to decide on those to court-martial is your responsibility, sir, but there might be a better solution." Woodward fished inside his jacket and pulled out a sheaf of papers. "The War Department holds a 'benzine-board' every year where a board of officers passes judgment on anyone submitted. It's not a court-martial, but an adverse ruling by the board will remove an officer."

"Kidd would be reassigned?" Ben thought on this. "That hardly seems punishment enough for his gambling. He is so consumed by placing bets that he neglects his men."

"That might not sit well with the other officers, either, sir. White officers don't look to be popular with black soldiers."

"I don't look to be popular, I aim to be the best commander of the best cavalry in the West!" Ben said. He cooled down a little. "Submit Kidd, Armes and Cox to the 'benzine-board' and let them rule on it. And proceed with Graham's court-martial. I see no way of avoiding what might be construed as a direct order from Sherry-dan."

"Very well, sir."

"Wait, Sam. You look pleased. Why's that?"

"Colonel, the lists have already been sent. I took it on myself to forward the request with the morning courier. By now it is registered at Fort Leavenworth that there will be a change in company commanders here."

Ben didn't like Sam going over his head like this. If he had chosen to continue with court-martialing Kidd, he would have looked like a fool. But Woodward knew the politics of the Tenth Cavalry better than he did.

"Thank you, Sam," he said.

"And sir, you know how news travels around fast on any post. The men in Kidd's company request your presence."

"I see," Ben said. "I should tell them directly, but perhaps it would be better to inform Kidd first."

Sam Woodward held the door and let his commander exit. Assembled on the parade ground, in perfect ranks, stood Kidd's company. Seeing Ben, they struck up a jaunty melody, "Red River Valley." It was almost without flaw, although it had never been intended for drum, fife, and bugle.

"They appreciate you, sir," Woodward said softly.

"They must. They're playing in tune." Ben Grierson was secretly pleased at the support his troopers showed.

He stepped up to inform them of the change in their company commander, although it was hardly news to any of them. Again, Sam had proven his worth by careful spread of rumors. Ben appreciated his adjutant as much as he did the ease with which he had removed Kidd.

Deep into Texas

January 30, 1871
Weatherford, Texas

"Four men dead?" asked Ben Grierson. He shivered as sleet pelted his heavy jacket and stung his face. But he wasn't sure it was only the cold that made him shiver so hard. The Kiowa had shown the year before that they were becoming bolder about winter raids. Major Kidd had tried repeatedly to run Satanta down and had never found him, whether through the Kiowa chief's cleverness or Kidd's lack of determination Ben had never decided.

But Kidd was gone now, the "benzine-board" finding him unfit for command. Ben knew that meant little. He should have court-martialed Kidd and seen him thrown out of the Army for his gambling. But that was history, and he had the present to deal with.

"Yes, sir, them Injuns rode in as bold as brass and started stealin'. Anything that caught their eye, they just up and took. Sort of like a crow goin' after shiny things to carry back to its nest, you know?"

"The men they killed," insisted Ben. "Tell me about them."
He looked up and down the snowy street of Weatherford.
Other than being preternaturally deserted for this time of
day, nothing seemed out of place. Yet it was. Big Bow and
his braves had come to town, possibly accepted as potential
customers, probably watched carefully for any sign of
treachery. It had certainly come to that, Ben knew, but some
of the residents must not have watched carefully enough.

"Four niggers," the man said. "Don't mean much."

Ben took a step forward and reared back, fist cocked,
catching himself at the last minute. The man hardly noticed.
He wiped the increasing flurry of snow from his eyes.

"Yep, four of the biggest, blackest sons o' bucks you ever
did see. They tried to talk to Big Bow."

"You mean they tried to stop him from stealing the rest of
your town blind," Ben said in a fury as cold as the Blue
Norther whistling down from the plains.

"Might be, might just be," the man went on. "Anyhow,
there wasn't no way we was goin' to do squat to the Indians
without a lot of us dyin'. Big Bow had more 'n twenty warriors with him, all armed to the teeth. Fact is, them niggers
mighta got us all killed by puttin' up a fuss."

"Which way did Big Bow go when he left Weatherford?"

"South. He ain't no fool. It's got to be warmer down
'round Austin or San Antone."

"What of the four men Big Bow killed?" asked Ben.

"What of 'em?" The man frowned, not understanding.

"Where are they buried?"

"In the potter's field, of course."

Before Ben left town, he stopped by the undertaker's
store and paid to have the four moved to the town's cemetery.

"Got to put 'em in a special spot, you know," the undertaker said, eyeing the gold double eagles Ben had stacked on
his counter.

"Why is that?"

"Don't reckon none of them were Masons. Most all of the cemetery's reserved for the local Masonic Lodge."

"They'll rest easy enough among ordinary folks outside the Masonic section," Ben said.

"Wait," the undertaker said as Ben started to leave. "You going after Big Bow?"

"Of course I am."

"Well it's about time. When you see Colonel Mackenzie, tell him he's doin' a damn poor job and that you ought to be in command of Fort Richardson!"

Ben laughed, but there was no humor in it. He had chased Big Bow all the way south from outside Fort Sill and not once had he seen a patrol from Fort Richardson. He doubted Mackenzie ventured out in inclement weather like this unless there was some good reason. However he sliced it, Ben doubted a "good reason" ever came up for Mackenzie or the men of the Fourth.

"We keep going south," Ben called to his adjutant. Sam Woodward had insisted on riding along, and Ben had not seen fit to deny him. Sam wasn't the marrying kind, but he had been sweet on the daughter of a settler a few miles from the post. Big Bow had raided her parents' spread, stolen all their livestock, and left the entire family dead.

For Woodward this was personal, and for Ben it was becoming more so with every mile he rode. How anyone in the town could dismiss four deaths simply because they were black men was beyond him. Not a single enlisted man riding behind him was white. And there wasn't a one he wouldn't trust with his life.

"How much of a start does Big Bow have?" asked Woodward.

"From everything said in town, at least an hour. Might be more."

"We can track him, then," Woodward said. "The scouts can follow a ghost through a snowstorm."

"That might be what we're up against," Ben said, looking over his shoulder. The dark roiling clouds promised more than sleet. Within an hour they might dumping inches of fresh snow on their heads and covering Big Bow's tracks for all time.

"Time's a' wasting, Colonel."

Ben let Woodward send out the scouts at a dead gallop. Ben knew they would find Big Bow's tracks. The Kiowa chief had a sizable band of warriors with him, and they drove fifty or more head of horses and mules alongside as their ill-gotten gains. But the temperature was dropping like a stone, telling Ben they had only a short while before the snow would begin covering tracks.

Ben wanted Big Bow brought in for a string of murders, ranging all the way from Indian Territory down into Texas, so bad he could taste it.

They rode hard, the scouts plying their trade expertly.

"That way, suh," a sergeant said. "We gonna get 'em in sight any minute now."

"Prepare for combat," Ben ordered. He heard the men grumbling about cold fingers and toes that had frostbitten on their hard ride, but there wasn't a one of the men with him who wouldn't fight and fight fiercely if the need arose.

"Sir, we have company," called Lieutenant Woodward.

Ben turned his attention from his own pistol to the top of a rolling hill a quarter mile to their right flank. He saw the cavalry banner fluttering in the brisk wind before he could make out the details of the riders. They were from Fort Richardson.

"Damnation," Ben said, then looked around to see if anyone had heard him utter such a terrible word. Woodward and the other officers were saying things even more fulminant.

"What are we going to do, sir?"

"Prepare the men. I want Big Bow—dead or alive. I'll warn off the Fourth detachment." Ben galloped across the icy ground in an attempt to stop the other Army unit from interfering with his attack.

Shots rang out, causing Ben to rein back hastily.

"What're you doing on my territory, Colonel?" An officer with braid on his hat rode forward, but Ben couldn't see the man's rank. Snow had frozen on his shoulders and a heavy scarf around the man's face hid any collar emblems.

"You'll ruin the attack. I've got Big Bow, just over that hill."

"Sergeant, prepare for an attack," the officer barked. The voices of the men carried in the cold, crisp air. Ben turned to signal Woodward to launch the attack before the Kiowa heard the newcomers and their rash, loud commands.

"Quietly," Ben said. "Big Bow has a large band with him. We have to strike quickly."

"You will not attack at all, Colonel." The officer pulled back his scarf. "I am Colonel Ranald Mackenzie, Fourth Cavalry. You have no authority south of the Red River."

"I've never had the pleasure of meeting the man who thought I was giving guns to the Indians," Ben said, surprised that Mackenzie had ventured outside his safe, warm fort in such vile weather. "We can discuss our differences later. Capturing Big Bow is paramount." Ben saw the expression on Mackenzie's face. He might as well have called the man a son of a bitch. Ben thought he knew the way around any argument now. "If you want the credit, take it. Fine. I want him stopped."

"Your men will withdraw, sir," Colonel Mackenzie said in a steely tone. "I doubt they'd be up to a good fight."

"Why's that?" Ben asked.

"They're all men of color, are they not? I believe General Sheridan mentioned that to me in some communiqué."

Ben turned and started to lift his arm to give Woodward the command to attack, but Mackenzie reached out and gripped him too firmly, almost pulling him from the saddle.

"My territory, my responsibility," Mackenzie said.

"Then attack, damn you!" Ben's angry outburst took him

aback. He had not realized Big Bow had affected him so deeply that he altered his speech so invidiously.

Colonel Mackenzie gave the order, but the Fourth formed a ragged skirmish line and made so much noise that a deaf man could have heard them coming. By the time they reached the top of the rise, Big Bow was long gone.

"We have to pursue," Ben said. "After your clumsy attack, it'll be more difficult because Big Bow knows we are close."

Ben swatted furiously at flakes fluttering in front of his face as the snow began falling more heavily. He heard Mackenzie ordering him back north. Then his scouts reported that the storm crashing down upon them was going to be a major one. Pursuit of Big Bow and the subsequent battle would have to be accomplished by luck rather than skill.

With ill will and great reluctance, Ben ordered his companies to swing about and find shelter. Colonel Mackenzie's demand that he return to Fort Sill immediately after the storm rang louder and shrieked fiercer than any wind gust during the night.

He had lost any chance of capturing Big Bow.

A Free Hand

May 29, 1871
South of the Red River, Texas

"General Sherman wanted to come along," Ben Grierson said. He took a deep drink from his canteen, then recorked it. The day was turning hot, and he would need the water later, when there wasn't time to stop and reflect on how to find the sweetest water from the Texas streams. "He's an old war horse champing at the bit to fight again. It galled him when he had to return to St. Louis so soon, after all that's happened."

"He certainly found enough to get his dander up," Sam Woodward said.

Ben nodded and considered taking more water. His mouth felt like the insides of a cotton bale. He gave in and drank more. They'd find another creek before the fighting started, and if they didn't, he would go thirsty.

"His tour of the Texas forts was certainly eventful," said Ben.

"Eventful? You've got a way of understatement about you, Colonel," said Woodward. "He barely missed being ambushed two weeks ago, and then Tom Brazeale stumbled into Fort Richardson with his story. That opened the general's eyes to what's going on, that's for certain."

Ben ran his fingers over the canteen, appreciating the damp canvas cover and wishing he could douse himself with the contents. Then he put aside such a notion. He was getting too old for field action, but he wanted to be here. His hot-tempered friend William Sherman wanted him to take personal charge after all the death and dying.

Brazeale's wagon train, loaded with corn, had been rattling across the prairie headed for Fort Griffin when it was attacked by an overwhelming force. Brazeale hadn't been able to identify the warriors, but there was little doubt they were Kiowa. Five of Brazeale's muleteers had been killed outright, and another six along with Brazeale had hightailed it for cover in a nearby stand of post oaks. Only Brazeale and four of the teamsters had made it.

Brazeale lost contact with the four and found his way to Fort Richardson. Ben couldn't help but wonder what Mackenzie would have done if Sherman had not been present—and had traveled that very road two days before the Brazeale massacre. Sherman had ordered Mackenzie and every trooper available in the Fourth to pursue the Kiowa raiders, onto their reservation if necessary, to retrieve the stolen property and bring the raiders to justice.

Ben knew the weather had been horrid, and Mackenzie was riding through driving rain. From the snippets Sherman had told him when he arrived at Fort Sill six days ago, Mackenzie had discovered seven mutilated bodies, a few dead mules, and the corn scattered across the prairie. The wagon train had not carried anything of value to a band of warriors, so they had taken their ire out on the dead and had tried to destroy the grain. Other than this obvious discovery, Ben reckoned Mackenzie would spend weeks chasing his own tail and not find anything.

Sherman had arrived at Fort Sill and had been impressed

from the beginning by how military the post was. Ben's only regret was that the round of festivities he had planned were thrust aside by events. Lawrie Tatum, the Indian agent, had monopolized Sherman's time because the Kiowa were to be given their rations at the fort on the 27th.

Ben wished he had been there when Tatum asked the Kiowa chiefs what they knew of the Brazeale attack. Satanta had launched into a bitter denunciation of Tatum and the United States, claiming the agent sought only to deprive the Kiowa of their due. Tatum had been thunderstruck when Satanta had openly confessed to the murders, then declared that he was going to assemble a war party and ride into Texas to show what a true warrior could do.

Ben had received a letter from Tatum warning: "Satanta, in the presence of Satank, Eagle Heart, Big Tree, and Woman's Heart, in a defiant manner, has informed me that he led a party of about one hundred Indians into Texas and killed seven men and captured a train of mules. He further states that Chiefs Satank, Eagle Heart, Big Tree, and Big Bow were associated with him in the raid. Please arrest all of them."

Further cementing Satanta's guilt was his parting statement to Tatum: "If any other Indian claims the honor of leading the party, he will be lying. I did it myself!"

Nothing could have stirred General Sherman more. He had ordered the Tenth Cavalry after the Kiowa and had given Ben carte blanche to do as he wanted, as long as the Kiowa threat was stopped. Ben took this to mean he no longer had to pay attention to Colonel Mackenzie's claims of territoriality and could pursue Satanta and the other war chiefs anywhere they ran.

He vowed to follow them all the way into Mexico, if he had to.

"Should we rest a mite longer, sir?" asked Woodward. "The men and horses are still tired from the ride."

"They'll get used to it. They'll have to, if we are to properly fight the Kiowa." Ben turned grim. "The Kiowa are not half the horsemen the Comanche are. When we face them, we'll find our stamina sorely tried."

"Yes, sir." Woodward shouted orders, got the troopers mounted, and started on the trail leading deeper into Texas. Before they had ridden a mile, two scouts galloped up, waving their hats and signaling for their comrades to be quiet.

Ben quickly passed the order to his junior officers and then to the sergeants: no talking, no noise. He felt his heartbeat quicken because the scouts must have found the Kiowa.

"Suh, we got them red devils," panted the lead scout. He pointed over his shoulder, at an angle to the road. "Must be thirty or forty of 'em."

"Not all of Satanta's men," Ben mused. He considered his chances of waiting to see if Satanta and this band joined forces. He wanted to engage all the Kiowa in a single decisive battle. They could hide and snipe at his men for years if he tried to pick them off a few at a time. While it might be hubris on his part, Ben thought his disciplined Tenth was more than a match for the Kiowa warriors, who were more accustomed to fighting singly than as a unit.

He wished he had some of Mackenzie's artillery. From here he could lob cannonballs over the hilltop and into the Indian camp. Then he pushed aside such a notion. The Tenth Cavalry's strength was speed and resilience. Racing fifty miles in a day to engage in a fierce skirmish would spell the death of most soldiers. Not his.

"Send out ten more scouts," Ben ordered Woodward. "Find out if there's any chance of more Kiowa around. When we attack, it will be full force, no quarter given until they surrender completely. I don't want Satanta or any of the other chiefs to attack our flank or rear."

"Suh, we know they's not behin' us," spoke up another scout. "Ahead's the only place they kin be."

"Thank you, Corporal. Act on this, Lieutenant. Get the men arrayed into a skirmish line. No one is to escape!"

Woodward saluted and trotted off. Ben spoke briefly with the scouts before sending them back out with more eyes to peer about. From what the scouts had reported, this wasn't Satanta's camp. But from the size, it had to be a significantly powerful Kiowa war chief's.

That would do for a start.

Slowly, quietly, Ben led his men in a long line to a spot just on the side of the hill away from the camp. He motioned for a halt, rode ahead, and studied the camp for a few minutes. The Kiowa were too arrogant to post guards. He wasn't seen. When he finished his scrutiny, he lengthened the attack line, set the ends in motion to come up on the Kiowa's flanks, then had his bugler sound the charge.

With loud whoops and sharp cracks from their carbines, three companies of the Tenth Cavalry burst over the top of the hill and down the far side into the Kiowa camp.

"It's Lone Wolf," shouted Woodward from a spot twenty yards distant. "I recognize him!"

Lone Wolf had not been named by Lawrie Tatum in his letter, but Ben paid scant attention to this oversight. Sherman had given him the authority to stop Kiowa raiding, and he had no doubt that the Indians in this camp were all on the warpath. Their paint, the way they set up camp, the lack of women and children and dogs, all bespoke of a raiding party. And they were off their reservation.

The ends of Ben's skirmish line curled in on the Indians and prevented escape. For a few minutes, the fighting was desperate, fierce, deadly. Then the Kiowa began surrendering. Ben was pleased that his men were well trained and did not kill any brave who had dropped his weapons. Of the forty Kiowa in the camp, ten were dead, another twenty wounded, and all others were captured, including Lone Wolf.

"I place you under arrest for murder and pillage," Ben formally told the chief. Lone Wolf stared at him as if he didn't exist.

"We missed the big ones," Woodward said.

"No, no, you didn't, suh," cried a scout. His lathered horse showed how brutally he had whipped it at top speed to arrive. The horse staggered with exhaustion, but the scout's expression told the story. "They's a mile to the east. Satanta, fer sartin."

Ben assigned the handful of his men who had been wounded or whose horses had become completely useless to guard Lone Wolf and the others, assembled the remaining troopers, and rode steadily in the direction given by his scout.

The Tenth Cavalry met Satanta and fifty of his warriors less than five hundred yards from Lone Wolf's camp. The element of surprise was lost to both sides, and some of Ben's men balked or tried to flee when they were attacked in the thicket. Their discipline took over as the noncoms regained some semblance of order.

"They're going to be hell to get outta there, sir," Captain Forbes called.

"Set fire to the woods. Burn the undergrowth," Ben ordered. "When they come out, fire at will." He then sent Woodward to the south to cut off escape in that direction and another company to the north. If there had been time and if he had brought more men, he would have circled the woods and sniped at Satanta until the chief ran out of ammunition.

The woods exploded in flame as the dry underbrush ignited. Some of the Kiowa warriors raced out, some mounted but more on foot. Ben's men showed them no mercy.

"South, some are fleeing south!"

"Woodward's there," Ben shouted. "Hold your position. Keep firing!"

The cry went down the line, and the buffalo soldiers fired until their barrels were too hot to touch.

"Reload!" shouted Ben. He waited for his men to be certain their carbines were in good order, then he gave the fateful order. "Charge!"

The ragged line advanced, firing as they entered the smoldering woods. If Satanta had thought the soldiers would not dare fight face-to-face, hand-to-hand, he was quickly dissuaded of such a notion. The soldiers took a fearful toll on the Kiowa.

"They're givin' up, Colonel!" someone shouted from the right flank. "All of them red devils!"

"Hold your fire, men," Ben ordered. His own emptied pistol hung in his hand. He had not bothered to unlimber the second six-shooter because of the way the battle was going. His men had been in command of the field from the first, and he knew it was only a matter of minutes before the Kiowa either were killed to the last man or gave up.

Satanta and Satank were the first to come out with their hands high in the air. Following them came the few uninjured warriors remaining in the raiding party. The rest had to be dragged from the woods, their wounds too grievous for them to walk.

"Sergeant," snapped Ben, "put Satanta and Satank in irons." He had brought shackles from the post stockade for this very purpose.

He looked around as the soldiers did as he ordered. The Kiowa chiefs had turned surly.

"Where's Lieutenant Woodward?"

"He lit out with a squad when some of the Indians got out of the woods. You want to send out a patrol to find him?"

"Never mind," Ben said, standing in the stirrups and shielding his eyes with his hand. The air was still filled with white gunsmoke, but it was clearing a bit. Enough. "There he is now." Ben grinned ear to ear. "Woodward's coming home with some prisoners of his own."

"Sir," Sam Woodward said, riding to his commander. "I wish to report that, after considerable pursuit, I have captured Big Tree and seven of his warriors."

"Well done, Lieutenant," Ben congratulated. Louder, he said, "Congratulations to every soldier in the Tenth Cavalry! When the prisoners are secured, water for everyone!"

Escape

June 8, 1871
Fort Sill, Indian Territory

"Congratulations from General Sherman, sir," Sam Woodward said, handing Ben Grierson the telegram.

"I'd venture that there's not a similar one from General Sheridan," Ben said. He took the telegram and read through it quickly. He smiled. "He knows who's responsible for the captures. He thanks the men of the Tenth Cavalry."

"He knows you're the one responsible for turning them into the best outfit west of the Mississippi, sir," said Woodward.

"Without the basic material, nothing could have been done." Ben tucked the flimsy sheet into his jacket. "How are the prisoners?"

"They know they won't be here much longer, sir."

"Amazing how quickly word gets around. Our sentries only spotted Colonel Mackenzie and his men an hour ago. Have they made any progress?"

"The rain is holding them back. I suppose the colonel

will use that excuse to explain his failure in tracking down the Kiowa raiders."

"I frankly don't care why he failed. I'm only glad that Sherman gave me free rein in tracking down those murderers. When Mackenzie gets here, greet him, but don't put yourself out. I'll be at home."

"You won't greet him personally, sir? That will be seen as an affront."

"Sam, of course it will. And if I am here, he'll see *that* as an insult. There's nothing that I can or can't do that Mackenzie won't find offensive. Considering my opinions of him and his abilities, not meeting him is a surer course. Let him report to Sherry-dan what I didn't say."

"I understand how you feel, sir, but you should greet him as one post commander to another."

"Send an orderly for me when you are ready to turn over the prisoners to him. I need to spend some time with my family or they'll think the Kiowa have taken *me* prisoner."

Ben knew he only avoided an unpleasant confrontation with Ranald Mackenzie. It was a small show of cowardice on his part, but he had fought too long and wanted a spot of peace in his life that didn't deal with political infighting. Mackenzie had Sheridan's ear and would turn in a report critical of the Tenth Cavalry, no matter what the truth might be. More to the point, Mackenzie was fuming mad that Sherman had directly ordered Ben to capture the Kiowa after the Brazeale massacre, regardless of where that chase took him and his troopers.

With Satanta, Satank, and the others securely locked up where they belonged, Sherman's orders would undoubtedly be rescinded because of Sheridan's protests, but it no longer mattered. The threat to the settlers from Kiowa in Texas was gone.

Ben spent a delightful two hours with his boys, keeping them from annoying their mother. Alice was ready to deliver any day now and was not feeling at all well. Edie did what she could for her mother, but the time Ben spent with his sons proved too short because the orderly arrived far too soon. With great reluctance, Ben pulled on his uniform jacket and prepared to speak with Mackenzie as he turned over the prisoners.

"Can I go, Pa?" asked Robert.

"You'd be bored. You stay and look after your brothers. George wants someone to play with."

"Aw, I don't like staying with a baby."

"He's not a baby, no longer. No argument. Stay and help your mother and sister." Ben let Robert fetch his horse and saddle it, then rode slowly back to the fort. Fort Sill had grown immensely, spreading out over the prairie. This was mighty attractive country for ranching or farming. One day it would be opened up for settlement rather than only permitting a few to work farms nearby, primarily to support the soldiers.

"He's waiting at the stockade, sir, and he's fit to be tied." Woodward looked worried.

"I expected no less, Sam. Don't worry. I won't lose my temper." Ben dismounted and marched to where Colonel Mackenzie stood impatiently.

"They wouldn't release Satanta until you gave the order, Colonel," Mackenzie said.

"It's good to see you, too, Colonel Mackenzie," Ben said. It rankled that Mackenzie was senior to him because of longer service as a full colonel in the Army. But this was Fort Sill, and the Tenth Cavalry had done what the Fourth could not. "Are you ready to take the prisoners back to Texas for trial?"

"We should hang them rather than turn them over to civil authorities," Mackenzie said. "But General Sherman doesn't want us to handle the matter militarily."

"Their crimes were committed against civilians, those crimes that caused us to go after them this time. Thomas Brazeale will certainly testify."

"We know what they did. Bring out Satanta."

"Get the prisoners," Ben ordered.

Mackenzie whistled, got his sergeant to form the guard, and watched as the Kiowa captured by the Tenth Cavalry were brought from their cells.

"They're treacherous, Colonel. Be careful with them."

"I don't need your advice, Grierson," snapped Mackenzie. He angrily motioned for his men to see the prisoners mounted. He grabbed the reins of his horse and started to mount when Ben stopped him.

"A moment, Colonel."

"What?"

"You forgot to sign the receipt for the prisoners." Ben held out the papers. Mackenzie scribbled his signature, growled like a bear, mounted, and moved out at a trot.

"I'm glad that's the last we'll see of those sons of bitches," muttered Sam Woodward.

"To whom are you referring, Sam?"

"Sorry, sir."

"I'll be in my office. Call me for band practice. I want to hear how the men are progressing."

Ben went to his office and carefully filed the papers dealing with the Kiowa chiefs, then dived into the more mundane work of running a cavalry post. An hour passed before Sam Woodward came running in.

"Ready for the band already?" asked Ben.

"Colonel, Satank's escaped!"

"What? That fool Mackenzie let him escape?"

"Looks that way, sir. Colonel Mackenzie sent a courier ahead and is returning with the rest of the prisoners. He wants us to go after Satank."

Ben issued the orders, got two companies into the field to find the runaway Kiowa chief, and then waited impatiently for Ranald Mackenzie to come stumbling back to Fort Sill.

"He got away! The red bastard ran," Mackenzie exclaimed

as he rode up. Mackenzie was flushed and had a wild look in his eyes.

"I dispatched troopers as soon as your courier reached me," Ben said.

"What? Why'd you send anyone out? There wasn't any reason to do that. I've got him. I only wanted you to know to expect me when I returned." Mackenzie pointed. Toward the rear of his column stood a horse with a lifeless body draped over the saddle. "Shot the red bastard. We got him before he'd ridden a mile."

Ben was filled with contrary emotions. Satank's death was hardly a tragedy, not after all the murder and mayhem the Kiowa had effected on his raids, but the body was still in shackles as it dangled belly-down over the horse. Ben found himself growing angrier by the second that Mackenzie hadn't recaptured his prisoner rather than gunning him down.

"I'll rest up a spell, then get back on the trail to Fort Richardson. You can bury that piece of offal before he starts stinking up the whole fort." Mackenzie got his emotions under control and looked more like a cavalry officer. Ben found this order to bury Satank more infuriating than anything else Mackenzie had done.

"I am taking charge of the remaining prisoners. You can go back to Fort Richardson unburdened by their presence."

"There's no need. My men should rest and get some supplies, and then we will get out of your hair with the rest of the Indians."

"The prisoners will be escorted directly to Jacksboro for trial by the civil authorities—and *my* men will escort them. Return to Fort Richardson, Colonel, or go to hell. That's your choice."

"You can't do this! I'm responsible for the Indians!"

"You returned to my post, Colonel Mackenzie," Ben said coldly. "I'll deal with this problem as I see fit. I assure you, sir, the prisoners will arrive in Jacksboro to stand trial—without any further bumbling on your part." He wanted to call Mackenzie a murderer but knew he shouldn't say anything more. It would only come back to haunt him.

Ben Grierson spun and marched to the stockade to make sure that the cells were secure and ready to temporarily accept the Kiowa prisoners again until they could be transported to Texas for trial.

Without Satank.

Orders

August 15, 1871
Llano Estacado, Texas

Ben Grierson wished that he had his adjutant with him, but he knew that Woodward's talents were better employed back at Fort Sill. He rode alone in many ways, in spite of having three companies of the Tenth Cavalry with him. Nothing over the past two months had gone right. Mackenzie had killed Satank, an outright murder in Ben's eyes. The Kiowa chief had deserved such an eventual punishment, but it should have been at the hands of a judge and jury. Without any further trouble, troopers from the Tenth had escorted the Kiowa prisoners taken from Mackenzie to Jacksboro to stand trial.

Ben's teeth grated as he thought of the ease with which Satanta and Big Tree were convicted of murder, and how quickly Texas Governor Edmund J. Davis had commuted their death sentences. The Quakers and others opposing the death penalty had petitioned mightily and the governor had listened. Commuting those murderers' sentences was bad enough, but Davis had released all but a handful to rove again across Texas, plundering and killing. Why it was all right for the Kiowa to kill but not proper for the state of Texas to execute was something Ben would never fathom.

But he did not have to understand. He was a military officer who obeyed orders. Even if they were orders he neither understood nor appreciated.

In the midst of his being ordered to Fort Richardson, Alice had given birth to Mary Louisa Grierson on June 23. Alice had taken the newborn back to Jacksonville, Illinois, to show the rest of the family, delighted at having another daughter. Ben missed her and his new daughter, but was glad they were back East among family, since Sheridan had not only ordered him to Fort Richardson but had placed him under Ranald Mackenzie's command.

The few months' difference between their promotion dates made Mackenzie the senior officer-in-rank.

"I'll pay for all my sins in this life," Ben muttered as he rode. "There won't be a need for punishment in the hereafter."

It had been with ill grace that Ben had ridden to Fort Richardson with five companies of the Tenth Cavalry to receive pointless orders that kept him from real work. He had discussed the matter with Sam Woodward before leaving Fort Sill, and they had agreed that the best course of action, for the moment, was to follow Mackenzie's orders to the letter.

That didn't keep Ben from grumbling. Mackenzie had sent him patrolling westward along the Red River and into the Texas Panhandle, across the Staked Plains, in search of Kiowa and Comanche that didn't exist. If Sherman's order had been reinstated, Ben knew where to go after Indians bent on raiding settlements and robbing teamsters of their goods.

"Suh, kin we take 'nutha break? My horse, she's 'bout ready to fall down."

Ben swiped at the rivers of perspiration on his own face. The weather had been stiflingly hot and utterly dry. At night the prairie fires burned so brightly that he could read by them. During the day, simply walking presented a chore. But Mackenzie had ordered him to take his troopers onto Llano Estacado, flat, dry plains that stretched endlessly into heat haze. And when he reached that horizon, there were only limitless more plains and heat and scorpions to endure.

"Sergeant, if you can find anything bigger than a mesquite bush for shade, you have my permission to halt for one hour." Ben craned his head back and studied the burning sun overhead. A rest would do them all good, but it would be even hotter when they started again on their futile patrol.

"Thank you, suh," the man said. His black face had turned almost silver from sunlight reflecting off the sweat. The sergeant was a powerful man but he moved as if his legs had been dipped in molasses. Ben knew how he felt.

"Sergeant," Ben said, calling to the man before he could pass the word to rest. "Do you expect the scouts back any time soon?"

"Cain't rightly say, suh."

"Then we ought not make it more difficult for them to find us. Bivouac for the night."

"Suh, it's not even three yet."

"We've kept a good pace all day, Sergeant. I hope the scouts have found us some water. If not, we'll be in a world of trouble in another day."

"Yes, suh. And thank you kindly."

The noncom hurried off to give the good news to the soldiers. Ben dismounted. His horse staggered and almost collapsed from the sudden relief from carrying him. As commander, he maintained his horse in as good a condition as possible, and it was about ready to die under him.

"Suicide, Mackenzie sent us on a suicide mission. There's not an Indian within a hundred miles because they're too smart to inflict this kind of torture on themselves."

Ben found a deep arroyo cut by long forgotten rains and settled down in the dubious shade offered by one bank. As he sat, the shadows lengthened and his horse crowded closer, appreciating the shelter from the merciless sun in a cloudless blue Texas sky.

If it hadn't been for the lack of rain, this would be fine farm and ranch land, Ben decided. His mind skipped and twisted about, touching on one thought for a moment before racing off in a completely different direction. He was half asleep—or half comatose—when a scout came running up.

"Colonel, we got ourselves a problem."

"Indians?" Ben snapped awake. He tried to judge the time from the position of the sun and finally fished out his watch to see that it was past five in the afternoon. There'd be hours more of the punishing heat, but at least it wouldn't get much hotter, and the sun's rays slanted in at an angle rather than hammered down directly.

"Out here, suh?" The scout laughed harshly. "No, suh. We got ourselves some comancheros."

"What's it look like they are dealing?" he asked. Ben pulled one of the detailed maps he had been making as they rode. He had tried to find decent maps of the region before he rode out and couldn't. Taking a page out of John Frémont's book, Ben had accurately recorded their path to turn over to a mapmaker when he returned to Fort Sill. The Tenth Cavalry would have adequate maps of the Staked Plains if anyone was foolish enough to dispatch them to patrol it again.

He studied the map and saw that they had pitched their camp near the rim of caprock. Ben pointed to the map, silently ordering the scout to show where the traders in illicit merchandise were traveling.

"'Bout here, suh. Count four wagons full of 'em. Might be as many as twenty men."

"That means we've got them cut off from a lot of empty land to vanish in, and if they ran, they'd have to scramble down off the caprock. Let's mount a patrol and see what they're carrying in those wagons."

"Yes, suh."

Ben got to his feet and mounted, his horse protesting mightily. But the animal had rested enough to carry him up the side of the arroyo to where the rest of his command stirred, still sluggish from the heat.

"Captain Alvord," he called. "Bring your company along. We've found some comancheros."

"No Comanche, sir?"

Ben snorted derisively. He waited for Alvord to mount his troopers, then set the scout on the trail back to the comancheros. His heart beat a little faster as they rode. Finding Indian raiders wasn't going to happen, but he could accomplish some small feat by arresting traders in illegal goods.

The flat land worked against them. Trying to sneak up on the comancheros proved impossible, but the teamsters driving the four wagons hadn't a clear notion where they were. The comancheros tried to escape to the south, only to find themselves on the brink of a lava cliff a hundred feet high. Paths—even roads—down the side of the caprock existed, but only at wearying distances apart.

"Hold up!" shouted Ben. "Colonel Grierson, Tenth Cavalry!"

His demand brought a hail of lead. The distance was too great for accurate shooting, but the heavy slugs ripping past caused their horses to crow-hop and rear.

"Captain, take half your company and circle. Cut off any retreat. Return fire only when you can shoot accurately. I don't want to waste ammo."

"Understood, sir." Captain Alvord took two squads and began circling. The sight of the cavalry detachment cutting off retreat drove the comancheros crazy with fear. They pulled their wagons into a square, got their mules into the middle, and prepared to defend themselves as they would against Comanche attack.

Ben rode closer, then shouted, "Colonel Grierson, commanding officer, Tenth Cavalry. Put down your rifles."

"Go to hell!" The curse was followed with a shotgun blast.

Ben was too far away for the shot to reach him, but he knew these were not innocent muleteers by the way they shot at an obvious military officer. The sun might be setting, but there was no way it didn't reflect from the braid on his uniform.

Ben rode along an invisible circumference as he studied the comanchero position for weakness. The simple investigation produced a flurry of shots, none of the slugs coming close. He tried again to reason.

"Surrender. Give up and we won't hurt you."

"The sumbidch is gonna kill us dead!" shrieked a scrawny man, with a beard that looked like moss, hanging from a tree limb. He leaped up to the driver's box on the wagon he had used for protection and began firing wildly. One bullet whined past Ben close enough to make him react.

Ben lifted his pistol, waited for his horse to stop moving, then squeezed off a shot. He was luckier than he was good. The heavy slug hit the man in the middle of the belly, lifted him, and tossed him into the square of wagons, spooking the mules. The animals smelled blood and panicked, braying loudly and finding their way out of the crude corral.

Half the mules escaped before the comancheros could stop the rest. Somehow, the sight of their mules running off did more to take the fight out of the smugglers and bootleggers than the death of their partner.

"We give up. Don't go killin' us now!" A shotgun barrel with a white handkerchief attached was poked up.

Ben signaled his men to be ready but not to fire, then rode forward slowly.

"What are you boys hauling?" Ben asked conversationally, as if the gunfight had never occurred and he was meeting them for the first time. The easiness of his question brought out the answer, and he reckoned it was the truth.

"We got a whole mess of rusty rifles and ammo that don't fit none of them. The Injuns pay big wampum for it."

"Where're these Indians?" Ben asked, more interested in

tracking down Comanche and Kiowa than comancheros with only four wagons full of worthless rifles.

"Hell, Colonel, we don't know. We jist ride on across the prairie here and wait fer 'em to come to us. Not often we get as far as Fort Griffin."

"Treat these men as prisoners," Ben ordered. "And burn their wagons with the contents."

"No!" cried the comanchero who had been acting as spokesman. "We paid damn good money for these rifles!"

Ben watched as the blaze rose skyward, engulfing the wood stocks and ruining the rifle barrels. Only then did he start back for Fort Sill, sick of this pointless expedition, with a squad of soldiers to guard the comanchero prisoners.

The rest of his troopers he left in Captain Alvord's command to patrol along the north fork of the Red River.

After another two weeks of searching, they returned without sighting a single Indian. Somehow, Ben didn't feel any happier when he learned that Mackenzie had returned to Fort Richardson with the same outcome.

Time wasted. Wasted. And the real raiders ranged wider and freer than ever.

LOSS

October 30, 1871
Fort Sill, Indian Territory

Ben Grierson sat in the front room of his house, staring out the window. He felt nothing inside. The curious hollowness had dwelled within him since their daughter, Mary Louisa, had died five weeks ago. Not even three months old, and fever had claimed her soft, small life. Alice had held her as she died. That gave comfort to the child but not the mother.

Try as he might, Ben had been unable to console Alice. Robert had come from Chicago, and Charlie and Edie had been a great help, but no matter what Ben did, he could not soothe the pain Alice felt at the loss.

"She was with us only a short time," he said softly to himself, "but there must have been some purpose." The emptiness within compelled him to admit that he was not sure if he was right. Was there any purpose to a life that burned brightly and gave such joy and then was snuffed out in fever so quickly?

"What's that, Benjamin?"

"Oh, I was thinking aloud, dear," he said. He got up and went to his wife, took her in his arms and felt only stiffness. She pushed away and sat in a large chair across the room from him.

"I don't want to stay here," she said.

"Perhaps it would be a good idea to return to Chicago. You can go to the family home in Jacksonville and—"

"If I hadn't been the perfect commander's wife, Mary Louisa would still be alive."

"What? Don't be ridiculous, Alice," Ben said, somewhat too sharply.

"I entertained almost constantly. Officers' this and officers' that, celebration for the troops, band concerts, touring dignitaries, you always away on patrol. If I had paid more attention to Mary Louisa, she would still be alive and sleeping peacefully in my arms."

"Dear, Providence is not always ours to understand. No amount of care would have saved her, and she could not possibly have been loved more."

"How do I do it, Benjamin? How do I find a way to go on without fretting?" Alice slumped, her hands folded in her lap. Her words rang with bitterness, but she appeared composed and at peace with the world. This dichotomy frightened Ben.

"Know that our other children, the ones who run and laugh and bring such joy to us, are well and love you."

"I'm not a saint, but neither am I a sinner. Why must I endure such punishment on Earth?"

"Go back to your parents for a while. I shall miss you terribly, but seeing your mother and father might perk you up."

"My mother is not well," Alice said. Ben knew that Susan Kirk had, as Alice's father said, "a softening of the brain" that produced degeneration. "Perhaps I can help my father tend her."

"The children can help. They are old enough," Ben said.

"I don't want you to go, yet a return to the city and your family might be just the antidote you need."

"Fort Sill is filled with so many ghosts," Alice said. She looked up and a small smile, the first Ben had seen in a month, flickered on her lips. "If you don't mind, we shall go to Chicago for a visit."

A New Uprising

April 23, 1872
Fort Gibson, Indian Territory

Ben Grierson stared at the cold, burned skeletons of the wagon train. He thought he had become used to the death and wanton destruction the Kiowa could inflict, but they always found new ways to prove him wrong. He walked among the bodies, now laid out in a long line by the soldiers from Fort Gibson who had discovered the massacre.

Seventeen. Seventeen dead and mutilated, before they were set on fire and turned to charcoal.

"Are you sure White Horse and Big Bow were responsible?" Ben asked.

"They've been making life miserable throughout Indian Territory for the past month, sir," said Captain Carpenter. "The Creek and Choctaw all complain about having their horses stolen, and a couple of weeks ago, Big Bow tried to kidnap a Creek settler's daughter."

"What happened? I didn't see a report about any captives." Ben's nose wrinkled. Three days of being in the hot sun only added to the incredible stench of the burned bodies.

He stopped pacing when he realized the crunching sound under his boots was an arm broken from the nearest corpse.

"The Creek settler fought them off. He was pretty badly wounded, but he'll live. Echoes from this raid are going all the way east to Tahlequah and the Cherokee. You know how powerful politically they are in Washington. They're seeing this raid as a way of speaking for all the Five Civilized Tribes, whether the other four tribes like it or not."

"A grab for authority," Ben said. "Not that I blame them. If such carnage can occur within miles of Fort Gibson, their capital is certainly in danger." Tahlequah lay a mere day's ride farther east from Fort Gibson. The Cherokee had suffered badly during the war, fighting among themselves as well as choosing sides, Federal and Confederate, and had fought a four-sided battle. The aftermath of the war had brought scant healing to their sundered nation, but they maintained powerful Washington political ties. Every time Ben heard from his friend, President Grant, there was always a line or two about the Cherokee delegation visiting him and Congress, bringing new requests.

"Big Bow and White Horse are flaunting their skills, sir," Carpenter said. "They are counting coup, in a way."

"It's not counting coup when they leave so many dead." Ben sighed. At least, the worst of the Kiowa were still locked up, securely imprisoned down in Texas. Satanta and Big Tree might have had their death sentences commuted, but they were going to be in a harsh penitentiary surrounded by stone walls and iron bars for the rest of their miserable lives. That knowledge didn't make it any easier for Ben to catch the younger chiefs who wanted to outdo those rotting in prison.

"Perhaps I should have said that they were taunting us, sir."

"That's why the Tenth Cavalry was summoned from Fort Sill. Are the facilities at Fort Gibson still as pleasant as they were when I commanded the post?" Ben remembered his time stationed at Fort Gibson with some pleasure. The quarters had been decent and the expansive fort had been beautiful, an oasis in the midst of turmoil throughout the rest of the Indian Territory.

"I can't speak for prior conditions there, sir, but everything there looks mighty fine to me. After riding from Fort Sill, my company was tired, hungry, and saddle-sore. The post sutler supplied everything we needed, quick as a flash." Carpenter took a deep breath. "Sir, we have to stop that war party soon. Remember how hot and dry it was last year? From everything I've heard, we ought to expect it to be hotter and drier this year."

"The *Old Farmer's Almanac* is never wrong, is it?" Ben said, knowing Carpenter had a copy sent him every year by relatives back in New England. "It doesn't matter how hot it'll get on the prairie, Captain. We will, I repeat, we *will* find and stop Big Bow and White Horse."

"What do we do, sir? Where do we start?"

"Give me the details of the ambush," Ben said. He pictured the landscape in his mind to get an idea how Big Bow and White Horse would plan their raid and where they might run afterward.

"The first wagon train was on the San Antonio-El Paso road and was attacked at Howard's Well. The Ninth chased the Kiowa in this direction, along the Red River, until it looked as if they were heading toward Fort Gibson," Captain Carpenter said. "We were summoned at this time. While we were riding to Fort Gibson, the Kiowa attacked another wagon train, with these results." His arm swept across the countryside, showing how the teamsters had been massacred.

"North-south," Ben said, knowing the terrain intimately. "The wagon train was coming from the north, going south. That means we go west to find the culprits. The Kiowa will head in that direction and then make camp to celebrate their slaughter," Ben said. "They wouldn't continue riding toward Fort Gibson and the garrison there, nor will they attack the

Cherokee right now. And the earlier raids Big Bow made were against the Creek. They aren't as well organized, so he will feel comfortable hiding out among them."

"Yes, sir! Westward ho!" Captain Carpenter shouted orders and got the three companies of the Tenth Cavalry that had sallied forth from Fort Sill swung into motion.

Ben watched his troopers and thought of a blue boat, gently bobbing along on the brown waves of the prairie. The Kiowa couldn't graze their ponies as well this year because of the drought, and that slowed them. That meant the blue-suited soldiers would overtake the Indians quickly because Ben's soldiers had fed and watered their mounts at Fort Gibson and were ready for a protracted sortie.

They made good time across the rolling prairie, but Ben did more than depend on his far-flung scouts for information about the raiders. He studied the ground, the land ahead of his column, every detail possible that might give him a hint as to the location of the Kiowa chiefs.

"Column, halt!" he ordered. The command passed down to company commanders and then to their sergeants.

"What is it, sir?" asked Carpenter. He looked around but saw nothing.

"A squad of men," Ben said thinking aloud. "Send a squad in a wide circle to the south. Have them come back up ten miles west of our position, then return eastward toward us, alert for Kiowa. If they find Indians, they are to whoop, holler, and fire as fast as they can lever rounds into their carbines."

"Are they ahead of us, sir? The Kiowa?"

Ben shrugged. He felt it in his gut. If he was wrong, it meant nothing more than most of his soldiers got a long rest while the squad sent out cursed him for eating dust and being burned by the sun all afternoon long.

"I'll have the men prepare for a skirmish. Where do you want the men positioned, Colonel?"

"Two companies up front, another in reserve behind to cut off escape or to give support should it be necessary. Long skirmish line, men five yards apart."

"That's a mighty wide front, sir."

"I don't know where the Kiowa will run when the squad flushes them. They're camped somewhere out there." Ben stared into the bright afternoon sun, knowing how dangerous this could be. If White Horse and Big Bow were flushed in an hour or two, the soldiers would be staring into the setting sun and the Indians would have that additional advantage. But Ben also knew the Kiowa would run in front of the weak squad. They would think those troopers had come directly from Fort Sill and had a heavy reinforcement force behind them.

Ben hoped White Horse or Big Bow didn't know he had already been summoned to Fort Gibson. If they knew this small morsel of information or simply decided to stand and fight, the squad of soldiers would be dead within minutes.

Riding up and down the line, Ben cheered the newer men who had not seen battle before and swapped stories with the older ones who had been with the Tenth Cavalry for some time.

"Do we git to play our songs, suh?" asked a corporal. "I bin workin' real hard on the bugle. I reckon I kin be regimental bugler any day now."

"When we get back to Fort Sill, I'll have a competition. If you're as good as you think, might be you can get the current bugler's post. But I warn you, Private Jefferson's a mighty fine player."

"So's I, suh!"

Ben laughed and rode on. Two hours of waiting had put the men on edge and dropped the sun to the horizon. Ben had to squint as he looked due west and knew any Kiowa riding hard would be on them before they could spot their long shadows.

Again, something spurred him to action. He gave the alert to prepare for battle minutes before faint gunfire reached his ears.

As the Kiowa burst across the prairie, running before the squad he had sent, Ben felt a moment of triumph. He had outwitted two of the more clever Kiowa chiefs.

Then his soldiers trotted forward into battle. Ben's victory was tempered. White Horse and Big Bow escaped, but they left behind forty of their brothers dead or wounded.

Disharmony

July 9, 1872
Fort Gibson, Indian Territory

"How dare they!" raged Ben Grierson. He slammed his hand down on his desk, sending papers scattering in all directions. "This is an outrage."

"Sir, what's wrong?" Sam Woodward stuck his head in from the adjoining office.

"The Bureau of Indian Affairs, that's what's wrong. They want to move Satanta and Big Tree to St. Louis!"

"Well, sir, is that necessarily bad? Satanta's family has used his imprisonment as an excuse to go on the warpath. Not that they needed much of a reason. The rest of the Kiowa, no matter what Kicking Bird says, are raiding more than they are on their reservation."

"It's bad, Sam," Ben said grimly. "If they move Satanta and Big Tree away from Texas, they'll be held by guards who don't appreciate the true viciousness of their prisoners."

"There's something else eating you, Colonel. Guards aren't stupid. Not that stupid, at least," said Woodward.

"This is a ploy to move the Kiowa chiefs to a prison with

lesser security. From there they will try to get them released. I've heard that Governor Davis is already filing a petition to pardon them. Not just commute their sentences, but to pardon them. Satanta, of all people! He wants to let Satanta go free!"

"There'd be blood flowing on the prairie, sir."

"Of course there would," Ben said, settling down a little. "We have our hands full now. The Comanche are raiding on a daily basis and the Tenth Cavalry is stretched from one end of the Red River to the other. The few raiders we catch are hardly worth the effort when so many more badger the Five Civilized Tribes."

"I, uh, have the latest reports on horse thefts, sir," Woodward said, pushing the paper in Ben's direction like he might feed a caged wild animal a haunch of raw meat. He jerked back, his hand still in place as Ben snatched up the sheet.

"All the news is bad. All of it," Ben grumbled. "Alice doesn't like the quarters here. We barely got the place at Fort Sill carpeted when I was transferred back here. These quarters are adequate, but nothing more."

"She worked hard to make a home at Fort Sill, sir," Woodward said diplomatically. The lieutenant gave way as Captain Louis Carpenter came up. He saluted Ben, then stood rigidly at attention.

"What is it, Captain?"

"Sir, may I have a word with you in private?"

"You can speak freely in front of Lieutenant Woodward," Ben said.

"Sir, I'll go," Woodward quickly said. "I have several more reports to finish and recruitment quotas to go over."

Ben made a shooing gesture. He was in a dark mood. Let his junior officers do as they pleased. Satanta being transferred meant the chief would be released soon. Ben had to write a letter immediately to prevent that miscarriage of justice.

"Sir, I know I can rely on Lieutenant Woodward. He's about your best friend in the officer corps."

"What? Oh, yes, he is, Captain. And you have proven yourself over these past few months to be both competent as a field commander and a loyal friend."

"Then you'll believe me when I tell you this, sir. Major Schofield is writing the vilest things imaginable in his reports."

"He's in charge of Fort Sill now. I have no control over him any longer."

"Sir, he's blaming you for every possible blunder and misfeasance. If even half the lies he's telling are believed, you will be brought up on charges in a court-martial."

"Don't be absurd. I know the major never liked me, but why the extreme animus?"

"Sir, he's like many officers on the frontier. He's regular Army and has strong ties with general officers who similarly graduated from West Point. They see any officer, especially capable ones like yourself, who did not graduate to be parasites."

"I stand in his way to promotion, is that it?"

"It runs deeper than that, sir. Every triumph you celebrate is a defeat for those officers who feel they are better suited—and who have not achieved similar victories."

"Mackenzie," said Ben, shaking his head. "He couldn't find—never mind. There's no reason to bad-mouth fellow officers."

"General Augur, sir, is likely to listen to Schofield."

"Augur, Sheridan, they are of a kind, aren't they? All bluster and no ability."

"Take steps to protect your reputation, sir. You have valuable contacts. Letting General Sherman know of your victories is not a bad thing. And President Grant could do more to bolster your position."

"I will not go begging, hat in hand, to the President of the

United States," Ben said tartly. "I fight my own battles. The one with Major Schofield can be done by scoring victories against the Comanche and Kiowa."

"Be sure you get credit for those conquests, sir. Please consider my suggestion that you more aggressively pursue a promotion. It will be harder for men like Schofield to attack you if you are a general officer."

"Your concern is noted, Captain. Thank you. I do appreciate it. But I have a letter to write now, an important one."

"Sir!" Louis Carpenter saluted smartly and left Ben to his letter.

Ben wrote several decrying the attempts to move Satanta and eventually free him. He felt better about this after he dispatched them, but still had Alice to deal with. And perhaps Captain Carpenter was right. A star resting on his shoulders again would be tribute to his devotion to duty and hard work.

Promotion, he knew, would already have come to him if he had not commanded an all-black unit, but Ben couldn't think of a finer group of soldiers than the Tenth Cavalry.

Inauguration Promise

March 4, 1873
Washington, D.C.

"This is the grandest event I've ever attended, Pa," Charlie Grierson said, eyes wide. Ben took great pride in his eldest son's awe of the inaugural festivities. He felt he could do so little for his family at times, especially his sons, because he was so engrossed in duties with the Tenth Cavalry.

"We'll speak with the President in a few minutes," Ben said. He smoothed his formal sash and settled his ceremonial saber. A quick glance at his epaulets showed the rank of colonel. He was one of the lowest-ranking military officers in attendance. In a way, Ben could be proud of that. He had met Grant early in both their careers and had maintained a friendship over the years. So many of the general officers here sought power and nothing more. Ben preferred Ulysses Grant's friendship to wearing a star on his shoulders again.

Still . . .

"Benjamin!" boomed President Grant. He thrust out his hand and pumped Ben's. "I'm glad you could attend. From your reports, Indian Territory needs you more than ever."

"Miss your second inauguration, sir? Never!"

"We should talk later. In private. I hate this social whirl, but it is necessary. Keeping all the damned politicians from raping the South and each other is a chore."

Ben saw Charlie stiffen a little at the president's bluntness. Although they lived on the frontier, Ben—and Alice—tried to maintain civility, And Charlie had been sent to Chicago for his education, so he wasn't as used to rough-hewn ways as many other young men from the frontier might be.

"You must be the eldest Grierson boy." Grant shook his shaggy head and then smiled. "You're no boy, not any longer. You're a young man. What are your plans, Mr. Grierson?"

"I, uh, sir, it's good to meet you." Charlie glanced at his father, then back at the president. "I would dearly love to become a soldier like my pa."

"If I had a dozen more soldiers like your pa," Grant said, "there wouldn't be an Indian problem. He's one of the finest cavalry officers in the history of the United States."

Ben felt embarrassed at such praise, but Charlie basked in the admiration.

"I know, sir."

"Mr. Grierson, if it pleases your father, I'd be proud to recommend you to West Point."

"An appointment to the Academy, sir. Why, I—"

"Thank him, Charlie," Ben said.

"Sir! Thank you, Mr. President!"

"Your country thanks you—and Colonel Grierson." With that Grant drifted through the crowd, shaking hands and settling into his second term as president.

Released

October 18, 1873
Fort Sill, Indian Territory

Ben Grierson stood stiffly, trying not to utter a word during the ceremony. He had fought long and hard against this moment, and it had done him no good. The Quakers, the Bureau of Indian Affairs, and even the governor of Texas had all spoken up, making Ben's voice less than a soft whisper in a storm. Only those who had fought against Satanta and Big Tree had argued against their release. Everyone else, especially the politicians in Washington out to appease politically powerful groups, had thought it was a splendid idea.

Satanta and Big Tree had been brought by special wagon from their incarceration in St. Louis to Fort Sill prior to release. Ben considered how long his court-martial might run if he ordered the Tenth Cavalry to level their Spencers and open fire on the two Kiowa chiefs. Such a court action would be over far quicker than the time it would take for Satanta to fall dead to the ground. But it might be worth it—his life against the innocent lives Satanta would take once he rode away from the fort.

"We are pleased to offer you a full pardon," the representative from the Bureau of Indian Affairs said pompously. Ben wanted to scream, to call out that the pardon was being given, not offered in barter. Satanta would grab at any chance at freedom. The way the Bureau of Indian Affairs official put it, the government was making an entreaty to the Kiowa chief and not just releasing him after too few years in jail for his heinous crimes.

"I am guilty of nothing?" Satanta spoke, but the question hung in the air. He had figured out he would soon be allowed to ride away from the fort, but Satanta couldn't understand why the white man freed him. Ben hoped the Kiowa never figured it out.

He wasn't sure *he* had figured it out. Did they think letting Satanta go would stop the vicious raids that tore apart the entire state of Texas? Satanta had nothing to do with the Comanche or their raiding. And released, he would again assume power in the Kiowa tribe and return to his old ways.

"Your pledge of peace is your bond." The Bureau of Indian Affairs official thrust out his hand. Satanta stared at it, as if the man intended holding him while he used a knife in his left hand to stab savagely.

Big Tree chattered something in Kiowa. Satanta nodded once, then clasped the official's hand. A cheer went up among the small group of delegates sent to witness what they thought was a historic moment.

No blue-clad soldier assembled to watch let out so much as a hurrah.

"We are pledged to peace, and your freedom is the first step toward harmony throughout Indian Territory and Texas."

Satanta stepped back, an evil leer on his lips. Again, Ben forced himself not to kill the Kiowa chief. Big Tree and Satanta leaped onto horses brought by a dozen warriors and galloped off, laughing and hollering in delight at being free once again.

To rape and pillage. At will.

Support—and Nothing More

September 28, 1874
Palo Duro, Texas

"You have to admit it's been mighty quiet, sir," said Captain Carpenter. "It's given us a good chance to whip the men into shape."

Ben Grierson said nothing. The autumn afternoon breeze carried just a hint of winter. It felt good after the stifling heat of the summer spent at Fort Gibson, enduring garrison duty and doing nothing more. Every time Ben had sent out a patrol, the Kiowa and Comanche had raced south into Texas, south of the Red River and out of his jurisdiction. That had brought relative peace to the Indian Territory and had made the Cherokee happy. Even the Creek and Choctaw had settled down, after the western tribes had been run off, also by the Tenth Cavalry.

"The Osage," Captain Carpenter said, "might be moving this far south. Or the Sioux."

"Apache," Ben said automatically. "We're chasing Apache. Or rather, Colonel Mackenzie is chasing them. All we're doing is support."

"The only men we've lost in the past year have been to disease, Colonel," Carpenter said.

"We're not out here to die of garrison diseases," Ben said glumly. "And we're not out here to hold Mackenzie's coat while he dukes it out with the Indians. I want to be in there, mixing it up, giving my men field experience."

"You make it sound as if you expect real trouble, sir. The Kiowa and Comanche are making a last stand and won't be a threat in another year or two, not to Texas settlers or Mexicans or anyone else."

"I wish I shared your optimism, Louis," Ben said. "Knock down one and two pop up. We still haven't run Satanta to ground."

"Do you think he might be down in the canyon?"

"I don't know," Ben said. "I wish Major Price or Colonel Davidson would share some of their scouting reports with us."

Davidson had commanded Fort Sill since Ben had been transferred back to Fort Gibson, and the communication between the two had been, at best, cool. Mostly Ben felt cut off from everything happening both to the south and to the west.

"Our scouts say Price's men are too exhausted to fight. Mackenzie is heading down into Palo Duro Canyon, and Davidson is guarding against any Kiowa escaping along the Salt River."

Ben remembered this land all too well. He had been sent out on a wild-goose chase years earlier and had mapped much of this country. It looked strange to him now, lush green from steady rains instead of the sere brown the last time he had been here. But he wasn't in charge of the attack and had been told to do nothing more than "support Colonel Mackenzie." That could mean anything—or nothing.

"How many trails down into the canyon are there?" Ben asked suddenly. "There are two full battalions in the field. That's more than enough to not only guard the canyon rim but to descend to the canyon floor."

"Colonel, your orders don't include going down with Mackenzie," warned Carpenter.

Ben smiled, then brushed at his thick black beard.

"You have misconstrued the orders, Captain," Ben said. "How can we possibly support Mackenzie if we are up here and he is down there?" Ben pointed into the distance. The level land seemed to stretch forever, but both Carpenter and Ben knew that wasn't true. Palo Duro Canyon was cut through the caprock and was deceptive. A rider had to be almost at the brink before even realizing a deep, vast canyon with sheer red walls cut through the flat lands.

"General Sheridan will have your head if anything goes wrong, sir." Carpenter laughed a bit ruefully. "Then again, he'll probably do the same if the battle goes well."

"I either let Mackenzie get in too deep or I'm trying to grab the glory. Neither explanation matters to me, Louis. We're here to fight Indians. Prepare the men for the descent, Captain."

Ben's mind raced. There were dozens of trails down the face of the canyon. If they made good time, two companies of the Tenth Cavalry could be on the canyon floor and in conflict with the Kiowa before sunset. He checked his pistol, then thrust it back into his holster. It had been too long since he had been in combat, although they had brought nothing but glory to themselves at the Wichita Agency.

Seeing Carpenter's signal, Ben raised his gloved hand, then lowered it, giving the silent order to descend. The trail was narrow and rocky, but his soldiers were well trained. Ben found his own route down, leading a squad to reach the bottom of the canyon at the same time as Captain Carpenter and his advance element. They joined forces again. Then Ben led the way to the river. He wondered if Mackenzie had already gotten his soldiers into position or if Ben would find himself in the position of attacking first.

That would force Mackenzie to support his Tenth Cavalry instead of Ben supporting the Fourth. Ben knew he would be boiled in oil in such a case, but it would be worth it if he recaptured or killed Satanta.

"Gunshots, sir!" came Carpenter's call from the far right flank.

"Forward, trot!" ordered Ben. His troopers picked up the pace and rounded a bend in the deep canyon to see a vast Kiowa village. Half the lodges burned and chaos reigned as women and children ran about, screaming in pain and shouting curses.

"Sir, there must be a thousand lodges," Carpenter said. "What should we do?"

"Engage the warriors!" cried Ben. "Cut off any escape in this direction and let Colonel Mackenzie prosecute the battle according to his plan."

Ben had no idea if Ranald Mackenzie even had a plan, but he deployed the two companies he had brought down to the canyon floor in a skirmish line and immediately engaged dozens of Kiowa warriors. In the twilight, foot-long tongues of flame leaped from rifles, and ahead of each muzzle ran a deadly bullet.

The fight continued well into the night, but the canyon was lit as bright as day by the burning Indian lodges. Better than an hour passed before the last of the Kiowa had been taken prisoner or run off.

It was a decisive blow to the Kiowa—but Satanta was nowhere to be found.

Transfer to Hell

November 3, 1874
Fort Concho, Texas

"I had expected more, sir," said Lieutenant Woodward.
He shivered although the day was warm and the light snow
from the storm two days earlier had melted.

"That's Fort Concho," Ben Grierson affirmed. He and his
adjutant had finished an informal tour of the fort perimeter.
They had arrived two days earlier and the men were settling
in as well as could be expected in the primitive quarters. "I
have some trepidation about this transfer, too, Sam, but
Sherry-dan might have done us a favor."

"Not much of one, sir," mumbled Woodward. "This place
isn't as good as an outhouse at Fort Gibson. I'd rather be stationed in a privy than here."

"It will improve. We'll see to that," Ben said, but he
shared his adjutant's opinion. Even after the Tenth Cavalry
had moved men and supplies into the ramshackle buildings,
Fort Concho looked more deserted than active. The troopers
who had been stationed here were gone for long weeks, but
the skeleton crew should have maintained it better. Weeds

grew on the parade ground. If he didn't have enough punishment details to police the yards, a week of close-order drill would trample the unwanted plants. This set Ben to thinking along more productive lines.

A few days of band practice might stir everyone's spirits. If it didn't, Ben knew he had a long, hard winter ahead of him.

"Sir, the Kiowa are nigh on defeated. The Comanche aren't kicking up the fuss they were. Is the Tenth Cavalry better off here than in Indian Territory?"

"Garrison duty in Indian Territory would be more pleasant, that I will agree," Ben said, "but I share the general's belief that this entire region is going to explode soon. You've heard the trouble Colonel Hatch is having with the Ninth in New Mexico Territory?"

"Of course I have, sir. The Apache are not taking kindly to being put on reservations."

"San Carlos sounds like a prison rather than a place for a man used to hunting as a livelihood. The unrest on the Mescalero Reservation is only the beginning. It will spill over into Texas." Ben considered the miserable fort. "It'll be here before we know it."

"Sir, we have unrest in our own backyard, and it has nothing to do with Indians."

"What happened now?" Ben almost didn't want to hear. Deciding how to improve Fort Concho was easier to deal with than what he knew Woodward was going to say.

"A dozen troopers were granted leave in town, sir. They were denied entry to the saloons."

"That's not a problem," Ben said. He knew his teetotaller opinions were not shared by everyone in his command, but being barred from a gin mill was nothing he would concern himself over.

"Sir, it is. Nobody in Saint Angela's willing to have anything to do with a black soldier. Worse, they make it appar-

ent the combination of black and in Union uniform will not
be tolerated. Two of the men were attacked by children
throwing stones."

"Any assault from the adults? I know Saint Angela is not
the most enlightened city in the state, but they are going to
accept my soldiers or I'll know the reason."

"You already know the reason, Colonel," Woodward said.
"The State Police is mostly black. Nobody in Saint Angela
has much truck with them. And I doubt there's a single man
in the county, much less the town, who doesn't have Confederate leanings. Reconstruction has not treated them fairly
or well."

"I will not allow them to abuse my soldiers. The War
Between the States is over, and we have new enemies. The
Kiowa might not be raiding on a daily schedule any longer,
but they are still a threat."

"And you said the Apache are a growing danger, sir, yes,
I know. But we have to deal with this. What should we do?
Cancel all leave?"

"No," Ben said slowly, considering the problem. "Soldiers
of the Tenth Cavalry will be well behaved. That is a standing
order. However, inform the town fathers that unless our
troopers are respected and served promptly and honestly by
businesses in town, I will approve leave, one entire company
at a time, and insist that the men not wear uniforms. Do you
catch my meaning, Sam?"

"Yes, Ben, I do."

Ben fumed. He had Fort Concho to rebuild, men to ac-
quaint with new territory, an increasing threat from an enemy
whose tactics might be different from those of the plains
Indians, and on top of it all the townspeople the Tenth Cavalry
was entrusted to defend were bigots. He couldn't change
that, but he could stop the overt discrimination. Allowing entire companies leave all at the same time insured no single
soldier would be attacked and ordering the leave to be in

civilian clothing sent the message that no military action would be taken should those soldiers retaliate. A hundred blacks descending on Saint Angela would force a change in behavior. Or else.

Ben turned back to planning the fort's renovation.

Family—At Last

September 5, 1875
Fort Concho, Texas

"I'm so glad to see you again, dear," Ben Grierson greeted. He looked around and didn't see any of his soldiers, so he hugged his wife. Such public displays were improper, but it had been so long since he had seen Alice that he could hardly restrain himself. "I've been working hard to get decent quarters built for you and the children."

"This place is as desolate as you wrote," Alice said. She appeared gaunt and drawn, as if the last year of separation had been harder on her than it had on him. She had spent much of the time in Chicago and Jacksonville with family.

"Bring the children along. I'll give you a quick tour of the post," Ben said. "Unless you're too tired from the trip. How was it?"

"Tiring," she said, smiling wanly. "It's good to be with you again, Benjamin. The life of an officer's wife is not an easy one."

"I know," he said. She had endured so many tribulations

alone. Her father had died a few months after her mother. Both deaths had chipped away at Alice's resolve and good nature. Her brothers and sister were hardly fit company at times, but they were family. At Fort Concho she was hundreds of miles from them and isolated from old friends, save by exchange of the occasional letter.

"How long will you be on the post before you go out on patrol?" she asked.

Ben sighed. "I've let my junior officers take on that chore. You know I've never appreciated horses, but signing reports written by Sam and checking requisitions to be sure we get everything we're supposed to is such boring work."

"You want to be in the field again," Alice said. The tiredness in her voice was more evident now.

"I won't go for some time, dear. I promise. Why, just today General Sheridan ordered me out to the Staked Plains again. He knows the precise spot where there are no Indians and insists on sending my soldiers there to squander their time. I see no reason to waste my personal time leading the patrol when it can give my junior officers a chance to see how their troops act in the saddle."

"You said the local ranchers are warming to your troopers?"

"We've stopped cattle rustling for miles and miles," Ben said. "A little of it was done by Indians. The majority was caused by white rustlers. Saving cattle and horses has improved relations with the locals."

"We drove through Saint Angela on the way here. What a . . . small town," Alice finished lamely.

Ben had to laugh. Saint Angela had potential. Lots of potential. One day it would begin to grow and thrive, but when was a matter of much discussion by the local government.

"They think renaming it San Angelo will help bring in more settlers," Ben said. "They argue endlessly over that and a dozen other insignificant matters. What will help most is for the Tenth Cavalry to stop all Indian raids and cattle theft. We've put an end to vigilante justice and the local settlers— almost—accept the State Police authority."

"That officer coming toward us at such a brisk pace. That's Captain Carpenter, isn't it?" asked Alice. "He certainly wants to speak with you, Benjamin."

"I'm afraid so. I'll dispatch him quickly. He's a good man, one of the best I have in my command."

"Colonel," Carpenter said brusquely, throwing a salute in Ben's direction. "Mrs. Grierson. I trust you had a safe trip."

"I did, Captain. Thank you. Why don't you speak with the colonel? I'll get an orderly to take us to our quarters."

"Can't this wait, Captain?" asked Ben, exasperated. He saw Alice's condition and wanted her to know he could care for her.

"General Sheridan has ordered half of the Tenth out into the Staked Plains."

"Half?" Ben's eyebrows arched in surprise. "Why so many? There aren't any Kiowa there anymore."

"Mapping, sir. That's what he said in his directive. He wants detailed maps."

"I made them myself years ago. Oh, bother." Ben threw up his hands. "Dear, go on to the house. I'll send a reply to General Sheridan and get this straightened out. We can't send six companies into the Staked Plains without jeopardizing patrol strength elsewhere."

"And putting Fort Concho at some risk from attack, Colonel," Carpenter added.

Ben saw that Alice and the children were taken care of by a small squad of orderlies under the command of his striker and then went to his office to pen a response to Sheridan's inane command. The Apache, be they Lipan or Mescalero, were a growing threat. Sending so many soldiers from the Tenth Cavalry into the Llano Estacado meant exposing the belly of central Texas to attack. Worse, he might lose most of his command to this foolish expedition if they were caught in a blizzard.

He could cope with the big problems. The little annoyances nibbled away at his patience.

Loved and Hated

July 30, 1876
South of Fort Concho, Texas

"We've found their camp, sir," said Captain Carpenter. "A whale of a lot of them, too. Might be as many as twenty braves. That's the most we've seen in one band for more than three months."

Ben nodded, shifted in the saddle, and wanted to rub his behind. That would be undignified in front of his troopers, so he simply rose in the stirrups, as if he peered into the heat-hazy distance.

"There's no question about them being the cattle thieves, either," Carpenter went on. "Scouting reports are accurate. They have more than fifty head penned up, waiting to be driven south."

"Are they Lipan Apache or Kickapoo?" Ben asked. It really didn't matter to him what tribe the cattle rustlers belonged to, but he needed it for his report to General Ord in San Antonio. Ord had transferred in recently and made little secret of his friendship with Phillip Sheridan or their shared ideas about how best to enforce peace on the frontier. Even worse, Ord had openly stated that he saw no reason for black soldiers to go on patrol and that they were best kept around for garrison duty and little else.

Ben felt he had to continually prove the courage and fighting skill of the Tenth Cavalry. The letters he had exchanged with his old friend Edward Hatch showed he was not the only one bearing the onus of buffalo soldiers in his command. Colonel Hatch and his Ninth Cavalry fought against overwhelming odds in New Mexico Territory and, had it not been for several brilliant skirmishes, the Apache would have boiled out of that area and throughout western Texas long ago.

But a bottle could stay corked only so long. Ben had to convince General Ord of this and get permission to chase down even the smallest band of Indians, no matter their tribe, and snuff out the raiders before an uncontrollable whirlwind swept through the entire state.

"From their paint, they're probably Lipan, sir," said Carpenter. "Don't hold me to that. We might find they come from several tribes."

"Oh?" Ben's mind was still focused five hundred miles away at General Ord's headquarters.

"We're seeing Arapaho joining bands of Lipan and Kiowa—strange bedfellows, I know, sir, but we've done well keeping them disorganized and on the run."

"They're camped on the tributary to the Trinity?" asked Ben. He wasn't as familiar with this territory as he was the land farther west. This was grassland, more like Indian Territory and even Illinois than the drier regions toward El Paso.

"We're ready for them, Colonel."

Ben saw that Carpenter had positioned the men well. Company H had already lit out, riding like fools in the hot sun, to circle far to the south and cut off escape. Neither Ben nor the captain thought the Indians would fight when running was easier and safer. These braves might wear war paint, but they were hardly more than common thieves after being stripped of their fiercest leaders. Satanta had surrendered on the Arapaho Reservation and had been sent to Fort Marion in Florida. Satank had been killed by Mackenzie. Kicking Bird was old, and the other Kiowa war chiefs were scattered and led only small bands of poorly armed warriors.

These cow thieves would not fight.

Captain Carpenter pulled out his pocket watch, flipped open the lid, and studied the face for a moment. Then he squinted up into the sun.

"It's time, sir."

Ben nodded assent. Carpenter passed the orders down the line and the troopers remaining in his command moved forward slowly, deliberately. Ben heard nervous muttering among those who had not been in a battle before, but they were few and interspersed among the veterans. What bothered him more was the repeated sound of the short-barreled carbines being cocked. The metallic noise carried on the still air and echoed like a drum beat.

Then he relaxed a mite. These weren't warriors he faced. They might not even have sentries posted.

And they didn't.

Carpenter's company trotted in formation into the camp before the Kiowa even noticed they weren't alone. The lowing of the cattle and a couple of bottles of whiskey lulled the Indians into believing all was well until it was too late.

"Surrender!" bellowed Captain Carpenter. Men in his company fired as the Kiowa reached for their rifles and pistols. And then all hell broke loose.

Ben found a target, fired, and fired again. By the time the wounded brave had thrown down his pistol and held up his uninjured hand, the skirmish was at an end.

"Four captured, sir. One dead, the rest fleeing. I'm sure Nolan's Company A will capture a few more of them."

"Well done, Captain," Ben congratulated. "We've recovered fifty head of cattle. Let's drive them back to their owners."

"Not too far this time, sir," Carpenter said. "The Rolling J is only a few miles to the east."

With their prisoners in tow, the company herded the cattle back to a grateful rancher.

"Surely do appreciate this, Colonel Grierson," Jerome Jensen said, taking off his hat and beating some of the dust off it. "Did you have to chase them varmints far?"

"Not far, Mr. Jensen," Ben said.

"For all the trouble they're causin', you kin chase 'em all the way into Mexico, for all I care."

"I wish we were permitted to do so, sir," Ben said.

"How's that? You mean you cain't go after them Injuns if 'n they cross the Rio Grande?"

"General Ord doesn't believe black soldiers should be stationed along the border, fearing the Mexicans wouldn't like it."

"That's the dumbest thang I ever heard," Jensen said.

"I agree. Why don't you let it be known that we could retrieve far more beeves if we could pursue wherever the thieves run, even into Mexico?"

"What do we care 'bout them Meskins, anyway? We done fought our way free of 'em before."

"I trust you'll get a good price for your cattle, Mr. Jensen," Ben said, not wanting to get too deeply involved in the politics of the matter. He was a soldier and obeyed orders, even if they were foolish ones. The Mexican government wouldn't get any more upset over a company of buffalo soldiers entering their country in hot pursuit of a cattle rustler than it would if the U.S. soldier was white.

But Ord thought so. General Sheridan did, too.

That meant the Tenth Cavalry had to work all the harder to show they were wrong.

Pursuit to the Limit— and Beyond

January 27, 1877
West Texas

"Make sure the men have enough water," Ben Grierson ordered.

"The scouts found a spring, Colonel," called Sam Woodward. "We've got enough sweet water to fill all our canteens."

"Fill the water barrels in the supply wagons, too," Ben said. "This is going to be a long campaign."

He watched as Woodward sent four of the supply wagons off the main road and into the foothills of the Davis Mountains. For more than a week, four companies of the Tenth Cavalry had sallied forth from Fort Concho searching for Mescalero Apache. A dozen raids had been reported, many of them perpetrated by Apache slipping away from their reservations in Arizona and New Mexico.

"Captain Carpenter," Ben called. "Continue along the road. The supply wagons can catch up."

"What's the hurry, sir?" asked Carpenter.

Ben looked at the dusty, winding double-rutted road meandering along through the desert in the mountainous foothills. Over those mountains lay the Rio Grande River and Mexico. Twice Ben had been forced to allow Indians to escape because of General Ord's standing orders for the black soldiers in his command to remain well away from the Mexicans.

"Because they don't like blacks," grumbled Ben.

"Sir? What's that?" asked Carpenter.

"Where's the Butterfield stage?" Ben asked. "It was due more than an hour ago."

"There might be all kinds of reasons, Colonel," Carpenter said. "The stage might have broken down or the driver could be taking his time. The road's nothing but chuckholes."

The San Antonio-El Paso road was vital to both the military and to the mail shipments carried by the Butterfield Stage Company. Supply trains were the primary target of Indian raiders, but the Indians weren't above shooting up a stage carrying mail, scalping everyone inside, and then stealing the horses. Somehow, the mail was always lost.

The few forts along the road were ill maintained and not properly staffed, forcing Ben to bring his soldiers from Fort Concho. If Ord had any sense, he would put all the West Texas forts under Ben's command, allowing the Tenth Cavalry to patrol the region properly. Ben took a deep breath. Wanting Ord to show common sense was like asking for the sun, the moon, and all the stars.

"Let's find the reason for the departure from schedule, Captain," Ben said. "If they've broken an axle or had some other breakdown, we can help. The Butterfield stations are only ten or twelve miles apart. We could even fetch fresh teams for the stage, should that be a problem."

"You're thinking there's another reason, aren't you, sir?" asked Carpenter. "Apache?"

"Colonel Hatch said another band had sneaked away from the Mescalero Reservation. There's no good evidence they headed this way, but two other parties have, as if they are gathering in this area."

"I've heard Nana and his band of Warm Springs Apache sometimes winter down around San Antonio," Carpenter said.

"Nana," said Ben, letting the name roll off his tongue. Nana was older than Kicking Bird and ten times as vicious. And Nana wasn't even chief of the Warm Springs Apache. A firebrand named Victorio had escaped the reservation twice, massacring soldiers both times.

Ben rode at the head of the column, eyes scanning the desolate land for any sign of life. Here and there a rabbit poked up to soak up the weak winter sun and watch the soldiers ride past before ducking back into his hole. The roadbed itself was undisturbed, showing that no stage had passed recently.

He looked to the top of a distant rise and saw one of his scouts waving frantically. Ben knew better than to question any of his scouts' conclusions. If one was this eager for the entire column to approach, the need was serious and immediate.

"Column, trot!" Ben called. The order rippled back through the soldiers and the dust cloud they kicked up was enough to warn an army of their approach. As Ben topped the rise and pulled up even with his scout, he saw the problem.

"Mescalero Apache, suh," the scout said. "Fifteen to twenty of 'em and they's goin' aftah that stage!"

"Column, full gallop!" Ben shouted. He led the attack down the far side of the hill to stop the Apache from killing everyone in the stage.

From what he could tell, the driver was already dead, but the shotgun messenger fired methodically, trying to conserve his ammunition and to keep the Indians at bay at the same time.

"First ranks, fire at will!" Ben called. He knew his men

were well trained. The soldiers at the back of the column wouldn't try to fire past their comrades. Already the sergeants were splitting squads off to form a large skirmish line, each half protecting the other as they advanced into the fray.

Ben whipped out his pistol and singled out a Mescalero, emptying the cylinder at his target. He doubted he hit the brave, but did keep him from killing the stagecoach guard. As Ben pulled up to get his second six-shooter from his saddlebags, the column swept past him, rifles blazing.

Even a disciplined army could not have stood longer than a few minutes against such an onslaught. As part of his men attacked, the rest watched and waited, ready to pursue when they saw any of the Apache making a break.

"Sergeant," he called to a grizzled, gray-haired noncom, "stay with the stagecoach and render what aid you can until Lieutenant Woodward arrives."

"Suh, yes, suh!"

Ben stuffed his emptied six-gun into his holster and hefted the loaded second one. He looked for a new target, but the Apache had already fled, whooping and hollering as they raced due west.

"Can they reach the border going in that direction?" Ben snapped at his scout.

"Purty much, they kin," the scout shouted to him. "Gotta cross the rivah if they wanta git to Mexico."

"Full pursuit, Captain!" Ben ordered Carpenter. "Don't let them get to the Rio Grande or into Mexico."

Captain Carpenter formed his company and took out after the Apache. Ben hung back and saw that the passengers were injured but alive. The only death had been that of the driver. He put his spurs to his horse's flanks and raced after Company M.

The Apache had the advantage of riding, every man for himself. But the Tenth Cavalry had chased enough raiders to know how to handle this. Rather than split their forces and end up being picked off one by one, no element smaller than a squad ever rode after any fugitive. Better to let most of the raiders vanish into the mountains than to lose any blue-coated soldiers.

Ben knew his tactic had worked out well enough before to keep the Kiowa and Comanche bands fragmented. Often, all it took was the arrest of two or three in a raiding party to put the fear of the cavalry's power into the rest.

Head down, determined, Ben caught up with the rest of the company and saw they followed the main body of raiders through a narrow mountain pass. Captain Carpenter was clever enough to know that they couldn't run their horses for long and changed gait constantly, letting the horses rest as they walked, then cantering or even galloping for a short distance.

The cavalry had the advantage of keeping up. The Apache had to evade them. In the narrow canyon and wider plain leading down to the Rio Grande beyond, this was difficult since the Indians were never out of sight of their pursuers. A shot from a scout now and then told Ben that his soldiers were keeping the pressure on the Apache.

"Sir, they've reached the riverbank. The range is too far for any hope of shooting them."

Ben caught up with Carpenter and saw the Indians frantically splashing across the shallow Rio Grande. In midwinter the current was greatly reduced from what it would be in only a few months. He cursed his bad luck that the Apache had found this ford at perhaps the lowest point in the river's flow.

"After them," Ben said.

"Sir, General Ord has ordered us not to—"

"Captain, I don't know how you could have made such a grievous error."

"Sir?" Carpenter looked from his commander to the escaping Apache. "I don't understand."

"That's not the Rio Grande. It's some other river. Some other river inside the United States. Now get after those raiders!"

Carpenter didn't argue. He worked his men down the slope to the broad bank of the river and hastily found the spot where the Apache had crossed. Ben followed, making certain all his junior officers understood their orders. None of them believed this to be anything other than the Rio Grande—and they were right.

But Ben had been pushed too far. Let the Mexicans complain to Ord that the Tenth Cavalry was keeping bloodthirsty killers out of their country.

The Apache reached the far side of the river in what they thought was a safe haven. Company M captured eight of them just after sundown and returned to the U.S. before midnight.

Black Horse

May 4, 1877
West Texas

Ben Grierson brushed dust off his uniform jacket, then sneezed as the brown cloud rose to catch in his beard and tickle his nose. He felt as if he had become part of his horse, permanently connected at his aching behind. For more than a week, he and two companies of the Tenth Cavalry had been in the field chasing after a Comanche raider. Since his capture of the off-reservation Apache in January, that group had been mighty quiet—in Texas. He got a weekly torrent of reports from Edward Hatch showing the pressure mounting on the San Carlos Reservation in Arizona again, but for the moment the Apache were his problem, not Ben's.

Ben still had the gut feeling that would change, but now his goal was stopping the Comanche from their new round of raids.

He hefted his binoculars and peered out into the distance. A curious combination of dust and haze from humidity hung in the air, obscuring his view beyond a couple of miles. How it could be so dry yet the air could hold mist was beyond him. The blue grama provided good forage for his soldiers' horses and for the Comanche. But he ignored the tall grass and focused on two riders slowly making their way west. Ben couldn't make out details in the haze because of the distance, but he saw the way they rode.

Comanche.

There was an easy joining of human to horse that was unmatched by anyone else, even other Indians. He could believe the Comanche boasts of riding a hundred miles in a day and then fighting fiercely. More than once the Comanche had simply outlegged his troopers, and not because his men rode inferior mounts.

"Did you spot them, too, Colonel?" asked Captain Carpenter. "A pair of Comanche braves."

"Heading west but not hurrying. Does that mean they're far from their camp or something else?"

"Scouting reports say that Black Horse is in the area. They might be scouts returning to report to him."

"Why ride slowly?" mused Ben. "That means whatever they found doesn't require immediate action."

"There's a wagon train making its way along the road, but it won't be here until tomorrow."

"That's what they want," Ben decided. "Supplies. Is there any ammunition or firearms in the shipment?"

"Only food, sir," Carpenter said. "It's our monthly supply going from Fort Griffin to Fort Quitman."

"Have the scouts found any spot along the route where Black Horse is most likely to attack?"

"Possibly, sir. There's a spring out yonder, about where we spotted the two Comanche. Water's not too good, a bit alkali, but still drinkable if you've got a big thirst."

"The wagon train's mules will be mighty dry. Come with me and bring a half-dozen scouts. I want to find appropriate cover for an ambush."

*   *   *

Ben Grierson was a man of action. Waiting in ambush wore heavily on him. He lay on his back, staring through the branches of a cottonwood, trying to make out the patterns of stars in the night sky. Locusts made some noise, but the wind soughing through the green leaves provided most of the soft, night-filling turbulence. His soldiers waited more quietly and patiently than he ever could.

Running down Black Horse was a fool's errand. Better to let the Comanche chief come to him for the fight.

Apache never fought at night, or so said Colonel Hatch. The best reason he could determine was their intense fear of rattlesnakes. But Ben had never found such behavior in the Comanche or other tribes. Night was as good a time for fighting as brightly lit noon.

He perked up when he heard the distant clank of chains and the creak of leather harness. Quickly following the first faint sounds were the brays from tired, hungry, thirsty mules. The wagon train had arrived.

Ben wondered if the Comanche were also laying in wait, neither soldiers nor braves knowing the other was already hiding.

He slid his six-shooter from its holster and put his thumb on the hammer. Ben knew better than to cock the pistol yet. The metallic sound carried in still night air and would warn any nearby Comanche.

The sounds of the wagon train grew louder, and Ben's heart beat faster. His senses magnified every smell, every small movement in the shadows, each sound. He swung around, squinted, and tried to make out who moved in a clump of mesquite at the top of a rise ten yards away. Carpenter had not placed any troopers there.

A shadow moved through deeper shadow, then momentarily came out in contrast against the starlit night sky. A Comanche.

Ben didn't like horses, but wished he was still mounted. But this fight had to be done on the ground, not racing across the prairie. Pursuit at night was always dangerous, and in this prairie dotted with animal burrows, he would lose both men and horses.

The cursing teamsters rattled to a halt a hundred feet away at the watering hole. A few fumbled in the backs of their wagons, hunting for bottles of whiskey. Ben wanted to warn them away from the fierce liquor. It would dull their response to the Comanche and deaden their souls.

Then he worried more about staying alive.

From the mesquite bush on the hilltop came four dark shapes moving like wolves in a pack. He waited a moment, then stood, braced his right arm against the cottonwood trunk, and fired.

The clear air began to fill with choking white billows of gun smoke.

"Attack! Charge!" Ben yelled. Crouching, he began methodically firing in the direction of the darting figures in the night.

"Charge!" he repeated, this time leading the attack. A dozen soldiers joined him. Ben reached the top of the hill and looked down on a small knot of Comanche milling about in confusion.

Ben started firing as he walked downhill, ignoring the surge of battle around him until a warrior yanked out a knife and slashed at him. Throwing up his gun arm blocked the thrust that would have ended his life.

He winced as blood flowed along his forearm, then ignored the pain and began fighting back, his life in the balance. Reaching out, Ben grabbed a sinewy throat with his left hand and squeezed. The Comanche twisted and thrashed about, then used his knee against Ben's belly to force himself back. As the Indian stumbled away, Ben lifted his pistol and fired.

This time he knew his target was dead.

"He's gettin' 'way!" shouted a soldier. "Thass him! Black Horse!"

Ben lifted his pistol and fired until the hammer fell with a dull metallic click on a spent chamber. Ben silently cursed his bad luck, although the weapon didn't have the range needed to bring down the escaping Comanche chief. But the rifles of his soldiers did. Ben wasn't sure which of the four privates who opened fire on Black Horse shot the chief from horseback, but one did.

Black Horse lay sprawled on the ground, dead. Ben was experienced enough to know Comanche raiding in West Texas wouldn't stop because of one chief's death, but it would slow.

And it did.

The New Pioneer Corps

February 14, 1878
Fort Concho, Texas

"Sir, I apologize," Captain Carpenter said. Beside him Lieutenant Woodward stood rigidly at attention.

"Colonel, I apologize, also. It was our fault the Apache got away." Sam Woodward looked as pale and drawn as if he had just stepped from his own grave. He tried to keep his hands from shaking as he held them at his side, but Ben saw.

"Are you ill, Sam? Did you pick up a touch of the fever?"

"N-no, sir."

"I court-martialed three officers in December. Captain Nolan went out on the Staked Plains and contrived to lose the lives of four fine troopers due to his negligence in providing food and water. He lost twenty-five horses and four mules, which we sorely needed. Along with him I court-martialed a sergeant, two corporals, and two privates for their foolish, unmilitary behavior."

"Yes, sir, we understand," Carpenter said. "Should we report to the guardhouse?"

"No!" raged Ben. "I court-martialed Nolan because he was a fool. He had no business being in this command or any other, not the way he blundered about with no thought to his men's well-being."

"We haven't caught a single Apache or Comanche in a month, sir," spoke up Woodward. "That's not acceptable."

Ben heaved a deep sigh and tried to calm down. These were his best officers and his closest friends, but he would have court-martialed them had their actions risen to the level of criminality Nicholas Nolan's had.

"You haven't lost a single soldier, either of you. Have you?"

"That's because we've failed to engage the enemy, sir."

"Do you consider me as guilty?" Ben asked. Both men jumped as if he had stuck them with pins.

"Of course not, sir," said Woodward. "It's not your fault we haven't caught any raiders."

"I must disagree," Ben said. "I am in command. Wait!" He held up his hand to silence both men. "I obviously have not laid out a proper battle plan if you cannot engage the Comanche or Apache." Ben rocked back in his chair, thinking hard. "We must develop a new strategy. The enemy we fight is mobile, fierce, and has nothing to lose, choosing death over return to the reservation. That means how we fight must change."

"How, sir?" asked Carpenter.

"They can hide from us. They know West Texas better than we do, in spite of a couple years of patrolling the region. That must change."

"More patrols, sir?" asked Woodward.

"Better mapping. I want every patrol to create maps showing watering holes, possible hiding places, roads, mountains, caves, anything that might be of use to the Indians—and us."

"We can do that, sir," said Woodward.

"How can we respond with greater speed, sir?" asked Carpenter. "We get news of Comanche raids days after they've occurred. By the time we mount a patrol and get to the spot, the Indians have a four- or five-day head start."

"Sam," Ben said to his adjutant, "do you remember the raid through Mississippi?"

"Yes, sir."

"The Pioneer Corps was the first real use of the blacks who wanted to help. They built roads, bridges, put back destroyed telegraph wires. I propose using the Tenth Cavalry for the same purpose."

"Road building, sir?" asked Carpenter. "I don't understand."

"Better roads mean we can travel faster when there's trouble. Better telegraph communication can speed us to the site of attack, cutting hours or even days off our response time. We might save lives instead of arriving so late all we can do is bury the victims."

"It'll be better if we can stop the Indians responsible," said Woodward. "The men will grumble about this, sir. It's bad enough being rousted out of a sound sleep for a long ride in the dark, but to go on patrol and do road work . . ."

"Make sure they take their musical instruments," Ben said. "Let them write songs complaining about their commanders."

Woodward had to smile. "They like you, sir."

"I know," Ben said. He had been better liked by his troopers than by his officers, and that dichotomy didn't bother him in the least. Much of the hatred by his fellow officers stemmed from him not being regular Army, from ambition, from the few command positions open—and from outright politics. Ben was not a vindictive man, but if he could send one officer to burn in hell, Phillip Sheridan would never again have to ask for a match to light his smelly cigars.

"We'll put your orders into effect immediately, sir," said Carpenter.

"Wait, both of you. You're good officers. This new scheme

is going to work, but I fear harder times are ahead. We'll need good roads for supply and for rapid deployment of our troopers."

"Is it something Colonel Hatch reported, sir?" asked Woodward.

Ben nodded, not trusting himself to explain further. To meet the new threat, the Tenth Cavalry was going to have to learn to ride farther and faster, and fight harder. And they were already trail-hardened veterans of long years of Indian fighting.

Typhoid

September 9, 1878
Fort Concho, Texas

Ben Grierson tried to take Alice in his arms, but she forced herself away as she had too many time before—and for the same reason. She looked at him with hollow, frightened eyes and held him at arm's length.

"She's dying, Benjamin," Alice said. "Do something."

Ben felt as helpless as a newborn babe. He sent hundreds of men ranging throughout West Texas to preserve life—and those stalwart men of the Tenth Cavalry obeyed without question. He held life and death in his hands.

This time, he could not grant life to his own daughter.

"I wish there was something I could do, Alice," he said. "Edie is in God's hands. The post physician has tended her with all the medicines we have. I even sent a scout out to barter with a Comanche medicine man to see if there was something else we could give her." Edith Clare had been unable to hold down food and liquids for days now. Steadily weakening from the fever, she was a mere wisp of her bright, cheery self.

"There has to be something more," Alice insisted. "She's my only daughter. Mary Louisa lived for such a short time. Edie can't be taken from us. Not now. Please, please." Alice broke down crying. This time she let Ben hold her. He felt the dampness from her tears soak into his wool uniform jacket.

"Be glad there's Charlie and Robert and Georgie," he began. Even as he called the roll of his surviving children, he knew what Alice would say.

"Kirkie died, too. Mary Louisa and Kirkie and now Edie. She lasted for thirteen years, Benjamin. We only had her for thirteen short years."

Ben fought for the words that would soothe his wife. Too many times he had agonized over the letters to wives and mothers of dead troopers. Some of those letters conveyed his regret, while others seemed devoid of emotion. He never figured out the difference and how to erase it. Each and every man in his command was important to him.

But not as important as his only daughter, and he couldn't find the right words to ease his wife's sorrow. Ben felt tears welling in his own eyes. Helpless. He was so helpless.

"Colonel?" The post physician came from the small bedroom where they had isolated Edie. "I'm sorry. There was nothing more to do. She died peacefully." The doctor fished into his pocket and peered at his watch. "Eight o'clock will be the official time of death." He snapped shut the case, closed his bag and left the Griersons to their sorrow.

Edith Clare Grierson was buried in the civilian cemetery outside the fort. Georgie helped Ben build a low rock wall around the grave site and every morning Alice went to sit, to read her mail, and to tend plants on her last daughter's grave.

Roads and Music

"More from General Ord, sir?" asked Captain Carpenter when he saw the sour expression on Ben Grierson's face.

Ben crumpled the paper and started to throw it away, then thought better of it and stuffed it into the front of his woolen jacket. A sharp wind blew across the monotonous West Texas desert to cut at his face and ripple through his thick beard, increasingly shot with gray. He studied the horizon and wondered what lay over it. Probably Mescalero Apache. Or Warm Springs Apache. Lipan? Comanche? Kiowa? He put his faith in Edward Hatch's reports of Victorio escaping the San Carlos Reservation and going on the warpath again.

Warm Springs Apache, definitely. The worst.

He sucked in another deep breath and hardly heard the activity around him. His New Pioneer Corps had toiled desperately, building roads and stringing telegraph wires, in spite of Ord's constant carping about misuse of cavalry soldiers. The new letter from his commander in San Antonio berated his efforts tracking down Indian raiders.

"This land is desert, Louis," he told Carpenter. "We ride across it, leave prints for only a brief moment, and then the wind erases all trace that we were ever here. No matter how hard we try to leave our mark, the land swallows it. 'One generation passeth away, and another generation cometh: but the earth abideth for ever.' "

"Sir?"

"Sorry, just feeling a bit down. How's the road crew doing?"

Carpenter rattled off a concise report, but Ben heard only every few words. The captain was an able officer. Ben really didn't need a report on routine projects. What he needed was a decent, verified scouting report of Victorio moving into their patrol area.

What he really needed was to forget Edie's death.

Ben had kept as far from Fort Concho as possible the past months, as much to avoid Alice and her constant recriminations as to bypass the stone-walled grave holding his daughter's body. The feeling of hopelessness that assailed him when he saw his sons vanished while on patrol. He was helpless to defend his family from cholera and other disasters, but he was good at protecting them and the Texas settlers from Indian attacks. He still didn't cotton much to horses.

"Sir? Sir!"

"What?" Ben jumped as if he had been stuck by a pin. "Sorry. What is it, Captain?"

"Signal mirror report, sir. From the scouts sent west toward the Rio Grande. From the message, there's a band of ten Apache looking for a ford."

"Continue your work, Captain. I'll take a company to stop them."

"Yes, sir," Carpenter said, saluting. "When you return, we'll have another mile of road improved."

"Don't drive them too hard, Louis," Ben said softly. "They're good men."

He shouted orders, got the column formed, and trotted off

toward the U.S.-Mexico border. Ord had been livid when he had learned of Ben's other incursion with buffalo soldiers. The best Ben could tell, the *peones* living on the other side of the river had welcomed the capture of Apache who scalped and killed their men and kidnapped their women and children. The *Federales* were corrupt and all too often patrolling elsewhere, like in some cantina with obliging señoritas. For two cents, Ben would have included a stretch of Mexico in his territory to protect. But General Ord had threatened to court-martial him.

At times, Ben wished the blustering general would stop threatening legal action and just get on with it. He wished the general would do *something*.

"That there's our scouts, suh," reported the company sergeant.

"I want a complete report," Ben said, galloping forward to join the three scouts.

"Suh, wish you hadn't wasted yo' time."

"The message you sent. Ten Indians."

"Suh, they got theyselves o'er the ribber."

"So quickly?" Ben's mind raced. The letter thrust into his jacket from Ord again castigated his tactics and lack of progress, yet the general had not appreciated his sortie into Mexico. "Are you sure they're over the border?"

"Sure as rain, suh." The scout hesitated, then laughed as he looked up at the cloudless blue desert sky. "I's from Al'bama where it do rain on 'ccasion."

"You know what this means, don't you?" Ben asked the scout. The man's eyes grew wide. "The company has to return to road work."

The scout grinned and tipped his head to one side. "Might cause a blister o' two, but them soldiers don't git shot at when they's shovelin'."

"Carry on," Ben ordered. He signaled the sergeant, got the company turned around, and returned at a slow walk. The men sang softly, accompanied by a few with harmonicas. Ben wasn't sure if he was disappointed at not catching Apache who had escaped from their reservation. He felt lighter at heart now than when he had raced off after them. Ben dismissed the company and sent them back to work improving the road.

"Captain Carpenter!" he bellowed. Carpenter came riding up. "Give the men the rest of the day off. But there's a price."

"Sir?" Carpenter wondered what had happened for Ben to return so quickly, but held his questions.

"A concert. Break out the instruments. I want a concert. I want to hear a dozen songs in the next hour. Then I'll decide if there should be an encore."

"The men will appreciate the break, sir."

"So will I, Louis," Ben said. He hadn't captured any Apache, and his immediate commander hated him and sent him scathing letters, but he felt better—good enough to return to Fort Concho and do what he could to console Alice.

Finally.

Warpath

August 29, 1879
Fort Concho, Texas

Ben Grierson spread the reports on the desk in front of him in a fan shape so he could see them all. A smile curled his lips. He brushed at the thick, bushy, gray-shot beard as his eyes darted from one number to the next. What a difference a year made.

He had marched the Tenth Cavalry more than thirty-four thousand miles patrolling all of West Texas. Fort Quitman and Fort Davis had been renovated and brought up to snuff. He looked out the open door of his office across the parade ground and puffed with pride. Fort Concho had been a miserable mud pit when he had arrived. Now it was the finest post in Texas, no matter what Generals Ord and Sheridan said. Ben closed his eyes and listened to the distant strains of the band playing. They were off-key, but that was because of an influx of recruits. Within a month, they would march and play as well as any band in the U.S. Army.

He wished Grant might come to see. Or his old friend Sherman. William Sherman had worked his way up the chain of command and was in charge of dealing with the Indians west of the Mississippi. His orders were harsh, but Ben found them sensible.

All Indians onto reservations. No exceptions. Extreme force to be used against violators. The Five Civilized Tribes in Indian Territory were a model for the rest. Keeping the Comanche penned up was a chore, but their star had set as more settlers moved into Texas. The vast plains they had raced over no longer existed. Fences marked off ranches and farms, plowed fields were dangerous to gallop across on a raid, and as important as anything else, the fire had left the Comanche chiefs. Their time was at an end.

"Three hundred miles of road improvement helped stop the Comanche," Ben said to himself. He shuffled more papers and saw the report from the State of Texas thanking him for stringing more than two hundred miles of telegraph line. Towns that had been isolated were now in communication, able to send for aid should it needed. More than once over the past year, a quick message had alerted him in time to field a company or two and capture Comanche raiders.

He leaned back and felt a glow of pride in the Tenth Cavalry. It no longer mattered what small-minded men like Sheridan and Ord thought of his black troopers. Ben had commanded men since before the war and, if he had been allowed to pick, would not have changed the current roster by even one name. His desertion rate was the lowest in Texas, drunkenness was low, and the people of Saint Angela had come to an uneasy peace with his troopers after he had allowed entire companies in civilian dress to enter the town on leave. The few bigots who would gang up on a solitary black soldier became mighty scarce when faced with dozens of soldiers, all obviously given free rein to defend themselves. There had been protests from the town marshal, and Ben had ignored them. The tense situation slowly became tolerable, and for the past six months, there had not been a single incident requiring his attention. Part of it might have been the demise of the reviled State Police, replaced by the newly formed Texas Rangers, but Ben preferred to think the improvements came because of his policies.

Even relations with Alice and the boys had improved. She still visited Edie's grave every morning, read her mail there, and spoke as if she carried on a two-sided conversation, but her grief was fading. Little by little, but definitely fading.

Ben had not thought he could be this content after establishing Fort Sill and being stationed at Fort Gibson, nestled in the lovely rolling green hills of Indian Territory. But he was.

With a sigh he swept up the reports and tucked them into a desk drawer before a cloud of dust came billowing in. He looked up to see Sam Woodward, flushed and looking edgy, jump off his horse at the hitching post and rush in.

"Colonel!" he said. "Bad news."

"What is it, Sam?" Ben asked. He wasn't going to be upset today. He felt too good.

"Telegram from Colonel Hatch, sir."

Ben sucked in his breath and held it.

"Victorio escaped the San Carlos Reservation. He took upward of a hundred braves with him, including his witch-sister Lozen and the old chief, Nana. Sir, he's on the warpath and he's coming our way!"

Captures

April 10, 1880
Peñasco River, Texas

"Any word from Hatch?" Ben asked, peering at the map spread on the ground in front of him. Rocks held down the tattered corners as he traced along the river.

"No, sir. We haven't heard from him since he caught the band of Mescalero," said Captain Carpenter.

"I know, I know," mused Ben. He rubbed his nose as he thought. Two weeks ago he and Ed Hatch had met to discuss strategy against the escaping Apache. Hatch worried more about Victorio and his band, although they had slipped across the border into Mexico, than he did the Mescalero. Ben had to agree with his old friend. Every knot of Indians Ben had come across was Warm Springs Apache trying to join their fugitive chief. A fierce fight in the Guadalupe Mountains had ended in a virtual stalemate. From everything his scouts said, the old war chief Nana had hightailed it south into Texas. Interrogation of prisoners gave a similar story: Nana would rejoin Victorio. In Texas.

That message had been conveyed to General Ord from

different sources. He had become downright panicked at the thought of Victorio ranging throughout the guts of the state he was entrusted to defend.

Ben had a new letter from General Ord tucked in his saddle-bags now. This one gave him a free hand to capture Victorio in any way he could. Ord would never give in and admit Ben and the Tenth Cavalry were the only ones to do the job. That meant pressure from above forced him to issue the orders. Sheridan? Possibly. But General Pope had given Hatch a similar mission.

Settlers, merchants, Mexicans—all worried that Victorio would turn the desert red with their blood.

"I need to know where Hatch's battalion is," Ben said. "We don't want to collide along the river and shoot at each other by mistake."

The Pecos meandered from New Mexico Territory into West Texas. The escaping Apache would follow it or the Peñasco River, depending on the water they needed to survive. The Apache both he and Hatch sought were not strictly war parties, either. Many had taken their women and children with them.

As tough as the Apache brave was, having his family with him would slow him and force different, easier routes.

"Victorio's sister? Have you heard anything of her?" Ben asked.

Carpenter snorted. "The scouts in the Ninth make her out to be more than human. They claim she has supernatural power to locate them. Lozen turns and faces in the direction where her hands turn hot. That's where her enemy is, or so they say."

"Yes, yes, but she's with Nana. That's what our captives have said. Victorio might be lured into a trap if we can catch his sister."

"She's a fiercer fighter than he is, Colonel. *That's* not superstition. I've read the reports. She fights with the best of the Apache, then goes and cooks and does women's chores."

Ben shook his head. So much of what they heard was mixed with rumor and outright tall tales. He didn't fault the settlers and others cowering in fear as the Apache raced past for embellishing the stories, but he needed facts.

"Nana supposedly has the supernatural ability to locate rifles and ammunition," Carpenter went on. "With Lozen, the pair is invincible."

"They are not," Ben said flatly. "We will catch them. We will catch Victorio, too. They are flesh and blood. All I need to figure out is where to look for their footprints so we can follow them."

"Sir, using them as bait to snare Victorio is a bad idea. If we find Nana or Lozen, we should capture or kill them on the spot."

"Perhaps you're right, but the Apache rally around Victorio. He's a natural-born leader. They'd never follow a woman, no matter how powerful her talents, and Nana is an old man."

"Don't underestimate him because he's old, Colonel," Carpenter warned.

"I know what he's done. I won't. But I learned to evade the Confederate cavalry during the war. Then I went after Nathan Bedford Forrest and almost caught him. That kind of guerrilla war is no different from this." Ben looked up across the mesquite-dotted desert. "The land is drier, and there aren't trees and swamps, but the tactics are the same. Lure your enemy into a spot he thinks is safe, then ambush him."

"What do you suggest, sir?"

Ben stood and stared at the map stretched on the ground. He knew where Hatch had been, where the Mescalero had been captured, where the ones that had escaped would go.

"I'm assuming Colonel Hatch and at least a battalion from the Ninth are still in the field and moving in this direction. That will flush the Apache he didn't capture along the river. Soon. Very soon. They won't have time to be careful."

"Should we deploy along both sides of the river, sir?" Carpenter pointed to spots Ben had been considering.

"Yes, there, but keep a company on fresh horses for pursuit. Has our supply train caught up with us yet?" The Twenty-fifth Infantry guarded his supply wagons, and he had five companies of the Tenth Cavalry to deploy.

"No, sir. I'm not sure when they will arrive. The foot soldiers travel slower than molasses flowing uphill."

"The river has boggy spots, just like I'm used to," Ben said, noting where the tules grew. They would provide decent cover for dismounted cavalry. Beyond, sloping up into the foothills, the ground turned rocky and was spotted with mesquite, sagebrush, and the occasional stand of salt cedar.

Ben and Carpenter finished their plans, and Ben let his captain go position the troopers. They would grumble about hiding up to their waists in muck among the tules, but they stood a better chance of surprising any Apache coming from the north. The one point worrying him most was keeping only one company in reserve. He wrestled with the idea and finally decided it was best to use the other four in combat and decisively end the skirmish.

At two o'clock Ben heard gunshots along the foothills. He felt rather than saw the tension among his hidden soldiers. At 2:30 the Apache appeared.

"Surrender!" Ben bellowed, riding out from where he had been anxiously waiting since the initial gunfire. He saw a dozen or more Apache, mostly women and children. Two were warriors who immediately lifted their rifles and fired.

The return fire was deafening. From among the reeds came a withering hail of bullets that ripped the two braves. One sank down on the spot, filled with lead. The other was spun about but managed to hobble to cover. Ben saw a lieutenant moving his men from the boggy area along the river to capture the fleeing Apache.

"Company I, advance!" Ben ordered. On the far side of the river, Company G already rode to the battle. The Apache were strung out in a thin line leading back into the foothills. The small group of women and children with the two warriors were already under guard. It was time to find if Nana, Lozen, and other dangerous Apache leaders were with this group.

Ben had ridden only a hundred yards when a bullet whined past his head. He turned, as if he could see where it had gone. A second round left a burning track along the back of his neck, warning him of a concentration of braves.

"Charge!" Ben drew his heavy cavalry saber and held it high so it would reflect the afternoon sun. The brilliant flash off it caught the attention of his men and gave them something to rally on. He put spurs to his horse's flanks and galloped forward.

An Apache popped up to one side. Ben had not seen him as he lay among a brown patch of sere grass until he brandished his knife. With a twist of his shoulders, Ben swung his saber to his left as he raced forward. The Apache surged, trying to reach him with the knife. Ben's saber opened a deep wound from belly to shoulder, sending the Apache staggering away.

Then Ben burst past and reached the crest of a small ridge. His eyes widened when he saw the battle raging below. Hatch and a battalion of the Ninth were in hand-to-hand fighting with a small army of Apache. Ben hesitated, got the sense of battle and how his four companies could best aid his friend, and then bellowed orders to his bugler.

The sour notes rang out, telling the men of the Tenth Cavalry how to advance.

A blue tidal wave poured over the ridge and down into the broad ravine. The Apache had been holding their own against the buffalo soldiers of the Ninth. Being suddenly attacked from the rear by another two hundred men broke their spirit.

Apache war leaders did little more than outline when to attack, leaving the individual fighting style to the braves themselves. Against concerted, coordinated assault they had only two choices. They could stay and die or they could flee.

Ben shouted to his bugler, "Sound pursuit! We're going after the ones who're running!"

The bugler's hand shook as he lifted the horn to his lips. A few notes brayed forth, then ended abruptly as an arrow pinned his right arm to his side. The bugler bent forward at the waist and dropped the bugle.

"After them!" Ben shouted above the tumult. "Don't let any of them escape!"

He swung his saber at another warrior who was trying to knock him from the saddle by using a rifle as a club. Rifle barrel and sword collided. Sparks exploded into the afternoon. The recoil of the impact almost unseated Ben, but it knocked the Apache to the ground.

By the time Ben fought his way back into the saddle, the fighting was almost over. A few stalwarts fought on, but the Apache knew they were outnumbered and had been outfought.

"Ben!" called Edward Hatch. The commander of the Ninth Cavalry rode over. His face was scratched and bloody, and his uniform was dark with gunpowder residue, but he grinned ear to ear. "Are you still in one piece?"

"I reckon so." Ben eyed his friend. "That's more than I can say for you. What happened? Did you attack through every prickly pear cactus patch in West Texas?"

Hatch laughed.

"We came on their trail a little after noon and then pursued vigorously. You were in the best position possible to bottle them up."

"If you'd let me know where you were, I'd have been there on purpose. As it was, I just guessed."

"That's what makes you such a fine commander, Ben. Your guesses are better than most generals' carefully laid plans." Hatch paused a moment, then smiled boyishly. "Do you want to report to Sherry-dan or should I?"

"How many have we caught or killed?" Ben asked. He saw Hatch's men making the final determination.

"Suh, we got danged neah three hunnerd," came the report from a corporal.

"How many killed?" asked Ben.

"There's the Indian agent. Russell's his name. He'll know for certain."

Hatch and Ben rode to where the agent sat on his haunches, scribbling notes on a scrap of paper. He looked up.

"I know what you want to know, Colonel," Russell said. "We captured two hundred fifty. Ten warriors killed. All of them are Mescalero off the reservation."

"Thank you, sir," Hatch said.

Ben was distracted when his adjutant came galloping up. Sam Woodward had been with the reserve company.

"Sir, we gave pursuit but some got away. Should we continue pursuit?"

"How many, Lieutenant?" asked Ben, fearing the number from the way Woodward looked.

"Can't give a good number, sir, but it looks to be twenty or thirty."

"They'll go straight south, Ben," Hatch said. "You might as well chase them, though I doubt you'll catch them."

"Why chase them, then?"

Hatch turned grim. "They'll meet up with Victorio. When they do, you'll definitely see them all again—peering down a rifle barrel with you in their sights."

Schemes

July 10, 1880
Grierson Springs, Texas

"There aren't many watering holes out here, Sam," Ben Grierson said, lounging in the shade of a cottonwood. The fitful breeze made it feel cooler than it was. Ben splashed water onto his face and let it evaporate, cooling him nicely.

"The Apache know every last one, sir," Lieutenant Woodward said. He walked around, wary of shadows and movements in the brush. All they had flushed that day were rabbits and snakes.

"If Hatch is right, Victorio will be here before we know it. He wants to recruit the Apache running from the Mescalero Reservation for his band in Mexico."

"He's raiding everywhere," Woodward said. "The border means nothing to him. Are you sure General Ord reinstated his order not to cross into Mexico?"

"A platoon from General Pope's command is feeling out the Mexican officials about more active pursuit into their country," Ben said. He knew Ord feared that Ben would cause a massive border incident and inflame already bad relations with Mexico. However, catching Victorio would do more to ease tensions. The corruption among the *Federales* was legendary, but Ben doubted they appreciated Victorio's raids on their villages and relatives any more than the settlers and merchants on the U.S. side did.

"We should have caught the Apache who escaped from us in April," Woodward said.

"There was some confusion between Hatch and me. If we had coordinated better, we could have made a clean sweep of the escapees," Ben said. "Twenty or thirty got away. We need to be certain we catch them now, along with Victorio. I've got a plan."

"Yes, sir?" Woodward looked more worried than ever. "We only have ten men with us."

"Don't you think the men of the Tenth Cavalry are a match for Victorio's riffraff?" Ben smiled. "Don't worry, Sam. I don't mean to say we'll go after them this instant. We need to use the roads we've worked on for the last eighteen months. And the telegraphs. We spread out, cover the water holes, and then rely on communication to reinforce the men positioned where the Apache show up."

"Sounds dangerous, sir. You know how difficult it can be traveling in the heat. Any delay might mean the scouts at the water hole would be in serious trouble."

Ben nodded absently, then said, "I want to take a squad to Rattlesnake Springs. If Victorio goes anywhere, it will be there."

He came out of his reverie and added, "I want you to alert Captain Nolan at Fort Quitman. I want his Company A to remain at the fort unless otherwise ordered. Have him telegraph you at Fort Davis with any information concerning Victorio. Then you ride out to report personally."

"You're going to be in considerable danger, sir," Woodward said.

Ben shrugged it off. The settlers and teamsters along the San Antonio-El Paso road were in more danger from the

Apache. The Tenth Cavalry was prepared to fight. Those civilians were more intent on living their lives and doing their jobs.

"We'll catch him. We won't let Victorio ravage Texas. Not while I'm in command of the Tenth."

First Skirmish

July 30, 1880
Tinaja de las Palmas, Texas

"It's good that Mother let me come, Papa," Robert Grierson said. "This is such grand adventure!"

Ben looked at his son and smiled. It was all that and more. While it was dangerous, he didn't think his son was in any greater danger riding with a detachment from the Tenth Cavalry than he was staying at Fort Concho. His mother could come up with all kinds of picayune chores to annoy him, and he deserved some small reward for having graduated from high school.

"I've taught you the two most important rules about your rifle," Ben said.

"I remember, sir. How to use it and when not to." Robert still bubbled with enthusiasm. Ben had missed that from his family. "This is lovely land."

"This? It's desert. Water is scarce and the plants are measured by miles apart. This is nothing like Jacksonville or even Chicago."

"I like it better. A man can be free here. I never liked

Chicago. Too many people." Robert took in a deep breath and closed his eyes.

Ben hesitated. His son was a man, but it was difficult not to think of him as a young child to be told how and when to do everything.

"You know we're hunting Victorio, and this is quite dangerous. I want you to promise to do exactly as I say, no questions. Agreed?"

"Sir, we've been over that before. Yes, of course, I agree. You know everything about the Indians, and I'm here to learn."

"I hope so," Ben said. His field headquarters at Eagle Springs was minimally staffed. Besides his son, he had a sergeant, five privates, and Lieutenant Beck. He worried more about the lieutenant than he did about his son's safety. Beck had ridden with him since 1862, risen to the rank of captain, and then at Fort Sill, had resigned as regimental quartermaster after committing slanders against Ben. Sam Woodward had recommended a court-martial, but Ben had been content with removing Beck. Beck had later been reduced in rank and reassigned to the Tenth Cavalry, to no one's pleasure.

"Should I tell you my ideas about where we ought to ambush Victorio?" Robert bubbled with enthusiasm. Ben saw Lieutenant Beck drifting from his post and going out into the bright sunlight.

"What is it, Lieutenant?" called Ben.

"Riders, sir, coming from Fort Quitman, 'less I miss my guess."

"Maybe they've located Victorio," Robert said anxiously. His tone had changed from excitement to one mixing in more than a little fear.

"We'll see," Ben said. He joined Beck.

"It's the ni—" Beck coughed as if something had caught in his throat. "It's that Negro officer, Flipper, from Fort Quitman. This might be what we've waited for, sir."

Ben pulled down his hat to shield his eyes better. Henry Flipper was the first black West Point graduate and from what Captain Nolan reported, a decent enough officer. Flipper had a great deal to learn, but on the frontier fighting the Apache who had lived in this desolate land forever, they all did.

"Sir!" called Flipper when he saw Ben's gold braid gleaming in the sun. "Captain Nolan sends his regards." Flipper dropped to the ground and saluted. He stood about the same height as Ben but was stockier and had a nervous air about him, his eyes darting about rather than looking either at Ben or straight ahead. "The captain got news from the other side of the river—"

"From Colonel Valle's force?" Ben asked. The Mexican Army colonel had a considerable force camped just across the river from Fort Quitman, but had fallen on sorry times. Ben had authorized Nolan to released several tons of supplies to support Valle's effort against the Apache.

"Yes, sir. Victorio crossed the Rio Grande just below Fort Quitman."

"Valle wasn't up to stopping him," grumbled Ben. He did not consider the supplies wasted since they had rescued many of the Mexican soldiers from starvation, but he wished there had been more action on the other side of the border. "Where's he heading? Victorio?"

"No one knows, sir."

"Tinaja de las Palmas is a likely spot," said Ben after a moment's consideration. "There's never an army detachment there, and the water comes from rainfall and isn't too abundant. This is the perfect spot for a man on the run."

"Orders, sir?" asked Flipper.

"Return to Fort Quitman. Tell Captain Nolan to get A Company out to Tinaja as quickly as possible. Have Captain Viele bring in C Company from patrol to support."

"And Captain Colladay, sir?"

"G Company," mused Ben. He stroked his beard, then

nodded. "If Colladay can reach Tinaja, we will have more than enough firepower to bring down Victorio. I know you had a long ride, Lieutenant, but I want you to repeat it."

"Twenty-two hours from the fort, sir."

"Eighty-five miles," marveled Robert, standing close to his father. "That must have been one hellacious ride through the heat!"

Flipper smiled, then came to attention. "Permission to water my horse and return, sir."

"Godspeed," Ben said. To Lieutenant Beck he said, "We need to arrange a reception for our errant friend, Chief Victorio. Pack as much ammo as you can, along with an adequate supply of water and rations. If something needs to be left behind, make it the food. Ammunition and water will win the day for us."

"Yes, sir. Will we depart right away?"

"The sooner the better," Ben said, his pulse racing. He might be wrong about Victorio heading for Tinaja, but he had studied the Apache chief's movement closely and didn't think so.

Vertical rocky cliffs rose to form a narrow valley. Ben's quick appraisal found the two spots where snipers could cover the pool of tepid water as well as the approaches. When Viele, Nolan, and Colladay arrived, they would provide both firepower and horses needed to run down Victorio, no matter where he darted.

"I feel mighty closed in, sir," Robert said. He nervously ran his fingers over the stock of his rifle riding under his right knee.

"Good, because we're going to be up there." Ben pointed to the tops of the cliffs.

"Each side, sir?" asked Lieutenant Beck.

"You take the far side with five men. I'll climb to the top of this cliff with the remainder."

"Me, too, sir?" asked Robert.

"Of course. How much ammunition did you bring for the rifle?"

"Two hundred fifty rounds."

"That ought to get us started, in case of a fight," Ben said. He knew the other soldiers carried similar amounts. For such a small band, they mounted more firepower than a full company of troopers.

"Don't go near the central pool of water," Beck warned his soldiers. "Find somewhere else to water your mounts. We don't want to spook the Indians."

"Good advice, Lieutenant," Ben said. "Get into position, keep an eye peeled and don't shoot at our own troops should they arrive before Victorio."

"You're mighty confident he's going to show up," Beck said, a hint of sarcasm in his voice.

"We'll wait up on Rocky Ridge until he does, Lieutenant," Ben said coldly.

He motioned and got Robert and the soldiers supporting him started up the cliff along a narrow path. They reached the crest and had a view of the countryside that was only a little bit less than spectacular, but Ben's attention focused downward.

"Pile up rocks for breastworks," he ordered. "Position men at equal intervals, Sergeant. See that everyone has their ammo in a pile close at hand."

"Yes, suh," the sergeant said. He barked orders and got the three soldiers toiling. Robert pitched in to help while Ben scanned the horizon with his field glasses. They had barely finished their work when Ben saw a cloud of dust rising. He waited before mentioning it.

"We have company," Ben said. "Looks like a courier from the fort."

"It's getting mighty dark, Papa," said. "Are you sure? It could the Indians."

"I'm sure," Ben said. From the way the rider picked his

way through the clumps of cactus, this was no Apache. He rode with single-minded determination to reach Tinaja.

They waited until the rider got to the edge of the watering hole before calling to him.

"Colonel Grierson! Word from a scout. Them Injuns're only ten miles 'way! They's comin' here!"

"Report to Captain Nolan and get Company A here as soon as possible," Ben said. He spoke to the soldier's back. The trooper had wheeled his horse about and raced away.

"What do we do, Papa?" asked Robert. He clutched his rifle with fierce determination.

"We do the hardest thing a soldier can do. We wait. Catch a few winks, if you can." Ben peered at his pocket watch. It was almost ten o'clock. The Apache wouldn't arrive until two or three in the morning, if they travelled carefully, alert for patrolling soldiers.

Ben made certain the sergeant had set a sentry, then settled down to take his own advice. He came awake, hand on his pistol, at 4 A.M. when Robert gently shook him.

"Sir, we've got company. Fifteen or twenty, from what Lieutenant Beck has seen."

Ben sagged a little when he saw the neat military column and caught occasional glints of starlight off brass. The column wasn't large enough to be Company A, but it was definitely military.

He made his way down to the watering hole to meet them.

"Colonel Grierson, that you?"

"Lieutenant Finley," Ben greeted. "Why did you come?"

"We found you were gone from Eagle Springs, so we rode out to escort you back."

"Your concern is misplaced," Ben said. "We have reason to believe the Apache will be here soon. Send a courier back to Eagle Springs for what support they can summon. I want you to post two scouts to warn us. Don't try to stop any Apache moving to the watering hole."

"Just alert you," Finley said. "I understand, sir. And the rest of us?"

"Up on Rocky Ridge," Ben said. "You have your choice of helping defend either Fort Grierson or Fort Beck." He had to chuckle at the notion that their few pitiful stones, stacked one on the other, could ever qualify as a fort.

"Yes, sir. Right away." Lieutenant Finley barked orders, set his sentries, and herded his men up to the top of Rocky Ridge.

Ben followed and settled down again. A quick glance at his watch showed it was almost four-thirty in the morning, and still no sign of the Apache. He dozed until his sergeant woke him for a light breakfast.

As they finished their meal, Ben's ears pricked up.

"The vedettes," he said. "Lieutenant Finley, report!" His quick command brought the lieutenant at a dead run.

"Sir, my sentries saw Apache coming, but they are swinging farther south. I think they saw the battlements on top of the ridge."

Ben cursed. He should have been more careful building the ramparts.

"Lieutenant Finley, take ten men and go after the Apache. Engage them, slow them, keep them occupied until Captain Nolan and the rest of our reinforcements arrive."

"When'll that be, sir?" Finley asked, his weather-beaten face turning pale.

"As soon as they can get here, Lieutenant. You know that."

"Sir, yes, sir." Lieutenant Finley barked orders and got his men moving down the face of the twenty-five-foot-high cliff and then onto their horses to chase after the Apache.

"Is it Victorio, suh?" asked the sergeant.

"I have every reason to think so," Ben said. He watched Finley's men open fire on the Apache. He saw a small cloud of dust some distance away, but could not determine its cause. Turning back to the encounter, he watched Finley begin to retreat in the face of overwhelming odds.

"Prepare to support Lieutenant Finley," barked Ben. "He's decoying them this way." He started to take his place, then made out the leading elements of Company A galloping along. Captain Nolan had arrived and would follow the Apache after Finley.

Victorio would be caught between fire from Rocky Ridge and that of Company A.

Ben put away his field glasses, took a rifle, and waited until Finley and his men were close to the cliff face before ordering his men to open fire. The sharp reports from the carbines echoed along the small canyon, and soon the air was white with gun smoke that refused to drift away on the morning breeze.

"I can hear 'em!" cried Robert. "They're shrieking like fiends!"

"Then shoot them," Ben said, choosing his own targets as carefully as possible. Curtains of lead rained down from above on the Apache. For a moment, Ben hoped they would foolishly continue to charge his fortified position atop the cliffs, but a single warrior shouted and drew the attention of the other Apache.

"Victorio!" Ben had never seen the Warm Springs chief but knew this had to be him. He aimed, squeezed, and fired but missed. Victorio never flinched as bullets spun past him. Ben had to admire Victorio's courage in the face of fire and his cool command over his braves. Because he didn't panic, Victorio led his warriors out of the ambush.

"They're gettin' 'way," the sergeant said. "Headin' west for the border. They want to get to Mexico!"

"They won't," Ben said, standing when the Apache had ridden out of range. "Viele and Colladay are in pursuit."

Three companies of the Tenth Cavalry now charged after Victorio and his band of warriors.

"We've got 'em on the run, sir!" crowed Lieutenant Beck.

Ben didn't share his lieutenant's enthusiasm. He watched the ebb and flow of the running battle through his field glasses, trying to make out the combatants through the heavy clouds of dust and smoke. He finally dropped the glasses, letting them swing on their cord around his neck.

"He got away. Victorio got away," he said, trying to hold back his anger. He turned to Robert and said, "There it is, son. The best and worst of being a soldier. We fight but we don't always win. What do you think of it?"

"This is wonderful, Papa!"

"Maybe you have it in you to be a soldier," Ben said, not sure if Robert understood that men had died and yet nothing had been accomplished. Victorio still raided off the reservation, and the Tenth Cavalry still had to track him down.

He marched down to the base of Rocky Ridge and waited for Captain Nolan to report.

Victorio had lost seven men. Captain Colladay had been slightly wounded and one of his soldiers, Private Martin, had been killed. But Colladay's injury had thrown his company into enough of a disarray to allow Victorio to escape.

Ben ordered the troopers back to Eagle Springs for a conference. The next time he met Victorio, the Apache chief wouldn't get away so easily.

Hide and Seek

August 3, 1880
Rattlesnake Springs, Texas

"How do you do it, Papa?" asked Robert Grierson. "The waiting is killing me!"

"Use the time to be certain your rifle is clean and ready," Ben said. "Sleep. Try not to worry about what will happen. These are all things a soldier must learn to do. If you try to second-guess the enemy, you'll only confuse yourself." Ben shoved his pistol back into its holster, having cleaned the mechanism of grit for the third time. He looked around the springs and saw his men lounging about in the shade of cotton-wood trees, trying to sleep in spite of the heat. Of all the killers in the army, boredom was a close second to lack of sleep.

"Is this what Charlie is learning at West Point?" Robert asked. "Can I go, also?"

Ben swallowed hard. Charlie had gone through difficult times during his second year at the Point and had a nervous breakdown. He seemed better now, but was hardly a fully functional cadet.

"It's difficult getting an appointment," Ben said. "If, after we finish this campaign against Victorio, you still want to be in the Army, I'll speak to General Sherman and see if I can get his recommendation. Senator Yates might also be willing to shepherd an appointment for you."

"I like this, Papa. I do," Robert said, his cheeks flushed. "And I'm not trying to outguess the enemy, but I think he's going to be coming here."

"To Rattlesnake Springs?" asked Ben. Amused, he had to ask, "Why's that?"

"When Victorio lit out for Mexico from Tinaja, he couldn't have possibly reached the river. If he had, Colonel Valle would have stopped him."

Ben said nothing since he wanted to hear his son's line of reasoning. But Robert had already made one deadly mistake: He didn't know all the facts. Valle had pulled up stakes and moved his entire army north toward El Paso, blocking Victorio's return to the Mescalero Reservation to recruit new warriors to replace the ones he had lost. Victorio might have continued into the rugged central highlands of Mexico. Rumors had it that he and Chief Yuh were blood brothers, though Ben doubted that. Yuh might give Victorio sanctuary, but his loyalties lay with Geronimo, whose sister he had married. The struggle for power between Chief Victorio and a pretender, Geronimo, would only tear apart Yuh's tribe.

Ben was certain Victorio had not crossed the border, but had wended his way through the network of forts and was now rattling about to the south. Rattlesnake Springs was the only sweet water to be had for dozens of miles. If Victorio didn't stop here, he had to ride another seventy miles to water his horses. After dodging the Tenth Cavalry in hot pursuit, Victorio's mouth would be like cotton.

He would come to Rattlesnake Springs.

Ben lay back and let the sweat trickle away from his eyes as he folded his hands under his head for a pillow. Lieutenant

Flipper was out near Van Horn and the most likely to engage Victorio's force. When he did, he would drive the Apache directly into Ben's ambush.

Then Victorio would be defeated. Then. Ben drifted off to sleep dreaming of an Apache-free Texas.

Defeat

"This battle will decide the fate of West Texas," Ben Grierson said in a ringing voice, addressing his troopers. "We will triumph over Victorio and his marauders. We will kill or capture them. We will show no quarter because they will not understand or appreciate any mercy on our part."

Ben saw the sea of dark faces, all grim, all preparing themselves for the fight to come. A courier from Fort Davis had arrived a few minutes earlier with word that Lieutenant Flipper had found and engaged Victorio as Ben had hoped. The Apache were fleeing before the lieutenant's company, unwilling to engage because Captain Nolan could reinforce from Fort Quitman and destroy Victorio's entire force. That meant the Apache would be tired from retreating, wary of any rider on their back trail and possibly less aware of what lay ahead.

Ben's Tenth Cavalry would destroy them.

"If we cannot defeat them in battle, if they choose to flee our guns, we will pursue. They will find no sanctuary this side of the border." Ben hesitated, knowing Victorio would try to escape into Mexico if the fight went against him. General Ord had been specific about Ben's earlier incursion. It was not to be repeated under any circumstance. But Colonel Valle was to the north and unable to engage Victorio—if he even wanted to fight such a fierce foe.

Ben tried to decide to if he would disobey and go after Victorio, then forced himself back to his speech to the soldiers. If all went well, there would be no reason to chase Victorio or any of the Apache.

They would be caught or killed.

"We will fight, we will pursue, we will be tenacious." Ben smiled a little now. "Before the fight, a tune!"

Four men with harmonicas began "Battle Hymn of the Republic." When they finished, the men were primed and ready for anything.

Robert came to his father's side and said, "You expect Victorio to get away, don't you, Papa?"

"Don't second-guess, son," Ben said. "We take this one step at a time. Victorio has to come to Rattlesnake Springs if he wants water, even if it is terrible. This place is named Rattlesnake Springs because the water would kill a snake. But not even the Apache with their legendary endurance can keep going without horses. The desert will pluck their animals from under them, one by one, without water."

"If he tries to bypass the springs, we'll pursue?"

"Yes," Ben said. He turned and spoke quickly with Lieutenants Beck and Woodward. Everything had to be ready. The scout reported the Apache on the way and his men were set to fight.

"There they come, suh!" shouted a lookout perched high in a cottonwood's limbs.

"This is it, Sam," Ben said softly to his adjutant. "I feel it in my bones. We win or lose today."

"We'll win, sir," Woodward said.

"Make it happen."

Ben motioned to his son to come over. "I want you to guard the horses, but be ready for the soldiers to come get them."

"Papa, I want to help fight!"

"You'll do as you are ordered. We cannot lose the horses. You will guard them with your life. Do you understand?" Ben knew his son would be as safe there as any place around Rattlesnake Springs. Any Apache brave would have to sneak past several rings of armed and alert soldiers.

"Yes, sir," Robert said, gripping his rifle as if he could squeeze the bullets out without touching the trigger.

Ben laid his hand on his son's shoulder. "Be ready, son. Be ready to ride."

He took his place in the middle of the troopers' skirmish line and waited. In less time than he expected, Ben saw an Apache rider appear in a draw not a hundred yards away. The brave reined back, wheeled his horse, and then whirled it around to stare toward Rattlesnake Springs.

Ben refused to order his men to open fire. He wanted more of the Apache in his sights.

Two more Apache joined the first.

"Do you think they know we're waitin', suh?" asked a private to Ben's right.

"They know. Fire!"

He snapped the order as the three let out war whoops and raced toward the springs. His men loosed a hundred rounds but missed more than they hit. Ben saw one Apache jerk. The others rode uninjured. And they kept coming. That worried Ben. When the Apache came within twenty yards, they wheeled and raced off. One was shot off his horse and the other two showed signs of being wounded by the heavy fire.

Ben was less than happy when he saw another half-dozen warriors appear just out of range.

"Sir, we should mount and go after them!" shouted Lieutenant Beck from the right flank.

"No!" Ben bellowed. "They're trying to draw us out.

Haven't you studied Hannibal's tactics against the Roman legions? Appear weak in the middle, draw the enemy forward, then attack with your strongest elements from the flanks." Ben clamped his mouth shut. Lecturing Beck was pointless, if the officer didn't already understand what Victorio was trying.

"What do we do? Just sit here and boil in the sun?"

"We have water, Lieutenant," Ben said angrily. "And they will attack from both flanks. Position your men to repel a flank attack!"

He saw that Woodward already had his men shifted forty-five degrees, no longer guarding the straightaway approach but looking to the side. Beck started to argue at the instant Victorio attacked.

From both flanks.

Ben rocked from side to side as the reports shook him, first from the left and then the right. Then the war whoops, rifle fire, and sound of arrows whistling through the air mixed into a heady wine that intoxicated him. He had fought through the war with only minor injuries in battle and felt a certain invincibility. His leg ached where he had been kicked but that faded as he concentrated on one thing only: seeking out Victorio. He knew the Apache war chief had to be in the vanguard of the attack because that's where *he* would be.

He had caught sight of Victorio once before. Ben knew instantly when the warrior galloped forward from the left flank. Twisting agilely, Ben raised his pistol and began firing at Victorio. The Apache chief straightened on his horse. For a moment their eyes locked. Each knew the other and saw destiny.

Then Ben's pistol came up empty. He resisted the urge to draw his cavalry saber and rush forward on foot. He was caught up in the fight but wasn't foolish. Neither was Victorio.

The first thrust had failed. Victorio signaled for his warriors to fall back, but Ben knew that was only a ploy. The twin attacks from the flanks had failed. That meant Victorio would reinforce his center and advance there, hoping the cavalry would ignore it since the opening gambit had been weak there.

"To the center, forward, face forward!" Ben yelled to Woodward and Beck. "He's going to attack head-on!"

Victorio did not disappoint Ben. The wily chief had maneuvered his reserves well, and the next wave of Indians came directly at the springs. Ben saw the rifle barrels on his men's Spencers begin to smoke from the rapid fire. If they weren't careful, they would fire so fast the barrels might melt and begin to sag. For a brief instant, Ben wished his troopers used bows and arrows. A trained Apache could loose six or seven arrows before the first hit its target.

"We're pushin' 'em back!" gloated Beck. "They aren't gettin' through here!"

Ben saw that the lieutenant was right. As much as Victorio might have exhorted his braves to press the attack, they were falling back in confusion. This was no feint, no trick. This was a rout. Ben had seen it in Confederate soldiers and he had seen it in *Federales,* too.

His men continued firing until their rifles started to fail. This provided enough of a break in the deadly curtain he had drawn around Rattlesnake Springs for Victorio to regain control and lead the retreat. Ben lifted his reloaded pistol and fired after the departing war chief. If Victorio had not been such a powerful leader, the Apache might have been slaughtered.

"Give me a count. How many dead or wounded?" Ben called.

"Sir," Woodward answered. "We got a—"

"I hear gunfire," Ben cut in. "What's going on?"

"That there's our supply train," came the answer from a scout who had run forward on foot and returned with the gasped-out answer. "Them Infantry boys're fightin'. So's Captain Carpenter."

Ben stopped and felt confusion swirling all around.

Carpenter's Company H could defend the supply train, especially if they were reinforced by the Twenty-third Infantry. But what did Victorio hope to gain by attacking the wagons?

"Prepare for another attack," Ben ordered. "Stick those rifle barrels into the water to cool them. You can't hurt the water. It's already bitter."

He watched as Beck and Woodward sent their men, squad by squad, to quench their rifles and prepare them for another assault.

"What's going on, sir?" asked Woodward.

"Victorio is going to attack the supply train, draw Carpenter off, and attack here again."

"That'll put his braves between us and the wagons, sir."

"He can pick off the infantry troopers later if Carpenter and his command are off chasing a pack of Apache while the remainder—under Victorio's command—are still here."

"Decoyed," muttered Woodward. "Do you think Carpenter will fall for it?"

"He has no choice," Ben said grimly. "He can't know if Victorio is with the raiders. His orders are to pursue. He'll commit Company H and the other three with him. We don't have much time to prepare. How are the men fixed for ammunition?"

"Well, sir. Each has at least a hundred rounds remaining," reported Woodward.

Ben started to demand a report from Beck when Apache braves again came galloping up the canyon toward the springs. This time they rode in silence until they were within a hundred yards of Ben's position. They let out their shrill, nerve-shredding cries.

Those battle yells were met with more withering fire. Again Ben spotted Victorio, but failed to hit him as he emptied his pistol. He itched to rush back to where Robert tended their horses, mount, and go after Victorio.

"Will they ever stop attacking?" moaned Beck. He bled from two wounds in his right arm that prevented him from lifting his pistol. Holding it awkwardly in his left hand, he came to Ben. "What are we going to do?"

"We will kill every mother's son of them!" raged Ben. "Get back to your position!"

Again his soldiers' rifles began to fail from overheating. But this time Captain Viele attacked from the direction of the supply train. Victorio found himself caught between dogged defenders at Rattlesnake Springs and cavalry troopers riding down his rear.

"There they go," Woodward said, limping over. He saw Ben's expression and smiled ruefully. "I'm all right, Colonel. I slipped on some blood and banged my knee against a rock."

"Whose blood?"

"A private's, but he is going to make it. The bullet caught him in the thigh."

Ben nodded. If a man didn't bleed to death on the spot from such a wound, there was a good chance of surviving it.

"Colonel!" shouted Captain Viele. "Do you need help?"

"Do you?" Ben shot back.

"We're in pursuit now, sir."

"A moment, Captain. What do you know of Victorio's supplies?"

"Captain Lebo captured Victorio's camp at Sierra Diablo three days back. And Kennedy with F Company rounded up a couple dozen Mescalero in the Guadalupe Mountains trying to join Victorio. They're already on their way back to the reservation to be imprisoned."

"Good," Ben said. "Victorio doesn't have any supplies, and he was cut off from reinforcements."

"Got a count for you, sir," called Woodward. "We killed or wounded at least thirty Apache. When we see how the supply train fared, it will be more. But we took a bigger toll on their horses. At least fifty killed."

"That puts quite a few Apache riding double on tired ponies," Ben said.

"Lebo captured most of their spare mounts, Colonel," said Viele. "Those horses ought to be dropping like flies under them. All we need to do is pick up the riders."

"Carpenter's already on Victorio's trail." Ben's mind raced as he considered where his best chance for success lay. "Captain Viele, remain with the supply wagons. Set up camp."

"The water's terrible here, sir," Viele said, making a face. "They say it's called Rattlesnake Springs because—"

"I know why," Ben said. "That's why I'm taking the two companies and joining Carpenter in pursuit. Six companies of the Tenth Cavalry ought to run down Victorio."

Ben mounted and set out at a brisk trot, wary of stragglers from Victorio's rout. His men picked up a few Apache, all wounded and on foot, but the main body of Victorio's force made a beeline for the Rio Grande.

To Ben's disgust, Victorio succeeded in crossing the Rio Grande just below Fort Quitman to gain sanctuary in Mexico, but it was the last time the Apache war chief would ever threaten U.S. soil.

Denied

"Any further word, Sam?" asked Ben Grierson of his adjutant.

"The good word is that we have verification that Victorio was killed on the fourteenth. The Mexican Army trapped him at Tres Castillos."

"We suspected that," Ben said impatiently. "What of Sergeant Perry?"

"Word from Company B is sketchy but it doesn't sound too good, Colonel," said Woodward.

Ben heaved a sigh. After he had heard the rumor of Victorio's death in Mexico at Tres Castillos, he had pulled back the Tenth Cavalry to Forts Concho, Davis, and Stockton for much-needed rest. The only patrols he had maintained were along the Rio Grande, mostly under the orders of Captain Nolan at Fort Quitman.

"Preliminary report?" he asked.

"The sergeant encountered a band of thirty or more

Apache, probably fresh off the Mescalero Reservation and on their way to join Victorio."

"Lucky devils," Ben said. "If they had left New Mexico Territory earlier, they would have been slaughtered by General Terrazos along with Victorio."

"Sergeant Perry was the unlucky one, sir," said Woodward. "They ambushed him at Ojo Caliente."

"Casualties?"

"Perhaps five. But the surviving soldiers chased the Apache across the river."

"Out of our grasp, just like Victorio," Ben said tiredly. He rubbed his eyes. The time away from patrolling had been good for his men. For him it had not. Alice had not been happy with him for risking Robert's life the way he had, and Ben couldn't make her understand their son had been safer with the Tenth Cavalry than he would have traveling across West Texas by himself. That was exactly what would have been required if Ben had sent Robert back to Fort Concho since every soldier had been needed for the fight against Victorio.

The final fight, as it turned out.

"Get me a full report when you can."

"It's little comfort, sir, but Colonel Hatch says he has both the Mescalero and San Carlos Reservations bottled up tight now that Victorio is no longer a magnet drawing the warriors away."

Ben nodded, closed his eyes, and then blinked when he heard a courier coming fast. The corporal jumped from his horse in front of Ben's office and hurried up the steps.

"Sir, message from General Ord."

Woodward took the courier's pouch and opened it. His eyebrows arched slightly and a little smile curled his lips. He handed Ben a letter.

"From General Sherman, sir. Do you think—"

"Let's find out," Ben said eagerly. He had been hoping this might arrive. He ripped it open and quickly scanned the letter from his friend. Sagging back, he tossed the letter onto the desk.

"Dismissed," he told the courier.

"No reply, sir?"

"Grab yourself some chow, then check back," Ben said. "I'm not sure I'll have any reply."

Ben saw Woodward straining to read the letter upside down. Ben reached out and spun the letter around so his friend could read it.

"I was put up for brigadier general," Ben said, all life gone from him. "Sherman fought hard for my promotion but Sheridan blocked it. Sheridan and the town fathers in San Angelo. They mounted quite a campaign against me, it appears."

"They never got used to black troopers coming to town as equals, sir."

"I hoped them changing the town's name would help their attitude change. It hasn't." Ben sat staring out the door, his jaw set.

"You deserved the promotion, sir. Sheridan knows you kept all of West Texas safe from the Apache over the past couple of years. What the Tenth did against the Kiowa and Comanche is well documented."

"Sherman says I might get my star when Sheridan retires. Or when hell freezes over." Ben laughed ruefully. "How cold does it feel to you, Sam?"

"Not that cold, sir."

"No, not that cold. Not yet." Ben turned back to his work, trying to put the snub out of his mind.

Court-marital and Reassignment

December 5, 1881
Fort Davis, Texas

"It's good to see you again, sir," said Captain Nicholas Nolan. "I'm sorry to hear about . . ." He inclined his head in the direction of Ranald Mackenzie, who squirmed in his chair so that he could position the stars on his shoulders in the sunlight, to be sure everyone saw.

Ben Grierson swallowed bile. Sheridan had pushed through promotion to brigadier general for his favorite in April. In spite of William Sherman's best efforts, and those of other powerful friends Ben still had in Washington, there was little chance he would ever be promoted now. In a way, he was victim of his own expertise. By eliminating the Indian threat in Texas, he had removed the need for many generals.

Mackenzie was a general, he wasn't. And that was likely the way it would remain.

"I'm sorry we have to cross paths again under such circumstances, Captain," Ben said. "It seems we meet at a court-martial more often than we do for purely social occasions."

"Sir, I'll always be thankful to you for your recommendation of clemency after I lost four troopers on the Staked Plains."

Ben waved that away. The court-martial had found him not guilty of criminal intent, and Ben had reconsidered all that had happened. He was glad he had suggested leniency on the charges Nolan had been convicted on. Since then, Nolan had fought well against the Apache and the mistakes made four years ago had never been repeated. He had turned into a competent officer because he learned and because he refused to give up.

"Tell me about Flipper," Ben said, although he knew this was improper. He was supposed to be impartial and weigh all the evidence after it was formally presented, but he felt better going into the court-martial with firsthand information, especially considering the ranking officer.

"We're friends, sir, and anything I say might prejudice you when you sit on the board."

"Tell me, Captain. We both know how little information is actually presented at a court-martial. Lawyers obscure the truth rather than expose it. I need background details if I am to come to a decent decision."

Nolan took a deep breath, then said, "He's my supply officer, sir. Colonel Shafter took an immediate dislike to him, and frankly, other officers in the Tenth Cavalry are cool toward him, also, but Henry is a good man."

"Do they dislike him because he's black?"

"Some might, sir. Perhaps Shafter, though I cannot truthfully say."

"Did he have access to the commissary funds he is accused of embezzling?"

"Yes, sir, he did. But that's garrison duty. A George duty."

"A duty no one wants but which gets assigned to the most junior officer," Ben said, knowing now where the trouble probably lay.

"Members, please take your seats," called the Fort Davis adjutant, acting as judge.

Ben shook Nolan's hand, then took his place beside General Mackenzie, silently acknowledging the man's presence. The other three officers on the court-martial board were from Mackenzie's command, making the charges against Flipper more serious. They were less likely to look upon a black as a fellow officer than some of those in the Tenth Cavalry.

Still, Ben thought the evidence presented by Colonel Shafter was weak. Flipper looked less like a thief than he did a sloppy bookkeeper. Considering his service in the field, Ben could pardon the man for not being as good at keeping a column of numbers aligned as he was at keeping his soldiers in line.

"The defense rests," Flipper's lawyer finally said.

Ben, Mackenzie, and the others exited to a small room off the officers' mess, where the trial was being conducted. Ben started to speak, then realized it wasn't his place. Mackenzie was the ranking officer. He settled down on yet another hard chair and waited for the prancing peacock to strut around, making certain everyone saw his stars before he said a single word.

"Lieutenant Flipper appears to have been negligent," Mackenzie said. "I vote for loss of pay and dismissal from the Army but no prison time."

Ben watched the emotions play across the faces of the other three officers. They felt as he did. He had always operated in the field under the premise that he should exploit any weakness in his enemy's position. Mackenzie had no reinforcements. Ben attacked.

"That is unduly harsh, General," Ben said, the title burning his tongue. He kept his distaste for Mackenzie hidden for Flipper's sake. "At worst, he is a dupe who allowed someone else to steal from the commissary fund. More likely, he is guilty of dereliction of duty and did not pay adequate attention to his duties in this regard."

"You vote for outright acquittal?" demanded Mackenzie.

"I vote for a letter of rebuke and dismissal of the more serious charges. We are all frontier officers. We spend more time in the field than in the garrison and, speaking for myself, I hate that time not on patrol because of the boredom."

"Your men have quite the band," Mackenzie said.

"For every hour spent practicing, an hour is taken away from some more military chore, but it keeps them honed as soldiers. Perhaps Lieutenant Flipper found other ways of fighting boredom when he ought to have been tallying numbers and wondering where the money went. There is no evidence presented that he stole it or the supplies."

"That's so, Colonel Grierson," said a major from Mackenzie's own command. "I'll go along with a letter of rebuke."

"And I, also," chimed in a captain.

The third officer, also a captain, nodded in assent. Mackenzie shrugged, as if saying he was magnanimous to go along with his subordinates in this dubious opinion.

"Very well. Let it be so recorded."

The major and the two captains quickly left. Ben thrust out his hand to shake. Mackenzie hesitated, then shook.

"Well thought out, Colonel," Mackenzie said. Then an ugly smile curled his lips. "Are you preparing for the move?"

"What's that, General?" Ben steeled himself for whatever Mackenzie had to say. It was like the man to save petty torment until he could personally witness the pain it caused.

"General Sheridan and I have decided that the Tenth Cavalry is better stationed at Fort Davis. Fort Concho will be shut down, of course."

"Of course," Ben said in a flat tone. It was as Woodward said. The Tenth Cavalry had done too good a job. The Indians were subdued. They had done their job and outlived their usefulness in Central Texas. Only the dusty frontier remained, and even this was more peaceful than it had been in a decade because of the Tenth Cavalry's valor.

"Life here at Fort Davis shouldn't be too bad for you and

your family. A bit dull, perhaps, but otherwise not too bad."
Ranald Mackenzie left the room, returning to the larger
mess hall, whistling off-key.

Ben took a moment to compose himself, then returned to
listen to the verdict being announced by Mackenzie. The
first black officer in the Army was acquitted of all charges,
strongly chastised, and exhorted to deal more closely with
his bookkeeping chores.

Ben Grierson sat in his chair long after everyone had left,
knowing this was to be his post, his exile, for a long, long
time. Then he stood and his mood lightened. If he had no
Indians to fight, then he could devote more time to his
music.

The Tenth Cavalry at Fort Davis would have the finest
band in the Army or he would know the reason. Alice and
the family would like that. And so would he, because he was
a soldier.

Epilogue

The rest of Benjamin Grierson's career was spent peacefully. The Tenth Cavalry was split up, half transferred to Arizona to fight Geronimo under the command of General Miles while the remainder, under Ben Grierson, was sent to Santa Fe, New Mexico Territory, for garrison duty.

After serving honorably at posts in Arizona, Santa Fe, and Los Angeles, Ben Grierson retired from the Tenth Cavalry after twenty-two years as its commander. General Sheridan died in early 1888, and on April 5, 1888, Grierson was promoted again to brigadier general after a twenty-four-year wait. He retired on his 64th birthday, July 8, 1890, splitting time between his sons' (Harry and George's) ranches at Fort Davis and his Jacksonville, Illinois, home. Robert was committed to an insane asylum, and Charlie became a lieutenant colonel, serving honorably in the Spanish-American War. Wife Alice died of a tumor in her injured leg on August 16, 1888, and Ben remarried in 1897.

At General Grierson's burial on August 31, 1911, a black man led the procession and his old friend, Lieutenant Colonel Sam Woodward (retired), performed the Ceremony for the Legion of Honor.

More Western Adventures
From Karl Lassiter

First Cherokee Rifles

                0-7860-1008-8   **$5.99**US/**$7.99**CAN

The Battle of Lost River

                0-7860-1191-2   **$5.99**US/**$7.99**CAN

White River Massacre

                0-7860-1436-9   **$5.99**US/**$7.99**CAN

Warriors of the Plains

                0-7860-1437-7   **$5.99**US/**$7.99**CAN

Sword and Drum

                0-7860-1572-1   **$5.99**US/**$7.99**CAN

Available Wherever Books Are Sold!

Visit our website at **www.kensingtonbooks.com**.